JOHN NICHOLS was born on July 23, 1940, in Berkeley, California. During his childhood years, Nichols moved frequently, living in California, Vermont, Connecticut, New York, Virginia, and Washington, D.C. At the age of 23 he completed his first novel, *The Sterile Cuckoo*. Published in 1965, it was greeted with great critical acclaim, earning for Nichols the reputation of a significant new voice in American fiction. The following year, his second novel, *The Wizard of Loneliness,* was published, solidly establishing Nichols as one of the foremost writers of his generation.

In 1968, after having lived in New York for over five years, Nichols moved to a small community near Taos, New Mexico. His interest in this region and its social, economic, and racial problems became for Nichols a great source of inspiration. He wrote several more books, both fiction and nonfiction, which examined the history and the physical beauty of the American Southwest. Perhaps the most famous of these works is his Mexican Trilogy, which comprises *The Milagro Beanfield War* (1974), *The Magic Journey* (1978), and *The Nirvana Blues* (1981). Also published during this time were *If Mountains Die: A New Mexico Memoir* and Nichols's fifth novel, *A Ghost in the Music* (1979) which was written between the second and last parts of the Mexican Trilogy and which represents a visible break from Nichols's other work at that time as it does not have for its theme the Chicano and his social and political problems.

His most recent novel, *American Blood,* was published in 1987.

AVAILABLE FROM SHORELINE BOOKS

Twentieth Century Fiction

Death in the Woods & Other Stories by Sherwood Anderson

A Fine Madness by Elliott Baker

A Ghost in the Music by John Nichols

Good Morning, Midnight by Jean Rhys

The Narrow House by Evelyn Scott

The Sterile Cuckoo by John Nichols

Testimony & Demeanor by John Casey

Tin Wedding by Margaret Leech

The Wizard of Loneliness by John Nichols

W · W · NORTON & COMPANY
NEW YORK LONDON

Published simultaneously in Canada by Penguin Books Canada Ltd.,
2801 John Street, Markham, Ontario L3R 1B4.
Printed in the United States of America.

ISBN 0-393-30473-6

W. W. Norton & Company, Inc., 500 Fifth Avenue, New York, N.Y. 10110
W. W. Norton & Company Ltd., 37 Great Russell Street, London WC1B 3NU

1 2 3 4 5 6 7 8 9 0

I am fourteen years old in Virginia.

It is about to storm, and one of the goats has broken loose. I am chasing her. I hate her, and by this time, having failed in every way to entice her into my grasp, I am panting, red, and screaming in exasperation, but nobody pays any attention to me. Mother is out back, picking ripe fruits off the pear tree, collecting them in her skirt, because, "If I don't pick them, the storm will ruin them," she says, and, needless to say, we all think she is crazy. Tim is in the kitchen fixing a supper for us which, knowing him, should turn out to be something like blueberry pancakes with mustard and honey sandwiches on the side, but then, he is only five and a half. Dave, who is well into his seventh year, is repairing the lower right-hand pane on the front door, while at the same time trying to read a Black Beauty novel lying open on the floor beside him. Mother blew up at him a little while ago and slammed the door so hard the pane toppled out. That makes the fifth time this summer: same pane every time. Dad is sitting on the porch ignoring us all, playing his guitar and singing bawdy French ballads, and sipping a beer. If I go up to him and say, "Pop, why can't we just let the damn thing run loose?" he will answer: "Are you tryin' to teach your old man how to suck eggs?" Clouds are dark and it looks like a good blow. The goat winks at me and cavorts away, and I collapse and bang my fists on the lawn, and begin to bawl insanely.

Later, after some thunder and a stiff wind, it is only raining. The main house is small, so I sleep in a big outside storage shack called the Tumble. I am surrounded by chicken dung, moth-eaten clothes, trunks full of old letters, and ragtag Christmas ornaments. I have my own corner with a bed, a bureau, a rug, and a chair. The door is open and I am alone. It is dark. In a moment the rain will stop, and the smell of dying roses will come over from the house. Fireflies will dot the warm night; a few may even be blown into me by a stray breeze.

I sit quietly on the damp threshold of my Tumble kingdom, looking at the darkened house where my family is sleeping, and that was eleven years ago, and it was the last summer we were all together.

This book, then,
is for MOTHER, TIM, DAVE, and DAD

And God knows he was lucky, so many ways, and God knows he was thankful. Everything was good and better than he could have hoped for, better than he ever deserved; only, whatever it was and however good it was, it wasn't what you once had been, and had lost, and could never have again, and once in a while, once in a long time, you remembered, and knew how far you were away, and it hit you hard enough, that little while it lasted, to break your heart.

JAMES AGEE: *A Death in the Family*

The Wizard of Loneliness

ONE

John T. sat easy on his motorcycle, and he wondered if his nephew, soon to arrive on the afternoon train, was really as big a pain in the neck as certain relatives had painted him up to be. If he is, that's all I need, I'll drive this motorcycle into a brick wall, he thought. But he couldn't get very excited about it: on a lazy May day like this he really didn't give a damn.

Ten yards away, a strong, relaxed-looking girl, Ercel Perry, sat on the parking lot side platform, her behind far back, leaning forward, her palms on the edge of the platform, arms taking half her weight. John T. grinned at her and she smiled back, loving him softly with her hazel eyes.

Behind Ercel, Bernie Aja, the gardener and general handyman to John T.'s father, Dr. Frederick Oler, stood on the track side of the platform, peering into the distance, his bald head shimmering gloriously in the sunshine. To Ercel's left, in a green 1940 Studebaker parked facing the platform, Dr. Oler and his wife Cornelia waited. The doctor rested his hands on the steering wheel and stared sleepily through the dusty windshield with totally unfocused eyes. His wife slumped near her door, knitting. The doctor's hands were large, the knuckles swollen with arthritis. He was wondering when he would wake up one morning without the use of those hands. He'd make a joke, of course: the detmoles giving his fingers a run for their money, Old Man Disease putting the screws on—It saddened him, though, and automatically he smiled to show it really didn't faze him at all.

Bernie Aja moved, and his head, flashing like a mirror, blipped a signal to the car. Cornelia glanced up at just the right moment.

"Train's coming," she said.

"Aah . . ."

"I don't see why it always has to be late." Cornelia wrapped up her knitting in jig time and stuffed it into the glove compartment.

"Oh . . . trains are always late . . ." the doctor said vaguely. He wiggled his fingers. Recently he'd taken to wiggling them a lot lest they stiffen on him unawares.

"Well, I don't see why." Cornelia got out and stretched. "I'll bet *he's* not on it," she said. "Nancy warned he was a troublemaker. For all she knew he might get off the train at White River Junction, spend his last nickel on a soda and a picture, not telephone or tell a soul, just let us all worry ourselves to death when he doesn't show up. She said he just loves those pictures. Says he even steals all the loose change lying around so he can go see them. Well, when I get my hands on that boy he'll change his tune. Grandson or no, he won't steal anything in my house, bet your life."

"She's comin'," Bernie called. "I heard her whistle. I got ears for train whistles. Must be goin' through Jactonberry right now."

Ercel Perry changed position so she could see down the tracks to where they bent out of sight behind some maples. Above the maples, the topmost rotted two-by-four of the burnt-out E. W. Snyder grain elevator poked into the limpid blue sky.

Softly, John T. said, "Here comes everybody's little surprise. I think I'll assassinate him when he gets here. Just on general principles."

"He won't be on it," Cornelia called.

"Don't worry, Ma—he'll be on," said John T.

"Not if what Nancy said is true. He'll be sitting in the White River Theater looking at the picture show!"

"Oh, I'm sure he's not," Ercel soothed.

"Well, what if he isn't on it, then what'll we do?"

"For God's sake let's not worry about that until we find out whether he's on it or not," John T. growled.

"Train, *train!*" screamed a small redheaded boy running off the Main Street sidewalk into the lot. Closing his eyes, John T. grimaced and whispered, "Who in hell invited the Indians?"

"The Indians" was followed closely by his mother, John T.'s older sister, Sybil, who carried a bag of groceries in her arms. She had wax-brown hair, a pretty but closed face, and a slight but athletic body. A blue silk kerchief graced her neck, unscuffed saddleshoes her feet.

Tom—for so the redhead was called—galloped across the lot and leapt at John T., screaming, "Let's rassle!" Obligingly John T. fell off the Harley-Davidson on top of him. Tom squirmed to free himself, and when he couldn't, began to yell, "Lemme up, *lemme up!*"

"I can't move," John T. gasped, clutching his stomach. "The Germans just shot me. I'm petrified."

"Oh, get off him, will you?" barked Cornelia. "You're going to hurt him, John T. *John T.!*"

"Yes'm?"

"You'll break every bone in his body. Get off this instant!"

"Ah cain't. Ah would really like to, but Ah cain't. Ah'm shot . . . in the gut . . . and Ah'm dyin' . . . today . . ."

Tom yowled. "Shut the little monstrouso up!" Sybil said, leaning through the back window of the Studebaker to put the grocery bag on the seat. To her mother she said, "Let Johnny squash him. It'll be good for him. He's made out of jelly anyway. He doesn't have any bones to break." She playfully bit her father's ear. "Hello, Daddy, you lecherous old yumkins. How's your gizzard?"

"Full of stones. . . ." The doctor's eyes focused; he kissed her cheek.

Tom succeeded in freeing himself. He stood and chanted defiantly, "Johnny and Ercel, sittin' in a tree, k-i-s-s-i-n-g. First comes love, then comes marriage, then comes Ercy with a baby carriage."

Cornelia clippety-clopped up the steps onto the platform. "There it is again," Bernie told her, pointing down the track. “We’ll be seein’ it any minute now. Told you I was a good whistle man.”

They all heard the next whistle. The doctor aroused himself; he and Sybil joined Cornelia and Bernie.

John T. dusted the seat of his pants and ran to the far side of the lot where tall grasses occupied a sunny strip just before the maple shade at the point where the tracks came into view. He ran awkwardly, his stride broken by a slight limp.

“Well, there she is,” Bernie announced, beaming happily. “Just like I said when I heard that first whistle.”

“Oh, yes, so it is. . . .” Cornelia shaded her eyes; she didn’t look at all happy. “If that boy starts stealing things . . .”

The train came into view, chugging sluggishly past the maples. John T. ran alongside the engine for a second, lost ground to the tender, and then to the first of three passenger cars. He cantered along in his odd gait, shouting up at indistinct passenger faces behind the reflection-filled windows—“Welcome to Stebbinsville, Vermont, Wendy baby! Welcome to Stebbinsville, Vermont, everybody baby!”

“John T., you quit that!” Cornelia hollered, her yell lost in the clanging of brakes and whooshing of steam.

“Yah-hey!” Sybil shouted.

And Tom opened his mouth in ecstasy as billowed air from the huge train wheels almost knocked him over backwards.

TWO

The man boarded the train in Hartford. As soon as he pushed open the door to the car and stood in the opening swaying a little, Wendall knew he was going to sit beside him. It was an instinct he had; he could always tell when something out of the ordinary was going to happen.

For example, two years ago in California he had felt sure of Helen's death the morning before she died. He woke early that morning and saw snow outside the window, and he could hardly believe in the snow, because kids in school had said the last time their parents could remember it snowing in that town was when they themselves had been children. Then, when Wendall opened the window, he found a dead sparrow which had flown into the pane, broken its neck, and fallen onto the ledge. And, even as he pressed the bird's fluffy breast against his cheek, a chill went up his spine, and he knew Helen would never come home from the hospital again. As simply as that he foresaw her death and felt her weight lifted off his shoulders. He closed the window and stuffed the sparrow into the toe of one of his Sunday shoes in the back of his closet.

During noon recess that day he called Helen and she didn't sound too bad. Having nothing, really, to say to each other, they only talked for a minute. At the end of the call, Helen said, "Make Fred wear rubbers," and kissed the mouthpiece. She could always be affectionate over the phone, never at home. Wendall hung up without a good-bye, and he felt no remorse though he knew it was the last time he would hear her voice.

The next day Fred came into his room about five in the afternoon. The snow had melted, warm air blew over wet sidewalks, kids were rollerskating across the street in a parking lot. Fred stood at the window, hands clasped behind his back. Wendall had been reading hunched up at the head of his bed, and he didn't look up when Fred came in.

All his father finally said was, "Helen's not coming home anymore." Wendall had to struggle not to smile. After an appropriate time lapse, he closed his book and said, "I knew she was going to die. I don't care. I didn't like her anyway." But when he raised his head, eager to see Fred's reaction, he found himself already alone in the room.

Two days later, on the night after the funeral, he finally cried about Helen. He had never loved her, nor she him: it was seeing her squashed into the bottom of a deep muddy hole by so much dirt that had done the trick. And for months following the funeral he had nightmares about after the coffin melted—not being able to move either his arms or legs, or daring to open his mouth because it would clog with dirt and he'd never get it closed again.

Six days after the funeral Fred came into the room and said, "What stinks in here?" Wendall said he didn't know. But Fred traced the stench to the closet and found the sparrow hidden in the shoe. He held up the bird and gazed at Wendall for a minute, then his face wrinkled like a monkey's and his mouth made a funny sound, and it was the most terrifying confrontation of the boy's life, because Fred was crying and he wouldn't turn around or leave the room or anything.

Shortly thereafter, Fred quit his job, joined the Marines, and sent Wendall east to spend two lonely uneventful years on Long Island with Aunt Nancy, his mother's older sister, a spinster who lived in a large Tudor house on the edge of a salty estuary near Oyster Bay. . . .

As the man came down the aisle, Wendall removed his sport jacket and books from the neighboring seat and arranged them on his lap. When the man drew abreast, he asked if the seat were taken, Wendall said it wasn't, and the man sat down.

Setting a small canvas bag on the floor between his knees, he leaned back in the seat, immediately closing his eyes. He had thick curly brown hair and a dark red beard. His cheekbones and eyebrows jutted harshly out of his face: one cheek and an area over his left eye were marred by scar tissue. Under his eyes the skin was bruised with fatigue. He wore a black jacket, olive-colored pants, and dirty combat boots laced loosely.

Six soldiers, cramped into facing seats, were sitting

across the aisle. One of them took out a harmonica, and the others began to sing along with his tunes—"On Top of Old Smoky," and "There's a Tavern in the Town," and "Home on the Range." Their voices were flat and hoarse, but most of the people in the car enjoyed the raucous noise.

Not so the bearded man. His eyes flew open, and he fixed his gaze straight ahead for a minute, his fingers twisting the ends of his bag's drawstrings. Then, turning sideways, he said, "I don't want to hear any more singing."

"You kiddin'?" The soldier on the outside of the opposite seat frowned.

"No, I'm not kidding. Your singing gives me a headache."

The soldier said, "Well, tough beans, Mister," and he and his buddies redoubled the volume of their voices.

The bearded man rested his head against the seat back, eyes trained on the ticket stub stuck under a brass fixture in front of him. The soldiers sang for a while longer, but when the train slowed down for Springfield they tired of their own noise and drifted into halfhearted banter, and then they sat quietly for a long time, waiting out the trip. Once past Springfield, the harmonica player took out his instrument again and blew a few bars, but the mood had changed, no one responded. Blue smoke came down from the ceiling, settling like a wing over Wendall. Sleepily he rubbed a clear space in the window and watched the tail end of night rattle by. His eyes were starting to close when someone tapped his shoulder.

"Where you going?" the bearded man asked.

"Stebbinsville." One-word replies were automatic to the boy.

"Hey that's funny. Me too. You know, the minute I walked in that door and saw you I said to myself, 'That kid is going to Stebbinsville, too.' How about that? You ever been there before?"

"Once."

"What—you got folks there?"

"My grandfather."

"Who?"

"Doctor Frederick Oler."

"Oh, sure: Doc Oler. How old are you?"

"Ten, going on eleven."

"You always wear glasses? I mean, you don't see very many kids your age wearing glasses, you know."

"I'm very nearsighted."

"Sure. No offense meant. I mean, don't let it bother you, my talking to you like this. If it does you say so, I don't want to bother anybody. People are bothered enough without me. Did you hear those bastards singing a while ago? It gave me a headache, it really did."

"I don't mind singing."

"Yeah . . . well—hey, I sure am a talker, aren't I? Old blabbermouth, that's me. I could blabber your ear off if you let me. By gosh . . ."

He settled back. Night lifted outside. Trees put on their pale morning foliage and a river slid among them like a snaky mirror. Then dawn colored everything.

"Do you think I'm young or old?" the bearded man asked abruptly.

"I don't know."

"Well, I guess I'm pretty young. Yes, I'd say so—definitely. But I'm old, too. It's a secret. I'm a very secret fellow. . . ."

He lapsed off. In silence they traveled across northern Massachusetts into Vermont. The day turned into a beautiful one, sun streamed through the windows, warming the car and waking the passengers. The soldiers cursed and grumbled, and women with children shuffled back and forth between their seats and the bathroom at the end of the car. A food vendor came on at White River Junction. Wendall bought a sandwich and a carton of milk. He ate part of the sandwich, then the bearded man said:

"You know, I didn't think I was hungry, but now that I see you wolfing that thing down, damned if I couldn't use some nourishment at that. How about a bite?"

"I guess . . . a little one if you want—"

With three quick bites the man polished off the half sandwich Wendall handed him. "Milk?" he asked. "Just a swig?"

"I don't know . . ."

He grabbed the carton anyway and quickly sucked up the remaining milk, inhaling loudly even after the straw made a sputtering sound.

"By God," he said, "I didn't know how hungry I was, did I? My old belly must be a heck of a lot emptier than I thought."

He crushed the carton and juggled it between his hands. Coldly, Wendall took a book—*A Farewell to Arms*—from his jacket pocket and began to read. But the sun streaming through the window made him sleepy, and soon he closed his eyes. The soldier across the way blew some mellow notes on his harmonica. Wendall wondered what his grandparents would be like. Whatever they were, he didn't really care; they wouldn't understand him, that went without saying. They'd get on him right away, there'd be fights, and he'd always be on the defensive, but so what? Had it ever been any different?

A hand disturbed his back pocket; he awoke with a snap. The bearded man held up his wallet.

"Only a dollar," he said quickly. "That's all I need." He took out a bill. "See? There's a five in here, too, but I'll just keep this one."

"You put that back," Wendall threatened.

The man dropped the wallet on the seat between them. He squeezed the dollar and stuffed it in his jacket pocket.

"If you don't give that back I'll do something rotten to you," Wendall said tightly, returning the wallet to his pocket.

"Oh, you shut up," the man said, nervously looking away.

"I want that damn dollar back."

The man slid over harshly, cramping Wendall against the window. "I said shut up about it!" Then he relaxed, and backed away. "Look, I'm sorry. I don't mean to be angry. I'll pay you back. And anyway, I could have taken the five. You're lucky I didn't. But I could have if I'd wanted to. I'm sorry . . ."

"Like hell."

The boy's head swelled with anger. In *A Farewell to Arms* a man had just been killed near some railroad tracks. It was this man beside him, Wendall decided; and he himself had fired the fatal shot. And now, standing over the wet, prostrate body, he spit, and the spittle landed on the man's beard. Then the boy took out his billfold, crumpled up the five-dollar note and dropped it distainfully on the dead man's stomach, and walked away. . . .

Well, he wasn't afraid of the bastard. The adult wasn't made yet who could take the measure of Wendall Bates Oler. The man touched his shoulder, saying, "Look; don't be angry," but the boy ignored him. He plunged back into his book, fairly ravaging the print with his raging eyes.

Some time later the train chugged slowly past the burnt-out grain elevator. "We're here," the bearded man said nervously. Maple leaves splashed against the window, the parking lot came into view. An older boy, shouting and waving his hands, ran alongside the cars. Then the train slowly passed a group of people, and forty yards beyond the group it stopped.

"All out," said the bearded man. "Nice to have met you. I enjoyed talking to you, I really did. I'm sorry about the dollar, but I'll pay you back, I promise. We'll probably see each other again real soon. . . ." Picking up his bag, he hurried out.

"You go to hell," Wendall whispered. Standing on the seat he wrestled his suitcase off the luggage rack and went forward. The conductor, who had just signaled up the go-ahead, said, "Better hurry it sonny." The whistle blew, Wendall hustled down the steps, and the train pulled out.

The boy set down his suitcase for a minute and stared up the platform at the Oler aggregation. He took off his thick-lensed glasses and slowly cleaned them with his tie. Then, bracing his shoulders and biting his tongue, and firmly resolved not to let any damn grandmothers or grandfathers push him around, he began to walk fiercely toward his new jailers.

THREE

The doctor stepped forward and said, "You must be Mr. Wendall Bates Oler. Better gimme that bag before it weights you over into a permanent bend and gives you halitosis of the elbow." Cornelia sucked in her breath, saying, "Oh, honestly, Frederick—" and Wendall said he could handle his suitcase by himself, thank you, then hands were suspiciously shaken all around. Cornelia called the boy "Wendy," which prompted him to announce that his name was "Wendall" and if she insisted on calling him by the prissy diminutive he would be a "very gruesome child" to her. Before Cornelia could break through her shock with an appropriate reaction, the doctor exclaimed, "Lord love a duck!" and suggested they retire to Hood's, the local ice cream parlor.

Heading downtown in the car, Cornelia informed Wendall that both his manners and his posture were preposterous, and also his ears and fingernails were incorrigibly dirty, to which the doctor bellowed, "If all you scallywags don't shut up pronto, you'll get your heads clopped together!" It was a testy assemblage that tumbled out of the car and stormed Hood's.

In the ensuing exchange of greetings, Mike Stenatto, the thinly moustached proprietor of the parlor, pulverized Wendall's hand, and a minute later had the audacity to inform him that "frappe" was a hell of a thing to call a milkshake. Wendall earmarked him for some drastic future retaliation, and then, as John T. and Ercel went off on the motorcycle and Cornelia drove Tom and Sybil home, the boy found himself relatively alone and at peace with the doctor and Bernie Aja, strolling leisurely down Main Street, the doctor pointing out each place of business and giving a short summary of the people who worked inside. They passed Shoe Heaven, a barbershop, and Kahler's Market, then stopped in front of Jim's sport and news shop. "There's a fella in here I'd like you to meet," said the doctor, and in they went.

The store was small and unorganized, cluttered with all the paraphernalia indigenous to the sporting world. There was also a candy counter near the register, a wide magazine rack against the dark rear wall, and over it all a preponderously huge person reigned.

Short—just a shade over five feet tall—Jim was as wide as he was high. Sitting on a stool fenced in behind the handgun display case and the candy counter, chewing on a cigar stub and absorbed in his own copy of the *Sporting News,* he looked baleful as a basset hound, and he hardly noticed when the doctor, Bernie Aja, and Wendall walked in.

"This here's the fattest ugliest man in the world," the doctor said.

Jim lowered the paper a few inches and studied them over the tops of his rimless glasses. "Evenin', Fred—Bernie," he said.

"Showin' Freddy's boy here the ropes," said the doctor. "Name is Wendall."

"Spleasure, Wendall." And to the doctor: "Ballplayer?"

"Don't know yet. But if he ain't, we'll whip him into shape I reckon."

"I doubt it," said Wendall. "I don't like athletics."

He picked up two Butterfinger candy bars and held the five-dollar bill up to Jim, who stared at it a minute, then said, "On the house."

"I'd just as soon pay."

The doctor started to intervene, but Jim nodded, said, *"Mmpf,"* and made change. "Headstrong boy," he observed.

"Got cantankerous California blood," said the doctor.

"I'm independent," said Wendall, and while Bernie and the doctor hung around a little longer to shoot the breeze with Jim about pennant races, the boy slipped out the door and positioned himself on the front stoop. He tore the paper off his Butterfingers, wolfed the candy down, and wiped his fingers on his pants. Then he untied his shoes and put one candy wrapper into each one, and laced them up again, and he felt a certain satisfaction because even if someone scrutinized him closely, he would never imagine the Butterfinger wrappers were in the bottoms of those shoes.

The leaves of a lone elm tree on the Green, which was located at the intersection of Rutland Avenue and Main Street, shivered slightly as a breeze went by up there. Three clouds in the blue sky were as full and slow-moving as parachutes. A clock chimed four o'clock and Wendall sighed: he decided it was going to be a very long year, and he determined that before the month was out he'd steal enough money to make a getaway, and this time it would be a real getaway, it wouldn't be like the fiasco he'd pulled at Aunt Nancy's last winter.

His big mistake then had been in choosing, as the vehicle for realizing his escape, Aunt Nancy's small disintegrating sailboat which for a year had sat glumly on the grassy shore of its small slip at the fringe of the back lawn. But it had been the only thing on hand, and, recognizing the need for a large stockpile of food to carry him through his projected journey, Wendall began in September to steal various and sundry edible goods from the kitchen cupboards, and he stashed these eats under the deck in the bow of the boat, burying them beneath the old tarpaulins and cushions there. Right on through Christmas he built up his cache, and many an afternoon he sat hunched over in that cramped darkness, surrounded by food, giving full play to flights of fancy: he sailed shirtless and tanned into blue lagoons, he fought with typhoons while rounding Cape Horn, he quietly admired gigantic icebergs as he floated through a mirror-green arctic sea. . . .

And on New Year's Eve his dreams went up in smoke. Irritated at his aunt's dictum that the best place to welcome in the New Year was at home and in bed, Wendall waited until he thought the house was fairly bedded down, then he dressed warmly over his pajamas, hunted up a pack of Aunt Nancy's cigarettes, and snuck out to his escape ship to welcome in 1944 with a few illegal smokes. For an hour he sat in the frostly dark trying to puff through a couple of weeds while thinking about all the other places in the world that were better than the Godforsaken hole into which his father had banished him, but all he managed to do was catch cold and turn a grisly green color from too much smoke, and he only just did make it safely back to the house and up to his room where he needed but a few minutes to conk out dead to the miserable world.

No sooner was he gratefully asleep, however, than excited voices awoke him, and the first thing he saw were funny bright lights swimming over his walls. He ousted himself from bed, went to the window, and witnessed, much to his chagrin, the fiery demise of all his dreams. The boat burned brightly for almost an hour while several babbling people ran around the lawn, screaming every time a can of corned beef hash exploded. Later that night, after the excitement was over and all parties were snuggled back in bed, it rained, then with dawn the weather turned very cold so that when Wendall went outside to view the wreck, it was but an icy skeleton, symbolic, it seemed, of his entire life, his hopes, his dreams . . . that glassy blackened hull, so empty with despair, the vehicle of nothing but his doom . . . .

"Thought you'd flown the coop on us," said the doctor cheerily, when he and Bernie came out.

"Well: you just wait . . ." Wendall grumbled under his breath.

They crossed Perry Street, went by the First National Bank, stopped in at Bradford's Bakery for some eclairs, went by Harry Garengelli's Gulf Station where John T. worked, crossed Chestnut Street, and entered the shadow of elms in front of the Unitarian Church.

"I don't think anyone ever goes here," the doctor said, nodding at the church. "People say it's haunted."

"Ghosts are stupid," Wendall observed.

Ignoring him, the doctor said, "And the spirits who haunt it live right in this house." He was referring to the Svenson sisters, Dorothy and Marie, ancient twins who inhabited a run-down ghoulish structure next door to the church. They were sitting on their front porch in dilapidated rockers knitting long lumpy socks which they sent to soldiers overseas. They looked to Wendall like an extension of his Aunt Nancy down in Oyster Bay—fried grasshoppers who in moments of wrath were prone to say, "Don't you act up to *me,* you young whippersnapper!"

"Whatcha got there?" snapped one of the sisters.

"Freddy's eldest and onliest," said the doctor. "Come to spend some time with us."

"He wears spectacles!" shouted the other sister. "Isn't he young for spectacles?"

"Yes . . . well—good-bye . . . good day," said the doctor, a little ruffled by the turn the conversation had taken. Bernie bowed his lustrous head repeatedly as they sidled away.

"Those two old biddies seem like senile asses," Wendall said, working over his glasses with his tie again. Both the doctor and Bernie raised their eyebrows.

"If folks are lucky, they get to be that old," the doctor said quietly. "In the process they usually get a lot of detmoles in their rondo-sketiaptic dispellers, but it's still not good to criticize them, Skunkhead. People are tired when they get to that age, they've got a right to be a little snippity. But when they're only ten they ought to hang onto their tongues a little better." He said this last sentence apologetically, and ended up with, "They are a funny pair of hens, though, ain't they?"

"What are detmoles and a rondo-sketiaptic dispeller?" Wendall asked coolly.

"Oh, phenomolations. Make-believe stuff. Like I was sayin', when you get old, your brain goes a little mushy. . . ."

Three more houses and an empty lot brought them to the corner of Coolidge Street. Main Street ran off to the right up Killer Hill. Directly across the street in front of them was an old grange hall. Behind the grange, to the left, a wide lawn sloped down to the Willow River. On the other side of the river, atop a nine-foot concrete embankment, a bed of peonies flourished. Beyond it, a lawn rose gradually to a yellow three-story house of dubious architectural derivation: gables and wings poked out as if the carpenters were really drunk when they built it. A gravel driveway ran parallel with the river past the house, beneath a carriage port, and into a barn. To the right of the barn was a Victory garden growing tomatoes, beans, peas, squash, and asparagus—a narrow flower garden separated it from the main lawn. A smaller lawn lay between the other side of the house and Prescott Street, which ran parallel to the river and eventually terminated at Rutland Avenue. At the far end of this lawn, nestled in a small grove of lilacs, was a little two-story playhouse built by John T. when he was fifteen.

"There she is," said the doctor. "Number 4, Coolidge Street. What do you think, Skunkhead?"

"It's okay," Wendall said. He appraised the cupola riding the barn roof, wondering if people left it alone enough so that he might consider it a possible hideout.

They walked over the bridge, and, fifty yards farther on, entered the driveway. Bernie Aja said, "Think I'll go down see how them pumpkin vines are doin'." To Wendall he explained: "We're plannin' to grow a Victory pumpkin large enough to win a blue ribbon in the state fair come November. Want to see how we're startin'?"

"Oh . . . all right . . ."

Wendall trailed the handyman down to the garden, the doctor went inside. Upstairs, in the master dressing room, Cornelia sat with her back to a window, Sybil lounged on an overstuffed couch across the room.

"I don't know whether I'm going to love him or not, isn't that a terrible thing to say?" Cornelia moaned. "Do you suppose Nancy could have substituted some other little boy in his place? Frederick never told us he was like *this!*"

"I think he's just nervous, Mummy, I really do. You wait. He'll turn out all right, you'll see. I think he's a very intelligent boy, I really do."

"Well . . . yes; but he's also a rather queer little boy, isn't he?"

"I suppose so. . . " Sybil got up and went around her mother to the window. She could see Bernie Aja kneeling on the ground near the compost heap showing something to the boy. Wendall had his hands shoved in his jacket pockets, apparently listening attentively.

But while Bernie explained about pumpkin vines, Wendall was actually thinking: He doesn't know I have the Butterfinger wrappers in my shoes, he doesn't even suspect it, nobody suspects it, I could walk around here for days and they'd never catch on. This tickled him something fierce.

When Bernie finished discussing pumpkins, he spit to the side and began to draw thoughtful patterns in the earth with his index fingers. "Yeah; I been growin' them critters a long time," he said. "Fact is, I been here a long time. Come durin' the '27 flood for reconstruction and lived here ever since. I was around before that, though. Quit school in the sixth grade, went to Minnesota on a freighter outta Shelburne, come back and drove a team at a pulp mill, then put out to the real sea and wound up fightin' in the British Army. Round '16 they taught me how to fly a plane, but I got blown up pretty quick, went to Scotland for a couple a years, and met Mrs. Aja. Come back here and cut some granite, did a little sugarin', and durin' the flood I flew a mail plane 'tween Concord and Burlington, flew it nighttimes and damn near froze to death. Then like I said I come here. Mrs. Aja died in 1934, but I got two boys, Jerry and Joseph, that run away two years back. Gone and got themselves swallowed up by the world like I done when I was a pup. . . ."

John T. came into the driveway on the motorcycle. He waved, drove into the barn, guided the machine to the rear of the main room, and cut the engine. He lit a cigarette, blew smoke up at the ceiling, and thought about the war. Ever since Pearl Harbor the war had been eating away at him, undermining his pride because he wasn't in it, and he wasn't in it because in the spring of 1941 he had fallen out of a washtub suspended fifteen feet above the driveway between the barn and the house and broken his leg in four places. The tub was an aerial car he had rigged up just for the hell of it. The accident occurred when John T.'s closest friend, Duffy Kahler—who was on the second floor of the barn operating the old Ford engine that ran the tub—pushed the gearshift forward at a time he should have yanked it back, throwing John T. off balance and sending him crashing to the ground. Later, Sybil had suggested to John T. he join the war effort, in some capacity other than that of a soldier, but he had replied, "Push a pencil while guys are dying?" and, as far as John T. was concerned, that was the end of the Army forever.

Duffy got into the war, though. In his final year of high school he was Valedictorian of his class, captain of the football and track teams, Stebbinsville's delegate to a Youthful Citizens for Peace conference in Burlington, and the possessor of scholarships to attend Middlebury, Harvard, Yale—you name it, he had it, but he chucked it all to join the Air Force, and was killed over Morocco during the November 1942 invasion. His name, inscribed by his own father who worked for Tompkins Memorial on Rutland Avenue, was the only one so far on the Green war memorial.

Duffy's death had filled John T. with shame. For two years he attended Boston University, but he couldn't take the city and the war, so he finally quit school, came home, and went to work at Garengelli's contributing most of his small salary to the family till. He puttered around with victrolas and radios and cars, and he had even begun to build a kind of crazy jukebox—a chef d'oeuvre of mechanical claptrap that inhabited the cellar. He had also bought the powerful Harley-Davidson and tuned it to perfection. Sometimes he took the bike on short evening trips into the surrounding countryside, always alone, and usually when he came back after these trips he spent a few minutes in the dark at the rear of the barn, smoking a cigarette and calming himself down, unwilling to face his family right away.

Getting off the Harley, he rocked it back on the stand and leaned over to flick up the gas line stopcock. He unscrewed the gas cap, grasped the handlebars, and shook the machine, listening for the splash of how much fuel was left. Then he screwed on the cap and walked into the waning sunlight.

Cornelia had gone downstairs to the kitchen; but Sybil still stood at the dressing room window. She saw John T. leave the barn and hesitate on the wooden ramp. "You make yourself so unhappy, Johnny," she said gently, pressing her nose against the pane. She drew lines on the glass with her finger, and soon became absorbed with the lines which appeared only as faint smudges on the glass. She traced a face, and recalled her watercolor portrait of John T. that had taken first prize in a statewide contest her senior year in high school. For a second she was stabbed by recollection of the such high hopes with which she had embarked for Bennington College, only to be bounced from school toward the end of April her freshman year, five months pregnant. Then, rather than return to disgrace at home, she'd broken off all contact with friends and family, gone to New York City, had the baby alone, and late in 1940 she married a man called David Matthewson who a year later enlisted in the army, and only then did she and Tom come home at last. David had been away now three years: his boyish figure suddenly clouded out John T., and Sybil said, "I pray for you, darling—every day."

She smeared her palm across the window, and, as she prepared to leave the room, heard her father, who was huffing up the stairs, say, "You're bedded in on the third floor with Tom the Terrible, Skunkhead. You just follow me so you don't get lost and we'll have you settled in jig time."

Behind the doctor, Wendall grimaced. That's all he needed, being caged in with that little redheaded son of an ostrich! You would think they'd have at least had the common decency to realize he valued his privacy!

Maybe he should just set fire to this house the way he'd set fire to Aunt Nancy's sailboat: *fizz, pop, crackle,* and the whole lot of them would look like Christmas sausages!

Well, it was going to be a long year all right: *if* he stuck around for it, that is.

FOUR

When the bearded man got off the train, he crossed quickly out of Wendall's sight of the station. He waited until both the motorcycle and Studebaker had left the parking lot, then circled to the track-side door of the waiting room.

Inside, he sat on a bench, closed his eyes, and wished his headache would go away. It had been the fault of the soldiers seated across the aisle from him, all their singing and cigarette smoking. Everywhere you went, there was too much smoke. People sucked on cigarettes as if they were sucking on life itself. Well, no more trains for a while. He'd come home; he was through with them.

"You sure are keyed up," he whispered. "Come on, take it easy. Use your upstairs."

His upstairs. That made him laugh. How many times had his upstairs cheated him in the past six months? Whatever he did, he always had to remember that his brain was laying for him. Even if he thought he was thinking clearly he had to keep in mind that maybe he was making a big mistake. It was like having an opposing football player dressed in the uniform of your own team always ready to tackle you unsuspectingly when you thought you were in the clear.

His eyes circled the waiting room. Two posters peeled off the wall beside the main door, the smaller a timetable and explanation of fares, the larger a War Loan advertisement. Before the war more trains had run through, coming down from Montreal, and there had been a ticket office. Now passengers bought their tickets on board, the office was closed, the glass behind the grill was broken.

Going to the front window, he watched some kids on bicycles pedal across the parking lot. They disappeared into a trail he knew came out by the grain elevator. Did people still try to climb to the top of that dangerous old skeleton? He'd done it a few times Against the sky he had been where he was all his life going to be: on top, healthy, in the clear air. Kids gaped at him in awe, they thought he was really something—A dog trotted across the lot, following the bicycles into the maples.

"Think," he said. "Come on, call the play."

He was getting nowhere. If his hands were only strong the way they used to be, that might make a difference. In the old athletic days all he had to do was hold his hands up and let them go to work. They could fix anything, catch anything, throw anything. Nowadays they trembled so he could hardly hold a match. And the fingers on his left hand, where they'd been broken, were misshapen, he probably couldn't throw or catch a thing.

He felt he was losing control. His mind couldn't stick to anything, it was pulling out on him when he needed it most.

"Do something, will you?" And then: "All right, I'll take a leak. No problem. Everything works just fine and dandy down there."

Bent over, his lips awry with frustration, he hurried into the bathroom. After he had relieved himself, he leaned his head against the wall over the urinal, thinking: Maybe I'll just stay with my head against this wall until they come in and find me and take me away and kill me.

And then he saw his own name written in pencil; he'd been rubbing his nose across it without even realizing. It took a minute to remember when he had written it—one summer, two summers ago? No, before the war. It had been before track got laid through Willow Falls, and this station had served both Willow Falls and Jactonberry. There had been a baggage room then, and he had worked part time in it one vacation.

The baggage room.

Excited, he rushed out and tried the neighboring door, but it was locked. Still, there was a way to enter. Back in the lavatory, he was delighted to confirm that the wall on the sink and urinal side of the room extended only a few feet above head height, it nowhere near approached the high ceiling.

He climbed onto a sink and looked over the partition. Below him several trunks stood on end in one corner of the room, a few burlap sacks were piled on the floor nearby. An only window, facing the Main Street side of the parking lot, was covered so thickly by dust he could make out nothing through it except color blurs.

Smiling, he returned to the waiting room and sat down. Sunlight mixed in warm pools on the floor. He heard a few cars moving around downtown. He relaxed, fell asleep, and dreamed. The fresh handsome face of his prewar youth came into the dream. His hair had just been cut; he had combed it with water, the water had dried and some of the hair had begun to frizz out a little. Dressed in a white track uniform, he was running. Lovely autumn leaves framed the path on which he ran. Sunlight, dulled and diffused by the leaves, splashed over his face. Breathing deeply in time to his strides, he descended a hill and crossed a small wooden bridge, turning out of sight behind some tall ferns. But a minute later he came down the hill again and ran across the bridge and disappeared behind the ferns. And then he jogged down the hill once more and ran over the bridge. The dream began to disturb him, but it was too pretty to be a nightmare. . . .

He awoke in a semidark station. Outside, the sky, a dull pink color, was giving way to dusk. He sat up, startled. Only by a miracle had no one entered the station while he slept. His luck wouldn't hold out much longer. Upturning his satchel on the bench beside him, five pocket westerns, a fountain pen, some little cakes of soap, two candy bars, and a pair of fur-lined gloves tumbled out. He tugged on the gloves; they were stiff, hampering the movement of his fingers. All winter his hands had frozen, but not until three weeks ago had he seen the gloves in a store window and been inspired to steal them.

The sky dimmed, gaining momentum toward night. He gathered his belongings, went into the bathroom, climbed on the sink, and hauled himself onto the partition. In doing so, his foot kicked on the faucet. He rolled over, lowered himself down the wall, and hung for a second, preparing to drop. Before he could decide, his fingers gave up, he fell, his legs buckled, he struck his shoulder on the floor.

Lying still, he listened to the running water. The sun went down altogether, leaving him in darkness. The water soon lulled him to sleep. The boy from whom he'd taken the dollar appeared before him. His dark eyes burned with elliptical madness behind the thick lenses of his glasses. Slowly, he uplifted his hand and said, "You give me that dollar." He moved closer; the man couldn't back away. "You give me that dollar," the boy whispered through clenched teeth, his wizened little eyes peering right into the man's eyes, his gaze like a spider creeping around the inside of the man's head, inspecting all the nooks and crannies of his befuddled brain—"You give me that dollar. . . ."

Voices woke him. He heard a shout, someone yelled good-bye, and car couplings made wrenching sounds as a train pulled out of the station. An automobile left the parking lot. Whoever had gotten on the train had turned off the faucet in the bathroom. He sat up.

The gleam from a distant streetlamp burned foggily in the window; little of the light penetrated into the room. He got to his feet and tried to open the window, but years of weather had warped it tightly shut. No matter. He circled the room, tapping lightly on the walls. All his thoughts came up blank. He reversed direction and tapped around the walls for five more minutes and things cleared a little.

The baggage room was made for him. If he were careful, sleeping most of the day, leaving only during the night, no one would discover him. He could scavenge some articles to fix up the room a little . . . But first things first: he was hungry, he needed to eat. For a few minutes he circled the room, talking softly to himself; and then he knew where he could get food.

He dragged a trunk across the room, set it on end against the partition, emptied the bag and wrapped the cord around his wrist, struggled over the wall, and left the station house.

He walked along the railroad tracks. The rails gleamed like long silver threads, the sky stretched clear and full of stars toward a dark meeting with the horizon. The moon, in its first phase, came into sight hovering resplendently in the sky, framed between the upper black timbers of the grain elevator.

Laxly, he jogged down a grassy embankment and pushed through knee-high weeds surrounding the base of the elevator. He kicked a bottle and some beer cans, and skirted the rusted hull of an old car. A path took him through a twenty-yard stand of sumac and poplars into the lot lying between the backward fences of two houses on Liberty Street. A tall oak with a tire hanging from a lower limb dominated the center of the lot. Quite nonchalantly, he walked by the tree to the sidewalk, and, going diagonally left, crossed the street, walked past three houses, and turned right at a fence bordering a dirt path which ended at an incinerator situated on the fringe of a bare area behind the Miss Stebbinsville diner on Rutland Avenue.

Being an all-night diner, the Miss Stebbinsville was well lit. Above and beyond it loomed the dome roof of the Imperial Theater. He edged sideways, staying in the shade of some bushes. When his boots felt the spongy grass of the Episcopal Church lawn beneath them, he could see past the diner up the street to where Prescott branched off Rutland. The post office–town hall on the far corner was darkened, as were all the homes on Prescott starting twenty yards beyond the municipal building's backyard.

He moved out of cover. No one left the diner as he went by. In a minute he regained darkness and hurried along Prescott Street. By day, this section, the poorest in town, was a noisy place of wailing babies, dogs, and cats. Now, however, all the lights were out; crumbling wooden tenements stuck up through angles of low-slung telephone wires like prehistoric phantoms, and the street was extra quiet.

He began to trot. At Perry Street he veered right, ran another forty yards, and stopped for a minute on the bridge, his eyes probing the backyards on the far side of the river. Not a light burned anywhere; it was going to be so easy he had to hold his breath to keep from laughing.

Just short of Jim's sport and news shop he ducked off the sidewalk and swiftly covered the distance to the low fence behind Kahler's Market. Scaling the fence easily, he scooted around the back screen porch and rested a few seconds against the wooden door to a small shed on the right of the porch. Then, climbing on a garbage can, he gained the roof of the shed.

In front of him a low-hinged window was held open by a piece of kindling. In laying aside the stick of wood he became aware of his gloves, and, because his hands itched, he pulled the gloves off and left them on the roof. Rolling onto his stomach, he inched backwards, dropping his legs down through the window. His feet settled on an old kerosene stove. He brought his head inside and pulled the bag in after him.

The closet smelled of cleaning soaps. Just barely he could discern mop and broom handles lining the walls. The familiar smell nearly overpowered him, and his heart ached at the encounter.

He emerged into a hall, crept up the narrow way past an open storage room, some stairs, a wide chopping block that smelled faintly of blood, and, circling a new refrigerated meat counter, entered the market. Moving with an urgency, he hustled up front, and checked the sidewalk. Then, talking softly to himself, he worked down one row, up another, searching for things to steal. A quart can of tomato juice caught his eye; he jammed it into the bag along with a jar of mayonnaise and some olives, then added a box of Parmesan cheese and several tins of sardines.

"Wait a minute . . ." He needed useful goods, things he could eat. Swearing softly, he got rid of the mayonnaise, the cheese, and one can of sardines. He added a loaf of bread, a can of spaghetti, and some peaches. Then, setting his loot on the checkout counter, he held with his other hand punched the No Sale key, letting the drawer slide out. It was empty. While pushing the drawer back in, a noise made him glance sideways: Irma Kahler was standing in the doorway behind the meat counter.

She was a large and ugly woman: her little eyes were widened with amazement. The man dropped his hand from the register and the drawer banged out, ringing the bell.

"Don't scream," he said, groping for his sack. "I'm leaving."

Approaching her, he whispered, "Don't you dare make any noise or I'll hurt you."

Irma retreated a step so he wouldn't bump her going through the doorway. Once past her, he turned and walked backwards. He felt for the porch door handle, touched it, and backed outside, letting the door slam shut. Then he sprang around, rolled over the fence, and ran.

"Duffy?" Irma said. And then: "What are you doing? Where are you living?"

But she spoke to no one. Her son by this time had run well out of hearing.

FIVE

If he had to suffer living in the same cell with Tom, Wendall planned to at least make things excruciatingly miserable for the little boy.

The first night he decided to humiliate his cousin with the silent treatment. They lay in their respective beds, and although Tom made overtures of friendliness, asking all sorts of questions—when Wendall took off his glasses did the world look like in a "clidescope"? Had he ever shot a gun or ridden on a mototcycle?—the boy ignored him, keeping his mouth clamped so viciously shut that his jawbones soon ached. Finally, Tom turned on the lamp between their beds, sat up, and said, "Don't you talk at all?" Whereupon Wendall threatened, "If you don't turn off that God damn light I'll hit you."

"Can you hit very hard?" Tom asked.

"*Very* hard."

"Harder than Grandpa or Uncle John?"

"Look: just turn off that God damn light, that's all I'm asking you to do."

"Okay." He turned off the lamp.

"And shut up, too. I don't want to suffer a little child's babble all night, every night."

"Okay. Do you know any little moron jokes?"

"Yeah. Little Tommy dopehead is a moron." Wendall sniggered.

"What's so funny?"

"Don't you get it?"

"No. What's so funny?"

"The funny thing is you should shut up. Or I'll hit you. I'd do anything for a minute of God damn peace."

"What's God damn?"

"A swear word, for God's sake."

"Do you know any more swear words?"

Wendall thought for a moment. "Well, there's damn it all to hell."

"What's it mean?"

"It means you are angry."

"Are you angry?"

"Yes. Very much so."

"If I turn on the light and sit up will you be more angry?"

"Yes."

"Will you say swear words?"

"Of course. Now will you shut up pretty soon?"

A rustle: the light blared on.

"Say them," Tom said.

"Say what?"

"The swear words you said you'd say if I turned on the light."

"Turn off that God damn light, damn it all to hell anyway!"

Tom giggled, switched off the light, and wriggled deep into his covers. "The God damn light is turned off," he said.

A silence ensued, but it was no longer hostile. Wendall dropped his guard; fatigue overcame him, he drowsed, and he had an idea that perhaps his cousin liked him a little, and the thought excited him.

So when Tom said, "Sometime can I look through your glasses?" he smiled, replied, "Mm-hmm," and fell into a sound and contented sleep.

In the morning when the boys awoke, Wendall was reluctant to undress in front of Tom. In fact, only once since his appendix operation several years ago had he undressed in front of anyone.

He had been invited to a birthday party at the home of a girl whose parents had a swimming pool. Wendall couldn't swim, but the girl said the pool had a shallow end for waders, and anyway, Helen had insisted, she bought him a bright red suit, wrapped it in a gorgeous yellow towel, and made him take it to the party.

When the time came to swim, the boys undressed in a bedroom. Wendall tried to wait until everyone had left the room, but some boys kept hanging around and asking, "Come on, aren't you gonna get in your suit?" so finally, facing a wall, he stripped down. But before he had a chance to tug on the suit, one of the boys peeped around him and said, "Hey, look at Wendy's scar," and the other boys crowded in to look. Even when Wendall had yanked his suit on, the big purple tail of the appendix scar showed above the waist.

"That's where they stuffed in all the books," one boy said, and the others took up the cry. Forever after that boys and girls alike would come up to him in school halls or classrooms and say, "Hey, Wendy-girl, show us the place where they stuffed in the books!" as if it were the biggest joke in the world. One day after lunch some seventh-grade boys captured him on the playground, wrestled him to the ground, and pulled off his trousers and underpants, all the time laughing and shouting, "Hey, where's that place where they stuffed in all the books?" and when they saw it they bellowed, "Looks like they sure got in a lot of books, you must be a real smart kid, Wendy-girl," then they ran away. Wendall pulled on his pants, drawing the belt so tight it hurt his stomach, but he knew a lot of kids, including girls, had seen him naked from the waist down. After that, whenever he walked around the school he felt titanically ashamed. And he had never again undressed in front of anybody, not even Helen or Fred.

Tom had little modesty, however: he solicited Wendall's help with the buttons on his shirt and his fly, and with his shoes. Then he sat on his bed, waiting for his cousin to shed his pajamas. Finally Wendall said, "Well, aren't you going to go down to breakfast?" and Tom countered with, "Aren't you gonna get your clothes on?" Whereupon Wendall gathered up his things, went down the hall to the john, locked the door, and dressed in peace.

As they entered the breakfast nook, the doctor said, "How's your gizzards?" Tom said "Full of stones," and dove headfirst into a bowl of oatmeal.

"How about it, Skunkhead?" said the doctor. He twirled the ash on his cigarette off into the orange bill of a battered tin penguin beside his plate. He pushed down a lever in the middle of the penguin's back and the bill tilted up, the ashes sliding into the bird's stomach.

"How about what?" Wendall said.

"How about your gizzard?"

"You're s'posed to say full of stones," Tom prompted.

"Isn't that sort of silly?"

"Now you listen here, young man!" said Cornelia, speaking through the window between the nook and the pantry.

"Whoa up," said the doctor quickly. "This here's a ornery critter from the West needs a little time to get adjusted to our ways, Grannie. We'll fit a eastern saddle on him one of these days, but no need to press it. What bronc ever ate from your hand on the first day?"

"He isn't a bronc," said Cornelia. "And if he doesn't mind his manners, I'll give him what's for, I will."

Sybil entered the nook, kissed her father's cheek, came around the table, said, "Good morning, Thomas, how's a wuzzley-wobble?" threw her arms around him, squashed her lips on his cheek and blew out—*"Blerrap!"* Then she pecked Wendall lightly on the ear. "Sleep well, Gruesome? You're lucky: you've got the lumpiest bed in the mansion." She sat down, shrieking, "Mummy, bring me my coffee this instant or I'll tar you and feather you and stick you in a cart!"

"Speak respectably," Cornelia called from the kitchen.

"All right. Mummy, bring me my coffee this instant *please,* or I'll tar you and feather you and stick you in a cart!"

"I don't want any more God damn cereal," Tom said, making a bitter face.

"What?"

"I don't want any more cereal," Tom mumbled, turning pink.

Sybil leaned forward. "What—did—you—say—the—first—time, Mr. Matthewson?"

"I don't 'member."

"I'll dismember you if you don't 'member, by cracky."

Tom squirmed.

"Spill the beans. I'm counting . . ."

Wendall was preparing to fight to the death, when Tom came up with the stock answer: "I heard you say it once, Mom." Sybil blanched, said, "Oh," and "Well, don't you let me hear you using it again or I'll tar and feather *you* within an inch of your life. . . ."

Afterwards, on the front porch, Wendall said, "That was very decent, your not telling on me."

Tom scratched himself, yawned, and emitted a series of professionally tailored belches. He said, "Want me to show you round?" and Wendall replied, "Certainly."

Tom led him through the Victory garden, along the edge of the river, and, as they walked through the flower garden, explained that John T. had once caught a "humbird" with a butterfly net there. They looked through the ground floor horse stalls in the barn, one of which had been repainted and the walls hung with old guns, then went upstairs where Tom pointed out the rusty engine that had powered the alpine bucket from which John T. had fallen. Next, they inspected the playhouse. "Mom says Uncle John's a genus," Tom said. "He builded it by himself."

Wendall cringed. "Genius," he corrected. "And built, not builded, for God's sake."

They went on to explore the cellar in the main house. Tom pointed out the furnace room, the preserve rooms and coal- and woodbins, and the jukebox John T. was building. "It'll hold a trillion records when it's finished," he said, and Wendall experienced a pang of jealousy as he scrutinized the heap of nuts, bolts, and metal joints and arms crowded into an ambiguous shape against a wall near the washtubs.

Then they toured the second and third floors, and ended up spending until lunch in the attic. As the morning progressed, Wendall got the feeling Tom was showing him everything much as a lieutenant might show his new commanding officer a familiar battle terrain, pointing out the enemy positions, what had been done and what was left to be done, what was important and what superfluous, reporting all this quietly and competently as a good inferior should while transferring responsibility into more capable hands, and Wendall hesitantly began to sense he might possibly be going to usurp John's T.'s position as the old general. This thought made his stomach twinge like a clam under lemon juice.

When at last they called time out for lunch, Tom deferentially let his older cousin lead the way downstairs. Wendall marched slowly, savoring his descent as must have Napoleon savored his entrance into many a forgotten and glittering ballroom of yore. The boy's heart beat suddenly—with such vigor that he felt weak: no one had ever admired him before, no one had ever suggested he *lead* anything. He watched himself approach the full-length mirror on the second-floor landing, and lifting his chin, he wished he didn't have to wear spectacles. Three feet in front of the glass he stopped, saluted, and held the salute. Tom snapped into place beside him and copied the gesture. They appraised their rigid selves in the mirror; it seemed to Wendall his feet were floating.

"Do you like us?" Tom asked.

"Well; perhaps a little," Wendall said snootily, but he had to fight hard to keep his stern eyes from betraying his growing inner joy.

After lunch Tom showed Wendall his pigeon-catching apparatus—an orange crate, a twig, some bread crumbs, and a long piece of string. They set up the trap on the cement walk leading to the front porch. The string, tied to the twig on which balanced one end of the crate, they trailed through the latticework between floorboards of the raised wooden porch and the ground. Crawling in behind the steps, they peered through the latticework's diamond holes, waiting for game to arrive.

"Grandpa'll give us a nickel or a dime for every one we catch," Tom said. "They grunce on the house and he doesn't like it."

The period of waiting was nerve-racking. Pigeons sailed down from the roof thirty seconds after the boys hid themselves, but once on the walk it took them forever to strut under the orange crate. They bobbled around, cooing and eating the bread crumbs that weren't scattered beneath the crate, while Wendall ground his teeth and Tom sweated and whispered "Now!" every time a bird so much as looked at the trap. So when one bird ventured halfway onto the shadow of the box, Wendall, who was teetering on the brink of his patience, yanked the string. Tail feathers and wing tips poked out for a second, but the bird's subsequent struggle carried it all the way under the crate. As he crawled into sunlight, Wendall sighed with relief—his first major mission in the role of commander-in-chief had been successfully realized. Nervously, he snuck his hands under the trap, grabbed the bird, and brought it out.

"We can take it to Grandpa right now," Tom said. "He doesn't mind."

They ran downtown to the doctor's office, which was on Rutland Avenue near the corner of Main—a trip of four blocks from the Coolidge Street house. All out of breath, they almost went busting through the wrong door into Wiggen, Cadwell and Hempe, Real Estate, instead of the screen door beside it, Frederick Oler, M.D., Consultations Mon. thru Sat., 9:00 A.M. to 6:00 P.M. Beneath the name and information hung a picture postcard depicting some goofy-looking drunks holding bottles with XXX written on the sides, and under them, printed in scrawly red letters, was the following:

THERE ARE MORE OLD DRUNKS IN THE WORLD
THAN OLD DOCTORS

Leaving the screen door reverberating behind them, and the doctor having no nurse for them to wheedle their way by, through the empty waiting room and into the office they plunged.

The doctor lounged behind a desk smoking, his profile against the window. Looking completely unruffled, he swiveled slowly around and said, "Well, if it ain't my doggone grandsons. How's your gizzards, boys?"

Before he could think, Wendall found himself saying unison with Tom, "Full of stones!"

Then the doctor said, "What in the world you numbskulls got there, a mouse?"

"It's a pigeon, Grandpa; don't be stupid," said Tom.

"Tryin' to teach your granddad how to suck eggs, are you, young fella?" He frowned severely, leaned back in his chair, and said, "Pigeon . . . hmm; how do you spell that?"

"P-I-G-E-O-N!" Tom shouted.

"But gosh darn it all, what exactly *is* a pigeon?"

Thus prompted, Tom recited: "The pigeon is any bird of a widely 'stributed family Columbidy of which there are many 'mesticated varieties such as homer trumpeter and tumbler derived from the rock pigeon of Europe!"

"Hmm . . ." said the doctor, apparently unimpressed by this energetic babbling of memorized knowledge. "I don't know . . ." With his stethoscope he listened between Wendall's thumbs on the bird's back to its heart. His face scrolled up seriously, until at last, letting the stethoscope slip down around his neck, he pushed out a deep sigh from his ample insides and leaned back in his chair, and his fingers slowly snuck into his vest watch pocket in search of what turned out to be a quarter for both of them. He teased a little longer, making the coins disappear and reappear between his fingers while muttering as how he wasn't at all sure he ought to be paying them on account of his not being one hundred percent convinced that what they had showed him wasn't a mouse or a duck-billed platypus or something, but he finally gave in, saying as the coins dropped into the boys' hands, "You skidaddle on out of here now, before you run me broke and into the poorhouse," and out to the sidewalk, smugly flipping their hard-earned wealths, Wendall and Tom jauntily strode.

"Let's get something at the ice cream place," Tom said.

Wendall hedged. "I don't know if I want to spend my money right away." After all, if ever he decided to run away, a small bundle might come in handy. "But I don't mind sitting with you," he added.

They installed themselves at Hood's counter, the pigeon still in Wendall's possession.

"Yessir," said Mike. "What you fellows got there?"

"We catched it ourselves," Tom said. "I wanna spustachio ice cream cone and a strawberry Coke."

"How about you, California?"

"I don't think I want anything. . . ." The pigeon's wings squirmed to be free beneath Wendall's palms. He wondered what would happen if he let the bird go. While Mike was leaning over the ice cream freezer scooping out the pistachio, he set the bird on the counter. Mike's head came up just as he took away his hands.

"Hey! Whattaya doin'?"

But the pigeon made no move now that it was free. It dipped its head and blinked its eyes; then it doodled on the counter.

"Grab it," hissed Mike. "Get that damn thing outta here."

Wendall stared at the bird, daring it to fly.

"Listen," Mike warned. "This ain't a pigeon coop."

"I don't see what's the matter with letting the bird stand on your counter," Wendall said.

"Oh, yeah? Look what your bird just done on my counter."

"That won't hurt the counter."

"Look, funny boy. Grab the bird, okay?"

"You don't have to be so nice about it," Wendall said.

Before Mike could think of a retort he grabbed the pigeon, swung off the stool, and stalked huffily outside. He stood for a minute, blinking in the bright sunlight, thinking about how much he disliked Mike. You couldn't trust the Wop; in fact, you couldn't trust anybody, not even the doctor. With a flash of puzzled amazement, Wendall wondered what was happening to him this day—he'd let his guard down more than once, and if he didn't watch out they were going to suck him right in, cooing and clucking like the good-natured doctor until they had him cooing and clucking, then sure as shooting they'd yank the string on him just as he had on the pigeon. He remembered Helen, the way she had had, before they became total enemies, of suddenly softening toward him and making guileful adult plays for his affection, only to turn on him when he didn't react the way she expected him to. He recalled in particular how—having claimed to be reconciled to his brainy reading—she had bought many novels that he had long wanted, then even read the books herself so as to be able to "converse" with him about them.

Well, their first and last conversation had been a real lolapalooza. It occurred over *Look Homeward, Angel*. When Helen asked him had he enjoyed it, Wendall said not really except for Ben's dying scene. "Why did you enjoy *that?*" she asked. "I didn't *enjoy* it," he said; "it just interested me, that's all." "Why?" she insisted. "I thought it was Fred dying," he replied quite simply. And that got her. She looked at him, her eyes going nutty, then she said, "You'd have liked that, wouldn't you? Something clinical for your little mind to ponder. Well, I'm sick of your mind. You aren't even a human being. I'm sick of your books and your cold shoulder; how am I supposed to be a mother to a book?" And she slapped him, screaming, "I should have died in childbirth, that's what!" and all he said was, "I think you need a psychiatrist," and marched unruffled from the room, in full possession of all his ascetic dignity, leaving her to launch the usual temper tantrum in solitude.

With all his might, Wendall threw the bird at the sidewalk, but as soon as it left his hands the wings snapped out and it flew swiftly over the curb, then rose in the air and flew over the store roofs across the street and out of sight. "That's for saying a frappe is a hell of a thing to call a milkshake," he muttered.

Inside Hood's, Mike said, "Is that kid balmy or somethin'?"

"He's my cousin," Tom said. "I like him 'cause he's different."

"That's about the only reason you could like him," Mike said, swabbing down his counter.

SIX

Irma Kahler sat on a chair in her dark living room, looking over dusty geranium plants on the windowsill to some burnished tree leaves across the street. She tried to think what Duffy's being alive meant; and for the second time in her life she felt herself on the verge of tears.

The first time she had cried was when she learned Duffy had been killed. Otherwise, as the fat and ugly daughter of a grocer, she had always been tough and unsentimental, impervious to the gibes and taunts of other children who poked fun at her. She grew up listlessly alone, never went to movies or parties, and from the age of twelve on she helped her father run the store (her mother had died, her older brother married and gone away). She learned the business so well that when her father died she took over. She ran a good store, but made no effort to expand. She chatted with customers who wanted to talk, but never cultivated a friend. And she was apparently destined to finish out her days in an indifferent and crisisless existence, when, shortly after her thirtieth birthday, a series of small incidents changed her life.

One afternoon a drab little German immigrant entered the market to buy a loaf of pumpernickel. He gave her his pennies, then automatically shook her hand. This startled Irma, for never in her life had she shaken a man's hand to conclude a deal, she had always folded her arms and nodded, and that had been that.

The next day the German came in, bought another loaf of bread, and shook her hand, and, noticing that his hand was very small, Irma avoided squeezing it so as not to hurt him.

Two days later, she fell down the back stairs and broke her right arm. She closed the store a half-day in order to have a cast put on her arm, and resumed business as usual in the late afternoon. The German came in not ten minutes after she had opened up, bought his loaf, and this time, instead of quickly dropping her hand and leaving, he looked up and said, "First time you break?" and she said, "Yes." "A shame," he said; "would you like to marry me?" "What do you want to get married for?" she asked. "I want a son," he said. "Maybe soon I'm gonna die. A son is the family name, a son would run the store after you are dead." They regarded each other, and, after a moment's reflection, Irma said, "All right."

On their wedding night they bedded down early, and when her husband had made love to her, Irma said, "That should do it," and Hank Kahler said, "Yes," and retired to her father's room which had been left untouched since his death. Their brief union did do it. Irma became pregnant and had a son, and she and Hank never slept together again.

The Kahlers took good care of Duffy, but they did not often kiss or cuddle him. From the age of two on it was evident Duffy would be everything the senior

Kahlers weren't—gay, handsome, gregarious—and they let him develop as he would. When by the time he was ten, Duffy was spending half his nights and days at friends' houses, it neither worried nor hurt his parents. Later, whenever Duffy invited them, they went to see him star in high school athletic contests, sitting dutifully on the sidelines, seldom cheering, but glad to see him excel. The store had more business as Duffy's fame grew, and people made less fun of Irma and Hank behind their backs, but by and large the Kahlers remained unaffected by their son's rise to glory; indeed, they were scarcely aware of it.

When Duffy said he had decided to put off college and join the Air Force instead, Hank said, "Good," and Irma said, "I'll fix you some sandwiches for the train," and they shook hands, then off he went.

The day they learned of Duffy's death, Hank Kahler drank half a pot of coffee after dinner and went to bed early. He lay on his stomach and thought: Tomorrow again we will try for another baby. Irma sat in the living room chair staring over the geraniums at the dark street, and though she felt little, tears worked their way out of her tired eyes, and it was the strangest sensation she had ever felt. On the following day, Hank suggested they try for another child, but she said, "Don't be ridiculous, it's much too late," and he never brought the matter up again.

Now Irma again sat in the dark living room, and she thought: Things are complicated, Duffy's alive, something terrible has happened, he's sick, he's afraid to come home, he's done something wrong, he must be living somewhere, but where? And if I tell the sheriff and they find him, could the thing he'd done be so bad they'll kill him or lock him in a jail or an insane asylum? Or maybe he hasn't done anything very wrong yet, she thought, and he should be found and stopped and helped. . . . But most of all, she should protect him, she should gain his confidence and find out before anyone else did what happened to him and what he had done. Yet, would he ever be back? Had she already frightened him for good?

Tears stung her eyes. After a while exhausted, she went upstairs to her husband's room, sat her great bulk down in a chair near his bed, and for the first time in their married lives the Kahlers had an argument.

"Why a light?" said Hank, rolling over and sitting up. "Is it morning?"

"It's night. Duffy is back."

"Duffy is dead."

"I heard a noise, so I went down to see. He was robbing the store. He had a beard but I know it was him. He said he'd kill me."

"You are talking silly."

"I tell you Duffy's alive, and all you can do is say I'm talking silly?"

"It is silly to say a dead man is alive."

"I know my own son."

"A nightmare. You dreamt. Duffy is dead. With my own hands I wrote his name."

"Duffy was down there and he's in trouble. We got to do something."

"With my own hands—"

"—you wrote his name. You're proud to have his name on the memorial? My son, not dead after all, and you want to keep his name on a memorial, you don't want him back."

"A thief I don't want back. A thief my son wasn't."

"I ought to clobber you."

"Go to the sheriff about the thief."

"Sic the sheriff on my own son?"

"Please. I don't want to argue. Do as you like. Let a thief rob the store. I don't care. I think best we forget about it."

"Duffy's alive, and that's all you can say?"

"I need sleep . . ."

"You don't care . . ."

"I care for my son who is dead. Nobody can give me back my son who is dead."

"Nobody can give you back your heart which is dead, that's what!"

"In a war everybody's heart is dead."

"I love him!"

"I loved him, too. . . ."

They stared at each other, stunned.

Late at night, by matchlight, Duffy was reading snatches of a pocket western, and the reading soothed him. He knew just exactly when something was going to happen: he knew the books by heart, he never made a mistake, he always called the play and had complete control.

But when he closed the book, a queer thing began to inflate inside his chest. He opened his mouth, and, getting on all fours, waited to see if the sensation would go away.

It stayed. He rolled over and rocked on his side. The thing didn't exactly hurt him, it prodded him in a soft extraphysical way, blooming in his guts like a wet wind-filled parachutal membrane. He wanted terribly to do something—hit out, or yell, or run—

He groaned and sat up. One of these days it would make him go into a tailspin, it would make him run completely amok.

And then, gradually, the feeling died, leaving him exhausted. He rolled forward and lay on his back, facing the ceiling. For an hour he remained that way, open-eyed, his muscles stones. A train came into the station, no one boarded, no one got off. When it had gone, Duffy shook the dust out of a burlap sack and climbed over the partition. He used the route which had served him last night, and again met with no one. On the roof of the woodshed behind the market he discovered, near the open window, a piece of paper weighted by his gloves. He tried reading the note, but it was written in pencil and he could make out nothing, so he put it in his pocket.

In the store, he partially filled his sack with a loaf of bread, jars of mustard and mayonnaise, cans of corned beef hash and peaches, and a coffee cake. He moved easily; gone was the bumbler of last night. Rising confidence took over his legs—he moved with a supple surefootedness reminiscent of his athletic days. He felt good: for the time being everything fit into place.

He paused in front of the meat counter. Had he forgotten anything?

Nothing. But wait a minute—a can opener, razor blades to shave off his beard and towels. These things he would have to get from upstairs.

But when he came to the foot of the stairs, his mother was sitting twelve steps above him on the landing. In the dim light her features shone with a brutal leaden coldness, her eyes faced him limply. For a moment they confronted each other, she searching his eyes for remnants of the old Duffy, he trying to see in her eyes an agreement to let him go on stealing uninterrupted for as long as he had to. Each found what he was looking for: then Irma said, "Duffy?"

Without answering, he turned and walked out.

SEVEN

It was after dinner, still light out, when Jimmy Wiggen, Stebbinsville's summertime general errand boy, brought a telegram to the Coolidge Street house. Tom and Wendall were on the front lawn tying strips of bacon onto arrow tips in preparation for a bat hunt they planned to initiate as soon as the day became dusky enough to wake up the bats and send them forth to the slaughter.

Jimmy skidded into the driveway on an old Schwinn bicycle. The handlebars of the bike were lavishly decorated with streamers, American flags, and squirrel tails; red and white paper snappers were affixed to the tire spokes. The messenger dismounted casually, let his souped-up vehicle flop into the lawn, and sauntered over to Wendall and Tom. Setting his hands arrogantly on the place where he had no hips, he reared back his crew-cut head, squinted one eye, lifted half his upper lip into a quasi-snarl, and said, "Who're *you?*"

"Wendall Bates Oler."

"Ya new in town?"

"No. I've lived here a couple of centuries."

"Whatta people call ya? I bet they don't call ya Wendall, do they? I bet they call ya Wen, or somethin'. Or *Wendy!* Hey, Wendy—that's a girl's name."

"Don't be so blatantly obvious."

"Listen, Wendy; ya watch yaself. I don't take crud. What're you guys doin'?"

"We're gonna shoot a bat," Tom said.

"With a bow and arrow? Ha! I'd like to see that."

"Stick around," said Wendall. "We'll pretend you're a bat."

"Ya looks blind'sa bat yaself, *Wendy.*"

Jimmy picked up the bow, bent it experimentally, grimaced, discarded it, checked out the arrows, sniffed the bacon, poked his fingers against the tips, then dropped them disgustedly in a heap and said, "Does a Mrs. Matthewson live here?"

"You mean Aunt Sybil," Wendall said. "Tom's mother."

"Who asked you, *Wendy?* When I wanna know something from you, *Wendy,* I'll ask you, *Wendy,* all right?"

Slowly, keeping his eyes on Wendall, Jimmy withdrew the telegram from his pocket, smoothed out the wrinkles in the envelope, and, reading through the cellophane window, said: "I got a telegram for Mrs. David L. Matthewson, c/o Mr. and Mrs. William Frederick Oler, Number 4 Coolidge Street, Stebbinsville, Vermont."

Wendall reached to take it: Jimmy slapped his hand away.

"Huh-uh, Wendy. Looky-looky but don't touch. Gotta get my tip, don't I?"

He scuffled insolently up to the porch. While waiting for someone to respond to his ring, he shouted, "You guys're nuts! Ya never gonna get a bat like that!" Then he focused his attention on Cornelia, received his tip, clumped off the porch, mounted his gaudy bicycle, and said, "I guess somebody died."

"Oh, yes?" Wendall said aloofly.

Jimmy pointed nonchalantly at Tom and said, "Yep; his old man." And, spinning his tires, he yelled, "So long, Wendy-girl!" and left.

Because his rage was so great he could hardly breathe, Wendall had to sit down. Tom quit tying bacon to arrow tips. Evening came on and they could hear river currents washing against the bottom of the cement wall at the other end of the lawn. A last robin left the grass bordering the flower garden.

Whistling came from around on Main Street, and pretty soon John T. walked into view. He moved leisurely through the shadow of elms, and then across the empty lot, his body naked to the waist, a T-shirt flung over his shoulder, advancing on the Coolidge Street house where only the third-floor windows reflected the oriole color of the setting sun. At the bridge he spied the boys and shouted, "Halloo!" The echo richocheted down the river as John T. smiled and sped up his pace. "How yew all makin' out?" he drawled, hopping over a round cement block marking the right side of the driveway. He tumbled on the grass beside the boys and rolled onto his back, totally at ease. His long blond hair shimmered against the dark grass.

"We're gonna kill a bat," Tom said. He raised his left arm, cupped the palm of his right hand in the pit, and brought the arm down sharply to his side, the squashing of his hand in the pit emitting a ripe sound.

John T. sat up and tried to bend his arms around to the hollow of his bare back where the grass had made him itch. "I suppose you're just gonna shoot an arrow up in the air and hope that by some stroke of luck one of those bats'll jump into it, is that it?"

"We're tying bacon on the tips," Wendall said defensively. "Going for it, they're liable to fly right into the arrow."

"My dead grandmother they will," said John T. "Bats don't bump into anything. There's exactly one way to bring down one of those little fellows and that's with a gun."

By the time this sank in, John T. had leapt to his feet, sprinted to the barn, and returned with his .410 and some shells. Breaking the gun, he swung it around a couple of times, squinting up the barrel at the sky. Then he loaded up, cocked the gun, and waited. There were several bats in the air; they were shadows that appeared for split seconds, flashes of gray against gray sky—and they were gone in less than no time.

"It must be difficult to hit one of them," Wendall said, fervently hexing John T.'s aim.

But: "It's like taking candy from a baby," John T. said.

The gun went off just as Wendall turned his head and saw the Studebaker, the doctor at the wheel, enter the driveway and come to a stop beneath the carriage port. Tom let out a whoop as a dead bat plunked miraculously onto the lawn. A second-floor window flew open, and Cornelia shouted, "What's the matter with you boys, shooting that thing off? Haven't you got any sense in your heads? Don't you know what's happened? Get out of here! All of you! Go away!"

The doctor straightened beside the car. He winked at the startled group on the lawn, and, cupping his hands to his mouth, shouted up through the carriage port roof, "You better come down here, Cornelia! Our son has gone and shot a hipppotamus and it's layin' in your pansy bed!"

"Oh—Frederick? Are you home?" She waved feebly at the spot on the roof under which it had sounded as if her husband were standing. "Frederick," she begged, "please come upstairs. You don't know what's happened . . ." and, his face darkening with concern, the doctor hurried indoors.

"What's going on?" John T. asked.

"I think someone died," Wendall said. "That lousy Jimmy Wiggen brought a telegram."

"It was my daddy," Tom said proudly.

John T. stared at the second-floor window. After a minute he walked to the Studebaker and drove it into the barn. When he came out he stood on the wooden ramp and dug a cigarette package from his front blue jeans pocket. He scooped his fingers in the pack, hunting for a smoke that wasn't there, until, giving up in disgust, he crumpled the package, and, as he stepped off the ramp, flipped it to the side onto the driveway and went into the house.

With a start, Wendall realized darkness had enclosed them. Beyond the barn an ochre moon was rising. Nobody seemed interested in putting him and Tom to bed, so, enjoying the authority involved, he took the initiative himself.

Tom wouldn't throw the bat away when Wendall told him to; he insisted on carrying it up to their room. When he brushed his teeth, he lay the bat on the sink rim; when he sat on the toilet, he arranged it on the lid of the shoebox nearby; and when he got into bed he moved the pillow over a little to one side so there would be plenty of space for the dead animal. Wendall drew the line there: Tom complained, but the bat was relegated to the table between their beds.

No sooner had Wendall turned off the bedside lamp, than the door opened and the doctor tiptoed in saying *shh,* it was only him. He sat at the foot of Tom's bed, and for a while no one said a word. Slowly, the doctor relaxed. Downstairs he'd been going through hell, and the boys' room, where no one knew much about love or bereavement or anything major, was a good place to unwind—a neutral corner as it were.

"Well, you old skunkheads," he said at last. "You won't mind if I skip the story tonight, will you? Your granddaddy is a little pooped. The detmoles are givin' him a workout again."

Wendall said, "Did her husband really die?"

"Yes. He was killed in the war."

Tom said, "Are they gonna fly him 'cross the ocean in a frigerator?"

The doctor said, "What do you mean?" and "I don't know," in the same breath.

Tom repeated. "When people're dead, do they really fly 'cross the ocean in a frigerator?"

"Now you rapscallions hush . . ." The doctor's voice was muffled with a soft gloomy note. He coughed. "I hear Uncle Johnnikins nabbed a flying rat. I mean, I saw it, I was there, wasn't I? Lord love a duck, but my brain's gettin' soft."

Maliciously, Wendall said, "It's getting blood all over the bedside table."

"Oh, well . . ."

The doctor started to get up, then sank down again and set to rubbing his hands together, the palms scraping against the scabby skin on his swollen knuckles. He pictured his daughter, lying pale and disfigured on her bed downstairs; he thought of his wife flapping around the room spouting a million unimportant and profoundly worried words; and he wondered how he could ever trudge downstairs and re-enter that room again, he wondered how he could ever force his lips into a calm competent smile and move among them, love and comfort seeping from all his pores. . . . And the more he sat in the dark with his grandchildren, the harder it was to get up. He wished that his life had ended twenty years ago, on a spring day during the first week in May, when, while walking along Main Street toward his new office, the air had suddenly become cool and snow had begun to fall, and he had felt his head would burst with the loveliness of it all. Forever after he had remembered the day, and he thought now: If only I could have sunk quietly to the sidewalk, never reached my office, never returned to my wife and kids. . . .

He got up slowly and said, "Good night; don't let the alligators get you," and Tom said, "We won't," and the doctor closed the door carefully and regretfully behind him.

Tom began to cry softly.

"What are you sniveling about?" Wendall asked.

"I don't want my daddy to be dead," Tom said.

"Kids whose parents are dead are lucky," Wendall said.

"I don't care," Tom replied.

"Well, I'm sorry about it if that makes you feel

any better," Wendall said. Vaguely he was disturbed, thinking he ought to say or do something else. Finally, softening, he allowed, "Well, maybe Fred will get shot to pieces, too."

"Who's Fred?"

"My father."

"Why don't you call him Daddy?"

"Because I always called him Fred. Daddy's pretty infantile, if you ask me."

"What's infantile?"

"Like you."

"Well, if he got shot to pieces, would we be twins?"

"Oh, sure . . ." Wendall said, turning away and clamming up.

During the night, Wendall slept very little. He heard grownups talking, their voices muffled up through the floor, or sharper when, listening at the open window, he heard his grandfather conversing with John T. and Bernie Aja on the front porch. The doctor handled the burden of this conversation: it concerned mostly the nice night, a moon that was so clear it seemed a man could almost touch it, and some asparagus that might or might not be ready for cutting tomorrow. Bernie brought up something about buying new hoses and new mole traps from Bitte's Hardware, and the doctor said he thought they ought to hold off for a while to see "what developed." Then he and Bernie speculated on how the Victory pumpkin would turn out, Bernie saying that soon as the little fellers were on the vine and grown some, he aimed to choose a healthy one and milk feed it, at which point Cornelia's strident voice interrupted, asking Frederick to come up to Sybil's room for a moment. A little later John T.'s motorcycle went quietly out the drive and Wendall guessed his uncle was going to see Ercel Perry, who worked in the Miss Stebbinsville Diner, and got off evenings around nine-thirty.

The boy dropped off to sleep, waking again to the rattle of the barn doors sliding shut. He went to the window, the driveway was deserted. Above, powerful gray clouds were becalmed in the night. Wendall felt angry and dissatisfied. Leaving the window, he leaned across his bed, grabbed the bat and the copy of *A Farewell to Arms* which he had not opened since the train, and tiptoed down the hall to the bathroom. He locked himself in and carefully inspected the bat, remembering the dead sparrow on the windowsill in California. He touched the animal's crusted fur, pinched its ears, and pulled out one wing that had three small holes in it where the shot had passed through. It certainly was a great triumph for John T. Wendall hadn't missed the admiration flooding Tom's eyes moments after the fantastic kill. . . .

Vengefully, he dumped the bat into the toilet, lowered the seat and the lid, sat down, and opened his book. For twenty minutes he read. When his head began to nod, he closed the book, and flinching at the noise, flushed the toilet, then scurried back to bed. He drifted off to sleep with Tom's raucous voice running through his head, chanting *Johnny and Ercel, sittin' in a tree, k-i-s-s-i-n-g. . . .*

EIGHT

Around the corner onto the crest of Killer Hill sped the motorcycle, John T. driving, Ercel clinging behind him, both bent and leaning as they cornered fast, zipping through dull lemon streetlamp glow, then straightening as they began to descend. The hill was steep, the pavement cracked and uneven with frost heaves. John T. went faster than he should have, and one third of the way down he hit a bump which knocked his front tire slightly out of line, and the machine started a shudder he couldn't control. He braked, geared down once, the motorcycle wobbled to the other side of the road, he jerked it away from the fender of a Ford, they recrossed the street, slewed sideways, lifted half onto a strip of grass bordering the sidewalk, and stalled.

"Jesus," said John T. "What did I have to do that for? All I need is for me to crack us up. That would really make existence peachy."

He backed the bike up until the front tire rested in the gutter, and lit a cigarette.

"Everything's blowing up," he said. "My whole house, my whole family, my whole life is rumbling like a volcano, just waiting to pop."

"What's the matter now?" Ercel asked.

"Oh—nothing's the matter now. Just my sister's husband got himself killed and she's about to lose her mind over it, that's all."

"That's a shame. I'm very sorry."

"Yeah. It's a crying shame all right."

John T. walked the Harley back, turned it around, and the engine caught on his first pump. He threw the cigarette onto the street, ran over it, and resumed the descent.

They bore left at the bottom, passed the grange hall and Coolidge Street, and continued up Main. Quite a few cars were parked along the right curb; the movie crowd had just got out and Hood's was jammed. Some elderly couples were coming out of the High Life Restaurant as they went by. Dim lights burned in the window of the Treasure Chest Gift Shop. They cruised through the Liberty Street intersection, went down another long block of stores, and turned into the railroad station parking lot.

At the other side of the lot, John T. geared down to first and nosed into the narrow bicycle trail. Leaves damp with dew slapped their faces. A few yards into darkness, John T. stopped for a minute. The Harley throbbed softly in the green gloom; the air, though humid, was just cool enough to feel refreshing.

Ercel kissed the back of John T.'s neck. "Please; wait here a minute," she said. She wanted just a minute of peace with John T. She knew he was seething; she knew in a minute he could erupt, angrily and confusedly, whining and bitching to her, and probably blaming her for one thing or another, transforming his frustration into accusation of herself, and this hesitation under the close leaves was just the few seconds she needed to draw in a deep breath, reassuring herself that she loved John T., loved all he had that was worthwhile and that would one day manifest itself when the self-pitying boyish bullying ended its cliché in him. And she also believed, to the battening of her own courage, that without her to vent his feelings on, John T. would collapse in a minute.

"It's pretty here," Ercel whispered.

"Yeah," said John T., his voice a thousand miles outside of the momentary lull. "Pretty as a picture."

They continued on to the open area around the elevator. John T. leaned the Harley against the car hull and joined Ercel, who had seated herself at the base of the structure. From their low position the grass in front was just high enough to block out the car and the motorcycle. They faced leaves, some dark, some whitish: the sky, starless, yet high, a lovely solemn color, neither blue nor black, was cloudless.

Ercel said, "Can I do anything to help?"

"What can anybody do to help? Hold our hands on the way to the graveyard?"

"How serious is her crackup?"

"I don't know. It's not a crackup really. She's just miserably unhappy. And Pop won't say anything: he's never said anything. He's afraid to open his yap. All he can do is stare at her."

Ercel waited patiently for John T. to go on. He avoided looking at her, bit a piece of skin on his lip, and sniffed.

"Pop is at the edge of his own life looking into a big darkness of disaster," he said. "And I wonder how it feels to be there?"

"I don't believe it. You always exaggerate."

"Oh sure. Actually everything is hunky-dory. Everybody sees affable old Doc Oler. Big smile. Twinkling eyes. Little kids love him. Old fogies cling to him. Set your bones and sew up your guts, yessir. But did he ever collect on his bills so maybe his own family would know where its next meal was coming from? Did he ever track his daughter to the city and find out if maybe she could use a little help? Did he ever give his oldest son one tip on women, so the poor boob wouldn't fall into the pot of the first pretty bitch that twitched her tail a him? Did he ever just put his arm around *my* shoulder and say, 'Okay Johnny; let's talk this over or that over?' Did he ever get *angry* at me? Or maybe jump for *joy* for me? I tell you, we've all gone through his life like his own damn proverbial clam through a gull, and boy, it's dawning on him; he is feeling it all right. I watch him just sitting in his chair, staring at Sibs, and all the potential defeat in that jolly old face of his is deafening! Oh, yeah. Everything is hunky-dory, no doubt about that!"

"That's enough, John T.—"

"That's enough yourself. If I had any sense I'd drive that God damn motorcycle right over a cliff into the Bixby quarry, bet your life on it."

"What a romantic way to solve everything."

"That would solve *me*."

"It would be the crown to adjust on your self-pity."

"Look: do I have to take that from you all the time?"

"I honestly think you should take it from somebody."

"And you've volunteered. Aren't you nice."

"I'd be glad to leave."

"No . . . I'll cut my griping. Why am I always griping? I must be really pleasant company. But if only I could feel right, if only I was doing something, establishing something, if only I was helping somebody else or even myself. . . . I work in a gas station. The Great Engineer, the Mechanical Genius, he works in a crummy gas station, can you beat it?"

"You could go back to school—"

"Yeah. Me and all the other flunkies. Listen to chalk-talks while our pals get filled full of holes."

"Pretty soon the war will be over—"

"Oh, you're funny as a crutch, you are."

John T. thought for a minute, then said, "There is one thing I am not going to do, however, and that is spend my life helping my folks sink into their old age. I don't care what happens. Things will get worse, always worse, but do you know they may not actually die until I'm forty? Well, I'm supposed to hang around that long? You can bet your sweet A double S this boy isn't!"

"I don't think you're being fair to them."

"All right, so forget it." John T. lifted his head and said, "Why doesn't anything good happen anymore?"

"Something good always happens if you wait long enough."

"Sure. When I'm eighty, something good happens: I drop dead."

Ercel brought her legs together, cupped a hand over each knee, and rested her chin between hands. "All I can say to help you, John T. is that I love you with all my heart."

"Sure. But you won't make love with me."

"'I explained that. . . ."

"I know. Good girls wait until they're married. Intercourse just for the hell of it is pornographic, we'd be bound to lose sight of love, et cetera. . . ."

"Yes."

"So meanwhile I masturbate."

She looked at him.

"Well . . . oh, hell, forget it, it was a stupid thing to say." He poked her shoulder with his finger, brushed back her hair. "Hey, lift up your chin. Don't die on me."

"You just stopped me for a minute."

"Look. I didn't mean it. I was a fool to bring it up."

"Is it a terrible thing to be driven to that?"

"No. You kidding? I said let's get on another track."

"Do you go with other girls?"

"In this little burg? Who? And where? And how without everyone including you finding out about it?"

"When you were in Boston, did you?"

"Yes."

"Often?"

"Every opportunity I had I took advantage of. A few times I paid."

"Are there a lot of girls in Boston who are willing to make love before they are married?"

"Some. Not a lot probably. But the war changed things. A girl with a guy on leave doesn't worry about consequences, that's all. I'm no soldier, so you can wait."

"I wish . . ."

"I said don't worry." He pushed Ercel back and lay beside her raised on his elbows. Her eyes were dark, her lips closed, her face altogether too serious. He began to kiss her. She reacted cautiously. To a certain point, she would respond with him. He touched her breasts with his hand, her thighs: she murmured, "Johnny . . ." and her hand clasped his, lifted it higher and placed it back over her breast.

John T. stopped kissing her, plunged his face into the grass, and after she had said, "I can't, I just can't . . ." he squeezed his eyes until they burned, he thought of his father standing at the edge of his life staring into a big black space filled with disaster, and he thought that in five minutes he himself would be standing at that same place in his own life staring into the same damn thing.

NINE

Right after David Matthewson's death, the Svenson sisters took it in their heads to twice invite Wendall and Tom over for luncheon in order to get them out of their bereaved grandmother's hair.

These meals were cruel mute engagements, the likes of which neither child, even in his worst nightmares, had experienced. They took place at a glass-topped table set with frilly pink mats, large wine-type glasses, and blindingly bright silverware. In the center of the table two giant white candles grew unlit out of skinny pewter candlesticks toward a sky-high ceiling. On opposite sides of the table sat Tom and Wendall: between them, snuff-colored and smelling of toilet water, Dorothy and Marie presided, their backs agonizingly erect, their chins tucked tightly into their long necks.

Savagely, Wendall bit through a crust of bread as if he were biting through one of the sisters; cannily he snuck a pad of butter on the tip of his knife beneath the table and smeared it over the underside of the mahogany wood; suddenly, on his right, Marie leaned forward, her ruffles rustling, and said, "Eh?" The sharp wings on her nose twitched. Wendall stopped smearing butter, couldn't remember what they'd been talking about, smiled sickly, and smelled a pomander ball somewhere urging him to sneeze. "Yes, ma'am?" "Well—" blurted Dorothy: her little ticky-tucked chin ground back and forth in her neck like a loose joint, and her myopic peep eyes stared glitteringly at him. He felt as if the room were jam-packed with dust. There was dust in his head, dust clogging his nostrils, dust stopping his pores, dust choking him. . . . He shifted his eyes from Dorothy to poor sweating Tom across the way—

There was a pause, then trumpeting music from a distance, followed by the muffled cloppeting of horse hooves. Wendall leaped upon his chair, then onto the table. The plume in his cab swept the air, the buckles on his boots clinked with joy, the cool emerald-studded handle of his shining sword slid greedily into his palm. "Avast!" he shouted, sending candles, cups, and saucers flying with one swift boot. *Swish-swash* sang the sparkling shaft of his sword, and two gray heads toppled from Svenson shoulders, thudding on the floor like soft footballs. They spun on the rug for a minute, but they didn't spray blood, only sawdust and mouse droppings. With apocalyptic whoops, Wendall and Tom upturned the table and stomped into oblivion whatever glass remained to be broken, then, like the swashbuckling hearties they were, they grabbed hold of the drapes and exited in the only befitting manner, swinging through the closed windows. There was a tremendous crash, the tinkle of cascading glass . . . startled, Wendall looked up. "Oh, my *Lord!*" gasped the sisters in unison, the air quivering with their birdy shudders: he'd just tipped over and broken his water glass!

As they stumbled down the steps after this disastrous adventure, Wendall snarled, "Those bitches ought to get a medal for being a pain in the gludial maximus."

"What does that mean?" Tom asked, running to keep up.

"It means God damn," Wendall spat out through tigerishly contorted lips.

The second and final meal also terminated somewhat prematurely when Wendall, having been offered a large helping of creamed spinach, dropped his baked potato in the center of the milk-green mishmash, and said, "If you force me to eat that stuff I'll gag and vomit all over everything." Later, after the sisters' belligerent telephone call to the Oler household and after the doctor had gently reprimanded Wendall for his bad manners, the boy called the Svensons senile asses again, and locked himself in the third-floor bathroom with copies of *Tom Swift and His Wizard Camera* and *David Copperfield,* which books he read, alternating chapters, for five hours before coming out.

Cornelia made him write a note of apology to the sisters. He complied readily enough, then snuck into the kitchen when it was deserted, squeezed the juice out of a lemon, and, using a quill pen, wrote "senile asses" again and again between the lines in tincture that soon dried and became invisible. He hoped one of the old derelicts might accidentally hold the letter over a candle flame, thus exposing the true nature of the epistle's soul.

But of course, there'd be no such luck. Miss Murdstones and Mr. Murdstones—the world absolutely crawled with them!

There was, however, a deeper way in which David Matthewson's death affected Wendall: it served as the touchstone from which he flung himself wholeheartedly into a fanatical "war consciousness." The fascinating aspects of annihilation, mass or otherwise, suddenly intrigued him no end. He felt, vaguely, as if he had been close to death all his life, for in a way his loneliness at times could not have been far from the absolute suffocation death suggested, like the thought of the terrible immobile loneliness under the earth that had made him cry for Helen. Yet, though he had often thought about death, it had always been like thinking about how far away a star is, or about how many and what kind of people are right this instant standing on the balcony atop the Empire State Building. For though you could be completely assured that the farthest star had a distance and that people were right now congregating atop the Empire State, it was nevertheless impossible to measure that distance or count and know those people.

Now, somewhat against his better judgment, Wendall decided to ask the members of the family for their opinions on the subject. Not that he expected much from any of them: in fact, the only ones he guessed it might be worthwhile grilling were John T. and Bernie Aja. He could imagine his grandfather joking about it—*Death? That's when the detmoles clog up your rondo-sketiaptic dispeller;* his grandmother would most likely have a fit—*What do you want to think about that for? It's morbid. Go out in the sunshine where it's healthy, etc.* And as for Sybil—because of her recent close affiliation with dying he could picture her staring at him with preoccupied eyes, silently piercing through him to the milky space behind his head he would never in all his lifetime see, the space where the real lumpy form of Death hulked . . . and that gave him goose pimples. So it was first to John T., then to Bernie Aja that he went.

John T. stopped tightening a bolt on his jukebox, rubbed his nose with the handle of the wrench he was using, and tapped the invention with the wrench.

"Like this thing, sort of," he said. "You could stand here until hell froze over waiting for it to do something, and it wouldn't budge, wouldn't even twitch, because it's dead. One of these days, though, when I get the motor all built, I'll plug it into a wall socket and give it life with electricity."

Bernie Aja shed no greater light on the subject. "Well, now; dead is just like . . . dead," he said, making a vacuous gesture with his hands.

"Have you ever touched a dead person?" Wendall asked.

Oh sure, Bernie had touched millions of them during the first war, but when Wendall pressed him to describe the experience, he replied, "I don't know. You don't really feel nothin'. If they only been dead a few minutes, they're warm. If they been dead a few hours, they're cold and pretty stiff."

"But don't they feel as if there's something about them that isn't really dead? I mean, even though their hearts have stopped beating, don't you think they still might be thinking of something, or able to feel something, or maybe even try to open an eye and say something?"

"Nope. Dead people is dead. They don't even sneeze if you tickle their feet. . . ."

Wendall climbed up the rickety circular stairs to the cupola atop the barn, and there, seated on a crate, surrounded by mounds of pigeon dung, he toyed with a definition synthesized from what he had been told, and came up with the following, which was quite unsatisfactory:

DEATH IS A JUICELESS JUKEBOX THAT, WHEN YOU TICKLE ITS FEET, DOESN'T SNEEZE.

Obviously, then, he was on his own. He descended from the cupola and went to the pantry to have a look at the shelves of old crockery, china, and glassware there. He yanked the chain to a dim light bulb in the ceiling. The bumb cast a dry yellow glow that gave to the surrounding shelves and all they held an unreal gilded quality.

Wendall studied the designs, shadows, and faint translucent colors. His favorite pieces were hand-painted Bavarian plates, petal-edged, with centers of roses onto which bumblebees were about to land. Next to the plates, he regarded his miniature reflection—so small as to be nearly featureless—in a fishbowl made of a fine glass thinner than the most delicate eggshell. It gave out reflections which had to them a predominant lavender tinge that was always changing, ever uncertain. In this same bowl, the light bulb, a mere pinpoint deep in the glass, vacillated between a natural yellow to a fairy green color, and shadows that were suspended in the glass took on an ambiguous mother-of-pearl tint. But he leaned too close, his breath tarnished the bowl's surface, and all colors drained into the transparent heart of the globe.

Wineglasses that Wendall had never seen used extended in orderly rows along a higher shelf. The most beautiful ones, of a faded cherry color, were octagonal and reflected light repeatedly in panels. Other glasses were tinted amber and butterscotch as if age had very slowly, over centuries of time, smoothed its way into their delicate bowls. The glasses, when he lightly touched them, were neither warm nor cold: they were without temperature, politely reflecting subdued colors into each other's transparency. The feel of them made Wendall shiver.

Standing in the center of the dim passageway, gazing at the reflections cast by the glassware and trapped in it, the boy felt quite awed. He closed his eyes and leaned back against the cellar door: a laziness took hold of him, the manifestation of some eternal drowsiness crept into his veins—he felt as if his heart and his blood would stop, and he would soon open his eyes and find himself in a land of tall wineglass trees and giant fishbowls and Bavarian plates, and the dignified, total silence of glass would be in everything, including himself . . . heart of glass, veins of glass, hair of glass . . .

"Don't slouch like that!" barked Cornelia, backing with a tray through the double doors at the sink end of the pantry. She clacked the tray on a kitchen counter and shouted, "What are you doing there all alone? That's no place for a growing child to be. Go outside and play. It's a scandal for a child your age to stay in dark places when the sun is shining."

"I don't like the sun. It makes me sweat. It fries me. You'll walk out and I'll just be a crisp on the lawn."

"Oh—go trap pigeons. I've got enough to do without fighting with you. I'm going to speak to Frederick, though. You're a nasty little boy, and things have got to get straightened out mighty quick. And keep your dirty fingers off my doorjambs . . ."

"I can't keep them off your silly doorjambs."

". . . and don't forget to change into your old shoes or sneakers if you're going crawling under that dirty porch," Cornelia continued, filling a basin with soapy water and plunging some dishes in. "Have either of you boys been using my rubber gloves? I can't find them anywhere."

Wendall spotted the gloves lying on the floor at her feet, but he said, "I saw Tom yesterday with your pinking shears cutting off the fingers," and retreated before she could blow a gasket about that.

He did not go outside, however: he went up to the third floor, climbed a rickety wooden ladder, uplifted a trapdoor with his shoulders, and entered the attic, where he planned to further ruminate on things.

Before him were sleigh beds, carriage lamps with kerosene wicks, quilting frames, old blue silk parasols, and silly brown linen mobcaps. To his right were a bicycle with a seat higher than his head and three giant hogsheads. To his left was a hollow dressmaker's jenny, beside it was a tin hip bath, and stuffed in the bath was lots of stiff old horse equipment, plus a spiked collar for weaning calves. And behind him were crazy quilts ravaged by mice, big green glass demijohns in wicker casings, carpetbags with dusty Oriental patterns, and the model of a square rigger, the masts crumpled across the decks as if toppled there by a miniature typhoon, the rigging dripping down as still in the airless attic as ropy icicles.

Wendall sat on a trunk flanked by some unpainted duck decoys and two chamberpots and kicked a cracked leather strap of sleigh bells, which jangled rustily. He bent over, untied his shoes, and dug out the Butterfinger wrappers. He smoothed the papers on the top of the trunk, and with a stub of blue crayon wrote, I HATE GRANDMA on one, and I HATE JIMMY WIGGEN on the other. For a minute he mulled over his work, then, lacking further inspiration, he returned the wrappers to the toes of his shoes, and, resting his chin in his hands, noticed that there were really a lot of locks in the attic. In fact, there were hundreds of them. They turned up everywhere, round, heartshaped, square and crudely fashioned: in some big keys were rusted fast in half-turned positions; in others the backings were exposed, showing mechanisms cluttered with cobwebs, pellets of dust, and scraps of paper.

In a wicker basket Wendall discovered a ring of very small keys, none longer than his little finger. They had probably once fitted into the locks of jewel cases, music boxes, and the fragile drawers in the top parts of desks where secret letters were normally stashed away. And of course some of the keys, the hollow ones, had undoubtedly been used to wind clocks.

And clocks, more in evidence than anything else by the very fact of their size and number, ruled the attic. Against one wall, towering above Wendall's head, stood a grandfather clock with a bashed-in casing and a broken crystal: its fleur-de-lis hands had stopped at 12:25. Of what year? Wendall wondered. In what century? He thought: 12:25 occurred on a certain day under certain circumstances. He thought: David Matthewson had suddenly stopped—at 12:25? or 3:15? or 9:30? never more to draw a breath, tick off a minute, move his hands. . . .

Wendall approached the blank face of a white wooden clock hanging from a nail, reached up, and with his crayon drew in hands pointing to five o'clock. This was, he decided, the exact time Fred had walked into his room and said Helen wouldn't be coming home anymore. Standing on tiptoes, he wrote H.O. in the narrow space above the twelve.

On a larger clock face which had a ship painted over the twelve and whales lunging out of blue puddles every quarter hour, he drew in an 8:15 in the morning for David Matthewson. Of course, he had no idea what time his unseen uncle had died, but he gathered most soldiers were killed in the morning, when the light was best and the enemy, rested after a night of sleep, could aim better.

But on the most elegant clock of all he was helpless to work his changes, for the crystal was rusted shut and no amount of prying with, among other things, a straight razor, a bayonet, and a pair of spurs could get it open. The face of this clock was sunken into a carved wooden pagoda. In the back of the pagoda a hole opened into the complicated innards. The clock's chime was located just inside the hole. Wendall snapped the clapper against it with his finger; the resultant sound was crystal clear, its tone entirely rustless, so that for the longest time afterwards he could hear its note off in a corner dying.

The hands pointed to 11:10: evening, Wendall surmised—almost midnight. It would be his time for the people who hadn't died yet: for his father in the nighttime jungles of the Pacific; for the bearded man; for John T. who one icy night come winter might skid off the road on his Harley, and they would find him, high in the frozen branches of a tree. . . .

Wendall followed a beam thick with dust toward a small cobwebbed window at one end of the attic. About his feet tiny wings flashed: they were gone in a second, disappearing into the low shadows wherein nail points gleamed, leaving phantasmal turbulences in the sunbeam. Ahead of him, silhouetted against the dusty window, wasps, dryly doubled over in death, dangled from the end of spider web strands. Occasional breezes through a crack in the molding stirred them, but there was no question as to whether they were alive or dead—they were beyond death, preserved in the dry air, mummified.

He stood at the window looking down on the street. Behind him the attic air pulsed in a mysterious way. Was it ghosts, or mere boy's imagination giving birth to supernatural wavelings in the unstirred air? Was it possible that the voices of all the 2:25's and 5 o'clocks and 8:15's that had ever been were trying to whisper to him from some land outside time—from perhaps, the land of wineglass trees and Bavarian plates, the ultrastill land of grassy silence?

His body relaxed, he drowsed. Something sad and precious hovered just out of reach: it was as if all the dust-covered inactive things were going on, or the resonance, the echo of their usefulness and the personalities of the people who had used them could still be felt and even defined by him if only he had the key, if only, in closing his eyes for a minute, he could be dead. . . .

TEN

Wendall submerged himself wholeheartedly in the war. He began a scrapbook of pictures and articles, and his ardent, often premature scissor attacks on the Boston newspaper soon had Cornelia stewing.

"He's doing it on purpose, he steals my sewing shears and makes them dull cutting all that paper," she complained one night. The doctor, who was sitting on the john smoking a cigarette, tapped some ashes into the sink.

"Buy him scissors of his own," he suggested wearily. It had been a dull day: he felt submerged under the weight of picayune things. He had, for the past hour, been trying to think of a casual and happy activity to do with the family, but his mind had drawn a blank. And though it was late, he disliked the idea of bed, knowing that as soon as his head touched the pillow he would be wide awake, and his knees and hands would intensify their aching.

"Buy this, buy that, throw away money here, throw it away there, spend, spend, spend," Cornelia said.

"Fifteen cents, maybe twenty-five cents." The doctor dropped his cigarette in the sink. He flushed the toilet and, standing before the medicine cabinet mirror, took out his teeth.

"If we had all the fifteen cents's you've thrown away over the past fifteen years we'd be about fifteen thousand dollars richer right now," Cornelia called, turning down their beds in the other room.

The doctor nodded to the mirror and gargled an antiseptic foam in his mouth. He pouted, spit into the sink, rinsed his hands and smoothed the palms down his pajama front. Opening his mouth wide and tilting his head at an angle, he inspected his teeth, tongue and the back of his throat. "Aah . . ." he said, thinking of all the millions of mouths he had looked into, all the millions of throats that had opened to him while he stuck in "the old Popsicle stick." For kids, the old Popsicle stick; for middle-aged people, the old Popsicle stick; for the dying, the old Popsicle stick—and it had always made them smile. Right now, the thought of it didn't make him smile, though: in fact, for just a few seconds he disliked it with uncomfortable intensity.

Cornelia hovered at the half-open bathroom door. "If we had all the money people owed you, we'd be millionaires."

"Yes, wouldn't we?" He held up his hands and looked at them a second, then shrugged, and went into the other room.

"Your turn," he said, getting into bed.

Cornelia switched out the overhead light and shut

the bathroom door behind her. The doctor pulled his covers up under his chin, arranged his hands on his stomach, and closed his eyes. Now, while the bedside lamp was still lit and his wife was making her pre-bed noises, he felt drowsy. He listened passively to the water faucet, first hot, then cold, in the bathroom. There was silence, the toilet flushed, the faucets went on again for a short time, the medicine cabinet snapped open, there was toothbrushing, spitting—Cornelia came out and walked around his bed to her own and got in, turning out the lamp. Darkness brought the doctor out of his slumber. He opened his eyes, and his hands, his knees, his toes began to ache.

"Sybil have a good day?" he asked quietly, knowing he might just as well find out now, as it would only be brought up later.

"She did some reading, but hardly ate a thing. If she doesn't begin eating right away she's going to waste to a chit, she'll die of malnutrition, that's what I think. Frederick, don't you have any little pills she could take?"

"She'll be okay. Everything will turn out fine."

"That's all right for you to say—"

"How's Wendall?" he interrupted.

"Oh, *him* again. Well you've got to talk with him, do something this time, I don't care what, I'm at the end of my rope. I don't want him playing with little Tomas any more if he's going to be the way he is. He'll turn the child into a gangster, mark my words. That boy is evil, there's no other way to describe him. Did you speak to him about the newspapers?"

"Three days ago."

"Well, I wish he would run away. He's going to drive me crazy. I think you should give him a good lambasting."

"What he needs, apparently, is for us to love him."

"How can we love him? He doesn't give us a chance to love."

"Oh . . ." But what was the use? "Time will tell . . ." he said vaguely, unhappy.

"Bitte's sent their bill over today. Did you know

Bernie bought two new mole traps he never told us about three weeks ago? Those traps cost two dollars and fifty-nine cents each. I told Bernie—I called him to the carpet today—I told him he wasn't to buy anything without your consent because things were a litle tighter than usual, but he didn't look me in the eyes, I don't think he even listened. I tell you, there's something shifty about Bernie Aja: it's getting shiftier every day. I want you to speak to him, make it clear . . ."

"Of course . . . Is that a dove I hear?"

"A what?"

"Outside. There's a bird or something making a noise."

They listened for a minute. The doctor thought about mole traps, then about Bernie Aja who for fifteen years now had been getting shiftier every day. He wondered what time it was where Fred was right now. And was his eldest son sleeping? fighting? dying?

Cornelia snuggled her head into a pillow of worries and slipped quickly off to sleep. Not so the doctor. For over an hour he lay on his back, wondering how his affairs could be so continually depressing. His hands throbbed; he wriggled his fingers.

Then it dawned on him what he would truly like to do with his family, something he had not done for years. All he needed was a sunny spring or early summer evening around five o'clock. He imagined himself coming in from the office and shouting, "All right, all you scallywags, into the bus on the double!" Down the stairs came Freddy—serious, shy, carefully marking a place in a book he was reading; out of the barn ran John T. and Sybil, fresh from some devilish shenanigans; and from the kitchen, untying her apron and smiling, strode Cornelia. They all piled into the car and went for a ride, it was as simple as that.

Before Freddy left and kind of broke up the family, they used to go on two, sometimes three drives a week. They drove along dirt roads, and the air was pungent with fresh manure smell, the fields were green, the trees bursting with leaves, and the far mountains were veiled in blue haze. And sometime during every drive they inched around a deep-rutted turn in one road or another, and Sybil screamed, "Look Mummy, look Daddy, look everybody, there's Camel's Hump!" and they all craned their necks, and sure enough there it was, distant, vague, almost lost, and it was Cornelia who always said, "That's the prettiest mountain in the world," and at that moment the doctor felt not only was Camel's Hump the prettiest mountain in the world, but also his family was the prettiest family in the world, and how lucky they were to be alive.

Now he wished they could be once more all together in the car on a quiet evening, about to turn a corner and bring Camel's Hump into view. But not since the war began had they gone for a ride. And anyway, he could envisage what would probably happen if they did get together one evening for such an excursion. He'd be at the wheel, Cornelia would be in the front seat, but not at all close to him, and the kids would be silent in back, and he knew that as they turned a special corner, someone might say laxly, almost in passing, "There's Camel's Hump." and Cornelia would halt her yapping for just a second, John T. would glower a little more ominously, Sybil would say "Oh," startled, and then they would turn another corner and the prettiest mountain in the world would swing out of sight, and rightfully so, poking its magical height up for only a younger, less embittered family to marvel over.

The doctor switched his thoughts to Fred, trying to bring his eldest son into focus, and after a minute two incidents came to mind. The first had to do with his penguin ashtray. Fred had given it to him as a Christmas present some nineteen years ago. The doctor had unwrapped it, held it up, and everyone in the room except Fred had crowded around and oh'd and ah'd, until Sybil shrieked, "But Daddy—*you don't smoke!*" And Fred, who had been sitting tensely on the piano stool, shouted, "That doesn't matter!" clammed up, and no matter who tried to tease him out of it, he wouldn't respond for the rest of the day. The very next morning the doctor bought his first pack of cigarettes, and he lit one up right after dinner. At first it had been miserable, though he never let on, of course, and by gosh, after a month or so he began to smoke a lot, and pretty soon he was inhaling.

The other incident had to do with a pony, Dolphin, they'd had for several years, and who'd been drowned in the '27 flood. Fred had cried for days afterwards, his nose and eyes running continually. Finally, the doctor had grasped him by the shoulders and said, "What are you tryin' to do, start a second flood or somethin'?" and Fred had wrenched loose, crying, "You don't feel anything!" and hid for hours in the ravaged barn before they'd found him.

The doctor sat up, startled and sweating. Then he smiled: stuff and nonsense—what *was* the matter with him? The damn detmoles must be having a field day inside his decrepit old noggin. He eased himself backwards, sadly shaking his head.

Life had been reduced to mole traps, leaky hoses, the payments on a mortgage, on insurance policies, on medical supplies and equipment, on fixing up the house, and on its taxes. . . . He had a heartsick daughter, a belligerent grandson who needed loving care, a son, John T., in whom every day seemed to etch a bitter trace, and another son who might be dying somewhere, might be dead, and a wife who, in trying to keep the ship afloat, was actually blabbing it under —Well, he loved her, he loved them all: and things weren't really much worse than they'd ever been, and if you loved—Hell, he didn't even know what love was unless it was just sticking together, riding out all the storms, pulling your weight with the team. . . .

But why had they all become so tense? Why couldn't they have fun anymore? Was it the war? Or himself? He wriggled his fingers, feeling that pain might consume him. Later he drifted into uneasy sleep and dreamed of the May day when it had snowed and when he should have collapsed to his knees on the sidewalk, given a last thankful nod to the budding tree branches above, and died.

The dream erased his pain: a phantom looking in the window after midnight would have caught him smiling.

ELEVEN

Wendall prepared himself and Tom for war. He discovered, in the umbrella stand beside the front door, a dueling cane which he limped around on when Cornelia wasn't present to make him put it away, and which he brandished upon occasion, when, all out of ammunition and severely exhausted, he would turn like a wounded lion on the crest of the lawn, his back to the locust tree by the carriage port, and face single-handedly the charge of ten million Nips or Krauts (authentically portrayed by Tom, appropriately costumed in a tricornered hat, Lone Ranger mask, ratty elbow-length gloves, and tan grass-stained football pants). Wendall always repelled such charges with a maximum of effort, sweat, and theatrical flair, and sometimes (though not often), as Tom lay bubbling up blood on the roots of the locust, he would stagger, pale from loss of blood, onto the center of the lawn and collapse, and, amid operatic never-say-die admonishments to the rest of his army, he would condescendingly expire, much to the elation of Tom, for whom these small triumphs were the magic elixir that renewed a hundredfold his willingness to play without a squawk and until hell froze over the doomed part of the dastardly enemy.

Their day's activities were usually inspired by the content of the Boston newspaper which they received, seated side by side on the top front porch step, during the blissful somnolent hour after lunch and before

Tom was sent to take his nap. Or, more properly, it was an hour that might have been blissful had not Jimmy Wiggen been in charge of delivering the news. For every afternoon as Wendall and Tom eagerly awaited the paper, they just as uneagerly awaited Jimmy Wiggen—and with good reason, too.

It was Jimmy's habit, pedaling by on his bike, to fling the triangularly folded paper onto the front porch, or at least in that general direction: most often the paper landed in some daffodils beside the house, or skidded to a ripped and dirtied stop under the carriage port—anywhere, that is, but where Jimmy aimed it. Yet, soon after Wendall and Tom took to stationing themselves on the steps, Jimmy developed a curiously accurate aim, and, facilitating this aim by slowing his bike down (and sometimes actually stopping it), he repeatedly tried to hit one or the other of the smaller boys with the paper.

Each time he reared back to throw, Tom and Wendall scrambled out of the way, then hurled insults at Jimmy's vulgar form, but the insults got them nowhere.

"It's our property, our porch," Wendall complained to the doctor. "We have the right to sit on it peaceably whenever we want."

"Well . . . if you don't like to be bothered, just don't sit on the porch when he comes by, that's all there is to it," the doctor replied.

After this brief exchange, Wendall growled to Tom, "I am going to do something dire to that son of a bitch: we have inalienable rights to sit on our own porch steps unmolested and I am going to see that they are protected."

But his brain was functioning groggily, and several days passed during which he could strike upon no adequate plan of revenge. Then Tom inadvertently came up with a solution to the problem. He said, strictly off the cuff, "Why don't we shoot him like in the war?"

"No." said Wendall. "You can't just shoot somebody. No, that wouldn't be right."

He said no, then thought about his no, then wondered a bit, and as he wondered he thought how satisfying it would be to plug Jimmy Wiggen, and the thought grew, it burgeoned and blossomed way out of proportion, it became an obsession, and one afternoon he tiptoed into the barn to have a look at the guns, most of them old, rusted, and useless, hanging on the wall of a room that had once been a horse stall.

One gun was in excellent condition, of course: John T.'s sleek and dangerous-looking .410. Wendall reached up and touched the shiny butt; then he slunk away and thought some more.

Next morning he returned to the barn and took the .410 off its hook and felt its weight in his hands until a noise outside scared him into hanging the weapon up and effecting a hasty retreat.

The following day, after sneaking a shotgun shell from a box in John T.'s desk drawer, he went to the barn where not only did he take the gun off the wall, but after several minutes of experimentation he also learned how to cock it and pull the trigger. He broke the weapon open, held the barrel up to the light, and squinted through it as he remembered John T. doing the night he had killed the bat.

Then he inserted the shell into the chamber, closed the gun, pulled back the hammer with his thumb, and stood in the center of the room for five minutes thinking how all he now had to do was aim the gun at Jimmy Wiggen, pull the trigger, and forever after receive his newspapers in peace. He pictured Jimmy in agony, doubled over and gripping his stomach, screaming as his bike wobbled up Coolidge Street, bucked the bridge railing, and plunged in poetic bloody flight down to the river. Piranha fish stripped his body to a skeleton in fifteen seconds; a church bell tolled. Should Wendall phone Van Duren's Funeral Home and have them send over a plastic bag for the bones? Should he phone Mr. Kahler and order one tombstone appropriately inscribed? A wet squirrel tail and a paper snapper floated to the surface and drifted slowly downriver . . . the skeleton washed ashore on a sandbar beyond the railroad tracks . . .

Well, that was a bit overdoing it, he decided. Actually, he needed only to aim the gun somewhere in the vicinity of Jimmy and his bike just to give him a thorough scare and let him know where he stood. So thinking, he raised the gun, fitted the butt against his shoulder, took careful aim at the single small high window in the room and pulled the trigger.

For days afterwards Wendall wondered groggily how he could have been so utterly unprepared for the blast that followed. The gun butt jarred his shoulder with such force that he snapped around and his glasses flew off: he did not even have time to be terrified by the magnitude of what he had done, because, as a few small pieces of glass from the window rained on his head, he passed instantly through the entire register of emotions into shock.

It took Cornelia, hotly pursued by Bernie Aja, thirty seconds to thunder into the barn and find Wendall standing in the same spot, staring up at a few strands of spider web that wavered in the paneless window. Cornelia fell to her knees and hugged the boy. Her face red as a beet, she sputtered, "Oh God, oh misery, oh *God!*" The gray smells of her hair and tight skin penetrated Wendall's shock; her dry lips touched his cheek, her arms squeezed him tight, and it was all he could do, under the circumstances, to keep his head turned away from both the grownups so they wouldn't see him crying.

"Golly," Bernie said. "By golly, he blew out the window . . ."

Cornelia held Wendall out at arm's length, and they both began to giggle hysterically.

"It's not funny!" blubbered Cornelia.

"I *know,*" Wendall countered.

But they guffawed and boohooed to beat the band.

TWELVE

The penciled note Duffy found under his gloves on the shed roof read:

> DEAR DUFFY,
> I know you aren't dead. I know it's you who took from the store. I don't care if you take things. I want to help you.
>
> M.

Duffy returned the following night. He tried the screen door to the back porch, found it unlocked, padded quietly down the hallway, stopped short of the stairs, and leaned forward to peer around the corner: his mother was sitting on the landing.

Each had been expecting the other; neither jumped. They locked eyes for a few seconds, then Duffy drew his head away and walked out.

The afternoon of that same day, Irma Kahler left the store and went up the street to the Green. Her hands shoved deep into the baggy front pockets of her pale yellow dress, she stood beneath the sprinkling shadows of the elm, looking at her husband's work on the memorial. She stayed for three minutes; during that time she felt a peculiar sensation inside her; it made her giddy, almost as if in her womb a child were experiencing its first life throes. She thought even the nipples on her flattened breasts were prickling. When the feeling became too much for her, she hurried back to the market.

For a while, Duffy came to the store nearly every night. Sometimes Irma sat on the stairs watching him while he raided the store, but she refrained from speaking to him, afraid that if she were to break the silence he would never return. One night when she slept through his visit, Duffy got upstairs and stole two knives, a spoon, a can opener, some soap, a razor and blades, a box of wooden matches, and two towels. As soon as he got back to the baggage room he shaved off his beard, and his face felt so good minus the hair that he had to go for a walk. He followed the tracks of the grain elevator, scrambled down the embankment, and approached the old car buckled on its rims in the weeds near the strip of poplars and sumac. To his great joy, the rear seat, though mildewed and full of small holes, was still intact. He wrestled it out of the car, lugged it back to the station house, and worked it over the partition.

To celebrate the find, he opened a can of peach halves, but as he was eating them his guts suddenly floated up and swelled against the sides of his diaphragm, and, groaning, he circled the room, his hands patting, then beating the walls. But the thing inside him grew, driving him on, and then out again. Whimpering, he tipped up his climbing trunk, grabbed one of the kitchen knives he had stolen, and scaled the partition.

The cool air cleared his head, his stomach settled. A mist lay along the tracks, dew sparkled on the rails. He walked purposefully up to the tracks where they crossed Main Street. For as far as he could see down the street there was not a car parked at the curb, not a person on the sidewalk. Mist shrouded the elm tree on the Green, it seeped out the leaves like smoke.

"Go ahead. Walk right down it. Don't be afraid."

The light at Rutland and Main clicked red. Holding the knife at his side, Duffy advanced cautiously to the Green where he paused a minute to read the inscription on the war memorial. He was surprised to find his own name, and, when he went on, the idea of having that name on a memorial for the dead exhilarated him. He wondered: if someone looked out a window right now would he think him a ghost? Or had he changed so much that even if he walked up to a man and said, "I'm Duffy Kahler," the man wouldn't recognize him?

He elongated his stride for half a block, then began to jog. He speeded up going past the gas station, ran by the Unitarian Church, and slowed down, winded, shortly before the deserted lot. At the other side of the grange hall he dashed over the lawn into the shadow of a brick wall and circled the building. In the rear he bore left and came to the end of the lawn, where ten feet below him ran the river. Bearing right, he followed the grass to its termination in the backyard shrubs of a neighboring house. A little further on, the wall descended and broke onto an open muddy spot near the water, and the river narrowed slightly, going through a shallow pebbly rapids.

Duffy waded across, wetting only his sneakers and the cuffs of his jeans. On the other side he pushed up an incline through lush grasses, skirted a recently plowed plot, and crouched in the shadow of the barn. Mist swayed over the river like the soft dispersed tails of smoky cats. It searched the cement wall, touching and leaving, and went under the Coolidge Street bridge going against the river's flow.

Duffy advanced swiftly through a line of weeds, keeping his eye on the darkened windows of the main house. The front porch light still burned: a few exhausted moths fluttered around the bulb.

Hunched over, he scurried across the driveway and went through some lilacs that lined up with the edge of the back porch. He found the door to the playhouse open and sat in one of the wicker chairs for a while, then climbed to the second rung of the ladder and poked his head into the small attic. Some cardboard boxes stood against the far triangular wall; closer by lay a broomstick with wooden wheels at the base and a crude horsehead nailed to the other end. Duffy was sure he remembered the exact day John T. had built the toy for Sybil. . . .

He left the playhouse and snuck alongside the main house, zipping the tip of his knife on screen windows. At the corner he rose one step onto the back porch.

Some flower pots arranged in low cardboard trays lined the side of the house. A hose, patched with rags, ran from a spigot underneath the dining room bay windows, over the porch and through his legs. He followed the hose to the slanting cellar door and cocked his head, listening. Hearing nothing to cause alarm, he settled the knife with utmost care on the lid of a garbage can, stooped over, and grasped the handle to the door.

It lifted easily; he descended into the stairwell. Webbing tickled his nose; upright wooden pillars obstructed his way; the metal on John T.'s jukebox gleamed—the invention gave him a start, then evoked a smile.

His body juices went warm, making him supremely relaxed and confident. He'd walked right in without a hitch. Gingerly, he poked open the door to the tiny furnace closet, seated himself, and folded his hands in his lap, feeling the chill in his feet drain out through his wet sneakers.

"Nobody knows you're here," he whispered. "Nobody has even the faintest idea. When you leave, don't forget the knife on the garbage can."

On the third floor, Wendall's eyes flew open, drawing him instantly out of a deep sleep. He prickled all over with the sensation that somebody new was in the house.

And down below, Duffy's confidence suddenly tailed off. He began to sweat. His feet got cold again. And in a minute he had to flee from the cellar. In his hurry he forgot to take the knife with him.

THIRTEEN

With the Fourth of July imminent, really dehydrating weather set in. The river, which had once been dangerous enough to warrant a warning a day to the boys about going too close to its edge, dried up so that the one actual danger of falling in was no longer that they might drown, but rather that they might break their necks when they landed on an exposed rock or sandbar. When at home, the doctor went around singing "The Bluetail Fly," his summer song, but his voice was dry, it cracked with fatigue. At most given hours of the day, Bernie Aja could be found either on his hands and knees in a flower or vegetable garden, puttering around with a trowel and yanking weeds, or else seated in semi-darkness on piled-up crates in the barn toolroom, smoking his pipe and looking very bushed. Sybil slept long and late, did a lot of reading, and helped her mother around the house. She ate little, grew noticeably thinner, and went daily to pray for an hour or so at St. John's Church. John T. continued to work hard at the gas station: what little free time he had he divided between Ercel Perry and the cellar. The jukebox, so far as anyone could tell, was progressing: it looked like an upright piano someone had dropped a boulder on, but John T. swore that one day it would work and they'd all be millionaires.

In reply to this, Sybil said, "Then, when winter comes, we'll paste thousands of dollars on all our trees. We'll listen to the money leaves rustling in the wind at night. We'll wear armbands of thousand-dollar bills, and our salute will be 'Heil Rockefeller!' "

"I'll buy a hundred pink motorcycles," said John T., "and I'll throw them away when their gas tanks are empty."

"Daddy can retire and we'll buy him a baseball team to play with," said Sybil. "Hell, we'll buy him the Boston Red Sox if he wants. We'll even buy him Boston. And we'll buy back Freddy from the Marines. And we'll buy a diamond asparagus fork. And a sapphire-studded muzzle to put on Mummy when she talks too much."

"I don't think that's funny," said Cornelia woefully. "It's not healthy to joke about money when you don't have it. If this family would do a little less joking—"

"—it would fall apart, way apart," Sybil interrupted. When Cornelia looked hurt, she touched her mother's cheek and said, "I didn't mean it," left the living room, and ran upstairs. John T. scowled, bit his fingernail, and said no more.

Wendall sprinkled all his escape money onto the bed. He sat at the head of the bed arranging the coins in piles, gloating over their abundance. All told he had most of the change from the five-dollar bill Aunt Nancy had given him, plus $3.35 he had assembled through his own wit and dexterity, including one quarter he had an hour earlier lifted from Cornelia's purse.

There was too much, it gleamed too brightly, it weighed too much, it was too hot to keep in a sock in his closet anymore, that was for sure. So he decided to transfer his treasure to the great outdoors where the possibility of its being stumbled across would be infinitely less.

But traipsing through the kitchen he accidentally jingled the money in his pocket. Cornelia looked up from a breadboard on which she was kneading dough for a pie, and said altogether too calmly, "Going somewhere?"

Wendall made his eyes as wide and innocent as they could go.

Cornelia said, "When are you going to return to me the quarter you filched from my purse this afternoon?"

"Huh?" Wendall's brow squinched into a sincere and well-practiced frown.

"You stole a quarter from my purse this afternoon," said Cornelia, "and don't think I don't know it, either. I'm on to your ways, young man. I know that some of the change that's been disappearing around this house hasn't just been flying away or going to pack rats. Now: are we going to have this out in the open right here, or do I have to tell Frederick on you?"

"I don't know what you're talking about." Wendall drew himself up, composing his face and frown so that both were inscrutable. "I don't know anything about your quarter. *I* certainly did not steal it. There is nothing in this town that is worth buying anyway."

"Nancy warned me," said Cornelia. "She told me about your sticky fingers. She told me the trouble you'd be. She said you'd steal us blind behind our backs, and I wouldn't be surprised if that's exactly what you're doing."

"That's exactly what I am *not* doing," said the boy, straining to keep his voice calm. These scenes were completely familiar to him: he had utmost confidence that he could get out of this one with no trouble at all.

"I don't know why I don't have a stroke the way people in this household treat me," Cornelia said. Abruptly, she sat down at the table.

"I don't know why you don't either," said Wendall, holding back an impudent smile.

"I'm just trying to be helpful and keep things going," she said, opening the drawer to the table and taking out a handkerchief. "But we'll all be burned in hell before anybody listens to me. I'm not likable, I know that, and my ways may be stern, but I've come a sight further than you, Mr. Know-It-All, I have come through fifty-two years, that's what I have, and if you think they've been easy—oh dear, I think I'm going to have a cry . . ."

Wendall had always thought of Cornelia as a kind of feelingless scarecrow stuffed with straw and sand, and the tears honestly shocked him, though it turned out to be one of the shortest cries he had ever witnessed. Cornelia sobbed no more than three times, rubbed her eyes energetically, and put the wet handkerchief back in the drawer. She sighed once, deeply, took several huge breaths, blinked her eyes, and stood up.

"Well, there's no time around here to be crying," she said. "I ought to be whipped myself for being a fool. But I don't want to see you anymore for a while, I've had enough. And don't walk out of here with a smirk on your face, young man, because I'm giving a full report to Frederick, and don't think he won't do something. And before you leave you can just get a sponge from the sink and wash that spot where you've been smearing your fingers."

Obediently, Wendall scrubbed off the doorjamb, then rinsed out the sponge and went outside. Morning glories strung up the rickety back porch pillars displayed wilted blossoms: a new kind of butterfly with brown jagged wings flew off one of the flowers. He followed it into the sky, feeling more unsettled by his encounter in the kitchen than by rights he should have.

In the barn, at the end of a shelf lined with mostly cracked flowerpots, he found a glass jar. Hiding it beneath his shirt, he walked nonchalantly along the barn, turned the corner, and followed the base line to the far side of the building. There, he unscrewed the cap to the jar, dumped in the money, screwed on the top, crawled a few feet under the barn, and hid the jar behind two bricks. Then he backed out, went around the house side of the structure, and climbed to the cupola.

A pigeon heard him coming too late: he shut the wooden door and, in one jump, placed himself in front of the window hole. The bird flapped frantically for a minute, then perched uncomfortably on a small beam. Wendall leapt and caught one wing. He hauled the bird in, clamped its wings together, and held it close against his chest as he looked out the hole, past the house, up over roofs and treetops to the park.

He could see the upper half of the grassy slope cleared for skiing: two small figures were on the slope, sitting in the warm sunlight—Tom and Sybil: his aunt was painting.

Wendall touched his cheek to the pigeon's head. He felt lousy, unsettled by his kitchen confrontation with Cornelia. The triumph of his financial escapades had faded; for a moment he wished he'd never taken any money—and then a minute passed in which he actually entertained the thought of casually returning the various coins, sneaking them back into purses and pockets, and into the cuff link receptacle on the doctor's bureau. In fact, he became so dotty for a few seconds that he chucked the pigeon out the window hole.

That bumped him rudely awake. What in tarnation was he doing, kissing away a possible quarter?

He growled at Cornelia: it was all her fault. As he descended the rickety stairs, he wondered where her purse was now. He pictured it lying in a chair or on a sofa somehere, soft and pliant and pregnant for the plundering.

His eyes lit up fiendishly, and he growled again. Pity that poor purse if he ever got alone with it!

FOURTEEN

At five o'clock on the morning of the Fourth, John T. shook Tom and Wendall awake. Mysteriously *shh*-ing them, he helped Tom dress while Wendall clothed himself in the bathroom. Then John T. led them downstairs, and from the umbrella rack beside the front door he withdrew a large paper bag. Grinning demoniacally, he ushered the boys out into the lime-colored morning.

"What're we doin'?" Tom asked.

"You'll see . . ."

They followed him up Coolidge Street to the bridge where he paused and opened the mouth of the bag. Tom and Wendall looked inside—their eyes bulged.

"What are you going to do with all *them?*"

"Oh, just tell a few people to rise and shine. Come on."

First they lit a string of twenty-five crackers on the Svensons' front porch. Midway through the string an upstairs window flew open and one of the sisters screamed, "I'm going to call the po-*lice!*"

"Go ahead!" Wendall shouted back, tingling all over with sweet revenge. He had a brief vision of himself lighting the heavy cord wick of a scrumptiously fat stick of dynamite jammed under their front porch.

A minute later the house erupted off its foundations and rose lazily into the air on a geyser of purple fire and smoke, then it disintegrated, and Dorothy and Marie tumbled head over heels like boneless monkeys down to earth amid a cascade of boards, bricks, shingles, torn drapes, knitting needles, and silverware. . . .

They lit out like all hell afire, turned right on Chestnut Street, and invaded the short slum along Prescott. Fifty yards down the stretch, Tom fell: John T. scooped him up and carried him piggyback. They heaved strings of firecrackers onto the second-story porches, into open doorways and ran like Mercuries. Going full tilt, they hit Rutland Avenue, leaving behind two blocks of cursing grownups, wailing babies, and barking dogs.

Sunlight lit up the morning: it glistened off the hoods of idle cars and glinted in the windows of both the Stebbinsville Tavern and the Pavilion Hotel. By the time they were through with both structures, the upstairs windows were filled with irate heads, but the boys were already disappearing from sight, off to the right along Conroy Street. Where Conroy leveled out and terminated at South Maple, they caught their breaths, chucked several cherry bombs back the way they had come, then headed north toward the park.

A block and a half later they ran out of ammunition. Wendall touched a match to the last cherry bomb fuse, John T. hurled it into a flower bed at the base of a house, and, as shreds of pansy petals were blown back at them, they sprinted uphill another hundred yards to the south entrance of the park. Once safely in its houseless protection, they slowed down to a walk. Wheezing like a bagpipe, John T. let Tom slide off his back. Trees shaded their path, but already the day seemed hot, it was going to be a scorcher.

John T. led them along a dirt road through a pine woods where some crows had gathered and were cawing. Now that they had slowed down, blood rushed into Wendall's head, he staggered and said, "I have to stop a minute . . ." whereby, with as much dignity as he could muster, he removed his glasses, stepped behind a tree, and for half a minute was violently sick.

"Boy, you must be in lousy shape," said John T. when Wendall navigated shakily back to them. The boy chose not to risk a worded reply, but made, rather, a halfhearted attempt at stabbing John T. with a glare, which came out as more of a plea than anything else.

Emerging from the woods, they went by Bloody Pond: John T. explained that in the early 1800's there was supposed to have been a triple murder by drowning there. The pond looked anything but bloody now, however; its placid surface was disturbed only by the darting forms of water skeeters. To their left, the ski slope went by, then they walked through the north entrance onto blacktop and descended a curvy road, the beginning of Coolidge Street. When they got home, the lawns were already beginning to wilt under the searing sun, and early hummingbirds were hard at work in the flower garden.

"Well, we sure blammed them," Tom said. "I bet they thought the war was in Vermont."

John T. smiled, said, "Yeah, I guess we really had them thinking," and then he dropped his smile and went inside.

Tom belched, not once, but thrice, and stretched his arms out. Wendall was feeling better, and impulsively he pointed a finger at his cousin and fired point-blank into his belly. Taken by surprise, Tom lurched and staggered back; his eyes bugged, his nose wrinkled, and his lips curled into a rabid snarl. Wendall fired again; Tom twitched and shivered and pitched onto the floor in a corner. He bridged, his breath coming out in huge hoarse rasps, and just before he expired he managed to get his pistol from its scabbard, and he squeezed off one shot in Wendall's direction. The bullet struck its mark. Wendall bounced off one railing after another, his hands flopping and his tongue lolling, his body went lazy from loss of blood, and, smiling dazedly, he collapsed to his hands and knees, unloosed a final shot at the quivering mess of Jap flesh in the corner, then died, his head plopping comfortably onto the WELCOME mat.

"Lord love a duck," said the doctor, who had witnessed the double killing from behind the relative safety of the screen door. "Looks like that compost heap is gonna get some high-grade fertilizer after all!"

At four o'clock in the afternoon, the doctor and Jim took Tom, Wendall, Ercel Perry, and John T. to a Dual Cities baseball game. The Dual City Tigers were an amateur team sponsored by Stebbinsville and Willow Falls.

Once installed in their seats at the game, the doctor straight-way bought Tom and Wendall some hot dogs, Cracker Jack, and Royal Crown Colas, then he launched into an explanation of how to keep score—lines diagonal here on the scorecard, this and that blacked out there, numbers . . . 1–3, 5–4–3, letters . . . FO, S, 2B . . . "A lot of cantankerous mumbo-jumbo if you ask me," Wendall said. The doctor went on to explain what was going to happen before it happened, and when it didn't happen as he said it was going to, he knew exactly why not, and it was all so obvious he should have seen it all beforehand, must be that his rondo-sketiaptic dispeller was clogged with detmoles, etc. Even though the Tigers eventually lost 15–3 to Twin Cities (Montpelier–Barre), his enthusiasm never once waned. He was in it for the game, for the green grass and sun, for the carnival smell of the stadium, for the guys who razzed "Stickit iniz ear!" and "D'umpbeatziz wife!" He was in it because for a couple of hours it didn't matter who won or lost, the only object was to enjoy himself, and nobody was going to come blithering up to him wailing about some unauthorized person who had bought mole traps to kill off the animals that were ruining the infield. He argued right and left, up and down, with anybody over anything, and after a heated exchange, he would turn to Tom or Wendall, nudge him with his elbow, and burst out laughing. "Oh, I got him runnin'," he would sputter happily. "You watch old Bill over there: I wouldn't be surprised if in a minute he exploded, so hang onto your hats, boys!"

Jim, on the other hand, went at the game more scientifically and without all the fanfare. A real student of baseball, he furrowed his brow in such a way that his eyebrows descended to, and were almost burned by, the stub of his cigar, making him look like an inventor who had just patented the game, and who was tensely watching it in its maiden operation, his hawklike eyes on all areas of the diamond at once searching for bugs in his creation. While concentrating on what was to happen next, he whispered, or rather coaxed, in a constant but almost inaudible line of chatter—"They're gonna go for the squeeze, watch it now, pitch him inside, inside and high . . ." He, more often than the doctor, called the play. And when he did, instead of bellowing "I told you so!" to the neighbors, he merely relaxed his brow, tapped the ash off his cigar, nodded to the stub, replaced it in a brown hole between his teeth, and refurrowed his brow for the next crisis.

John T. didn't care much for the science of the game. The important thing to him was that D.C. win: consequently he viewed this particular contest with his nose wrinkled in disgust. As for Tom—he didn't mind the game so long as he had a soft drink in one hand and a box of Cracker Jack in the other: eats, and plenty of them, were all he needed to be satisfied.

But Wendall wasn't yet ready for baseball. He squirmed, complained of the heat and of a stomachache, and was soon inwardly purple with rage at the American Pastime about which he understood nothing, and which was making him suffer so, and he soon wondered why in hell he hadn't had the sense to go to the matinee at the Imperial with Bernie Aja. By the fifth inning he finally figured out who the opposition was, and seeing that they were lambasting Dual Cities afforded him his only pleasure of the afternoon: he gloated joyfully when it became evident the massacre was going to be a near total blitzing.

"Perfect execution of the squeeze play," said the

doctor, when in the seventh inning Dual Cities bunted across their initial run. "I told you they were gonna try it."

Wendall clapped his hands over his ears. "I don't care what it was: I'm hot and I hate baseball. When I become President of the United States I'm going to abolish it."

"Games are very important to a boy," said the doctor. "They teach him to pull his own weight with the team. They teach him to be a part of something and to be dependent on others, and also to have others dependent on him."

"Well, I'm not dependent on anybody," Wendall said.

"All right." The doctor smiled. "If you're goin' to be such a sourpuss, why don't you go wait in the car? That way you won't make the rest of us miserable. That face of yours is so long it looks like you're gonna bump your chin on the ground."

"Oh, I'll stay," grumbled Wendall.

"Don't do us any favors," John T. said. "Boy, how you ever got to be my brother Freddy's kid I'll never know."

Wendall flushed. "Fred doesn't like sports either. We never went to any games together. He's too educated for that, to scream and yell over nothing."

John T. said, "Oh, have you ever got it wrong, pal. Helen didn't like sports. Freddy was the best high school skier this state ever had, and he wasn't so bad a skater either—"

"Hey, now, *hey!*" protested the doctor.

"Well—tell him go soak his head," said John T.

"All right, if that's the way you feel—" Wendall got up and made his way down the grandstand. The crowd let out a whoop as Dual Cities scored their second and third runs. Settling back, Jim said, "That'll be the scoring for the day," and he was right.

In the car after the game, Wendall mumbled, "I didn't mean to be such a sourpuss . . ." It was a guarded apology that took them all by surprise. The doctor said, "Heck, we were all feelin' a little blue around the gills with the thrashin' those bums were handin' to us, ain't that right, Jim?" and Jim said, "Right, Fred," and everyone felt better. They stopped at a roadside stand and picked up a watermelon, the plan being they would drop by Hood's for ice cream, then head home where they would carve up the melon on the front porch and listen to the tail end of the doubleheader from Boston.

They were seated at the counter in Hood's telling Mike about the game, when Sheriff Flood came barging in. He was a short powerful man with a big lump-covered nose and mammoth hands, and he looked flustered to within an inch of his composure. Motioning urgently, he hollered, "Let's go, Mike! Vandals over to Olers' residence! Close up quick and let's get!"

"Why, that's us," the doctor said, clambering stiffly off his stool. "What's wrong?"

"You know that little house on your property?" the sheriff said. "Well, your wife gimme a call, and she stated there's vandals in that place bustin' out all the windows. She thinks they got guns. Maybe Nazi prisoners from the war camp over to Jactonberry. Said she's so scared she don't dare stick her head outn' the house. Let's go!" he shouted back at the counter where by now only Jim and Tom remained.

"I'll watch the kid and the shop," Jim said. "I ain't too fast."

Mike and Wendall piled into the back of Sheriff Flood's pickup truck, the doctor hoisted himself into the cab. As soon as the sheriff had said "Let's go!" John T. had run from the shop and started up his motorcycle. Careening around the corner of Main onto Coolidge, Wendall spotted his uncle just ahead of the truck, bent low over the Harley, and at that instant the truck hit a bump going onto the bridge, and, rising into the air, the boy caught sight of two guns, a rifle and a shotgun, lying on the floorboards near the back of the cab. They clacked loudly as he tumbled almost on top of them and his glasses skidded across the floorboards.

Then people hopped all over him, doors slammed: Mike Stenatto grabbed the guns and tossed one to the sheriff. The doctor, who had his shirt cuff caught in the door handle, shouted, "John T., you let the sheriff take care of it!" and just as John T. was crossing the front walk, Cornelia flew out the door, ran down the porch steps, and practically tackled him, and Ercel Perry ran by behind them. The guns, the people—all disappeared around the corner of the house, leaving Wendall alone.

But not for long. He located his glasses, scrambled over the side of the truck, and encountered Bernie Aja jogging into the driveway, sweat streaming off his shiny forehead.

"What's all the commotion?" Bernie asked.

"A Nazi!" Wendall shouted. "He's got a gun!" And hell bent for leather he went where the crowd had gone. He came up behind it as Sheriff Flood, a shotgun ready in his hands, was saying: "You better come out of there, you. I'm the sheriff here, and I got a gun, and I don't want no one to get hurt!"

For an answer, another window was broken. Cornelia shrieked at the noise; the rest of the group retreated a step.

"You come out of there 'fore there's gunplay, I'm warnin' you!"

Evening had quickly drained most of the color from objects, you had to squint to make out the shape of the playhouse through the bushes. Off to one side of the lawn, several cars, having noticed the commotion, had stopped along Prescott Street. Now, a few people with their arms folded leaned against the sides of automobiles, waiting for what was to happen.

"All right, then," shouted the sheriff, "here's a last warnin'!" He pointed the shotgun at the ground about ten feet in front of him, pulled the trigger, and clods of dirt and grass rose and pelted into the lilac leaves.

"I mean what I'm sayin'!" he shouted.

Sounds, soft and birdlike, came from the darkness behind the lilacs, and everyone hushed. It was hard to tell if the person was singing, or laughing, or crying, or even if the voice was masculine or feminine, because it sounded of no sex, it sounded almost divine. Wendall thought for just a minute that it was some wonderful big animal from a fairy tale that had accidentally blundered into the house and broken the windows simply in trying to escape. The animal that came to mind was Pegasus, the winged horse.

There was a crackling in the lilacs, branches snapped as something pushed toward the open. Then Sheriff Flood dropped back and let the gun hang loose in his hand. Cornelia drew in a deep, shocked breath: "Oh my God, I forgot to check her room!" she said.

Sybil emerged from the lilacs. She wore a white blouse, a tan skirt, and no shoes; her bare feet sank into the lawn grass. She stopped, staring at the sheriff and her family behind him. In the dark sky above her head the first of the rockets in a fireworks display at the picnic grounds a half mile out of town exploded, casting a glare over the lawn. Sparks fell, a faint boom carried over, followed by a series of explosions, another rocket, and more sparks.

"Everybody can go home now," Sybil said quietly. "Show's over." Then she wilted. It looked as if she were going to be sucked up by the grass, disappearing like water, for like water she descended, but in the end she was still there, a glowing spot of white on the lawn.

A long time when no one did or said a thing passed, then the doctor went to her. As soon as he disengaged himself from the group, the people watching moved to go, engines sputtered, cars pulled away from the curb—in less than two minutes the Oler family stood alone.

The doctor bent over Sybil. He couldn't go down on his knees, nor could he squat beside her to lay a soothing hand on her shoulder. He had to make do with bending at his waist; his long arm hung awkwardly down, his finger tapped repeatedly against the base of her spine.

"I should have gone to the ball game," Sybil said.

"It's all right," the doctor said. "Now gosh darn, it's all right, nothin' to worry about."

All this happened miles away from Wendall, and from miles away came John T. and Cornelia and Ercel Perry and Bernie Aja—they converged on the spot like ghosts of familiar yet unidentifiable people walking out of a mist. John T. helped Sybil up, and Wendall heard her say, "Daddy, you can revoke my allowance if you want; Mummy, don't look so scared . . ." and her voice trailed off as John T. and Cornelia guided her into the house.

The doctor straightened painfully. His dark shape presented itself to Wendall, the head raised . . . booms carried over from the picnic grounds. Sparks fell, and died out, and the ashes dropped unseen through the night.

When next Wendall knew, he was alone. He heard the doctor scuffling around in the playhouse: pieces of glass chinked when he stepped on them. Sitting in the cool grass, the boy couldn't for the life of him figure out what had happened. And he all of a sudden wished more than anything that he hadn't been such a brat at the baseball game that afternoon. He wished he had listened to his grandfather: he wished, for the sake of the doctor, that he had been able to like baseball. His desire to have done this became so great that he rolled over in the grass and had to struggle not to cry.

Inside the playhouse, the doctor looked out a broken window at the dark lump of his grandson on the lawn, and all he could think about was the mole traps.

"I wish it hadn't happened," he said aloud, but he didn't wish that at all, he couldn't wish a thing. He couldn't feel dismayed or angry, even fatigue seemed to be denied him for the moment.

The one clear thing that overwhelmed his mind was the mole traps.

Half an hour later Jim drove over in his station wagon with Tom and the watermelon. Wendall opened the door, and, in spite of the serious nature of the occasion, he almost burst out laughing. There stood Jim, that short blimp of a man, with a watermelon tucked under one arm and Tom tucked under the other. Tom, his face hidden behind massive splotches of chocolate ice cream, was talking like Donald Duck and wriggling something fierce.

"I tried to clean him up," Jim said.

He set Tom down and shifted the watermelon to his other arm. Wendall remembered Jim had paid for half the melon, and when he suggested they cut it up right away, Jim smiled and said he would be delighted. From among the tackle boxes, fly rods, loose plugs, and wicker creels in the back of his station wagon he extricated a Case knife of suitable size, plugged the melon first, and, satisfied it was ripe, cut it in half and divided it up from there.

The three of them sat on the porch steps and listened to the distant thunder of fireworks. Midway through their first slices, John T. and Ercel came onto the porch and for a moment sat with Jim and the boys, splitting a piece of melon between them.

"If you made much more noise eating that thing," said John T. to Tom, "somebody might think you were trying to swim in it instead of eat it."

"It doesn't taste good unless you make noise," Tom said.

A minute later John T. wiped his hands on his jeans and said, "Well . . ." and Jim answered, "It can't be helped . . ." and Ercel said, "No . . ." then they both said good-bye and went to the motorcycle. Ercel waited until John T. had pumped the starter a couple of times; when the motor caught she climbed behind him and slid her arms around his waist. Quietly they moved out of the driveway, John T.'s shoe scraping along the gravel; slowly they went up Coolidge, crossed the bridge, and turned out of sight onto Main.

Once in a while a car cruised by slow and thoughtful, hunting, perhaps, for remnants of the excitement. Tom and Jim and Wendall didn't pay attention: they spit out watermelon seeds, and the seeds clicked against the front walk like little beetles.

FIFTEEN

On the Monday afternoon a week following the playhouse incident, Wendall answered the doorbell and found himself facing a big-headed skeletal thin man who stood but a little over five feet tall, and who was one of the ugliest persons the boy had ever seen. Dark eyes popped out of his face like the eyes of an embryo; the skin on his thin nose was crisscrossed with swollen blue veins; his lips were thin, straight, and smudged-looking, like orange lines drawn with a wet crayon; and his upper teeth were worse than buck- or rabbit-teeth—they protruded like a cowcatcher, and when he talked, his lower lip came up on the b's, v's, and other labials, jiggling a loose front incisor. Then his chin slanted into a scrawny neck notable for a prominent Adam's apple lodged in the throat like a cartoon spoon or some equally buffoonishly swallowed object.

His name was Marty Haldenstein; he was twenty-eight years old; he lived alone in Margaret Simpson's boardinghouse on Conroy Street. Marty looked sick, and he was. Even during the hot days of summer he wore an overcoat; in the pockets he carried several large handkerchiefs into which he was frequently obliged to cough. Doctors had once told him to go to the Southwest or some similarly less severe climate for his health, but Marty deeply loved Vermont and had doggedly refused to leave. When the war was imminent, he had wanted very much to volunteer for the Army—he had, in fact, taken the physical examination, and he was, of course, rejected. Now the town's head librarian and the organist at St. John's Episcopal Church, he had lived in Stebbinsville all his life except for a four-year academic absence at Yale; yet in spite of his long residence, probably not ten people in all of

Stebbinsville were even roughly acquainted with Marty. In fact, he was not even known enough to be considered mysterious for the lack of what was known about him.

Marty said, "Hello, I don't believe we have had the honor of being introduced, my name is . . ." all very fast and squeaky, his Adam's apple bobbing frenziedly in his throat. Mastering his initial surprise, Wendall shook Marty's limp hand, saying, "You play the organ, don't you? In church?"

"Oh, well . . ." Marty blushed. "Is your, uh, grandmother on the premises? And if so, may I have the pleasure, should she not be otherwise occupied, of speaking with her?"

Wendall hailed Cornelia from the kitchen. She said good afternoon to Marty and invited him in, but he said no, he really didn't want to inconvenience the household, he hadn't dropped by but for a minute knowing how busy everyone was likely to be.

"Nobody around here is busy," said Cornelia. "Come on in, make yourself comfortable. Coffee on the stove. Or tea if you like."

"Oh, no, that is awfully kind of you, but it isn't necessary. If it is any trouble at all for you to talk a minute now, I would only too gladly return tomorrow or the day after, as I am in no hurry, and what I have come to ask you about is in no ways important—"

"Nonsense," said Cornelia; "you must come in."

Marty worked the doormat over with his toe. "I would really prefer to try again tomorrow. It was silly of me to come without first calling."

"Right now's fine. If you won't come in, at least speak up."

"Well, what I would like to know," Marty said hesitantly "is would it disturb you people greatly if I were to take some photographs of the hummingbirds in your garden? I have noticed they are rather abundant down there, and it would afford me much pleasure if you would condescend—"

"Nothing would please me more," interrupted Cornelia.

"Of course, I will give both you and the doctor copies of all the photographs I take. That goes without saying."

"Oh, that's very sweet of you but it won't be necessary."

"Well, uh, one other thing. I wonder if it would be all right with you if I set up a blind, a large box for camouflage, that is, on one of the paths. Of course I wold not dream of harming a single—"

"You go right ahead and set up whatever you want."

Marty shuffled his feet, was very profuse in his thanks, and withdrew his hand and extended it to bid Cornelia good day. He bumped into the screening, apologized, opened the door, then first Cornelia, and after her, Wendall, shook his hand.

"I am very much obliged," he mumbled. "I won't bother you at all. Don't you worry about a thing . . ."

Wendall held his breath, wondering if Marty was going to stumble down the porch steps or not. He made it down the steps all right, then, almost running on the walk, looking backwards and waving his twentieth good-bye, he tripped over the box trap and lost his balance, yet, defying all gravitational forces, he attained the sidewalk still upright, and, smiling, sickly, ran away.

The next day a blind appeared in the middle of the garden. About six feet high and wide, it was constructed of tar paper that had been drawn and tacked tightly over a wooden frame. A ribbon of window ran across the front of the structure at Marty's eye level. The bottom rear half of the blind, cut away at knee level, served as the entrance. The box weighed very little; it could be lifted up and fitted over the head like a big frozen dress.

This was also the most logical way to carry the blind, and carry it Marty had. He set out early in the morning from Simpson's; there was no one on the streets. Down the steep incline of Conroy Street he hobbled, or rather the blind with a pair of human feet went. Turning left on Rutland Avenue, he clomped past the Pavilion Hotel where Sheriff Flood's beagle, General Patton, fell in behind at a safe distance and began to whine, dragging his tail between his legs.

At Prescott, Marty veered left, entering the slum area. There he passed Chad and Tabby Spender, the ten- and eight-year-old son and daughter of the town's notorious garbage man Joel Spender, both of whom were up early because their mother had sent them out to filch a quart of milk from some unsuspecting neighbor's porch. Seeing the curious box struggling by, they dropped their plans and joined up several yards to the rear of General Patton.

Once past the slum section, nearing Perry Street, the troupe tramped by Harry Garengelli's bungalow house. Harry was just leaving for the gas station; but instead he fell into step behind Chad and Tabby. They crossed the street and filed by the entrance to the Jubilee Café, a tiny all-night lunch counter. Willie Bayle, the gray-haired owner-cook of the café, came out the door, followed by an unshaven truck driver from downstate. They scratched their heads and joined the parade.

When Marty tired a short distance down the block and stopped for a breather, everyone else halted with him. They moved on again only when Marty lifted the blind and sweated through the final several hundred yards to the Oler house. There, he staggered along the driveway, cut over the lawn onto a garden path leading to exactly the place where he wanted the blind to be, set the box down, crawled out from underneath it, and stood up, stretching to snap the kinks out of his back. He coughed for a minute and cleared his throat into a handkerchief, then looked up and saw facing him, leaning against the railing that ran along the sidewalk three feet above the street side of the lawn, Willie Bayle and the truck driver, Harry Garengelli and the Spender kids, and Sheriff Flood's beagle.

Troubled by their perplexed expressions, Marty cupped his hands to his mouth and shouted, "Good morning! It's for hummingbirds!"

The truck driver sucked in his cheeks and said, "Aah . . ." Willie Bayle raised a hand to his chin and said, "Ah-haaah . . ." Harry Garengelli ran his hand through his unkempt curly hair and said, "Oh . . ." then, with a smile, ". . . sure . . ." Spender kids said in the same breath, "Hummingbirds!" as if that were the exact and only thing at the farthest other end of the thought spectrum from stealing bottles of milk off neighbors' doorsteps.

Then Willie Bayle and the truck driver shoved their hands in their pockets and headed back to finish off their cold coffee at the Jubilee Café. Harry shrugged, and, smiling sagely, followed them. The Spender kids clung to the fence a half minute more, perhaps to see just exactly how the tar paper box was for hummingbirds, then they too went away. General Patton stared glazedly at Marty for a short and suspicious while: in the end he yipped sharply once, and, confidently upraising his tail, trotted away.

Marty stood with one hand on the top of his recent burden; the heads and leaves of flowers, blue with dew, were scalloped with a faint pearl color as the sun prepared to come up. Marty felt pleased, yet very tired after his exertions; his chest ached. He stifled another fit of coughing so as not to break the stillness. The sky beyond the grange hall, a deep pastel blue color, was fading.

And Wendall, kneeling with his chin on the third-floor windowsill, took off his glasses, making Marty disappear into a blurred gray collage of garden shapes. When he replaced the glasses, Marty was gone.

The following afternoon at two when Marty came to set up his gear and start taking photographs, he did not discourage Wendall from helping him. They drove three long stakes into the ground, and to the top of each affixed a simple rig consisting of an upside-down honey bottle fitted with a rubber stopper out of which a tube descended. They placed each apparatus in such a way as to be camouflaged by flower blossoms.

"Not that hummingbirds mind the bottles," Marty said. "But disguising them among the petals makes for a more aesthetically apropos photograph."

Wendall said, "Yes . . . of course . . ."

"Are you a photography buff?" Marty asked. "You look a little like one."

"I never had a camera," Wendall said. "Fred never took pictures either. Helen, my mother, did, but just of people. Always standing and saying cheese in front of a house door or a car. They weren't very interesting."

"Who is Fred?" Marty asked.

"My father."

"Oh. Frederick. Of course. We used to know each other. He was in a photography club with me at the high school. He had a sense of proportions when it came to catching his subjects in a favorable setting, and I think his knowledge of lighting was brilliant. I thought him a very decent fellow. What is he doing now?"

"He's in the war. The Marines. The Pacific."

"Oh. He told me once on the St. John's annual picnic at the Bixby quarry that he was afraid there was going to be a war. He said it would be an all-encompassing struggle that would reach out to touch everyone in the world. He had a vision many years before it came about, and he was right."

"Are you an Episcopalian?" Wendall asked.

"No, I am nothing, really. A benevolent atheist is what you might call me. Though there is much that is commendable in the church or synagogue, I am inclined to believe that for the most part churches are but religion's hypocritical trumpets. After all, how can I justifiably and with dignity align myself with any denomination when my father blindly informs me that the Catholics, the Episcopalians, and all other non-Jewish denominations and sects are ignorant uneducated pagans, thereby undermining the very tenets of the religio-social philosophy he holds himself, and of course tried to instill in me—namely that the religious man and his concepts of a decent life, being above prejudice, is the only worthwhile being upon this earth? Playing the organ in St. John's has a therapeutic value, not only for myself, but for the others who sing, I think. That is why I do it."

"Would you mind," Wendall asked timorously, "if I sat in the blind with you just once for an hour or so to see what it's like? I've never seen a hummingbird up close."

"That is a very capital idea," Marty said gravely, and fifteen minutes later Wendall joined him for an inaugural session.

Right away Marty's presence in the hot and tarry darkness did something to Wendall, it made the hair prickle on the back of his neck and balanced his stomach on the edge of queasiness. It was a little as if Marty were a component of the sensations the boy had felt in the attic: something sad, precious, and archaic; something secretive; a being, almost, from another—perhaps a past or even a future—world. . . . Was it possible that Wendall had stepped into the box with his own self of fifteen years hence? For he could sense an unusual bond between himself and the librarian, and neither of them, their shoulders barely touching, dared speak.

Not five minutes had gone by when Marty began coughing. Listening to the deep complaint from his lungs, Wendall became aware of a soft pressure far behind his own eyes—the gentle nudging tears made long before they became large and then real. He thought of the Butterfinger wrappers crushed into the toes of his shoes, and desired to take them out and show them to Marty. And it also crossed his mind that nothing would be more normal than to take off his clothes right now and show his scar to Marty, because the librarian would not tease him about it or ask if it were the place where all the books had been stuffed in, but rather he would understand, and touching it with his fingers, he would say, "That's a scar, all right; it must have hurt—" And Wendall knew beyond a doubt that Marty had a scar exactly like his own, and he would maybe even be willing to open his shirt and drop his pants a slight ways to show that scar to Wendall. Then, perhaps later in their relationship, they would come to joke about their respective marks, saying, "Hey, Wendall old fellow, how *is* that place where they stuffed in all the books?" and so forth. It would be a warm joke, a bond of friendship, a mutual secret, one of the things that would make their being together more meaningful. . . .

Wendall began to feel strangely at ease beside Marty, and although the tears became no more real, they still pressured him deep behind his eyes. He wondered if Fred had shared some of his innermost thoughts with Marty. After all, they'd been in a photography club together, they'd gone on that picnic—and he wondered, with growing excitement, if Marty would one day tell him all he knew about Fred. It might not happen unless Fred were killed in the war, however. Or it might never happen, and then some day, when Marty died and doctors cut him open to perform an autopsy, a ball, small and smooth like a pearl, would clink against their knives as they probed around the snug places lining Marty's stilled heart, and they would scoop the ball out and set it on an aluminum table, puzzled at its radiant shine, embarrassed by the secrets it revealed to them. . . .

"Here comes one," said Marty. "Oh, And here's another. . . ."

Hummingbirds came by the score. They were unafraid—even willing to pose, it seemed. In the hour, Marty shot fifteen pictures with his old Graflex. Each time the lens clicked, Wendall jumped a little no matter how much he prepared himself in advance for the noise. He would see the hummingbird come in and hover, touching its long bill to the mouth of a tube, and he would say to himself, Here it comes, this is it—then, without fail, when the shutter went off he jumped anyway, because the sound was so big, like shovel blades sliding against each other.

"Why are you taking all these pictures?" the boy asked.

"Well . . . first it is because I am on vacation for a week from the library. Secondly, I guess it is because hummingbirds fascinate me. After all, they are the most vertiginously coordinated things under the sun. Did you ever stop to think how incredible that little bird is? The velocity of its wingbeats, the strength it takes to maintain such constant rapidity, and yet, at an almost ultrahigh frequency of speed it can maneuver as slowly and gracefully as a feline; it can wend its way precisely, almost nonchalantly, among the flowers, seemingly relaxed, stopping, restarting—Why, it is the most exactly tailored and sure-moving bimotional thing on earth!"

A bird appeared like a flash from out of nowhere; it hovered near a tube like a fat bumblebee and pricked its bill into the honey as carefully as Cornelia threaded a needle. A second later the bird zipped away faster than it had come, leaving the ghost of its tiny form to fade out of sight behind it.

"What are you going to do with the pictures?" Wendall asked.

"What do you mean?"

"Are you going to give them to somebody?"

"To whom would you have me give them?"

"Do you have a girl friend?"

"No. I don't have a, uh—girl friend."

"Did you ever want a girl friend?"

"Oh, well . . ." He broke off coughing. Wendall wondered if there lived anywhere on earth a girl ugly enough to be Marty's girl friend. A girl with scraggly hair, a short girl—very scrawny, and a girl with big horse-teeth, including one tooth that moved with her labial words and maybe even squeaked a little. . . .

Then it struck the boy that he might have embarrassed Marty by bringing up girl friends, so he said, "Well, me neither—I've never had a girl friend. I wouldn't give ten cents for one, either. They are definitely the most irksome thing a person could ever have around him." He curled his lips into an appropriately scornful snarl which Marty missed because of the darkness. A hummingbird zoomed by, disappeared, then dropped like a spider and came to a sudden stop at the end of its invisible thread even with the mouth of a tube. Then:

"You could give some to me," Wendall suggested softly. "The pictures, I mean. I've been saving up some money; perhaps I could buy a couple."

"Oh . . ." Marty moved. His shoulder bumped Wendall, then his hand touched the boy's knee, brushed off it awkwardly, located Wendall's hand, and clasped it. He mumbled something unintelligible. His hand was damp. For a fraction of a second Wendall wanted to object, then he realized there was no need to. Marty applied no pressure; he held on limply, and Wendall felt remarkably at peace. A locust that had been buzzing monotonously stopped its noise; two hummingbirds came at once and danced around the honey feeders, their wings whirring like little electric motors. Wendall couldn't hear Marty's breathing—was he holding his breath? At the end of thirty seconds, the librarian let go, saying, "All right, I will give you some of the photographs." After a pause, he added indecisively, "Well . . ." and something mysterious seemed to have been settled between them.

They crawled into the sun: light spread them apart, making them timid.

"I'll see you tomorrow?" Wendall asked.

"Oh. Yes, tomorrow." Marty buttoned up his camera.

"Get anything good?" shouted Sybil. She had climbed out her window onto the front porch roof and, dressed in a white swim suit, was lying back on the inclined surface taking a sunbath.

"We shot two hummingbirds, one Japanese beetle, and a lion," Wendall said. He thought that for just the fleetingest part of a second a smile warmed Marty's face.

SIXTEEN

The doctor came out of the house onto the back porch. Tom and Wendall were lying with Sybil on the lawn; fireflies winked above their heads. Bernie came around the side of the house coiling up the punctured hose that had been watering the Prescott lawn. Over by the barn ramp John T. was taking advantage of the last glimmers of light to tinker with something on his motorcycle.

"Hey!" the doctor called over to John T. "If you ask me, looks like that tub of bolts ain't gonna go another inch."

"Don't you worry about this thing, Pop. She's more polished than a Parisian whore."

The doctor smiled: that was his expression, and it always gave him a little thrill to hear his expressions in John T.'s mouth. It meant that when he was dead and gone there would still be someone to lean back at the table and say, "Boy, I'm stuffed as a Thanksgiving turkey"; there would still be someone to go through the "How's your gizzard—full of stones" routine.

Watching his son, he wondered if that were all there was to life. A few expressions surviving out of all the things you'd done or hadn't done. And was it more than most folks had? Or less? He'd seen so many old people die, but not once had a man told him why he had done all the living he'd done. Oh, some of them moaned and carried on, not so much afraid as just plain sick and uncomfortable and impatient to get it over with, but they never said whether they'd been happy or unhappy to have done all that living, or if it had been worth it or if it hadn't. They were simple folks who took their deaths straight, no cream, no sugar, people of the earth going back to the earth, leaving lots of sons and daughters, and never saying much about what it had been like, or what they reretted or didn't regret. Death was quiet, solid, and drama-less in this part of the country—John T. stood up.

"She'll go like shit out of a tin horn, now," he said.

"Well—don't go gettin' yourself wrapped round a tree. I'd have to fill out a long report."

John T. gathered up his tools and carried them into the barn. Smiling sadly, the doctor walked to the edge of the garden where spears of asparagus gleamed in the ebbing light. He sat down, and remembered back to a chilly October day in 1939 . . . It was raining, he was alone in the car, driving to Montpelier to see Mike Stenatto's son who was dying of polio in the hospital there. Midway on his journey he spotted a hitchhiker at the side of the road, slowed down, and picked up an old man carrying a violin case. After the man warmed up a little, he took out his violin and began to fiddle.

Sitting now, overlooking his garden, the doctor could hear the strains of that violin as clearly as if they were coming from just out of sight around a corner of the barn. Waltzes he had played, the doctor didn't know which ones, but they were all old tunes he had heard before and that he guessed came from Europe. The man said the rain did something to the violin strings, and he apologized for the quality of the music, but the doctor thought it sounded just fine and told him so.

Then the man lay the violin in his lap and, staring out the flooded windows, said, "Usually it makes me cry to play those songs, but I see Mother Nature is doing it for me." A few miles farther on he returned his violin to its case. "I get out here," he said. The doctor peered to both sides, and, seeing no houses, said, "But we're in the middle of nowhere." "That's all right, I get out here," the man repeated. "I've been going in the wrong direction. I sure am a fool." So the doctor braked and let him out.

When he got to Montpelier, Mike's boy was dead. They showed him the body; there was nothing he could do but drive back to Stebbinsville. All the return trip, in a rain that never once let up, he expected to come upon the violinist by the side of the road, but he didn't encounter a soul.

When he got back to Stebbinsville, the doctor called Montpelier and arranged to pay Mike's entire medical bill. The Italian had just bought Hood's and the doctor knew he was having trouble trying to coax it into a smooth and profitable operation. He talked the thing over with Mike, who refused at first to allow him to do it. After much prodding he agreed to accept the money as a loan, but the doctor wouldn't hear of it. "I don't believe in loaning money to people," he said. "That's the surest way to lose a friend. Pretty soon he can't pay you back, so he starts avoiding you, and before you know it, he's not your friend anymore, and every time you meet up with him by chance he's ashamed and unhappy as all get out. Nope, if you've got it to give, then give it, and if you don't have it, well give what you can, but don't ever loan money, because that's just like giving it to the devil."

In the end, he talked Mike into accepting, and the money saved his life, he didn't have to give up the ice cream parlor. When Cornelia found out, she and the doctor had quite a row, because the money, part of her once ample inheritance, had been destined to send John T. and Sybil, on the heels of Fred, comfortably through a good college education.

Now the doctor could use that money. He could use all the money he'd given away through the years, that he hadn't collected. But he'd never been able to stop his giving, he'd been like the man in the car that day who, realizing he was headed in the wrong direction, went there nevertheless thinking he might be able to lift someone's spirit with his music, or perhaps simply because he wanted someone to hear his music and tell him it was nice. . . .

Sybil's laughter came from the lawn. The doctor

rose, brushed off the damp seat of his baggy trousers, and went over to his daughter and grandchildren.

"Well, now, if this isn't the most motley crew I've seen in a long time . . ." he said.

SEVENTEEN

Kneeling, Duffy Kahler drank from the river. The night, light and reflective, returned the image of his face from the water. His eyes and white cheeks shimmered below him. He opened his mouth and splashed his finger in its reflection, then, cupping his palm, tried to skim off his watery face.

The light going off in John T.'s room made him look up. For a second a halo seemed to hang around the house, then darkness took over, the sides of the structure glowed subduedly, the open windows blindly faced him.

The night was hot and muggy; Duffy slapped a mosquito off his head, stood up, and waded across the river. At the foot of the barn he waited a minute, preparatory to heading up for the house—then the blind in the garden caught his eye.

"Wait a while; be smart," he whispered, and crawled under the barn. Lying on his back, he faced strong but rotting timbers, the cracks between beams dripped with dust hangings. He felt proud at being so cautious: every day he was becoming more clever, learning more control. Now that he had established himself in a safe place to live, things were quiet and beginning to shape up the way they should. He squeezed his eyes shut and stayed perfectly blank for a long time. When he began to have trouble breathing, he ducked into the open. He shook his hands and that helped. His chest felt a little constricted, but it didn't hurt.

So long as he experienced no pain he was all right. His muscles tightened, he tensed a little, then relaxed, sighed, and breathed as deeply as he could. He closed his eyes and softly nodded his head.

He was in control.

Moving silently, he traversed the Victory garden, being especially careful not to break any asparagus spears. Sticks with small tomato and bean vines afforded him some cover. Then he slipped safely into the higher stalks of the flower garden. A sensitive perfume, wetted and exposed by the night dew, came to his nostrils. On hands and knees he crawled up one path, went left, and came to the blind. Without hesitation he entered it and stood up. Through the eye slit he could see the entire house, but of course they could not see him. He lit a cigarette, smoked, and calmly, supremely, regarded the house.

Only a minute had gone by, when to his surprise the front door opened and the boy he had sat next to on the train, dressed only in his pajamas, came out. He stood on the porch a minute, listening for telltale rustlings in the house behind him. Then, to Duffy's utter disbelief and dismay, he snuck off the porch and came swiftly across the lawn into the garden and down a path directly toward the blind.

At supper, Cornelia had informed the gathering that tomorrow both Tom and Wendall had dental appointments in Willow Falls, and when she announced the time of these ghastly engagements—two P.M.—Wendall groaned and said, "I'm sorry but I can't go."

"What do you mean you can't go?"

"I've got things to do around here."

"Well, you just tell your 'things around here' to wait on you for a few hours," Cornelia said. "I may be a terrible grandmother, but I'm not going to have my grandchildren's teeth rotting out of their mouths. If you don't take care of yourself now, you'll wish you had later," and deeming it useless to argue further, Wendall lapsed into grouchy silence.

Nevertheless, once in bed, the boy couldn't get to sleep. Tomorrow Marty would come to take photographs and he wouldn't be there. Marty might think he had been offended by the hand-holding episode of the day before, and their relationship would be ruined. Wendall worried for about an hour, then he hunted up a pencil and a piece of paper, went down to the bathroom, and wrote *I can't be here today because I'm going to the dentist. I will see you tomorrow I hope. Good luck.* He folded the paper, waited still another twenty minutes when he thought the household would be asleep, then left his room and crept downstairs and outside.

Ten yards from the blind he thought he saw something move through the eye slit, and stopped. He waited, then said, "Hey, hello; who's in there?" No one answered. "If someone's in there, I'm not coming to hurt you or anything." He detected a slight wisp of smoke in the air above the blind. "You're smoking a cigarette, aren't you? Well, don't be afraid. Now . . . I'm coming all the way."

"Don't come in," Duffy said. "I don't want you to."

"How come *you're* here?"

"I just came. If you go away, I'll leave. I won't ever come back again. I promise."

"You've been here before, haven't you?"

"No. This is the first night. I just wanted to see what this box was."

"You're lying. I know you've been around. I've felt it."

"Look. I want to leave. Will you go away?"

"Where do you live? Do you have a place to live?"

"Yes."

"In town? I never see you around. Are you hiding? Did you do something wrong?"

"No. You shut up, I said."

"You don't scare me one bit. I think you're sick, aren't you? Are you a soldier?"

"Shut up. If you don't leave I'll hurt you, I mean it. I can too, if I want."

"Oh, shut up yourself. I don't have to do what you or anybody else tells me to do. Where's my money?"

"You shut up about your money. I don't owe you any money."

Duffy stooped out of the blind and straightened up. Wendall backed up for a short distance. "You don't have a beard," he said. Only for a second did they face each other, then Duffy ran away. He broke some asparagus stalks and knocked over a tomato stick. Wendall heard him splash across the river, and, a moment later, followed him with his eyes through the bushes along the far riverbank and out of sight into the darkness under the trees behind the grange hall.

Then he wedged his note into a crack between the wooden upper ledge of the eye slit and the tar paper in the blind, and returned to the house.

Mounting the stairs to the second-floor landing, he saw Sybil's dim reflection like a ghost deep in the mercury of the full-length mirror. For a suspended moment he dared not turn around to face her actual self. Then, just as he had made up his mind to say something, she retreated into her room, closing the door with a soft click.

Wendall lay in bed and thought: The man on the train is probably cracked, he is also probably a peeping Tom, and I think he was more frightened of me than I of him.

Perhaps, Wendall thought, I can find out where his hideout is and turn him in to the sheriff. There might even be a reward.

In any case, it would serve the bastard right for stealing his dollar on the train.

He switched to thinking of Marty, hoping he would find the note. He tried to picture how pleased the librarian would be to get word, realizing, as he read the note, how thoughtful Wendall really was.

The train man ran frantically through his slumber, chased by pretty little hummingbirds. Wendall and Marty laughed at the sight, and joined their hands, and laughed some more.

EIGHTEEN

On Wednesday, following the hour of picture taking, Marty asked uncertainly, "Would you like to come see where I make my humble abode?" and Wendall said he would be delighted.

Glowing with excitement, the boy walked beside Marty to Margaret Simpson's boardinghouse on Conroy Street. A thin old man sat in a chair on the front veranda, cinnamon shots of sunlight rippling through leaf-holes onto his scowling features.

As they came up the steps, the old fellow's mouth went through several rubbery shapes, and his eyes did not swing onto them—they clicked from one position to the next, first sideways, then up a few degrees to the level of Wendall's, then Marty's face.

"Hello, Mr. Twine," said Marty. "Did you have a good lunch?"

The eyes clicked, the mouth flip-flopped, and Mr. Twine said, "Ah-ha, ah-ha . . ."

"I'm glad to hear that, sir." Marty guided Wendall by him into the main hallway. "B. J. Twine," he explained as they ascended the carpeted stairs. "He retired from the presidency of the bank in 1928, and has lived here ever since. He has a nurse, of course, and spends his time on the porch during the summer, in the parlor during the winter. He used to be a voluble man, but in recent years he has quite forgotten how to talk. I think senility is a great pity, particularly when it occurs in the once articulate, don't you?"

Marty opened a door at the head of the stairs. Wendall had expected a somber and disordered room; instead, this one was clean and sunlit—there was in it a bed with a gay yellow spread, a large bookcase, a comfortable leather chair, a roll-top desk, and, in a corner in front of a cushioned window seat, a small table with a vase of daffodils on it. Marty slid open the door to a shelved closet stacked neatly with photographic equipment, and put away his camera. Then he took Wendall through the bathroom into a small darkroom where he did his developing: already hanging on a wire were some negatives of the hummingbirds shot on the first day. Back in the main room he said, "I think it would be much more agreeable if we went out to the yard. I have rigged a hammock, and it is really quite pleasant. I often dawdle away a free hour or two there. Do you like apples?"

"Sure; I'm pretty fond of them."

Marty stooped into the clothes side of his closet and came up with a bag of apples which he upturned on the bed. The librarian watched nervously while Wendall chose two of the largest and reddest fruits, then he scooped the others back into the bag, and, as he was sliding the closet door shut, he said, "Have you ever had occasion to read *Green Mansions?*"

Wendall said he hadn't.

"It is by W. H. Hudson, and is by far one of my favorites. And I think that, though perhaps a bit Victorian, it is really very beautiful. I would like to introduce you to it anyway. . . ."

The backyard was small, bordered on three sides by shrubs and flowers, and in the rear by a low chickenwire fence. Slung between the trunk of a crab apple tree and a sturdy post was the hammock, a large blue and white nylon one that stretched very wide—"From Mexico," Marty claimed.

"Down in the more native parts of Central and South America, everyone uses just such a hammock to sleep in," he said. "They sleep crosswise." He demonstrated, entering shakily and almost tipping over before he got settled right, the hammock spreading for him like a big elastic wing. "Often whole families occupy the same hammock. You can get in any way you want, now. I assure you it won't throw you over."

Wendall took off his shoes and tackled the hammock. His feet sank into the webby material; cautiously he positioned himself at right angles to Marty, his toes touching the librarian's waist.

"I'll begin reading," Marty said. "At first, of course, you may not like it, as it takes a while to meet Rima, she is the bird girl. But I think, or I would at least hope, that once we are into it you will really enjoy it. You may eat both the apples if you wish: I am not very hungry."

Wendall bit into an apple and Marty began to read. At first his voice was a little strident, then it lowered and settled into pace with the book and the day. Wendall lay back his head; leaves above him did not move; shadows lay on his face like pieces of wet silk cloth. From far away sounded the usual buzzings of a summer day: close by a butterfly flew through the yard, a bird landed out of sight in the apple tree and gave a call. Marty's voice lulled the boy, he began to drift off. Names of jungle places came and went, seasonal rain fell, some drinking with savages was done, there was talk of sleep—and then a new place was described, there were birds, songs, a first look at the forest girl, a snakebite, then thunder, darkness. And as the hero, Abel, dropped into a cloud of foliage, so also did Wendall, clutching desperately at consciousness for a while, fall eventually into a deep slumber.

Marty touched the boy's foot, then withdrew his hand. The other apple had rolled against his ribs. He picked it up, breathed on it and polished the smooth skin, holding his breath to keep from coughing. He wanted to wake Wendall and go on with the reading: he would like to have read the entire book in one afternoon. The sun turned in the sky, rimming the outer overhead leaves with gold. Marty did not move for fear of waking the boy, and he wondered: how long—a day? a week?—before he would lose him.

Whatever his thoughts, the still leaves above, their undersides gilded in transparent shadow, would not deny them.

The next day clouds darkened the sky, and, although it did not rain, the ominous light was bad for photographs, so Marty didn't show up. Sneaking downstairs early from his nap, Tom made friendly overtures to Wendall, suggesting the gamut of activities from pigeon trapping to rustling around in the attic, but the boy wasn't interested, he sat sullenly on the front porch, and later, after brusquely dismissing Tom, he retired to do his brooding in the privacy of the cupola.

Fresh in his mind was the moment the day before when he had come slowly out of sleep and encountered Marty sitting on the ground not two feet away, staring at him. There had been between them a look of such penetration, that after a few seconds Wendall had turned away feeling uncommonly ill at ease. Marty had suggested he go home, and the boy had readily acquiesced. All the way to Coolidge Street he had wanted desperately to shake his head, to clear it and understand the relationship between himself and the librarian. In the cupola he searched the clouds but could not even begin to think, for he had no idea what he was supposed to think about.

The sky cleared on Friday and Marty came to take pictures. He and Wendall were in the blind for an hour, during which time Marty twice sought out the boy's hand. After these moments of brief physical contact, the librarian opened up and talked at a feverish pace: about religion, politics, the war, literature, medicine . . . almost as if he had saved for years to give his opinions to someone, and had never dared to until now. Wendall listened politely, offering an opinion or two, perplexed, anxious to please—and sometimes he thought a certain happiness was welling up in Marty, a frantic all-too-serious joy letting loose, and, although often his prattle became too complex to follow, the boy sensed that in a way they were really communicating.

When the session terminated, Marty again invited Wendall to return home with him. This time they did not read in the hammock. Instead, Marty led him to the graveyard at the lower end of South Maple Street.

"I often come here to read of an afternoon," he

said. "The solitude of the dead carries a wonder in it. I think there is something clear and intrinsically immortal about these stone heads, the lives that in death have been simplified to the name on a tomb, some dates, a little grass—None of the suffering is evident in this, the final, immobile façade."

Wendall got the funny feeling he had had in the attic and again during the first hour he had spent in the blind with Marty. While the librarian perched on a dark gray stone and passionately read to him, Wendall lay on the grass, his ear to the ground, listening for the earthy turnings of the dead. He imagined bony fingers straining up through the rich loam toward sunlight, and flat on his back, his body woozy, he allowed the hands to glide up on either side of him and tug him under, but he could still see everything clearly through the roots of the grass: leaves and sky, the undersides of birds flying over, Marty's knees. . . . And he was neither dead, nor even afraid to open his mouth. Bravely he parted his lips: no crumbs of earth tumbled in. He opened his mouth wider; his spirit soared as he drew in pure air, sucking on it until his lungs were filled to bursting. Then he became alert; hearing Marty read:

"Have you ever observed a hummingbird moving about in an aerial dance among the flowers—a living prismatic gem that changes its color with every change of position—how in turning it catches the sunshine on its burnished neck and gorget plumes—green and gold and flame-colored, the beams changing to visible flakes as they fall, dissolving into nothing . . ."

Wendall sat up: Marty broke off reading. Beyond the librarian, toiling up a dandelioned slope on the arm of a nurse, Wendall saw the old man, B. J. Twine. The thick hot air extended both the old man's and the nurse's body lines beyond their natural boundaries, making them glow fuzzily like sunlit hair in a photograph. Following Wendall's eyes, Marty said, "Yes, he comes here sometimes with the nurse. His family is buried on the hill, and there is a small patch of grass beside them for himself. I would imagine it is the spot where he feels most at home nowadays. I think he looks forward to taking his place beside the rest of them."

Then Marty went back to the book and Wendall listened attentively, afraid to miss even a word. Marty's voice read steadily on throughout the afternoon, and the boy lost himself in a blue sky over Venezuela: only when the sun was nearly set did he remember he'd almost missed his supper, and the threat of Cornelia's forthcoming bickering jabberwocky put him on his feet and sent him winging home.

It rained on Saturday afternoon, pitifully, the sky emptying its reservoir, sputtering dry for the summer. Marty came later than usual: once again Wendall spent an hour in the blind with him, an hour during which each held his silence and neither touched the other. The flowers, dripping with water, were more beautiful than Wendall had imagined they could ever be. Looking out the slit, he was forced to concentrate on what was intimately before him: the form of raindrops, the slick veins on wet leaves, the sparkling of hummingbird colors and movement—everything was imprinted strongly on his memory.

At the end of the hour Marty fiddled with his camera for a minute. Reluctantly, he said, "I think that I have imposed myself on your grandparents all that I should."

Wendall experienced a sinking sensation. Beside him Marty moved, he touched the boy's face; even in forming a kiss his lips could not close completely over his protruding tooth, and Wendall felt it against his cheek. Pulling quickly away, Marty said, "Thank you . . . I'm sorry . . ." and before the boy had time to respond, he had ducked out of the blind.

The sun hurt Wendall's eyes when he emerged. A slight wind had cleared the sky, and in the west a dim rainbow was fading into a warm blue background. Marty closed his camera and put the plates in a leather briefcase while Wendall gathered the torn film papers. When all was in order, Marty said he would return the following day after church to collect the blind. They shook hands like very serious gentlemen.

"It has been my most sincere pleasure . . ." Marty said.

"Mine too . . ." What was the librarian making it sound like a farewell for?

Marty nodded. "When I have developed the pictures I will bring over some of the more satisfactory ones for you."

They shook hands again. Then Marty went away, and Wendall stared desolately after him.

When the librarian returned to take away the blind, Wendall missed him, having been dragged out to the picnic grounds by Sybil, John T., and Ercel Perry. On Thursday of the next week Marty dropped off a large portfolio of blown-up photographs at the house, but once again Wendall did not see him because he and Tom, having trapped a pigeon, had gone downtown to cash in the bird with the doctor.

The pictures were beautiful. The hummingbirds, with their wings stopped, their eyes bright and intelligent, their body feathers unruffled, dipping their long bills into the honey, were even more magical than they had been in real life. Also included in the portfolio were pictures Marty had taken of other subjects: among them were several shots of butterflies, one of a huge caterpillar monster, some bizarrely twisted close-ups of autumn leaves, and five magnificently enlarged photos of snowflakes.

But Wendall was never again to spend any great length of time with Marty. As suddenly as it had begun, their friendship ended. Occasionally Wendall greeted the librarian on the street. Always Marty stopped and shook hands, asking how his health was, but their conversations never developed much beyond that. The only prolonged time Wendall was able to see him was from afar, playing the organ in church on Sunday.

One week after they parted, Wendall went to the library to check out a book on his grandmother's card, thinking he would talk to Marty and perhaps be invited up to the boardinghouse again. The librarian was formal, hardly recognizing the boy when he brought the book to the desk. He said hello, asked perfunctorily after his health, and commented on the heat. Wendall, in turn, found himself miserably speechless: he could but stare at Marty's hands while they stamped the book, took the card out of the rear inside envelope, and filed it—his face remained inscrutable even on discovering the book was *Green Mansions*.

Finally, Wendall said, "Are you still taking pictures?" To which Marty replied, "Yes, of course," his voice seemingly edged with impatience. Wendall said, "Oh"; Marty shrugged, fiddled with a pencil, and arranged a paper.

"Well," Wendall lamely ended, "I guess I'll see you. Thanks a lot."

He took his book: Marty did not call him back: he went home.

Thereafter, they continued to meet from time to time on the street. They nodded in passing: these times Wendall felt ashamed; he knew Marty did also. Sometimes the boy dreamed of walking straight to the door of Margaret Simpson's boardinghouse, pushing determinedly by old B. J. Twine, and charging up to Marty's room. "Now you look here, Martin Haldenstein," he would say. "Let's talk this over, man to man, let's find out just what happened between us, because frankly I don't know why we aren't friends anymore, I don't understand anything that happened, and personally, I think it's a damn shame. . . ."

But it was only in his dreams that he went there. He finished *Green Mansions,* reading it with Marty's voice, going through it with the librarian's eyes close to his, or again with becalmed leaves suspended over his head, or again in the graveyard with the old man and the nurse in the background toiling up the slope to have a look at past and future grave sites. . . .

Tom was glad to have his general completely back. At first, noticing Wendall's delicate condition, he was careful not to step on his toes for a few days. Then he belched joyfully as Wendall at last condescendingly trudged outside with him to review the condition of their various battle stations.

Where the blind had stood a yellowish patch of grass remained for a little while, then it grew out and was gone.

NINETEEN

A wire pen behind the playhouse had once been used for the sole purpose of harboring skunks. These animals abounded in the Stebbinsville area; most of the either courageous or stupid dogs in town had been squirted a few times, as had several of the either courageous or stupid human beings. Among these latter—and, in fact, heading the list—was John T. Oler.

During his middle teens, John T. had gone through a skunk "period," much to the consternation of Cornelia, the amusement of the doctor, and the varied reactions of the other children, depending on how close they happened to have been dragged into the heart of a capturing or descenting operation when a squirting occurred.

It is a fact, however, that during this redolent epoch, John T. became the county's foremost authority on skunks, and he was even written up in the Sunday magazine section of the Burlington *Free Press* once, with accompanying pictures of himself, the family, and some of the animal retinue.

Now: although it was years since the last skunk had bitten its way through the rotting chicken wire and made for the hills, often during evening meals one of John T.'s skunk adventures would come up. The story was inevitably recounted by the doctor in a very boisterous manner, while John T. nodded humbly and corrected any mistakes, and Cornelia, shaking her head and frowning, let out peeping protestations.

And the more the family reminisced, the more Wendall thought he was getting to know a lot about the subject of skunks. A time came, as it was bound to, when he guessed that with all he had heard and learned, he was definitely equipped to catch one of the black and white animals. In fact, he felt he would positively enjoy catching one, and he bragged a little to Tom about how he would do it when the opportunity presented itself, and when Tom asked him wouldn't he be scared, Wendall said of course not, what was there to be scared of in a puny old skunk?

"Just the same, I'd be scared," Tom said.

"There's nothing to be scared of," Wendall said, "so long as you keep your head."

Then, quite suddenly, the opportunity for Wendall to "keep his head" presented itself one muggy evening when the boy was alone beneath the front porch impatiently waiting for pigeons to walk under the box trap. Just as he was about to yank the string on a hapless victim, he heard a slight scuffling to his rear, and turning around, beheld—not four feet from him and barely discernible in the dim light—an animal doing some kind of horrible dance. Its teeth bared, it was stamping its forefeet very rapidly like a child throwing a tantrum. Wendall stared at it, wonderstruck, then it did the craziest thing he had ever seen an animal do. It backbent its rear end all the way over to a position above its head, and there the boy was—face to face with a skunk's posterior. The animal gave him little time to think or move: it squirted, then scrambled away as Wendall opened his mouth and unleashed a bloodcurdling scream.

Crawling from beneath the steps, he thought for sure he was going to suffocate in the stench that had been dealt him. His eyes smarted so sharply he thought he was going blind, and whatever it was that had been olfactory in his nose had been repulsed all the way to the inside top of his head where it clung by its sticky nodule feet upside down like a terrified lizard. Even the skin on his hands, as if attacked by flames, seemed to be shriveling, the skin splitting banana-like and peeling back off each finger.

Disaster was a magnet to Cornelia: she reached him quicker than she had when he'd gone hunting cobwebs in the barn with John T.'s .410.

"Oh Lord!" she shrieked. "A skunk!"

Bright deduction. Wendall removed his glasses, surprised that the plastic frames hadn't melted or at least been bubbled a little. He stood up shaking and squinted onion-sized tears out of his eyes. He pinched his nose, the nostrils of which burned witheringly, and the pinching only made the raw pain worse. He thought: if it hadn't been for the war, Fred would never have gone overseas, he himself would never have gone to Aunt Nancy, Aunt Nancy would never have sent him to Stebbinsville, he would never have met his grandfather, his grandfather would never have urged him to trap pigeons, he would never have crawled under the damn porch. . . .

The doctor made his appearance, took one look at the boy, roared with laughter.

"A skunk got him," Cornelia sobbed.

"A skunk?" said the doctor. "Could that be what I smell?"

"Frederick, this is no time for joking. Look at the poor child. Oh how he stinks!"

Tom, trailed by Sybil, came onstage holding his nose. He added his two bits: "Wow!" and a noise through his lips that sounded like boiling chocolate pudding.

"Spit on him," grimaced Sybil. "Maybe he can't swim."

Between tears, Wendall flashed the assemblage a galvanizing glance of concentrated hatred.

"Welcome to the club," said Sybil cheerily, sticking her feet between the rail dowlings and leaning forward. "Potent little feller, wasn't he? Daddy, what are we going to do, use him for fertilizer?"

"Just leave him in the driveway to stink to death." The doctor laughed again and his nose went very red.

"How about a bath in tomato juice?" Sybil said. "Didn't that used to work with Johnny?"

Wendall leaned back his head, closed his eyes, and bellowed, "What am I going to do? I don't want to stink one minute more! I hate all the bastard skunks that ever were invented!"

"Huuup!" gasped Cornelia. "There's no need to swear, young man."

"Oh, Lord love a duck," said the doctor. "Call John T., there's a skunk on the prowl."

"Get your clothes off," Cornelia barked, taking command—at last—of the situation. "You, Frederick, stop your gawking and get some of that laundry soap. "Bernie!" she called to the handyman who had come up from the garden to see what the fuss was about. "Is the hose hitched up?" Her eyes went heavenward, rolling into their whites: "If ever this family gave me a moment of peace, the shock would kill me, it really would."

"Does it hurt?" Tom asked gravely.

"Yes—it—hurts."

"Did you try and catch him?"

"No—I—didn't—try—and—catch—it."

"Where'd he go?" Tom asked.

"I don't care . . ."

"Do you wanna try and catch him later on?"

"Can't you shut your mouth for a change?"

As he unbuckled his belt, Wendall remembered about the scar, but he was too miserable to give it more than a passing thought. Dropping his pants, he felt, overall, like a burnt marshmallow. His head went dizzy: the doctor returned and tossed him a bar of brown sandpapery soap. Bernie Aja connected a piece of hose to the outdoor faucet near the back porch and turned on the water. Wendall discarded his glasses in the grass alongside the driveway, and, with Bernie standing back several yards shaking his head sadly, he scrubbed himself, and while he scrubbed he planned his revenge. He imagined himself sitting on the bridge railing, a long bamboo pole in his hands. Attached to the end of the pole was a thin white cord, and hogtied to the end of the cord was his friend from under the porch. For the five-hundredth time he dipped the pole a few inches, submerging the skunk in the river. He counted to ten and raised the pole: dangling drenched and bedraggled, the skunk implored him with repentant eyes to have mercy. He replied, "Ah-ha, ah-ha," like old B. J. Twine, smiled sadistically, and dipped the pole. . . .

But it was John T. who eventually shouldered the task of revenge.

He assumed that with darkness the skunk might sally forth to plunder the garbage cans located near the slanting cellar door. Therefore, at the conclusion of supper, Tom and Wendall were appointed an observation committee of two to keep vigil over the back porch through the dining room bay windows. Not ten minutes had passed when they noticed a blackish something the size of a cat scratching around the base of one of the cans. They informed John T., and the hunt was on.

In the living room, John T. stripped to his underwear, and, after ceremoniously shaking all hands present, he left by the front door, armed only with a flashlight. The others sneaked into the dining room and gathered around a window to take in the action, which was not long in coming.

Past the corner of the house crept a round spot of light: it slithered sinisterly along the driveway, searched the foundations of the back porch, skimmed over the cellar door, and spotlighted the skunk. Cornelia sucked in a deep breath; Bernie Aja gave a soft whistle.

"If he gets squirted, I don't know what I'll do," Cornelia whispered tensely. "This family is crazy, that's what it is."

The skunk froze; John T. did likewise.

"Now you . . . just . . . watch . . . this . . ." said the doctor, smiling confidently in anticipation of the feat his son was about to perform.

John T. took a step forward, then another.

"Never get it thataway," Bernie said, shaking his head. "Looks skitterish to me. Gettin' ready to let him have it right now." His hand went slowly up to his chin.

"Don't you move!" Cornelia hissed.

"Attaboy, Johnny," Sybil coached. "Daddy, he's going so slow it gives me the willies." She took her father's hand and squeezed it.

The skunk blinked, twitched its tail, and stared mesmerized into the flashlight. Wendall wondered when that little pink heart of a rear end was going to flip over into position. It didn't seem fair that John T. might get through unscathed.

"Slowly . . . slowly, that's the way . . . show 'em that golden Oler touch," whispered the doctor at each of John T.'s careful steps. The skunk waited, perplexed, stunned by the light.

"I just know that darn animal is going to squirt him," whined Cornelia. "If people in this family wouldn't be such fools . . . oh, I can feel it, just as sure as . . ."

"Shush," said the doctor.

John T. tread carefully among the coils of the hose Wendall had forgotten to curl up, and then he was safely by the obstacle, not three feet away from the window, right at the edge of the porch, and suddenly Sybil made a spouting sound and began to giggle, because John T. in his droopy underwear stalking a skunk with a flashlight was just plain too funny. At the very instant she opened her mouth, there was a lot of movement, both internal and external. A cry from Cornelia, a shout from the doctor—the flashlight flew out of John T.'s hand, richocheted off the edge of the porch, and rolled across the grass into the driveway where it came to rest, its beam cutting onto the front lawn.

"Got him!" said John T. The doctor threw open the window. "Judas-pries', so he does!" he shouted.

John T. held the skunk up by the tail. A great grin split his face—he hadn't lost his touch. Each time the animal wrenched around to try to get its teeth into him, he gave it a hearty shake to straighten it out. He was in no danger of being squirted, skunks being helpless to discharge their fluid without their feet on the ground.

"Now what the devil do you plan to do with it?" asked Cornelia.

"I'm gonna give it to Wendall," John T. said.

"I don't want it," Wendall promptly replied.

"If you let him go, he'll hie himself back under the porch and muss up the first passerby," Bernie Aja said.

"Let's put it in Mummy and Daddy's bathtub and squirt eau de cologne up its bottom with the chicken baster," Sybil said.

"Hush!" said Cornelia, batting the air with her hand. "Stop all this silliness."

"Wait a minute—I got . . . a great idea of what to do with it," said John T. "I think maybe our dear neighbors, the Svensons—"

"I won't hear of it!" interjected Cornelia, but the matter was out of her hands, it was already settled.

"Okay. Who's going to hold this thing while I get back into my togs?" John T. asked.

"How about the original skunkhead, here?" the doctor suggested, ruffling up Wendall's hair with his hand. "How about it, Skunkhead; you game to hang onto that critter while Johnny puts his britches on?"

"Certainly not!" Damned if he was going to get plastered again.

"Bernie—?"

"Well, I'd rather not. Never can tell, y'know."

"I'll hold it," said Sybil. "Let the women save the day, Jonathan old sport." She ran out of the room for the front door.

"I won't have it," moaned Cornelia. "Oh Lord, does she have to be squirted, too?"

"Nobody gets squirted," said John T. "Sib knows how to hold them, Ma—honest."

Hustling around to the front porch where the company met him, he handed the skunk to Sybil, who promptly took charge of the situation, giving it a tooth-rattling shaking to let it know who was boss. When—as John T. hurriedly put on his clothes—the skunk attempted one last time to flip itself out of the girl's grasp, she gave it such a thorough chastising that afterwards it hung pathetically upside down, its little eyes shining imploringly, its paws dangling limply in the air —as if, Wendall thought, it had just emerged for the five-hundredth time from the cold water of the river, and he was filled with peace.

"You're all a bunch of little cowards, aren't you?" said Sybil, drawing herself up proudly. She took a step forward and went "Skaah!" at her mother, who scurried inside, slamming the screen door behind her. Wendall edged over to the carriage port steps in case she should decide to pick on him. The doctor lit a cigarette, but stayed his distance. Sybil chuckled quietly to herself, then a little louder, a soft hesitant laugh. And then tears wet her cheeks, but she kept on laughing. A moth catapulted down the porch light and got its wings momentarily tangled in her hair. As it escaped, John T. came out and Sybil transferred the skunk to him.

"Attababe, Sibs." He kissed her. She smiled and, nodding to the rest of the family, quickly went inside and ran upstairs.

"Now I'll be doggoned," said the doctor.

"She used to help me all the time," John T. said. "Remember? She held them for me while I gave 'em the gas before taking out their stink. Okay—them's as is gettin' aboard better get."

"Tomas, you can't go," said Cornelia. "You're too young to be a member of a foolhardy plot like the one those oafs are planning. You come with me, we're going to bed."

But she said nothing to Wendall. Bernie Aja went along on his way to the movies, as did the doctor, despite Cornelia's parting shots about old men playing at kiddies' games. "Next thing you know you'll be wearing diapers to the office," she said in disgust.

Wendall walked down Coolidge Street between John T. and the doctor, Bernie Aja on the outside, and they were all four of them pals coming back from the war, walking into an empty town on this blue night.

Leaves rustled, and frogs and crickets in the hills over town sent their voices down into the empty streets, into the empty houses, and on they walked, the warm pavement a white road they had traveled for ages, leading through the silent streets, and all about them, a companionable loneliness touched their skins like a breeze, a breeze carried over from the war where soldiers lay in sunny meadows, killed in the morning, and on they walked, four abreast, home from the war, together, pals forever. . . .

Three minutes later, while Bernie Aja and the doctor (in due respect to their ages) waited on the sidewalk in the shadow of an elm tree, John T. and Wendall snuck around back of the Svenson house. At the slanting cellar door, John T. halted.

"Test it, see if it's open," he whispered.

Wendall tugged on the handle; the door lifted.

"Lift it all the way back, then get set to shut it and run," John T. said.

Wendall followed instructions: he waited nervously, his hand on the upraised door. John T. approached the threshold.

"I'm gonna count to three," he said, "then pop her in, and you shut that door faster'n you've ever shut anything before. Ready?"

"Yes, sir."

He counted. "One, two . . ." then, as he brought back his arm, he bellowed, "Jesus—*shit!*" and in the same breath, "Run!" Wendall let go the door; he and John T., going in opposite directions, collided, and, as John T. started to gallop frantically over him, Wendall caught a flash of black and white fur not two feet away where the skunk had landed after slipping from his uncle's grasp. Then he was bowled over, John T. fell with him, and, hopelessly entangled, they were gassed like sitting ducks.

"Damn! Damn! Damn!" howled John T., pounding his fist against the grass. At his third damn, a light from upstairs dropped onto the lawn. John T. rolled off Wendall. They jumped to their feet, and, stumbling every inch of the way, fled for their lives.

Only when safely out of reach on the bridge did they stop and wait for the doctor to catch up: Bernie had gone on to the movies. Wendall felt nauseous; his stomach turned over; he hung himself on the railing and let fly. John T. tore off his T-shirt and dropped it like a soiled diaper into the river, then slapped Wendall's back, and said, "Jesus H. Christ, can you beat it?"

The doctor came around the corner of the empty lot, advancing very nonchalantly, delicately holding his nose. He drew up to the boys, shook both their hands, and then, unclasping his nose and making a twisted face, said, "Lord love a duck. I never . . ."

"Pretty inept of us, wasn't it?" John T. said ruefully. "Sibs will be madder'n a wet hen when she hears."

They leaned on the railing, luxuriating in foul odor. Below them, reflected like a dim moon in the water, shimmered the outside light bulb on the rear corner of the grange hall. It cast a galaxy of light across the water, defining the flow as a swath of gleaming ripples. A fog was forming: on the water several water-drop gyres ringed out and disappeared.

"Lord love a duck," sighed the doctor again. He chuckled; John T. joined him.

"Guess the old lady'll really hit the ceiling, too," John T. said softly.

"She'll put a dent in it," said the doctor, gently punching his son in the arm.

After a moment, Wendall moved closer, touching his shoulder to his grandfather's arm. The doctor looked down and smiled, but said nothing. They looked at the river, then they gazed at the sky, and no night in Wendall's life had ever been so suddenly beautiful as that one.

TWENTY

The peak of summer closed over Stebbinsville. Drought, which had been well on the way to finishing off a good many crops by the end of July, had—by the second week in August—almost finished the job. Folks conjectured that maybe the world had moved a little too close to the sun, or the sun too close to the world, or something along that line. People sweated themselves dry, and the dogs—the poor dogs—roasted. General Patton lay on the front stoop of Kahler's Market, his head on his front paws, his mouth open, tongue lying extended on the cement, and one day as Wendall walked by, he saw a little river of sweat running off the dog's tongue down the steps and onto the sidewalk.

The sidewall itself was so hot you could fry an egg on it, and fry an egg on it is exactly what Carl Hatcher, a young reporter for the Stebbinsville paper, did. And not only was Wendall present for this occasion, he helped Carl do it.

The frying took place in front of the *Reporter* office in Main Street, directly across from Kahler's Market. It took place at noon: the word had been spread several hours earlier, so there was a sizable crowd on hand when Carl came out of the newspaper office wearing a camera slung over one shoulder, an apron, and a tall white chef's hat on his head. He held up an egg and a spatula for all to see, and announced the temperature in the shade was 104°, in the sun, 111°.

Then he looked around, spotted Wendall, and asked him to step forth. Carl handed the boy an egg and fitted the chef's hat on his head. Wendall backed away, thinking he must look ridiculous, expecting the crowd to break into catcalls, but Carl urged him forward, the crowd stayed relatively calm, and his fears were somewhat allayed.

"You know how to crack an egg?" Carl asked, handing Wendall the spatula.

"Do you doubt my dexterity?"

"Huh?"

"Yes. Of course I know perfectly well how to crack an egg. I'm not a dunderhead."

"Oh, okay. Listen, I want to get some snapshots, so you just crack it open and drop it on the sidewalk when I say to. Try not to break the yolk."

Carl unslung his camera, made some adjustments, and gave Wendall the go-ahead sign. The boy laid the egg on the sidewalk; he tapped it gingerly, then a little harder, with the edge of the spatula. Five times he had to tap, growing more nervous with each delicate blow. For a second he imagined the whole thing was a farce: the egg was really made out of stone, and in a minute Carl, his camera full of mocking photographs, would crack up with laughter, inform him of the joke, and headlines next Thursday would be SUCKER SWALLOWS EGG LINE: STONE FAILS TO GET SHELLED.

But then the shell cracked. Wendall lifted the egg an inch or two above the pavement and dug the two shell halves apart with his thumbs, dumping a blob of albumen and yolk successfully onto the sidewalk. People surged forward and intently peered at his handiwork. Those behind who couldn't see shoved and complained, some angry words broke out, they were quickly stifled. As for the egg, its underside took on a whitish tinge.

Wendall said, "It isn't exactly sizzling up a storm, is it?"

"It's cooking," Carl exclaimed, snapping a close-up of Wendall observing the egg.

Five, ten, fifteen minutes went by, the albumen whitened, the yolk hardened. Every three minutes Carl carefully lifted the egg with the spatula, shifting it to a new section of sidewalk. Several times he had to marshall back the crowd, which had a tendency to push too close and cut off the sun.

At the end of forty minutes, Carl pronounced the egg done, and Mack Yater, the managing editor of the paper, produced a plate, a fork, and a salt shaker. "Who wants to do the honors?" he asked. No one jumped eagerly forward, leaving it up to Carl to volunteer, which he did, eating the egg while Mack Yates took a last photograph.

"Okay, folks. You've seen it with your own eyes," Carl said. "That's it, believe it or not."

Wendall surrendered the chef's hat, but hung around a few minutes while Carl and Mack Bates held a short gabfest with some of the onlookers. A few men shook Wendall's hand, saying he'd done a damn sight better job than their wives ever had.

Once home, Wendall felt so happy that instead of going straight into the house, he climbed up to the cupola and for a while surveyed his domain like a small astute God, loving every inch of it. The thought occurred to him for the first time that this was a "home," and this town was "his town." Silently he mouthed "home" and "my town," then he said them aloud, and it made him giggle in a funny way that was almost tearful.

Then he went to the kitchen and said, "I guess I can fry an egg all right," but when Cornelia asked, "What brings on a fool statement like that?" he replied mysteriously, "You wait and see," and his eyebrows grabbing the ceiling of his forehead in daffy nonchalance, he strode jauntily off to busy about his own affairs.

The following edition of the paper was, in Wendall's opinion, by far the greatest *Reporter* ever to hit the stands. The back-page headlines were HEAT SOARS AT 111: SIDEWALK CHEF FRIES EGG, and almost the entire page was dedicated to photographs. There was Wendall cracking open the egg, Wendall again in a close-up staring at the first signs of whiteness, and Wendall once more, still wearing the chef's hat, standing beside Carl Hatcher while he tucked away the egg.

Wendall hunched in his chin, raised his eyebrows, let his eyes glaze over with world weariness, twiddled both sides of his imaginary black—and very waxed—mustache, and decided that now, as he'd become a bona fide celebrity, he must dedicate himself to being very brusque and superior with Tom.

So the sidewalks sizzled, as did most of the Stebbinsville citizenry, and pretty soon just about everybody had been backed into one kind of bad humor or another. It became very evident that on one of the days in the not too far future the war would come to an end, but people were too fatigued to even think about rejoicing. In fact, all that a potential armistice made many folks do was worry. And the closer the end of the war came, the more they worried.

Probably the biggest worry in Stebbinsville was the old can factory. One of the few factories in Vermont to have a war contract, it produced blood plasma containers, machine-gun belt links, and milk containers for the Army. The workers in the factory were poor: yet before the war, they had been much poorer, so that as victory loomed closer, an undercurrent of dismay, even of panic, spread among the workers who feared that any day the government might cancel the contract, meaning half of them would be laid off, and the other half would be reduced from as high as a fifty-four-hour week to a thirty-hour one, and at lower wages. This uneasiness, coupled with the oppressive weather, caused several fights to break out on Prescott Street, and in one of the fights, Joel Spender was stabbed and almost killed. His wife, Lucille, a gaunt, gray-haired woman, and her eldest son, Chad, drove the truck around town collecting the garbage for nearly two weeks while Joel was recuperating in the Montpelier hospital.

Another thing people found it easy to fret over was rationing. They were fed up with coupons and quotas, fed up with being told that so many Red Stamps were good for so many points on meats, and stamps thus and so in War Book 4 were good for five pounds of sugar, and that butter was 16 points to the pound, and so forth. Nothing had greatly changed during the two years of regulated buying, but as the weather and tempers turned rotten, folks became testy when they couldn't travel to where they wanted, or when they had to wait a week or a month for a new tire, or when they tried and failed forever to get a part for a burnt-out electric refrigerator or vacuum cleaner. Meat was hard to come by, fruits were plentiful, so naturally everyone wanted meat, no one wanted fruit.

To top this off, infantile paralysis spread far and wide; many more cases were reported nationally than in previous years, so conscientious or naggy mothers were worried about that, constantly telling their kids to wash their hands after wee-wee, and not to play in filthy places, and every day in the papers new cases were reported in such and such a town, and in such and such another town. . . .

The long and short of it was that everything combined to make Stebbinsville a pretty crabby little town. When you met a friend or neighbor on the street you didn't talk about anything because it was too much of an effort in the heat to think up a conversation, and the war had long since ceased to be a topic of mutual interest. So the Russians attacked Warsaw, so Goebbels said the Germans would mobilize for a total war effort, so the Nazis had a new silent robot bomb, so the Americans entered Brittany, so the Marines took Guam, so what was keeping them, why didn't they hurry up and get it over with?

On the home front, Boy Scouts kept coming around with wagons to cart off anything you had (in, around, or on top of, the house) that had a papery quality, and that got to be downright irksome. Outside of town, two barns burned within a week of each other; the fires were caused by spontaneous combustion. And the Boy Scouts came around again; this time it was old clothes they wanted. Then Dallas Wiggen, older brother of Jimmy, was reported killed in some insignificant place in France. And the Boy Scouts showed up, back on the paper drive again.

At the Coolidge Street house, the doctor felt as if he were being slowly comsumed by fatigue. His hands, knees, and elbows always ached; Cornelia fired petty problems like little darts into his skin night and day; he tried his best to be cheery, but lacked all animation—

numerous were the times he begged out of reading his grandchildren an evening story because the detmoles were giving him a going over. Cornelia's life as always revolved around the kitchen where it was can, can, can, day and night—onions, tomatoes, beans, hot steam and enough sweet sickly sugar smell to drive you wild, and if that wouldn't do the trick, the sight of her leaping from pot to bubbling pot, red and sweating like the devil's wife herself, would. Desipte such activity, she always found the time to make life miserable for Wendall with her pet peeve, namely fingerprints on the doorjambs. This became such a fixation of hers that soon the boy was spending the better part of an hour a day sponging smudges off her precious woodwork. Several times he was tempted to martyr himself by chopping off his hands with the carving knife and leaving the bloody little things to drain in his grandmother's sink—maybe *that* would make her happy!

Sybil had occasional bursts of energy and fancy, but for the most part she remained subdued. She framed some of her old paintings and did some new watercolors, and arranged for a show in Barre, but at the last minute the show fell through, and she took a part-time job in the Treasure Chest Gift Shop.

When you came right down to it, Tom emerged as one of the very few people with whom Wendall had more than a partial contact, who looked as if he would —through the present heat spell—retain what might be called his human-beingness. So despite his fame from the egg-frying escapade, Wendall continued to allow Tom to tag along after him, as always ever-ready to be the butt of his ideas. Enthusiastically, then, they went on with their war games, augmenting their battle days with various side trips into butterfly collecting when, sporting nets made of cheesecloth, broomhandles, and coat hangers, they industriously wrecked the flower garden by swopping off the blossoms of sweet peas, nasturtiums, and poppies as they attempted to snag swallowtails, morning glories, and monarchs.

As to other fields of diversion, the pigeons had wised up a good deal, so trapping them was almost altogether abandoned. However, the asparagus grew to gigantic proportions and went to seed, forming a ticklish forest through which the boys were able to construct a complicated network of crawl-size tunnels.

Life, Wendall decided, was going to be almost supportable—then Tom went rotten.

It began when he tried to catch a black snake three times longer than himself down in the pumpkin vines by the compost heap, and the damn thing bit his hand bad enough to keep it (the hand) wrapped up in gauze for four days, and to keep Tom cranky for the same amount of time. Then, the minute the gauze was removed, Tom caught poison ivy. Not just regular poison ivy, the kind that can be combated with calamine lotion—a little bit on the arms, a few painful bubbles between the fingers—oh, no, not Tom: the way he caught poison ivy you would have thought he'd gone out and purposely rolled in the stuff. His eyes swelled shut, his cheeks puffed out, his ears cauliflowered, and to help things along, temperatures hovered around a hundred degrees—the humidity was reported daily to be between eighty and ninety percent. Tom was stuffed between sheets, swabbed with lotions, and given a barrage of shots and pills, and all he did for hours on end was whine, whine, whine, making it well nigh impossible for Wendall to talk him into doing a belch, a Donald Duck soliloquy—anything.

"Well, if he is going to be so damned crotchety, I'll leave the little bastard alone," Wendall finally mumbled.

And he did.

So, with August grinding slowly into its final devastating weeks, as long ago must have the Greeks, the Byzantines, and the Huns, so did Wendall stand on the front lawn in the rubble of his fallen empire, shaking his fists at the third-floor window, shouting slanders. . . .

TWENTY-ONE

Sybil was painting Stebbinsville from a point midway up the cleared skiing slope in the park. Alone, she painted lazily, giving in to the sun. After a while she felt as if her hair were filling with dust, and, setting aside her paints, she went down the slope to Bloody Pond. She knelt on the bank and splashed water over her arms, face, and neck, then dug her hands into the mud a foot from the bank and dipped her hair into the cool water. Raising her head, she swept the wet hair back, allowing it to drip onto her blouse.

That is when she spotted a figure standing off the road where it cornered with the small pine woods. A man, tall, angular, and pale, his eyes, in a stiffly drawn face, rimmed with black, was watching her. They regarded each other, and it didn't take long for Sybil to put the features together and realize the man was Duffy Kahler. Standing up, the fact *Duffy Kahler is not dead* so overwhelmed her that she accepted it almost instantly, and raised her hand in a stunned wave which he did not return.

Next, she traversed the edge of the pond, gained the road, and continued along it to a spot in line with Duffy where she paused. Fifteen yards away, Duffy stood in shadow, his hand on the trunk of a tree. Sybil thought: He is probably crazy, probably dangerous. Intently facing him, she thought: I must be careful, I must do nothing to frighten him.

"Is it really you? Duffy?"

He nodded, shoving his hands into his pockets. In back of him a blue jay squawked and he jumped a little.

"May I come near you?"

He nodded again. Yet, as she measured her steps

over the distance between them, he backed into the solid shadow of the close pines. On the edge of sunlight, Sybil hesitated for just a moment, then entered the woods.

Above their heads white flecks of sky like stars broke the balanced somberness of pine branches. Duffy took up some needles and switched them from one hand to the other, then he dropped them on his thigh, dusted them off, and said, "Well—hello, I bet you're surprised to see me, aren't you? You thought I was dead, didn't you? Everybody thinks I'm dead, can you beat that?"

"What happened?"

"Oh no." Smiling slyly, he touched a finger to his lips. "That's a secret. Everything's a secret."

"But what are you doing? Where are you staying? Why is it that no one knows you're back? Your parents—?"

"That's just the way it's going to be." He gazed into the thicket of branches overhead. "You won't tell on me, will you?"

"What do you mean, tell on you?"

"That I'm here. I don't want anybody to know I'm here. They can't, don't you see? They all think I'm dead. If they found out I wasn't dead—"

"Duffy, have you been home?"

"No."

"But what do you do? How do you live?"

"I've got a hideout. I've fixed it up real nice. I've got a bed and books and some trunks and lots of magazines and provisions, I've got everything I need, you'll see."

"Are you inviting me there?"

"What? Where?"

"Are you inviting me to your hideout?"

"I didn't say that. Nobody knows where my hideout is, and nobody is ever going to know." He drew up his knees, and his eyes, suspiciously askance, regarded her.

"Duffy, you've been hanging around our house,

haven't you? There was a night where I looked out the window—"

"No!"

He sprang to his feet. His legs planted firmly in front of her, Sybil thought he was going to kick, yet she did not raise a hand to protect herself. She concentrated on the worn knees of his pants; thin flakes of drying mud peeled off them. His hand came down and gently posed on her head, the fingertips applying no pressure.

"What's his name?" Duffy asked.

"Who?"

"The little boy?"

"Tomas . . . ?"

"The little red-headed boy. You know who . . ."

"Tomas."

"How old is he?"

"Four and a half."

His hand slipped off her head; he walked away; Sybil lifted her eyes.

"Is he . . . mine?"

"Yes, of course."

"If you hadn't forced me to, he wouldn't be alive now."

"That's right. But I'm glad he's alive."

"You love him?"

There was no need for Sybil to respond.

Duffy shuffled farther away, then folded onto the ground, grasping his stomach. He moaned and breathed loudly for a minute. Sybil could see only the underside of his chin: then his head moved, and his eyes, bright and pained, came into view.

"I had him in August of that year," Sybil said quietly. "I lived alone in New York, and he was a good baby. That autumn was quite beautiful. I wheeled him all over the city. We basked in the sunlight on a lot of benches like fat old turtles. Sometimes we thought of you. I didn't want to pray for you because I realized you really hadn't a part in creating the baby. For you it was a small, disgusting, unhappy act like taking a drink to break training. Do you remember how I talked you into it, how afterwards you whimpered and said it wasn't your fault, as if there could be a fault in a thing like that? You didn't understand I suddenly had to bust the virginity myth before it became bigger than me. You were so unhappy afterwards, and I felt so nil—but I thought at the time it had saved me. I didn't care a whit about you, though. That is, until you were reported killed—then I prayed for you. . . .

"In New York I met a man, David Matthewson. He was a dreamer from the Midwest who'd gone to Yale, but, believe it or not, he was working with the City Parks Department when I met him. We were married. At first I was content to live day to day with my child and husband. But then the winter, the bitterness of it, changed me. I goaded David into returning to school, and both of us did, we enrolled at Columbia. I was so energetic; I thought I was really opening up to the world, and I was so involved in my own emergence that I neglected David and one day he told me he was quitting school and going into the Army. His farewell sounded like an apology, and I suddenly couldn't bear myself, I came home, I wrote David a million letters and received vague answers. I prayed for him, and in August 1943 he asked for a second tour of duty. He came back from the Pacific on leave, was in California for most of it, then planed east for a few days before going to Europe. I flew to New York to meet him, but such a heavy fog shrouded La Guardia that the plane was rerouted to Hartford and grounded for twelve hours. We missed connections, and by the time I made the city, he was gone for good. So I loved him, but never showed it much until he'd left, and then he was killed, too . . . I mean, then he was killed."

Duffy lay passively, listening.

"Now I don't know what to do. I haven't had time to think, of course. I always thought before news of your death that I would never like you when and if you returned. I imagined you would be a hero, decorated with ribbons. You really couldn't have returned as anything else. Well, there was a great to-do made over the monument, you know: Carl Hatcher wrote a sappy but very stirring memorial column in the *Reporter*. John T. cried when he heard you were killed. Later on he and I had a long talk. He said your death had made him want to commit suicide. I was a little angry that he loved you so much; I never saw in you what he did. It doesn't seem at all right, that you have come back. . . ."

She went and sat by his feet. "Your shoes are untied." She picked at the rubber toe of his sneaker.

"I don't care."

"Are you all right, Duffy? I mean . . ."

"Yes. I'm perfectly all right. Why do you say that? Does it look like there's something wrong with me?" He sat up, smiling ingenuously. "I'm the same old Duffy Kahler; heck, anybody can see that."

"What happened to your face?"

"Nothing happened to it. Don't talk about it." He licked his lips nervously and swung away from her.

"Something awful must have happened."

Duffy stood up. "I'm going away now."

"Do you come here often?"

"I don't know. This is the first time I came. Usually I sleep a lot during the day. I don't know if I'll come back because it might not be safe. You won't tell, will you?"

"Duffy, I think you need help."

"Say you won't tell. I could hurt you if you won't say it, I mean it."

"All right, I won't tell."

He disappeared through the pines. Sybil walked out into the sunlight and up the slope to her easel. The paint glistened garishly; she scraped most of it off, then began to lay on colors at random with a palette knife, smoothing out blobs, making little attempt to depict any form.

For fifteen minutes she applied paint to the canvas in this manner, then she scraped much of it off again, packed up her gear, and walked home.

TWENTY-TWO

John T. entered the Miss Stebbinsville and sat down in a back booth: he had fifteen minutes to kill until Ercel was off. She said hello, gave him a glass of milk and a doughnut, and when she got behind the counter she fished fifteen cents from her apron pocket and rang it up on the register. John T. ate the doughnut, brushed powdered sugar off his fingers, and with several large gulps put away the milk. He dug a nickel out of his pants pocket and flicked it onto the table as a tip. After the coin had spun and settled, he set the doughnut saucer over it.

Marty Haldenstein came in and took a seat at the counter. John T. thought, as he always did on seeing Marty: the poor bastard. He'd never said four words to the librarian, but anyone that ugly, that sick, you had to feel sorry for.

Marty ordered a cup of coffee and broke out coughing. The talk in the diner was subdued and Marty's coughs sounded loudly, tempting John T. to rise and walk over and tell him to get out because his sickness was damn depressing, things were bad enough without a walking dead man in your lap besides.

Marty Haldenstein's life stinks, John T. thought. Everybody in there's life stunk, in fact, including his own. And that was it; their lives never would be any bigger or better than they were at that moment in the diner. It was as if the life of Stebbinsville, and, worse yet, of the entire world, had been stopped at 9:25 P.M. of that late August evening, 1944. Thirty years from now a stranger might walk into the diner and be confronted with this same scene: Marty Haldenstein coughing out his guts and trying to drink a cup of coffee; Ercel, her face tired and lined, lifting the plastic cover off a stand of cherry pie slices; and himself shrugged into that last booth, waiting, always waiting, with one crummy nickel under his doughnut plate. The story of the universe in a hash joint. Jesus H. Christ.

He smoked. Marty Haldenstein paid and left. Ercel went out back to change, and returned, her hair combed, her face washed—she wore no lipstick. Regular as a dollar bill, John T. thought. Yes, sir.

"You forgot to pick up my plate," he said.

"Oh." She found the nickel, snapped open her purse, and dropped it in.

John T. spun the plate for a minute, unable to think of anything more to say. What he finally came out with was, "Saturday night is almost as lousy as Sunday, Monday, Tuesday, Wednesday, Thursday, and Friday night."

"I'd just as soon you stopped complaining," Ercel said.

"Oh, you'd just as soon, would you?"

She laid her hand on his. "Come on, now. It's too early in the evening to start a fight."

"What do we do this Saturday night, then? Drive around on the bike? It's already too late for a movie. Walk? Talk? Play cards? Strip poker?"

"I don't know."

"You don't know. Nobody knows. This is Nobody Knowsville."

"Please stop complaining, John T."

"All I want to do is unwind."

"All right. But let's not in here."

John T. dropped his butt into the milk glass; he held his hand over the mouth of the glass, watching the interior smoke up, the ash eventually die.

"There I lie," he said. "Come on, let's blow."

They cruised along Prescott Street on the motorcycle. Passing the Coolidge Street house, John T. said, "Give my daddykins a salute as we go by. He may need it." He accelerated, and said, "Let's go out to the lake. We could go swimming. We haven't tried that, have we?"

"We don't have any suits."

"Who needs 'em? We'll go skinny dipping."

"I'd rather not."

"Oh, hell. We'll see when we get there, then."

"You better slow down a little . . ."

John T. braked and stopped. "That slow enough for you, lady?" With the gearshift in neutral, he gunned the motor and walked the Harley forward. "That just about right for you, lady? Huh?"

"I'm sorry. I wasn't thinking. I didn't mean . . ."

"Well then, leave me alone when I'm driving. That's all I ask from everybody. I don't care what they tell me to do when my two feet are on the ground, but when I'm driving I don't want anybody to peep. Is that too much to ask?"

"No."

"Good. Now that that's straight—"

They started on again, and John T. kept the motorcycle at a reasonable speed the rest of the distance to the picnic grounds. There, with the engine cut, they rolled slowly over rough ground to the side of a wooden table and dismounted.

At the edge of the lake they stood a little apart. Only the old fireworks raft broke the calm surface of the water. Deep frog voices chunked; no waves lapped the beach.

"Come on. I really feel like going for a swim," John T. said.

"I told you, I don't want to. It isn't safe, anyway. Someone might come along."

"We'll walk around the shore a little ways to where the bushes are thicker."

"I don't want to."

"You don't want to do a God damn thing."

"I just don't like the idea."

"Look, I want to swim beside you naked in the water," John T. pleaded. "I want to touch you all over when you're up to your neck in water, and it's dark, and we're alone, can't you understand that? I wouldn't ask you to go any farther, I promise."

"Yes—you promise."

"Oh, hell with you then. *I'm* going swimming."

"All right."

"Coming? I need spectator support."

She followed him onto a dirt path that circled the lake. Some hundred yards along it, John T. veered off and pushed through thick underbrush onto a small rocky point. Ercel seated herself on a rock, her feet touching the water. John T. unbuttoned his shirt, took off his undershirt, and chucked the clothes in her lap. He unlaced his shoes, dropped his pants, and hesitated for a moment, then, self-consciously forcing his eyes to be disinterested, he removed his underwear.

He kicked the pants and shoes aside, and hands on hips, faced the black water. He felt small, hopelessly exposed. The night was not as warm as he had imagined it; his teeth began to chatter. He waded into the water and when it reached midthigh, he dove, disappearing into darkness warmer than the air. He came up gasping and began to swim the crawl. A good swimmer, he quickly gained the raft, and, scorning the ladder, lifted himself up with his arms. His foot slipped once on the wet planking, then he was upright, facing shore.

Hugging the clothes to her, Ercel kept her eyes on his small white form. Never before had she seen John T. naked. He'd stripped down so quickly that all she remembered of his body was it had no tan line where a bathing suit might have been worn. Lifting the undershirt, she pressed it to her face and smelled his body, feeling her own body stir as she did so.

A splash called her attention back to the water. Barely discernible in spite of the sputters his arms made, John T. swam a little off line, going full steam to show off. He looked up when he ran out of breath, corrected his direction, and in a minute strode boldly into shore.

"Whew," he said. "Who brought the towels? Gimme the undershirt."

She handed it to him, full of wonder that it should be so natural to do this as peacefully as she did with him only two feet away and naked. Hastily, he wiped water off his chest, thighs, and buttocks, then dressed.

"Cigarette," he commanded, still breathing rapidly after his exertion.

She gave him one from the pack in her purse. Folding his arms, he blew smoke at the sky and smiled.

"That sure felt good. Yes, sir."

She stood up, kissed him, and feeling him against her, wondered sadly if she would give in to him before they were married. He inhaled from the cigarette, they kissed, and she sucked the smoke into her own lungs. Stars swam like minnows a million miles beyond John T.'s shoulders, and it was a supremely quiet moment.

"I guess I'm unwound," John T. finally whispered.

On the way back he told her he planned to sell the motorcycle to Harry Garengelli. When she asked why, he said, "The old man could use the dough," and left it at that.

"Does he really need it?" Ercel asked. "Or are you just building a good tall monument to yourself?"

"Aw, Christ," moaned John T. "Lay off, will you? Just lay off me for one minute. . . ."

TWENTY-THREE

Early in the morning Wendall was awakened by the motorcycle. Poking his head out the window, he received the distinct impression John T. was trying to kill himself.

His uncle drove the Harley into the barn; there followed a moment of silence, then the machine roared out of the doorway, bounced over the wooden ramp and traveled on one wheel to the shade line of the carriage port where John T. hit the brakes, spun in a semicircle, gunned the cycle, and, bucking off at the same breakneck pace, shot back into the barn.

Wendall dressed, ran downstairs, and seated himself on a back porch garbage can. The Harley rocked and skidded out of the barn—John T. jerked up the front end and spokes spun like a disk of transparent silver. Then he spotted Wendall, came to a sudden halt, and gave a cheery good morning.

"What are you doing?" Wendall asked.

"Oh, just cutting up a little."

"What do you mean?"

"Just want to get a last workout on her before she goes, I guess."

"Before she goes?"

"Yeah, I'm selling her to . . ."

He cut off abruptly. The doctor stomped onto the front porch, asparagus fork in hand. He was dressed in a brown moth-eaten bathrobe; his slippers trickled strings of what might once have been the fur of some cheap, disreputable animal.

"Well, well," he said, "it's only you, Johnny my boy. For a minute I thought the sky was fallin'." He shuffled down the steps onto the driveway. "I think I better go and cut those sparagismos before the hot air comin' outta that infernal thing withers 'em to death." He walked onto the wet lawn, dewdrops flicking off the tips of his slippers.

"Who are you going to sell it to?" Wendall asked, when the doctor was out of earshot.

"Harry offered to buy it."

"But why sell it?"

"I don't know, just am. I've gotten my kicks on the bike, I don't need it anymore."

"Well," Wendall said hesitantly, "could I have a ride on it before you do?"

"You must be kidding me."

"No. I'm serious. I've never had a ride on it, you know."

"That's my fault? I thought you wouldn't be caught dead on a motorcycle."

"I've changed my mind. I'm not afraid anymore."

"Well, I'll be . . ." John T. thought for a minute, then he said, "Okay. Look, I just got this great idea. How about us two taking her on a last trip? We'll go fishing, an overnight job. Just you and me. Whatta you say?"

"I don't know how to fish."

"Who says you got to know how to fish to go fishing?"

One hour later, with sleeping bags, flashlights, cans of corned beef hash, a frying pan, fishing rods and reels, and other necessary and unnecessary paraphernalia strapped to the aluminum rack over the rear wheel or stuffed in the saddlebags, John T. and Wendall, mounted on the idling motorcycle beneath the carriage port, said their good-byes.

"I didn't give him permission," Cornelia wailed. "He'll fall off, and it will be the blow to end everything. But who in this family cares what I have to say? Learn the hard way is the motto around here. I'm telling you right now, Frederick, I wash my hands of the situation."

John T. let out the clutch. In a breathless surge of power, fire, noise, and smoke, they took off. Tom spit disgustedly on the porch, and buried his face in Sybil's skirt. "It's not *fair!*" he bawled.

Wendall thought that with the starting jerk his neck and hips had been dislocated. His cheek bounced off John T.'s shoulder blade, striking his glasses stems up to the sides of his head, but he dared not release his petrified grip on his uncle's belt to adjust them. All he could do for the first thirty seconds was shout voicelessly: "Stop, I don't want to ride, I don't want to ride, please *please* stop!" Then he passed out and on recovering was surprised to find himself still situated more or less vertically on the seat behind John T. Opening his eyes, he looked down, saw road screaming by in a gray blur, looked hastily up and saw Dorothy and Marie Svenson seated on their front porch flash by, followed closely by a blurred Unitarian Church. They slowed down, swerved—leaning almost to the ground!—and came to a halt beside the gas pumps at Garengelli's. Wendall oozed off the bike: his knees were so weak he fell down, tipping over a water can. Foggily, he got up and leaned against a pump, hungrily sucking down great portions of air.

"I think I'm going to vomit," he whispered.

"Nonsense," said John T. "We weren't even doing twenty."

"I don't care. I guess I am afraid. I want to go home."

"Okay. Be a chicken. I don't care. I'm going. You crawl back and face them if you want, not me."

"I don't care what you say. You can't make me do anything I don't want to do."

"Wouldn't dream of it. Put your tail between your legs now and whimper on home, sonny. I'll see you tomorrow."

"Well . . . I didn't say anything precisely about going back," Wendall said. "It took me by surprise, I'll admit; but I feel a lot better already."

"I'm not stopping every fifty yards to let you upchuck by the side of the road," John T. warned. "You make up your mind right now. If you want to come along, no more complaints."

"You don't mind if get sick all over you?"

"Turn your head to the side and it won't even touch me."

Grumbling, Wendall got resituated behind his uncle. John T. gave some coupons and a dollar bill to pay for the gas, Harry dug a handful of change out of his pocket, and with a "So long, kid," to John T., and a "See you, Slugger," to Wendall, he walked back toward the office.

The Harley kicked into gear and leapt away from the pumps into the street. This time Wendall had his cheek pressed staunchly against his uncle's back and the jerk of their take-off hardly affected him. General Patton barreled at them, yelping loudly, but John T. gave the gas handle a slight twist and left the beagle far behind, disconsolately shaking off their dust.

At the eastern end of town they crossed the railroad tracks heading out Route 684. Down the line the Sunday train south from Montreal diminished in size to an iron drop. And as they took the last bump over the tracks, Wendall brought back his head, astonished at the exaltation that had suddenly gripped him, dispersing all his previous fear and nausea. He leaned out to get the view past John T.'s arm. Bugs pinged against his face, they splatted over his teeth. He laughed and licked them off with his tongue and spit to the side, and felt wondrously happy.

They slowed down and climbed out of the valley. Below them on the right, blueberry bushes and dry yellow grasses covered a slope that ran down to a river. Across the river, green grass rippled, polished in silver streaks where breezes disturbed it. Beyond the meadow, birches flashed whitely and the dull lemon spears of poplars leaned slightly to the east. To the left of them, hills rose, rocks towered tall above them. Sometimes they drove through shadow, solid, of these rocks, then they burst out of shadow into sunlight where wind rushed hotly by and the country around them fell away to either side, far-reaching, mountainous, and green.

Eventually, thirsty and tired, John T. pulled off the road for lunch. They sat in flattened grass and ate jelly sandwiches, chewing thoughtfully, letting breezes fiddle with their hair. Then they faced down into the depthless blue of an abandoned quarry nearby; sheer sides of stone strained upward from the calm water. They explored among the rocks for a while, and John T. discovered a good-sized crevice with a small half-moon of ice lodged back in its tightest corner; Wendall came upon a few boulders loaded with garnets. John T. said Sybil would like the gems, so they dug some out with a pocket knife and stored them in the saddlebags —others they threw into the quarry.

As the worthless baubles sank from sight, they emptied their bladders and were off again. An hour later they turned onto an unused timber road. Branches slapped against their heads and shoulders, high weeds swished by, depositing crumbs of pollen on their thighs; burs caught in their pants cuffs. The last mile of the trip was spent in a green somberness beneath pines, where, because of the needles covering the ground, no weeds grew in the trail. Then slivers of silver light became visible between trees, and Wendall saw they were arriving at a small pond. The cycle lurched up a final slight incline and stopped, and silence overpowered them. They dismounted and wearily stretched their legs. After unpacking and rolling out the sleeping bags, they collected some wood and, having established a camp of sorts, put together the rods and went to the pond.

They located a large rock: John T. cast the two rods and handed one to Wendall. The boy made no effort to reel in and try his own hand; he was content to let his fly lie on the unruffled water. John T. cast often, lightly and perfectly, laying his fly on the water each time with hardly a ripple—but the fish were not biting.

The afternoon waned: Wendall could hardly keep his eyes open. He envisioned all sorts of gigantic fish rising up lazily beneath his fly like balloons. Then these fish turned into Jim the sporting goods man, and one after another they rose and spread out on the underside of the surface, bursting with nary a pop. Wendall opened one eye and said, "Do you know Jim very well, Uncle John?"

"Sort of, but not really," John T. said. "He's been here all my life, of course. A friend of mine, Duffy Kahler and I hung around his store a lot, we talked with him, were friends with him, but never really got to know him very well. Pop's the one good friend he has, I guess. In the earlier days they used to go to Boston a lot for Bruin hockey games or Red Sox baseball games. So I guess the bonds between them are pretty strong."

"Was he ever married?" Wendall asked.

"Who—Jim? Not on your life. He had a romance, though. There's a story about that. . . ."

It seems an old Italian, Frank Spinelli, who had eked out a living selling zeppole and calzone from a small store squeezed between Bradford's Bakery and the Gulf station, had a daughter, now Mrs. Mike Stenatto, who was at one time an uncommonly beautiful girl, so much so that, as she grew up, it became the general consensus she was headed for movie stardom. Her name, Claudia, got shortened to Clo, and Clo, through none of her own doing and much to her eventual consternation, was a freak.

For the prettiest girl in town—the one all the old Stebbinsville men, and middle-aged Stebbinsville men, and young Stebbinsville men, and even a few little Stebbinsville boys reached out for in their dreams, or kissed beneath the moon, or whispered "I love you" to in the shadow of a grape arbor—couldn't buy a date; everyone was afraid of her because she was the glamour girl who was going to be a movie star. Her father rejoiced at first; later he puzzled over the matter; then he despaired.

At this point, along came Jim, a shy young lad from upstate near St. Albans, freshly graduated from the University of Vermont, already addicted to generally unlit half-smoked cigars, and on the lookout for a comfortable business, perferably sporting goods, preferably in a small town such as Stebbinsville, and—the business having been shortly established—Jim rubbed the last stickum spots off his glass counters, sat his immense body down for the first history-making time on his stool, and his posterior comfortably lodged, a copy of the *Sporting News* open before him, he settled into the very same Jim, with the very same air about him, as the present Jim who ran the sporting goods store.

But the moment his first customer floated her exquisite little body through the door in search of sewing machine oil, Jim was a goner.

From then on, every day except Sundays, Jim, with his hair wetted down and combed and his glasses stored safely in a pocket, closed up the sport and news shop at noon, waddled across Perry Street, and, puffing from the mere exertion of walking, headed for, shortly to arrive in front of, Spinelli's little shop.

For a few seconds, he contemplated the three steps leading up into the shop. When at last he had summoned enough courage to continue, he would stretch onto his tiptoes, and, attempting to thrust a chin out of his neck, he would swing his arms once forward, once back for momentum, then hop ludicrously up the three steps leading to his love (who spent her days battling around globs of dough in a sizzling bin of fat), before whom he presented himself, rigid and scared, arms stiff at his overwhelming sides, a smile fading into a grimace on his face, as his cheeks, his eyes, and his lungs almost burst from his athletic display of enthusiasm.

There is no record of exactly how Clo greeted this impressive entrance, Most likely she continued batting the zeppoles around, or, if her brother Tony happened to be at work close beside her, perhaps she nudged him and said, loud enough for Jim to catch, "Here come the elephants again."

Whatever she said or didn't say, awkward moments of silence followed during which Jim switched his hands from clasped in front of him to clasped in back of him to clasped in front of him to hanging at his sides because he couldn't think what to do with them. His eyes would seem to be concentrating on the zeppoles bouncing around in their tub of fat making spattering noises, then, looking up quickly and evasively, he would ask if the zeppole or calzone were any good that day.

Clo would say she guessed it was as good as ever, which suited Jim fine and set him to scooping bits of candy bar paper, half-melted Life Savers, leader weights and other assorted odds and ends out of his sacklike pockets, searching for a few coins. Inevitably his glasses came out during this foray; accounts put the number of times he dropped and broke them on Spinelli's floor at around fifteen.

Then Clo handed him a greasy paper cone filled with fried dough blobs, and Jim handed her his money, and that was the instant when his heart did flip-flops as the sluggy tips of his fingers touched her fine appendages. And that is all he got each time—a quick touch, nothing more.

Purchase concluded, Jim would turn heel and shuffle out of the shop clutching the paper cone to his breast. Very slowly he would walk up the block, ruminating on his experience, and by the time he reached his own digs and had lugged himself up the steps one by one, he was a very sad man.

He couldn't stop, though. He strongly disliked zeppole and calzone, and he hated the way he jumped up the steps and the way he knew people made fun of him behind his back, imitating his short exuberant flight into Spinelli's shop, yet he couldn't change one single thing. Love had trapped him: noon in, noon out, it sent him through this painful ritual. Then one day, after Jim had been making a fool of himself to no avail for nearly three months, love released him—Mike Stenatto and Clo Spinelli eloped. And that's all there was to it: the affair ended, the Hollywood myth died, and people stopped making fun of Jim behind his back. . . .

The boys reeled in and broke down their rods. John T. fished two small boxes of raisins from his pocket, and they ate them while the pond cooled and turned an opaque color. Peepers began their nocturnal songs, bullfrogs chugged, a whippoorwill called—animals in the underbrush ceased their rustlings. A snake entered the water near them and set out for the opposite shore, leaving a silver wake behind it.

Walking around the edge of the lake to camp, John T. went off his rocker. He pretended to be an Indian, he crouched melodramatically, hand shading his eye, and, pointing to some scuffled earth, said, "Fox, him make easy track, him always drag tail." Farther on he stooped and picked up an imaginary something which he sniffed elaborately, and, scarcely able to conceal his pleasure over the discovery, pronounced: "Hmmm . . . Greater Abyssinian Kudoo shit. Still warm, too." He motioned Wendall down finger to his lips. "I can smell them," he said; "uh-oh—elephants. Rogue elephants, too. They're gonna take a trip because they're packing their trunks," and he snorted uproariously. Wendall stared at him, wondering what the joke was, or had he lost his mind, or what? John T. patted him on the head, saying, "Come, Bwana," and leapt into the air, waving his fishing rod like a spear. He misplaced his foot on a slippery stone and went sprawling. "Attack me," he squealed. "Leap on me, boy, I am the angry lion. Subdue me." At his feet, Wendall smiled and shrugged; but he had never wrestled for fun with anybody, and did not know how to go about it. "Well, never mind," said John T., springing up. "Let's chow."

Hungrily they devoured a supper of hash and bread. The day evaporated as pine boughs absorbed what little light remained. They washed their dishes at the pond, then threw water on the campfire. A cool wind came up and set to whirring in the pines. Wendall put on his pajamas, brushed his teeth at the shore of the pond, and slid into his sleeping bag.

Not far away, his uncle unwound weeds from the Harley's spokes. Wendall's eyelids drooped shut, a great snowy plain came into view, he and John T. on the motorcycle were crossing it, slewing from one side to the other, kicking up a white spray. Then trees—firs and pines—began to dot the snow and suddenly they were sliding down a slope into thicker and taller trees, branches hit their faces, and the motorcycle skidded away from them. Hand in hand they tumbled into a forest, slowed down, and came to a standstill in absolute darkness. "Don't be afraid," John T. whispered. "I'm not," Wendall replied, and John T. gave his hand a little squeeze. In the distance a bell chimed. Wendall recognized it as the voice of the pagoda clock in the attic. Above them a sudden flicker of light caught a brown branch, splashing off it like a pellet of snow. Farther away and nearer to the ground another light blinked and an irregular line of trunks spurted toward them. Closer, and above again, a third light showed, disappeared, a brother light answered, then another. The clock chimed. Soon the lights were everywhere, jarring through the forest. The resonance of the clock's bell lasted well over a minute. The lights, now sometimes identifiable as beams, worked in closer to them, dancing through the trees, illuminating the grotesque formations of low pine branches. Some lights, aimed straight for them, were round and small. They advanced unblinkingly for a few yards, then swayed, became elliptical, and sent out beams—flashlights. A minute later the area where they lay was blindingly lighted up as electric lamps emerged from all sides. "Stand up," said John T. Wendall obeyed. People surrounded them, aiming their flashlights discreetly at the ground. They all wore snowshoes. There was Marty Haldenstein in a drab overcoat; the doctor, dressed in his Sunday asparagus robe and slippers; and Jim, with a rolled-up copy of the *Sporting News* stuck in his front pocket. Also present were Mrs. Kahler and Bernie Aja and Ercel Perry and Tom and Sybil and Cornelia and Mike Stenatto, and even Jimmy Wiggen. . . .

"What are you looking for?" asked John T.

All together they mumbled something Wendall couldn't catch.

"Oh," said John T.

They nodded and shifted their feet. The clock chimed; Marty coughed.

"Lord love a duck," said the doctor. "Let's do something quick. It's cold as a frog's fanny around here."

Murmurs of approval greeted this suggestion. The people lined up behind John T. and Wendall, and John T. tapped the boy on the shoulder, saying, "you lead the way."

Wendall walked forward. Gray light filtered through the trees. They came shortly to the edge of the woods: ahead, many gravestones the same dim color as the dawn sky made uneven lines through a cemetery. There wasn't much snow on the ground: you could hear water rivulets like worms wiggling under the wet brown grass. Wendall led them up a hill to a small plot of washed-out yellow grass. Everyone gathered round. The boy stepped forward and tested the ground with his foot, patting the yellow grass as if to make sure it was solid, and when he stepped back, he said, "Guess that'll do." Then, one by one, slipping out of their snowshoe bindings, the others stepped forward to test the plot, and each, when he retreated, mumbled, "Guess that'll do." When half the people had tamped down the grass, Wendall turned away and faced downhill. Bleached flowers sagged against leaning tombstones; flared branches of black trees, clutching to a few crisp leaves, weaved a frozen tangle against the sky. "Guess that'll do," people murmured behind him. "Guess that'll do." Then there was a long silence, and Wendall had just begun to think everyone had finished, when somebody started shaking his shoulder. He turned around. . . .

"Shh. Wake up. Don't say a word."

He blinked, wide awake. Ribbons of gray light, as from many doors opened just a crack, crisscrossed the ground.

"We have a visitor," John T. said.

"What kind?"

"A porcupine. *Shh,* don't move. Here he comes."

Something deserted the campfire ashes and headed toward their sleeping bags. Wendall heard a new sound—quills clicking together. Unafraid, taking its own good time about it, the animal advanced to the foot of John T.'s sleeping bag.

John T. said, "Hello, you dumb old porcupine."

The animal lifted its head and stared at John T., shifted its gaze to Wendall, shifted back to John T., and for a second its frowning face resembled Jim's: then with a sneeze it waddled unhurriedly away, passing beneath the Harley without so much as half a glance up.

"Show's over," drawled John T., yawning prodigiously. "You can return to dreamland."

But Wendall couldn't go back to sleep. He put his hands behind his head and listened for sounds of morning. Beside him, John T. snored a little. And they were alone.

Wendall's eyes stayed open into dawn.

By five A.M. they were on the road again. The air was wet with a thin mist, and when ahead of them the sun burst out of cover, spraying the sky with rainbow vapor, John T. shouted, "How's your gizzard?" and Wendall answered joyfully: *"Full of stones!"*

Around eleven they crossed the railroad tracks into Stebbinsville and cruised thoughtfully and reluctantly along Main Street. At the gas station Harry slapped

Wendall on the back. "Well, Slugger, you don't look at all sick to me," he said.

"Of course I'm not. It was just a passing thing."

John T. emptied the saddlebags, untied the sleeping bags and camp equipment, and guided the motorcycle into the garage.

"Don't look like such an outcast," Harry said. "It's yours for the riding whenever you want it. Hell, I hardly know how to run the damn thing."

"I'll be back in an hour," John T. grumbled. "Gotta change."

"Take your time. Life should be slow."

They walked home. A glowering Tom was sitting on the porch railing—he uttered no word of greeting. John T. went on into the house; Wendall dropped his sleeping bag, and, to Tom's back, said, "What's the matter with you?"

"Nothin'."

Wendall took off his glasses, puffed himself up, and said, "I saw a porcupine!"

"I don't care."

"Okay, King Snot." Leaving his equipment scattered on the porch, Wendall fetched the dueling cane from the umbrella stand and began to cut at a few dandelions on the lawn. He shouted to Tom, "You know, I wouldn't be surprised if one day when I have the money I bought a motorcycle."

On "motorcycle" Cornelia clanged onto the porch and bellowed, "You come straight over here, young man, and pick up your things and put them away, then go straight upstairs and take a bath. You must be filthy!"

Wendall sighted along the sword at her chest, but then, instead of firing a snide answer, he lowered the weapon and obediently trotted up to the porch. On entering the house with his arms full of equipment, he tossed a parting shot over his shoulder at Tom:

"Don't turn into a stone, you little grump."

TWENTY-FOUR

Marty Haldenstein left the library at four-thirty and walked to the sporting goods store. He announced himself by sneezing seven times into a handkerchief. On the third of these painful blasts. Jim folded the Boston newspaper in half and acknowledged each successive outburst with a polite nod of his head. While Marty gasped and wiped his nose, the fat man lighted a cigar, slowly shook out the match, and said, "Afternoon."

"Please excuse my sneezing," Marty said. "I imagine there must be a rather high pollen count today, wouldn't you think so?"

Jim nodded and said, *"Hrmp."*

"You aren't busy at the moment, are you?" Marty looked furtively around the store.

Jim cast his eyes over toward the magazine rack and back and jerked his head slightly, meaning see for yourself.

"That is good," Marty said. "I have come to see about purchasing a gun. I was thinking along the lines of a revolver, not a very large or powerful one, you understand. I believe you carry them in small calibers, don't you? I would mean, for example, a .22-caliber. Isn't that a popular model?"

"Plinking?" Jim asked.

"I beg your pardon?"

"Cans; targets."

"Oh, yes, definitely. Targets. Yes, I was thinking of targets. Do you have targets, too?"

Jim pursed his lips, pushed his cigar out slightly, and lowered eyelids a fraction.

"That would be really awfully nice if I could get some targets, also," Marty said. "I had no idea you stocked them."

And they stalled, looking stupidly at each other for a few seconds.

"The, uh, revolver?" Marty said. "I don't mean to be, of course . . ."

"Regular .22 or a CO2 pistol?" Jim said. "I got both."

"Oh. Well, I don't know. I am not a real authority on guns as you may well imagine. What exactly is a CO2 pistol? I don't believe I have ever heard of that before. Is it something new?"

"You put in a cartridge. It shoots pellets 'stead of live ammo," Jim said. "Pretty powerful, though. Kills rats, chucks."

"That sounds very good. Does it come with instructions?"

Jim's eyelids deferred a little. He got off the stool, pushed it away to make room, and bent over to open the glass door to the handgun case. He came up with a slim red box, straightened painfully, stuck back a leg and caught his foot on a rung of the stool, and drew it beneath him again. Shifting the cigar to the other side of his mouth, he opened the end flap of the box and shook the gun onto the counter.

"This is how it works," he said. "Unscrew here, drop in the cartridge, like so. Then screw the cap back on, cock it like so without puttin' a pellet in, pull the trigger. That punctures the carridge. Now it's ready. Open the breech, pellet fits here. Single shot. Cartridge'll usually last a hundred shots. If it leaks, bring it back. Sometimes they leak."

"Does the ammunition come with the kit?"

"Pellets. Behind you, third shelf. The little round boxes. Hundred to a box. If you want targets, two shelves below 'em. I got standard, rabbit, crow, chuck."

Marty chose a sheaf of twenty rabbit targets and a box of pellets.

"Seven-twenty," Jim said.

"Oh, is that all it comes to? How interesting. I had been expecting something a good deal more expensive, You don't have a bag, do you? Of course, I realize there is a paper shortage, but just to carry it home in, you know. I could bring the bag back, this evening if you wanted it. . . ."

By the time he had finished saying this, Jim had the pistol, pellets, and targets in a bag. Marty took it, rolling the mouth down tightly against the contents.

"I do want to thank you very much for being so kind and patient. . . ."

"Na'tall," Jim said, bowing tersely.

Home in his room, Marty sat on the window seat and dumped the contents of the bag onto the cushion beside him. He pried open the carton flaps and shook out the pistol. For a minute he was afraid to pick it up, never having touched a firearm before, so he busied himself with the pellet box, dumping some of the hollow lead projectiles into his palm. They weighed next to nothing, could they really kill something? Gingerly picking up the gun, he slipped open the breech and fitted in a pellet. Raising the window, he cocked the gun and pointed down at the hammock. After a minute, he pulled the trigger—the pistol emitted a burp and he heard the pellet snap forcefully into the bark of the crab apple gree.

No doubt about it, then; the gun was strong enough to kill. He ran his fingers along the barrel and was overcome with despair. Pain, his lifelong companion, surged within his chest, forcing him to cough loud and long. He fitted the gun back in its box, and hid the box and the pellets in the bottom drawer of his bureau beneath some heavy sweaters.

He was too restless now to stay alone in the room. Closing the window against pollen, he dropped the sheaf of targets in a wastebasket, wondering as he did so if the magnitude of his act this afternoon would in the end be as great as he thought he intended it to be. Then he left the boardinghouse.

The walk up South Maple was not unpleasant. He entered the park, and the road carried him into the refreshing shade of the pine grove where sounds of the day were muted out. At one point he arrested his step and cocked his head, having been brought out of his reverie by what he thought were voices whispering.

Straining to hear, he stayed immobile for a long time, and just as he was about to attribute the voices to his imagination, he actually heard someone talking.

Cautiously, Marty angled left into the pines. He snuck from tree to tree, pausing at each one to wait for the voices to guide him. He had penetrated hardly more than twenty yards, when a short distance away he saw a girl's head move. Inching a few trees closer, he recognized the girl: Sybil Matthewson. A man's hand rose and touched her nose in a shy sign of affection.

"I think what you're doing is wrong," Sybil said. "You don't need to hide from this town, believe me. People will only want to help you."

"No," the man said glumly. "You don't know what I've done."

"What don't I know that you've done?"

"Oh, no you don't. You can't trap me into giving away secrets. I'm too smart for that."

"Have I said anything since the last time we met? I'm not trying to trap you. Can't you believe me?"

"I don't know. I have to be smart, I have to be careful." The man leaned forward and touched his lips to her nose, kissed her cheek softly, then abruptly drew away and said, "I'm crazy, aren't I?"

"No. You're sick. Not crazy."

"I have a bullet in the back of my head, low," he said, speaking quickly, confessing. "It's a Nazi bullet. I have two other bullets in my back. One is a Nazi's also, the other is a cop's. They sent me from over there to a hospital, they put me in with a lot of nuts, and I couldn't stand it, I walked right out and they didn't catch me. But I had no money, I was hungry, so in plain daylight I grabbed a girl's purse, and I ran . . . you should have seen me run. They couldn't catch me. They shouted and ran after me, and a cop shot me, but I ran them into the dirt. I can still run. My legs are fine. Feel the muscles on my calves."

He thrust a leg toward her and Sybil obediently felt his calf. "Yes," she said. "Your legs are strong. What happened after you stole the purse?"

"Oh no, you don't." He faced her angrily. "You're not going to make me tell anything. Nothing more. I must be crazy to tell you a thing. I . . . can't . . . control. . . ."

He clenched his fist and hit her in the stomach. Sybil doubled up, and his second blow as he was scrambling to his feet glanced harmlessly off her shoulder. He gave a cry and ran into the trees, passing well to Marty's left. Sybil moaned and rocked on the ground, fighting for wind. Marty started to go forward, but checked himself. What would he say to her? What would she say if she knew he had been eavesdropping? Before he could stop himself, he coughed loudly.

"Go away!" Sybil yelled. "I don't care about you at all! I never want to see you again!"

She cried bitterly, and while the pain in her stomach was still hot she swore to tell the sheriff and God knows how many others about Duffy so they could set a trap for him. But when the pain subsided, she wept long and quietly and resolved not to let the war kill her heart.

When Duffy bolted from the woods, he ran fifty yards up the road past the pond before realizing he should be fleeing in the other direction. He changed course, and in heading past the woods again, went by Marty Haldenstein.

Impulsively, Marty decided to trail Duffy. This was not hard to do, as the fugitive stuck to the middle of the road, moving with a strange slow gait that was hardly a run. Staying a good fifty yards to the rear, Marty followed him out of the park onto South Maple and then down Conroy and across Rutland to the path that went from the back of the Miss Stebbinsville over to Liberty Street. While in town, Duffy slowed to a walk and straightened his shoulders, and it amazed Marty that the few people Duffy passed took no notice of him, although a moment later most of them nodded hello to himself.

Some children swinging on the tractor tire in the lot ignored both of them as they went by wide of the tree and cut through the thicket to the grain elevator area. Marty waited in the protection of some branches, watching with amazement as Duffy climbed the embankment onto the railroad tracks and headed toward the station.

The librarian chose to take the bicycle trail instead of the tracks, and when he emerged onto the parking lot, Duffy was nowhere to be seen. Warily, Marty approached the station. He mounted the steps and peered through a dusty window—the waiting room was empty.

He circled both platforms, finally coming around to the northern end of the building. At first, when he looked in a window, all he could make out were some cans and newspapers scattered over the floor of an otherwise nearly empty room. Then his eye caught a movement off to the side, almost out of sight.

Duffy straightened his legs on the autoseat. Marty drew back from the window: he could not believe that in broad daylight, and through the heart of town, he had succeeded in tracking this man to his lair.

TWENTY-FIVE

It was a dog day: Wendall felt itchy and dissatisfied. He's read the Sunday comics and suffered through church in the morning, he was full of sluggish dinner, Tom was napping, and there was nothing to do. From his pocket he took the garnets he and John T. had picked up at the quarry the Sunday before, and desultorily arranged them on the porch floor. In doing so, he remembered John T.'s saying Sybil would appreciate them, and, gathering in the stones, he went upstairs.

"Hey, checkers!" Sybil kissed him vigorously on the cheek when he handed over the gems. "Wherever did you find them? No—wait a minute; let me guess. The old Bixby quarry?"

"I don't know where it was. I mean, Uncle John didn't say the name. But there was a lake and it looked rather deep." Wendall sat down on the unmade bed.

"I used to have millions of the pebbles," Sybil said. "Must be a crate of them somewhere up in the attic. John T. and I glued them into pine cones for Christmas."

She held each stone to the light. A ray of sunshine that penetrated past the side of a drawn shade caught in them and projected colored spots onto the walls.

"I know what: let's put 'em in a bowl," she said. "That ought to be pretty. Down in the pantry there's a sort of goldfish bowl, quite small. You know the one. We'll put water in it."

The boy went downstairs, filled the bowl in question with water, returned to the room, and Sybil dropped in the garnets. When all had sunk, they only just covered the bottom. Lifting the window shade a little, she placed the bowl on the sill. On the ceiling directly above the bed there appeared a blurry concentration of colored bubbles. Sybil touched the rim of the bowl, and the bubbles rocked and sparkled.

"Almost like the light through a stained-glass window," she said. And then, suddenly: "Did Freddy go to church much?"

"No. He never did. He stayed home, but Helen went, and usually dragged me along."

"You don't like church?"

"I enjoy the music, but I think Sunday school is horrendously stupid."

"What about praying?"

"I think that's stupid, too."

"Don't you ever feel like it?"

"No."

"Do you know that every night I kneel by my bed and I don't say anything fancy, I just say 'Please God, don't let Freddy be killed.' I talk a little bit like that about the people I love, or should love more. I do the same thing in church. Usually when it's empty are the times I like to go. If I'm alone I think there's more of a chance the powers that be might hear me. You wouldn't like to come with me sometime on a weekday morning, would you? It just takes a minute. I'm not trying to convert you or anything; hell, I'm the world's worst Christian, myself—most of the time I can't stand the stuff."

"Well . . ."

"I don't think you've ever voluntarily kissed me," she said abruptly. "Why don't you try it once? I'm not a monster, you know. A little show of affection wouldn't hurt you either, would it?"

"I guess not . . ."

As he touched his lips to her cheek, Wendall caught the movement of her hands starting to break and reach for him, then she controlled the gesture, and he drew back stiffly, saying, "I have to go, Aunt Sybil. I just remembered."

"What?"

He toed the floor, making up a fast lie.

"I promised to see Jim this afternoon. I promised and I almost forgot. Golly . . ."

He shook his head, intending to demonstrate that such were the foibles of youth, but instead of pulling it off smoothly, his face screwed up, he mumbled, "G'bye," and fled.

He took the dueling cane from the umbrella rack, thinking he would go down to the garden and slice up some butterflies, but the idea was no good because Sybil might glance out her window and see him. In fact, if he stuck around the house, somebody might start talking to him and she would hear, she would know he'd been lying. Why the hell he ever picked Jim, though, was beyond him, because what in the world could he see the fat man about?

Nevertheless, the safest thing to do under the circumstances was go downtown for a while, and with a heavy heart he set out. The sky was a nondescript color; the air had a buttery texture to it that made his skin feel smooth and poreless.

When he reached the sport and news shop it was closed. He knew Jim lived in the Pavilion Hotel, and, not intending to do much more than just drop by and see if the fat man was sitting around on the front porch or something, he directed his steps down Rutland Avenue in that general direction. When he arrived, there was, as he had expected, no Jim in sight. So, duty done, he walked by the rear of the hotel, heading toward a shortcut to Prescott Street—yet the green wooden fire escape on the back of the structure made him hesitate. He had nothing better to do: why not climb to the Pavilion's roof and see what the town looked like from up there?

Several steps below the fourth platform, he rested. A radio just above him was tuned in to a baseball game. He listened for a minute, heard "Red Sox" mentioned a couple of times, recalled his grandfather having said the Red Sox were one of the most important teams in a professional league, and guessed he might be just below Jim's room. Crouching low, he crept up the remaining steps to the platform and scurried to the side of an open window. Cautiously, he poked his head around the corner, and sure enough, there was Jim.

He was lying on a bed, dressed only in his underpants, and on his left hand he wore a baseball glove. Every few seconds he tossed up a big white softball which rose a third of the distance to the ceiling and came down in the glove. Just as the Red Sox made a double play, Jim missed the ball, it bounced off the side of his mitt, hit his stomach, struck the edge of the bed, and rolled across the floor toward the window. Wendall ducked out of sight, then leaned slowly forward. Jim hadn't seen him. The fat man's eyes were closed; he was going to leave the ball where it had rolled for a while. The roar of the crowd came out of the radio beside the bed, but Jim did not smile: in fact, his face remained startlingly motionless.

As quietly as possible, Wendall descended the fire escape and went away. Overhead, menacing clouds, their edges rough and ugly, lowered out of a high haze. Arriving home, the boy came upon Tom in the playhouse messing with some plastic soldiers, and he immediately took over, setting them up his own way. Tom fussed about it, they had a quarrel, Wendall knocked his little cousin down, and, bawling his eyes out, Tom ran off to tell Cornelia, and within seconds her shrill voice was calling his name.

Wendall retreated behind the barn to the garden, where Bernie Aja was hard at work weeding. His pumpkins were coming along pretty well, but when Wendall asked if he had chosen one to be champion yet, Bernie said no, he planned to wait and see what another week or two would bring.

At the foot of the garden, Wendall sat down and absently scanned the river for fish. As he did so, his mind went back to Jim. Dreamily, he concocted a scene. He and the fat man were on top of a small bald hill. All around the base of this hill lots of young and old Jimmy Wiggen–type people wearing baseball gloves hopped around and huffed and puffed, guffawing at each other's imitations, and screaming, "Show us the place where they stuffed in the books!" All he and Jim could do was join hands and view the sorrowful shenanigans from their little pinnacle of loneliness. That is, for a while this is all they could do: then Wendall felt his body go funny, and the dueling cane suddenly showing up in his grasp, he raised it like a wand over the heads of the mocking cavorters below, and bellowed, "I am the Wizard of Loneliness: *alakadetmole!*" When he uttered this, all the Jimmy Wiggen people fell to the ground, holding their stomachs and kicking their legs, their tongues flapping out of their gasping mouths, while their vocal cords rent the air with a furious din.

Between the writhing bodies ran Marty Haldenstein and Fred and the doctor and Bernie Aja. They charged up to the crest of the hill and joined hands with Jim and Wendall. Soon others mounted the hill: John T. and Sybil, Tom and B. J. Twine, and Ercel Perry, and even Helen and the bearded man from the train. They bunched closely together on top of the hill, and Wendall, the mighty Wizard of Loneliness, spoke:

"Have no fear, brethren," he said. "I will protect you!"

No sooner had the words escaped his mouth than from all sides sprang up waves of ugly people hippity-hopping and shouting, "Show us the place where the books were stuffed in!" They came like hordes of Oriental swordsmen, all with great purple tongues and bulging eyes. As soon as they were close enough, Wendall raised his wand and yelled, *"Alakadetmole!"* again. They all staggered, clutching their stomachs, and fell into heaps. On their heels came even more attackers, and, just as their predecessors had fallen beneath the magic wand, so also did they fall, their bodies eventually mounting almost to the summit of the hill whereon the small band stood.

And when the last attacker had fallen, evening lowered out of the sky; bodies stretched to the horizon. Stars and a moon ascended into heaven, and the little group of people on the hill let out sighs and sat down. Beneath them the pale limbs of the dead and dying glowed in the bright moonlight; last breaths rose like wisps of smoke toward the stars.

Then a lovely white grass sprouted and grew over the corpses. It grew quickly in the night, and soon only this grass was visible to the band upon the hill. Whereupon they stood up and ventured onto the vast plain. When they found the footing to be solid, they threw up their hands and laughed, they ran and tumbled and did somersaults, they threw their shoes at the moon, they ran like rays from the hill where they had made their stand. Only Wendall, the great Wizard of Loneliness, remained on the hill, sword in hand, ready at the least provocation to return once more to their aid, to utter once again the fatal and all-protective word . . .

" . . . alakadetmole . . ."

The sky turned black and a strong gust of wind nearly blew Wendall over the embankment into the river. One magnificent streak of lightning ripped apart the sky, and a thunderclap of such volume sounded that the boys half expected to be crushed flat beneath it. Hoe in hand, Bernie Aja hightailed it up toward the barn. His ears ringing, Wendall waited for the rain to fall, but nothing came.

Then the air filled with a golden snow as the wind stripped the leaves from a nearby locust tree. Yellow flakes were blown onto the river: soon a million of them floated on the water. It was as if a giant golden fish caught by the storm had, in the ensuing struggle for freedom, shed its every scale.

Yet rain refused to fall. Clouds descended momentarily almost to the tops of trees, then they began to lift, they lost their fierce dark color. Bernie Aja came out of the barn, shook his head at the sky, and shrugged.

An hour later the dull haze of the earlier part of the afternoon replaced the clouds. Wendall snuck into the house and up to the attic where the heat was almost unbearable. Little interested in what he was doing, he poked around for a while, then gave up and sat on the lid of a trunk, his body aching with the same intenseness of feeling he had undergone on the lawn the night Sybil broke the playhouse windows. It was the feeling that he wanted to do something for someone, and that he was very dissatisfied with himself. It made him more nervous and irritable by the minute, and pretty soon, his shirt soaked with sweat, he came down from the attic and landed smack in his grandmother's path.

"So there you are," she accused, folding her arms and sucking her lips in.

"I am in no mood to talk to anybody," Wendall said.

"Well, you just put yourself in the mood, young man. What's this I hear about you being a bully? Who do you think you are, hitting your little cousin?"

Wendall screamed, "I am not a bully!" and dashed to the bathroom, locking the door before Cornelia could get to him.

"I'm going to call Frederick up right away," she warned. "I will not have people locking themselves in rooms in this house, I absolutely refuse to have it!"

She went away, not to call the doctor as the boy knew she wouldn't, but rather to go moan about the kitchen and complain to anyone who made the mistake of passing through.

Wendall unlocked the door, snuck to his room, rounded up a couple of books he was in the process of reading, and reestablished himself firmly in the bathroom.

When the doctor came home at six, Wendall was still camped in the john. Cornelia rang the dinner bell, and when the boy didn't show up, the doctor went looking for him. He knocked on the bathroom door and said, "Skunkhead, you must be taking the longest bowel movement in the history of mankind. What's the story? Soup's on the table, you know."

"I'm not hungry. You go ahead without me."

"Well, I'd hate to have to break down the door one week from now and come upon a starved old skeleton," the doctor said. "Growin' boy's gotta feed his face sometime."

"I said I'm not hungry."

"Well, now, that may be true. But I'd at least like to get a look at you to make sure your ribs ain't pokin' too much through your scaly skin."

Wendall opened the door.

"Lord love a duck," said the doctor. "How's your gizzard?"

Wendall hung his head and mumbled, "Full of stones."

"That's all I wanted to hear. Now: if you feel like it, there's bound to be some jerky or somethin' left in the frige later on." And with no further ado he went downstairs.

Wendall got into his pajamas and went to bed. He lay still, thinking how funny it was to have the sun streaming through the window. After a while, he got out of bed and knelt on the floor. For a minute he couldn't say anything. He stretched his arms across the bed, pushed his face into the thin cotton blanket, brought his hands back and clasped them, and then he haltingly whispered, "Please . . . don't let Fred or Grandpa . . . be killed . . ."

And he bit the blanket and began to cry.

TWENTY-SIX

September brought the respite of leaves that blazoned red and deep purple for a while before dying, and a group of cool days came, followed by a week of rain. School resumed: Wendall marched into his first class hugging a new briefcase to his chest, his bright eyes arrogantly defying anyone to make fun of him, but surprisingly, no one did. That afternoon he hurried home, running full tilt down Killer Hill, and Tom, like a faithful old dog, met him on the bridge and tagged along half a step behind his elder cousin, listening to the boy's juicy castigations of Miss Flaxitte, the half-blind fifth-grade teacher whose stockings kept falling down, and whose lisp was enough to put anybody in hysterics.

Shortly after school opened, Wendall found an old softball mitt in an attic trunk, and hid it in his closet. There the glove sat for several days, until the boy slipped it into his briefcase one morning. After school that day, instead of heading directly home he detoured downtown to the sport and news shop where he self-consciously showed the glove to Jim, and asked how he could loosen up the leather to make it look a little better. Jim suggested a certain glove oil, which Wendall purchased, and, in the locked privacy of the third-floor bathroom, he rubbed the oil into the cracked leather until the glove's pocket was at least several shades darker and soupy enough so that any ball thrown with any velocity and caught would undoubtedly have made a splash.

Thereafter, Wendall carried the mitt around in his briefcase, and although he never dared take it out or propose himself as a competitor in a playground recess game, he often stood on the sidelines, watching the other boys, and he felt a part of their contest with his hidden mitt; he had budding hopes that one day he would just naturally evolve into a game. In the meantime, he began to take an interest, he began to learn what the point of baseball was, and on several occasions he actually ventured into the sports pages of the Boston newspaper to see what was going on in the professional leagues.

Leaf smoke clouded the town. Wendall and Tom and Bernie Aja and Sybil raked up the front and rear lawns, and stood around leaning on rake handles, watching their leaf piles burn. A zing came into the air, and Wendall remarked that he could now run downtown or home from school without feeling out of breath in the slightest. He flexed his muscles in the bathroom mirror and was sure he could detect biceps rising like long-dormant little mountains under his frail skin. In haling, he was sure never before had the chest of an eleven-year-old boy expanded to such Atlasian extent. And, through many refusals to submit himself totally to a barber's razor, he managed to cultivate a mildly moppish head of hair that looked somewhat tough, so he thought; at least when his glasses were off.

In the second week of September, Bernie Aja walked handily off with the local Green Thumb contest for the best Victory garden, and the family began to watch with interest the development of a particular pumpkin he had screened apart and begun to milk-feed. The contraption he rigged up to do the job looked much like Marty Haldenstein's hummingbird feeders: it consisted of a small bottle inverted and tied to a short stake, fresh milk in it each day, and a tube running from the bottle into the pumpkin which was already frighteningly big, although Bernie allowed it had only just begun to feel its oats and had a long way to go yet.

Around town there was suddenly much talk of V-E day, for France was rewon, and all that remained to be done looked as if it could be accomplished in a matter of weeks. Larger domestic struggles: the Presidential campaign, and the American League baseball pennant race, this latter, according to the doctor, being the more important.

Jim brought his radio into the sport and news shop, and the store became the center for baseball buffs of all ages and professions each day when news of the games was on. Men gathered there to make comments and maybe lay a few small bets on the outcome of the race, they talked and argued, and the quietest person in the ship was Jim himself, who just sat on his stool and called the shots, though never very loud, and never very wrong. Once he found out what was going on, Wendall took to devouring the sports news with almost as avid an interest as the war news, and he made it a point to come home from school by way of Jim's shop, where he was soon passing away the better part of his after-school hours.

Thus he happened to be on hand late one afternoon when Jim said that although at this point in the race it might look to some as if the first-place Detroit Tigers were going to take it, he would personally put his money on the St. Louis Browns, and the Yankees would be lucky not to wind up in fourth behind the Red Sox. The minute these words escaped his mouth, Mike Stenatto, who had wandered down from Hood's during a slack moment, said, "Jim, I'll bet you ten bucks the Tigers take it. I'll even throw in all the ice cream you can eat for a month, how's that?"

"Okay," said Jim. "Ten bucks?"

"Yeah," said Mike. "And don't forget the ice cream."

They put their money on the counter (it was later given to the doctor to hold), and the bet was on. The Yankees, as Jim had predicted, didn't last long in first and the Red Sox, as is their custom, all but rolled over and played dead, so by September 21, it looked like a race to the wire between the Detroit Tigers and the St. Louis Browns, with the Yankees still running an outside chance to back into the pennant. Jim initiated a daily chart in his window, and here is the way the teams stood on the chart going into the last week and a half of the season:

TEAM	GB
Detroit	—
St. Louis	1½
New York	4
Boston	6

By the 25th, the Browns were still a game out, and in Hood's Mike was saying with a confident grin, "Say, you ain't been down to Jim's lately, have you? Or is it still open?" His laugh boomed out the door and right down the block to the sport and news shop. Wendall stopped patronizing Hood's and took all his soda business to the Jubilee Café and the Miss Stebbinsville.

The very next day St. Louis beat the Red Sox, 3–0, and tied the Tigers for first. Jim read the *Sporting News* and chewed on his cigar and he never said a word.

"The Tigers are just givin' 'em a taste of first so's when the Browns lose, theyll have at least known what it was like," Mike said. "Them Tigers are first-class gentlemen."

On September 26, both the Browns and the Tigers won, and the standings remained, as Jim put it, "Co-pestetic." The Yankees were three games out; all three teams had five more games to play. Laughter came from Hood's—Mike said, "Me, I ain't worryin'. I like a close race. Makes it more painful for the loser." As for Wendall: not only did he clip out the war news and paste it into his umpteenth scrapbook, but he also began to clip articles out of the sports pages, and sometimes, when not very many people were around of an evening, the soft thud of a tennis ball against the barn doors could be heard.

The following day Detroit won, the Browns lost, dropping them again a game behind, and the Yankees won. Mike Stenatto gloated: "I'm goin' to get the State Police to come over and keep a twenty-four-hour watch on the roads leadin' out of town, just to make doubly sure Jim don't try to fly the coop." Jim frowned heavily; his eyebrows were almost singed by the tip of his cigar. Wendall threw the tennis ball harder against the barn door, and most of the time, it rebounded back through his legs and out the driveway into the street.

It rained out the St. Louis–Yankee game on the 28th, and the Tigers were idle, waiting to sink their teeth into the last-place Washington Senators. Mike said that tomorrow after the respective doubleheaders, Town Hall ought to fly the flag at half-mast in honor of Jim. At the Coolidge Street house, Tom, who had been recruited as ball boy by his bespectacled cousin, trotted panting up the driveway for the fiftieth time, and, in handing the tennis ball to Wendall, asked, "Who do you think is gonna win?" and Wendall replied, "The Browns, of course, stupid—who else?"

September 29 saw the Browns take two from the Yankees, while the Tigers split with the Senators, so once again Detroit and St. Louis were tied for first. Mike said it was too bad the Browns had used up all their wins against the Yankees in one day, since there remained two games as yet to be played between the teams and the Yankees were not ones to lose four in a row, especially to a spastic conglomeration of idiots and has-beens such as St. Louis. Jim merely erased the one after the Browns' name on the pennant chart in his window, replacing it with a horizontal line indicating tie. That same day Wendall switched from Butterfinger candy bars to Baby Ruths.

On the next to last day, the Yankees lost their third straight to St. Louis, and the Tigers beat the Senators. That means tomorrow would either decide it, or—assuming both teams won, or both teams lost—send the pennant into a play-off game. Mike spoke with a notably softer voice that wavered from time to time, and he laughed not at all. He hadn't planned on things going down to the wire like they had.

The final games fell on a Sunday. After dinner, the doctor, Wendall, and Tom walked to the sport and news shop. A few other men were there talking things over, running through the election of pitchers, chewing tobacco, and smoking cigarettes. The radio couldn't pick up the actual game broadcasts, so the gathering had to content itself with news reports that came in on the quarter hour.

Right away, the doctor slapped two ten-dollar bills on the green coin mat, then he paid Jim $2.75 for an official hardball, took it out of the box, and wrote *Pennant Bet, Oct. 1, 1944* on the cover. He signed his name with a flourish and passed the ball around to the other men present who likewise autographed it, Wendall and Tom drawing up the rear. "This thing'll go to the winner," the doctor said, putting the ball on top of the twenty dollars. "Every bet's gotta have a trophy, ain't that right?"

Before any results were in, Mike Stenatto dropped by with the Burlington paper open and folded to the sports page. He pointed triumphantly to an article that said Dutch Leonard, the Washington starting pitcher, hadn't beaten Detroit in seven starts against them dating back to 1941, whereas Dizzy Trout of Detroit had won twenty-seven games this year. And what Mike wanted to know was: "Who gave anybody the right to throw a bum like Leonard against an ace like Trout? It oughtta be considered a federal crime, the Tigers oughtta be thrown in the jug."

Jim said, "Does it mention Trout is startin' for the third time in six or seven days?"

"He could be startin' for the sixth time in six days and that wouldn't make no difference," Mike said.

Jim shrugged. "Trout's tired. I wouldn't be surprised if he gets shelled before the fourth inning."

Actually, according to the first sports bulletin, Trout's shelling occurred in the fourth inning when the Senators got to him for three runs. There was no news in from the St. Louis–New York game, only just under way in St. Louis. Mike went back to Hood's—silently.

There was a sudden flurry at the door, a swirl of creaking skirts, a snap of rusty bones, and, her sharp nose cleaving the air like an arrow, Dorothy Svenson burst into the store. The men grouped and backed up, staring at her while she leaned on the handgun counter, catching her breath. When some pieces of voice made the difficult journey up her taut esophagus, they exploded as, "Marie . . . better come help us, Frederick . . . she's having a stroke. . . ."

"Well, now, I guess we can take care of strokes!" the doctor boomed. "Dot, you just calm yourself or I'll have to bang you over the noggin and carry you piggyback right down the middle of the street, I will."

The doctor said he would be right back, and, taking the old spinster's hand, led her out of the store, whereupon the men relaxed and spread out again, lighting up fresh cigars and cigarettes. "Maybe it's her time," one man said. "Been a long one," another added. "Don't come much longer," a third finished, and all thoughts went back to baseball as the second report sparkled over the radio.

In the eighth inning the Senators had added an insurance run to the three they had scored in the fourth, and at St. Louis, the Yankees were out in front, 1–0, at the end of two innings. Mike came in and said Mel Queen, the Yankee pitcher, would hogtie St. Louis all day, so even if the Tigers lost there would have to be a play-off game tomorrow.

Jim shrugged and relit his cigar. John T., who had recently taken to working Sundays also at the gas station, stopped in for new developments to carry back to Harry. The question at this point was: could the Yankees hold onto their slim margin and force the two top teams into a play-off game? Wendall, for one, hoped so, hoped so with all his might, because it would mean another day in Jim's store, another day of excitement, predictions, friendly arguments, statistics—

Crouched in the semidarkness at the foot of the magazine rack with Tom beside him, Wendall listened to every word of sports talk, the turn of every phrase, he stored up slang, bad grammar, and names and accents as he incorporated himself into the world of sports for all time. And the smoke that rose to the ceiling recalled the smoke on the train when he was coming to Stebbinsville, the smoke of soldiers who were friends whether they really knew each other or not, friends because they had fought in the same thing, because they knew the same thing inside out, its fears, tensions, and yes, maybe even its joys for some, or at least its triumphs, its small and grand heroics, and that smoke then, Wendall concluded, hadn't been too much different from this smoke now which came from the pipes, cigarettes, and cigars of the men who were waiting anxiously, patiently, or simply with interest for the termination of a struggle taking place so far away and yet so near to every man's heart. The store smelled thick and close, quiet banter went around, a laugh sounded, somebody cussed, somebody else walked to the door and spit and stood there a while, relaxed, just looking out with nothing special in mind, and after a time he nodded, and then he turned when another bulletin came over the radio.

The Tigers scored only one token run before the end of their game, so Dutch Leonard had finally broken his jinx. And at St. Louis, the Yankees had a 2–0 lead going into the bottom of the fourth—then they blew it. A fellow named Chet Laabs homered for St. Louis with a man on board in the bottom of the inning, tying the teams at two-all. Mike came by, received the news standing no farther into the store than the threshold, and left immediately afterwards. And, no sooner had he turned his back, than the radio declared Laabs had hit another homer in the fifth inning, and another St. Louis player had homered in the eighth, and suddenly a sportscaster was telling them the Browns had won it, 5–2, and the entire World Series would take place in the Mound City.

It was over that quickly.

Mike's next and final stay a minute later lasted but a very brief while. He said, "You got your dough there, and the ice cream begins today," and off he slouched to Hood's with his tail between his legs.

The doctor hadn't returned, and no one stepped forward to make a presentation of the baseball to Jim. Mike's attitude had killed the fun; by rights he should have stayed around to be teased a little and take his loss good-naturedly. But he'd gone off in a huff, robbing Jim of his few triumphant minutes.

The fat man made no move to pick up the baseball

or the money underneath. Music played softly on the radio, he clicked it off. A few men stayed to talk about the World Series; they agreed—and correctly, as it turned out—that the victory belonged to the Cardinals, but they seemed not to care anymore. One by one they said good-bye and departed.

Wendall and Tom sat outside on the steps. Main Street could not have been more deserted. The sun setting behind the boys cast a long yellow strip along the far side of the empty street and over the sidewalk, and it burned red-orange in store windows. Jimmy Wiggen shot out of Rutland and pedaled like mad—streamers streaming, snappers snapping—toward the train station end of town. Then General Patton emerged from Rutland, took the center of Main as Jimmy had, but trotted toward, instead of away from, the boys. As he passed, they could hear, with each step, his toenails clicking against the cement. Shadows pushed the strip of sunlight off the street, off the sidewalk, and up the large windows where they erased the burning color. The sunset unloosed a yellow leaf that fell, and, carried by a breeze, whisked several yards along the street, until, released by the breeze, it fell to rest.

Wendall untied his shoes and took out the wrinkled Butterfinger wrappers and tore them into shreds, dropping the pieces on the step in front of them.

"What's that?" Tom asked.

"Don't you know enough to shut up?" Wendall replied.

Behind them, Jim rustled, locking up. His keys jingled mutely. Wendall slid to the side of the steps to make room. Jim lumbered down. He stood in front of them for a moment, trying to frame a thought or a sentence. He ended up by giving them a salute, a tentative salute where his right hand rose three-quarters of the way to his eyebrow, then, because of lack of conviction or strength, fell back to his side. His right pocket bulged where he had stuffed in the signed baseball.

"The Browns won," he said despondently.

"They sure did," Wendall said. "You called it, all right."

"Yes," Jim said, "I called it. . . ."

He walked off, swaying from side to side, and turned out of sight onto Rutland Avenue. Bitterly Wendall rose from the steps and threw an invisible stone that shattered against the pavement. "C'mon," he said to Tom. "Let's get out of here."

As they passed the gas station, John T. called out, "Who won?"

"Nobody," Wendall grumbled in reply.

TWENTY-SEVEN

The doctor sat forward in his chair, elbows on his knees, watching Marie Svenson die. Nothing he could do would help her now; only a very little air remained for the old body to push out. Being a spectator to these last moments was not painful, it was like watching a lone statue grow chill with the coming of night—the lack of motion and noise was almost prehistoric.

For quite some time the doctor had been aware of a suffocating closeness in the room; something dry and pungent in the air made him want to sneeze. So when Dorothy came into the doorway with a tea tray, he asked, "Is it all right to open a window?"

"There'll be a frightful draft on the poor thing," Dorothy said. "Won't it be bad?"

"It doesn't matter anymore, Dot. I think it would help, anyway, to air out the room a little."

"Well, you go right ahead, then." She moved from the doorway as he rose and threw up the window a little. Clean air rushed in; a crisp leaf which had been sitting on the sill for days tumbled inside, landing at the doctor's feet. He picked the leaf up, and absently twirling it in his hand, sat down again.

Setting the tray on a card table near the foot of her sister's bed, Dorothy went about preparing the tea. "One lump or two?" she asked, and "Cream? Or just plain?" She clinked a silver pair of pincers against the sugar bowl and tapped a little spoon against the thin sides of the old china cups. The doctor took Marie's pulse; a slow beat diminished even as he counted.

He sat back, took up his teacup, and sipped loudly. Dorothy gave him a slice of cinnamon toast. Marie's lips parted a little, they seemed to quiver; when the doctor listened closely he could hear a soft persistent flutter down in her throat.

He raised his head. Dorothy sipped her tea and stared at the open window. The doctor thought already the strength was going out of her eyes, too. Well, these girls were old, they had held their ground a damn sight longer than most. He noticed a third cup on the tea tray. That was really all there was to dying, when you came right down to it. People stop pouring into your cup for a while, then somebody new acquisitions it. No long darkness, only a muted sense of loss for a moment.

His hands pained him. As again he felt for Marie's pulse, he was really only aware of the throb in his own knuckles. Fresh air rubbed the dying woman's face with a faint autumnal hand.

"I won't be able to bear it," Dorothy said, putting down her teacup. "It's a horrid thing to do on her part."

The doctor nodded.

"Being alone will kill me," she said quietly. "Who'll come to talk to me, now she's gone? Not that I did much gabbin' anyhow, but—"

"Why, heck," said the doctor, "I'll have to come by to make sure you're not cavortin' with any of the young bloods behind our backs."

"Oh, hush . . ." A handkerchief sprouted at her fingertips; she carefully wiped the sharp down-dips at each corner of her mouth.

"I thought we was both to be struck down at the same time," Dorothy said. "Thought it sure as I'm born.

But I wasn't in the room. Ain't that careless of me? If I'd been in the room, I wouldn't be settin' here now like a fool, I'd be right in there beside her, and we'd be goin' wherever she's goin' together. What a fool I was. . . ."

"Dot. When this is over you and me'll go out and get drunk," said the doctor. "And I wouldn't be surprised if you saw me down the pipe in the end, I wouldn't at all."

"Oh, that ain't so."

Something in the sound of her voice brought the doctor up short. He stared at her, and she averted her eyes. Then his stomach shrank: it shrank and shriveled right down into his toes, leaving him dizzy. He thought: I'm not cheering her up at all: she doesn't think I'm one bit humorous. In near terror, his body squeezed out sweat. Why had he never noticed the eyes and voices of people before: had it been this way all his life? and with everyone? Had they all just tolerated him, while being secretly disgusted behind his back? All his life had this professional jocularity been in bad taste?

Quickly, he took Marie's pulse again and could feel nothing. He listened at her lips and thought he could hear a very faint tremor, then even as he listened that went away, and when he lifted her eyelids he saw that she was dead. Death, he remembered, was quiet and solid and dramaless in this part of the country.

"That's it," he said. His voice sounded funny—far away as if his ears were clogged.

"Gone, eh?" Dorothy finished her tea, put down the cup, and blew her nose. "Didn't take her long. She did a smart job of it."

"Yes, a smart job," the doctor said. "Maybe you better let me call up Van Buren's, 'less of course, you got other plans."

"You go right ahead, Frederick. I'd appreciate a few minutes to get my loose ends drawn up in a bundle before all those busybodies come pokin' around."

The doctor left the room. Dorothy folded her hands in her lap, sniffed deeply a couple of times to clear her nose, and regarded the scrawny composed face of her sister. A gust of air came through the window and blew the leaf the doctor had been playing with off the chair he had just vacated. Sun was setting outside, and you could hear the tree leaves rustling. It was a pretty sound.

TWENTY-EIGHT

At first Tom didn't want to be any part of it, but Wendall said he'd twist his arm until it broke off if he didn't help out, and thus encouraged, Tom reluctantly agreee to pitch in.

It was forbidden, under threat of dire punishment, for anyone but an adult to pick anything from the Victory garden, so they had to be sneaky about it. Whenever Bernie Aja was in the house or fooling with the Prescott side lawn, Tom went on lookout at the ramp into the barn, with orders to give a whistle when he saw Bernie coming, and Wendall dove into the garden. There were mostly squashes to be had, some small pumpkins, late carrots and tomatoes, onions, and two heads of cabbage. Wendall hastily plucked the vegetables and ran with them to a cardboard carton stashed beneath the barn. When the box was full, he lugged it down to the river, waded across, and hid the loot underneath a bush on the far shore.

Then he and Tom went around by the bridge, crossed behind the garage, picked up the hot vegetables, and puffed down to the Svenson house and up to the front porch.

Wendall rang the doorbell, sucked in his breath and wet his lips, going over one last time the speech he planned to give. Tom rubbed his perspiring palms together and was more silent than was his wont.

Dorothy opened the door and squinted at them.

Wendall opened his mouth, and what he had planned to say was this: *Miss Dorothy, Tom and I have been feeling guilty for our behavior back last June when you so kindly invited us over for several luncheons, so we would like to make amends and in doing so, express, at the same time, our sincerest sympathy to you . . .* at which point the carton of vegetables would be hoisted and presented with moderate but humble flair, and Dorothy's soft shining look as she accepted the generous gift, and more importantly—the thought behind the gift—would be more than enough recompense for their pains.

But he clutched. Face to face with the woman he became confused, past sins addled his brain, and he only just managed to stammer out. "We brought this stuff . . ." Then, in raising the carton for her to accept, Tom lost his hold, and the box tipped over, spilling its contents at (and very much onto) Dorothy's feet.

"Away!" the old woman screamed, slamming the door with force enough to send a pumpkin and some onions skittering across the porch.

Livid with rage, Wendall stamped on a squash, splashing it over the porch, his shoes, and Tom's legs. Next, he kicked a pumpkin, which struck against the dowelings of the porch railing and burst apart. Then he picked up a tomato and pitched a strike against the center of the door. "We wanted to be nice!" he raged, gathering ammunition in his arms. "You hear that? We wanted to be nice!"

"Nice!" Tom echoed, joining the fray. "Nice! Nice! Nice!"

When Wendall hurled an oinion through one of the windows flanking the front door, they both turned and ran down the porch steps—right into the arms of Sheriff Flood, who was very quick to answer a call.

He didn't say a word, just spread his legs and shook them both until their teeth snapped, rattled and clacked against each other like castanets. Then he dragged them bawling to his truck and drove angrily over to Coolidge Street.

"That does it," said Cornelia. "I won't have them

playing together anymore. That's all there is to it. I forbid it."

"That's not the answer to anything," said the doctor.

"That's the answer to the way I feel," Cornelia said. "That gangster can play by himself!"

The doctor turned to her and before he could stop himself, said, "Well, the way you feel happens to be stupid."

And, after a moment of speechless shock, Cornelia left the room.

"You see," said the doctor to Wendall, "stealing to make amends isn't right. It's a twisted way of tryin' to have things come out right. Even if you mean well, it's bound to go amok. If nothing had happened over there, Granny or me'd have found out over here, and there'd have been the same hell to pay."

"You don't even believe we meant well," Wendall said. "Everybody thinks we picked all those vegetables expressly to throw at that ass's door."

The doctor frowned. "You call somebody an ass and expect people to believe that you intended to do something considerate for him?"

"Well, it isn't fair anyway!" Wendall said brokenly.

"No, not much is fair, I'll grant you that," the doctor said. "But the sooner you learn to be honest, the easier it'll be to understand things. An honest fool's worth ten of anything else."

"She never gave us a chance," Wendall said. "She wouldn't let us explain."

"I believe you," said the doctor. "And I'm glad you wanted to do something for Dot. I guess if we can just straighten out your old rondo-sketiaptic dispeller, maybe next time the whole operation'll come off without a hitch. Now why don't you just go off and lay low for a while before Granny bumps into you again and aims you at a briar patch."

Wendall went off, oddly ashamed at not having been beaten with a belt, or switched, or at least having been issued the sort of tongue-lashing Cornelia would have been only too happy to administer had she been allowed the chance.

The way things were, his blood and his brain felt like poison. He lifted the dueling cane from the umbrella rack and went outside and whacked all the seeds out of a sunflower. He wondered where the man from the train was. If he so much as dared to show his head around here, Wendall would give him what's for: run him through with the dueling cane sword and cart him wriggling down to the sheriff's office, that's what he'd do.

"Argh," he growled, stabbing the air. *"Argh,"* he muttered, spinning away from a dying foe. *"Argh,"* he snarled, leaping into a mass of cowering old ladies, sending their arms and ears and noses flying.

Then he tripped, nimbly stabbing himself in the bare foot. For a minute he sat on the lawn and couldn't believe his eyes. Blood came out of the wound, and his foot began to throb. There was no one around, the sun was hot, and when he opened his mouth to call for help, no sound came from his throat. He moved his leg and fainted.

When he came to, Cornelia was at his side, a cold compress, which she had just removed from his forehead, in her hand.

"It serves you right," she said nastily, and not without satisfaction.

And Wendall smiled and felt at peace, because she was right—it certainly did.

TWENTY-NINE

The days were cool now. Although several times Duffy Kahler went up to the park and waited at the edge of the woods, Sybil did not show up to paint. One day it rained, and Duffy stood a little in from the edge of the cleared slope, watching wet yellow leaves, unloosed by the wind and rain, carry halfway across the open area toward him before falling into the brown grass. Dry yet chilled, he waited an hour, thoughts whirling through his head like the leaves, each similar and different and dying.

Later, when he brought his attention to the area below the slope, he saw that many leaves floated on the surface of the pond, a surface plucked by raindrops, much as his brain, his heart, and all his muscles were right now being plucked by the tip ends of his nerves. His thoughts were leaves that went nowhere in their dying: he shut his eyes and thought of Sybil, and he desired her, although he did not know how or in what way—as a friend? a lover? a confidante? an enemy? She ran through his head with the little redheaded boy, sometimes laughing, more often grave, her soft hand cupped his own, her fingers touched his cheek . . . and sometimes she was stone cold, hunting him, walking down through the pine grove, touching each tree as she drew nearer to him and asked what happened after he stole the purse. In her hand was a knife with which she planned to dig the bullets out of his back and the base of his head. He retreated from her, but when he came to the edge of the pines, a line of skinny boys with big heads and large glasses faced him, and their eyes, so big and yet wizened, looked deep into him and understood everything about him. In all the boys' hands were small yellow pads and pencils, and the only sound was the sound of lead scratching paper as they wrote all the things they could see in his heart and his mind. He fell down in the wet grass and felt the knife cutting into his back and into the base of his head, and when he looked up he could smell blood and the bespectacled little boys were in a circle around him intently taking notes while he screamed. . . .

When no Sybil came, and after the rain and wind had slackened a little, Duffy walked onto the slope and collected some leaves, selecting only the largest, yellowest ones. When his hands were full, he returned to the pines and laid the leaves about a foot apart in a row on the ground. Soon he had a line of them winding through the trees. When he had gathered and set down the leaves for an hour, he began walking at the beginning of his line, following it, weaving among the pine labyrinth, returning always to his beginning. Soon he felt very sure of himself, and he crouched, feeling his legs go supple. He danced on his yellow path, patting his hands off trees, touching the trunks for a split second, then pushing off and turning a circle for the sheer delight of movement, his hands quickly coming up to ward off another tree, his steps light and dazzling. He pranced, entirely in control, and finally laughed from the pure ecstasy of his fluid movement. He danced along his selfmade path until he was warm and elated and confident, then he ran away. The next day, when Marty Haldenstein came to inspect the woods, he puzzled for a long time over the systematically laid leaves, but could make neither heads nor tails of them.

And neither heads nor tails was Duffy's game and Duffy's dilemma. He slept sometimes fifteen hours a day, and was always sleepy except for rare bursts of nervous enthusiasm. Several times he had found bundles of clothing and magazines on the back porch of his parents' store, but no longer did his mother keep watch on the stairs; she had stopped it as soon as he quit going there every night. Only two or three times during the month of October had he seen her on the steps, staring longingly at him while he took what he needed from the store, and these times she dared not speak for fear of losing him. On a couple of other nights, when she was sleeping, he had mounted to the second floor and puttered around in the dark living room, but so far he had successfully curbed the desire to go upstairs and look in on his father. Once, during the day, he walked by Tompkin's plate-glass window and saw his father working, and he paused for a minute, looking in, wondering if his old man would glance up and spot him, and if so, would they each recognize the other? But Hank Kahler had kept his head bowed to his work; the glass window between them represented years of a silence as solid and polished as an unmarked tombstone.

One night Duffy tried the back door to the sporting goods store and found it open. He crept into the store and stood in its center, his eyes taking in all the equipment that had once been the awesome extension of his personality, the root of his very life. He tried on baseball gloves, smoothed bats through his hands, and gripped footballs that were soft and not yet fully blown up. Then he eyed the rifles and shotguns hanging on the walls, but was afraid to touch them. In the end he stole some sports magazines and a couple of pocket books and went quietly out. When, a week later, he tried the door again, it was locked.

He continued also to visit the Olers' house, though less frequently than he had earlier in the summer. With the fall rains, the river had risen and was much colder to cross, and sometimes, having forded it, painful cramps attacked the soles of his wet feet. And although he yearned for a meeting and reconciliation with Sybil, and often thought of entering the house, even going up to her room, he was afraid of the queer little boy who wore glasses and seemed to know everything about him.

So most of his time was consumed in sleeping. And his sleep was not always deep: often he drifted for hours through a hazy semiconsciousness, his skin warm, all his muscles relaxed, his mind floating freely through a fog of misty shapes and unclear forms. The walls of his room closed comfortably around him like warm flat arms, and, when darker sleep sent his body into total intoxicated slackness, he dreamed of himself on the Green beneath his monument, hibernating under an incessant leaf-fall through the deaf-mute world of a golden autumn giving gently way to winter.

And in these deep unexcited dreams Sybil's low voice caressed him, her hands traced smiles onto his face and tickled his eyelids, and he was always in a house looking out a window instead of outside looking in, and what he saw outside were lawns white with sunlight, empty of people, but with maybe a robin, or a sprinkler, or a baseball glove lying deserted in the grass, and then, sometimes, through the heart of his deepest slumber, he himself as a boy ran, his hair freshy cut and combed, a boy in a clean white track uniform who ran down a hill and who crossed a wooden bridge, and disappeared behind some ferns: a dream that was too pretty to be a nightmare. . . .

Duffy slept.

THIRTY

The doctor tooted the Studebaker's horn: several Prescott kids scrambled out of the gutter. They gathered in the shadow of a porch and watched the car park. It was the last hour of a mid-October evening; the chill air smelled of leaf smoke. The doctor had taken Wendall with him on his rounds, and this was their last stop.

"Up and at 'em, Skunkhead." The doctor bounced several times on the seat as was his custom, searching for an easy position from which to rise. "Let's go in and see if there's any legs or arms need sawin' off." He heaved himself sideways and out. "Grab the old tool kit, will you?"

They skirted some plastic pails, a wheelless wagon, and chose their way carefully up some decaying steps onto a porch. The doctor had to duck his head to avert a low clothesline. An inverted umbrella lay on the threshold; the door itself had been unhinged and stood at one side of the entrance into a dark hallway.

The doctor knocked on a ground-floor door: interior voices stopped. The door opened a crack, then all the way, and Lucille Spender smiled.

" 'Lo Doctor," she said. "Didn't know whether you'd find time t'see us or not. Come right in."

She backed up: the doctor and the boy walked in

and looked around. Newspapers were scattered over the floor. Directly in front of them at a long wooden table sat the entire family—Joel Spender, Chad, Tabby, and four other kids, three of them boys, the smallest a girl. To the right a stove was cluttered with pots and a frying pan; beside the stove a yellow sink was piled high with dishes; scattered beneath it were some soap boxes, one of them tipped over with a blue drizzle of powder coming out the cardboard spout. On the other side of the room, in opposite corners, stood sagging brass beds, each unmade and piled high with drab quilts and articles of clothing. Between the two beds, a doorway led into a back room; a sheet tacked to the molding served to close it off, but there was a large rent in the sheet, darkness beyond.

"This here's Doctor Oler I called about Chad," Lucille said.

"Well, shoo, I guess I know Doc Oler all right, don't I, Doc?" Joel pushed back his chair and got up, wiping his hands on his coveralls. He hadn't shaved in a couple of days, little particles of food were caught in the stubble. The children left off eating and stared as Joel and the doctor shook hands.

"Yep, I guess we know each other, now, ain't it a fact?" Joel said, tilting his head to one side and winking an eye. "Shoo, now—ain't that so, Doc? Who sewed me together with that knife stickin' in my ribs if it weren't the doc here, eh?"

"I reckon if you say so." Wendall detected a change in his grandfather's voice, a slight nasal adaptation of Joel's twang, intended, most likely, to make Joel feel more at ease.

"Damn straight of you t' make the effort t'night," Joel said. " 'Course, it ain't nothin' serious, jus' the old lady got her tail heated up over a triflin', and I don' spect there's much you're likely t'want t'do. . . ."

"I forget which one the missus told me was the dead body," the doctor said, giving his head a conspiratory little twitch, his eye a flicker in the Joel Spender manner. "All them sprouts over there look fat'n'sassy as Thanksgivin' turkeys."

"Eldest'n," Joel said, pointing to Chad. The boy lowered his eyes. "Come here, boy, show the doc what you been crybabyin' about. Look to it, now."

Chad slipped out of his chair and limped around toward them. But at the near side of the table he was reluctant to leave its support in order to take steps necessary to reach his father.

"God dammit, boy, come here I say!" To the doctor, Joel said, "I whipped the bejesus outta him a'ready, like t' lifted his hide for walkin' like that, but he won't quit it, damn him. This ain't no sissy family, mind you."

"Well, let's take a look, see what's the problem," said the doctor. "Looks like he's busted a leg, maybe we'll have to shoot him."

"Haw, haw, shoo, Doc, I like that!" Joel tapped the doctor's arm in a familiar manner. "Luci-bet, go fetch the rifle, we got a young'n with a broke leg needs dispatchin' of." When his wife gave no reaction, Joel grinned and abruptly rubbed his chin. "How 'bout it, sonny?" he said, directing his words at Wendall. "You think that colt needs shootin', huh?"

Wendall shook his head. Lucille drew up a chair for the doctor beside the table, and he sat down. Chad remained very still while the doctor leaned over and examined his leg, touching it with his large hands, probing gently. The lower part of the shin was inflamed and swollen. After a cursory inspection, the doctor said, "Let's get this walkin' mountain of misery over to that bed before he drops dead on us."

"Git on over there!" barked Joel, jerking his head at Chad. "You heard the doc, boy, he tol' you t' git on over there." He hooked his thumbs in the coverall suspenders and rocked back. "I tell you, Doc, just look at him. Ain't nothin' wrong a good whippin' can't cure." He hawked some sputum into his mouth and was about to spit, then thought better of it, swallowed, and repeated. "Yes, indeedy, a good whippin'll git the devil outa that leg, or so help me, I'll kill the boy. Git over to that bed, hear?"

Chad let go of the table and took a step. He stopped,

his leg lifted tenderly, the toe just touching the floor. In two strides Joel was beside the boy and slapped him hard. Both Wendall and the doctor flinched; Lucille and the children remained impassive. Wendall thought to himself: This must be the most unhappy home on earth. He wondered how any God, if there was one, could have let Joel live through his knife wound last summer.

Apart from the red flush spreading on his cheek, Chad gave no indication of having felt his father's blow. He took two more quick steps and might have fallen had not the doctor butted in.

"Looks like we're goin' to have to hit him with a sledgehammer to get him movin'," he said, expertly lifting the boy by the underarms and carrying him to a bed. "Why, he doesn't weigh but an ounce. What you been feedin' him—feathers?" he exclaimed, gently pushing Chad back onto the bed. Then: "Oh, would you come here and look at this leg. Judas-pries', if it ain't somethin'! Bring me that tool kit, Skunkhead. I don' know's I got a big enough saw."

"There ain't nothin' wrong," Joel insisted, glaring at his wife as she hustled by him to the doctor's side. Wendall brought the bag to the bed.

"He's done a pretty good job on himself, he has," the doctor said. "Old Man Disease has laid his grinders into this boy. Take a look at this. Drawn a map, he has."

Lucille sat on the bed beside Chad and helped the doctor drop the boy's shorts. Joel sauntered over; he grimaced: "I tell you, Doc, there ain't nothin' the matter with that boy. I ain't gonna pay you t' give pills and crap t' that kid, I ain't just a foolin' neither. God damn little brats don't wanna go t' school, that's what it is."

"Blood poisoning," the doctor said. "Look at this." His finger, beginning at the red swelling, drew a circle around the inflamed area, then moved up the leg to the inner thigh just above the kneecap where a red line under the skin began and ran up to the groin. "End of this road there oughtta be a bump," he said, pressing his fingertips against the groin. "Yep. There she is, all right. Here, you give her a poke, Mrs Spender."

Lucille allowed the doctor to guide her hand to the swollen lymph node: she touched and withdrew.

"That's the dam," the doctor said. "That's the place full of a lot of little fellers called phagocytes that are keepin' Old Man Disease and his little red line from going any further." Looking up at Joel, he said, "I'm gonna cut him open down there, drain the pus out."

"What you gotta do that for?" Joel lifted his head, turning it slowly and suspiciously. "I don't see nothin' a good whippin' wouldn't cure."

"Well, now, you just watch." From his bag the doctor took a small scalpel, some gauze, a cotton ball, and a bottle of alcohol. He swabbed the swollen part of the leg with alcohol, then told Chad, "You just give a good holler when I touch bone," and with a deft motion, he cut a neat slit in the skin. Wendall expected blood and was preparing himself to feel faint at the sight of it: instead something ten times worse, a large gray-green bubble of pus pushed out the sides of the cut. Chad made no sound, his leg gave a slight jerk. The doctor swabbed off the pus as it oozed out. Wendall's stomach felt suddenly as if it had been stuffed full of pricklebburs; Lucille's countenance did not alter in the least. Joel folded his arms and said *"Hmphf!"* and bit his lips. The kids did not leave the table to see what was going on, nor did they commence talking. The doctor squeezed the wound and the last of the pus came out, followed by some blood. Wendall broke into a sweat and sat down on the floor with a bump.

"Now we're gonna stuff him up some," the doctor said. He fiddled a minute with a thin strip of gauze, folding it into a tight little wad which he inserted in the cut. Then he wrapped the wound loosely and said, "I'm gonna give you a prescription for some pills. All you have to do is feed him a couple every few hours and in no time he'll be so healthy you can whip him double if you want and he'll make nary a peep. Tomorrow I'll come back and snip off a little of that drain, and I'll bet you my left earlobe Old Man Disease will be lyin' all shriveled up on the floor at the foot of this bed gaspin' for air."

"We don't want no pills," Joel said.

"I tell you, it's a good idea," the doctor advised, going to the sink to wash his hands. "He's got a good little fever to go along with that poisoned leg."

"We ain't even got enough to pay for that cuttin' up you done," Joel said. A bargaining tone entered his voice. His upper lip curled into a nasty smile, his winking eye closed. "How much you figure we owe you for that? Huh?"

The doctor flicked his hands in the air. "Well, seein' as how it's a Tuesday evening and the moon is full, and on top of that you all are my ten-thousandth customers, I guess I'll have to give it to you free, don't see no other way out of it." He hurriedly packed his bag and wrote out a prescription on a slip of paper.

"Well . . . haw, haw, God damn, Doc, well haw, haw . . ." Joel's face lit all over with a crude triumphant smile. "Now ain't that straight of you. By Jim, ain't a straighter man in all of town. I swear t' it, there ain't. A straight-shooter all the way, Doc. God damn."

"Thank you," said Lucille, shaking the doctor's hand. Wendall regained his feet and possession of the tool kit, but his face was still a little pale and his stomach still felt crammed with burs.

"How 'bout a drink t' celebrate the successful operation?" Joel said. "Got me a jug of dandy jack over there, have a swig with me?"

"Oh, no. No thanks," said the doctor. "I left my iron-coated windpipe at home. Maybe tomorrow night when I drop by I'll bring it along with me."

"Yes, indeedy, you do that, Doc. And you and me'll have a straight one as between men who knows their likkers, won't we?" He touched the doctor's shoulder; the motion was open, vulgar, friendly.

"You leave him in that bed, stuff him full of food, and don't let him move, and don't give him that whippin' for a while," the doctor said.

"Shoo, hell. About that whippin', you knowed I was jokin'," Joel said, opening the door for them. "Shoo, Doc, you know I'm a jokin' man. Get a funny streak in me longer'n a rattail, I do. Shoo, now. You didn't believe . . ."

He closed the door. It was dark. The white bodies of near-naked children stopped in the darkness across the street. The air was extra still, as if a huge wind were waiting just around the corner. The low-slung telephone lines were only just blacker than the sky, cutting thin scars across an unfolding front of cloud that obscured the moon. The doctor and the boy climbed into the car; it was some time before the doctor started it up.

"Where would this world be if we didn't help each other out," he said in a hushed uncomfortable voice. He felt strange; his shoulder felt dirty where he had allowed—no, encouraged—Joel to touch it. He turned the key, a red light on the dash went on. "Uh . . . you won't tell Grannie about that, will you?" he said, turning to Wendall with a tired smile.

"About what?"

"Well . . . about me not chargin' anything for cuttin' up that dyin' horse of theirs."

"Why?"

"Well, you know how she can get to be awful persnickety sometimes, and she just might not take kindly to it, that's all." He flicked the key, the car started up. "Lord love a duck," he exclaimed as they pulled away from the curb. "I'm so hungry I could eat a Chinese elephant."

They drove down the street, past Harry's bungalow, past the Jubliee Café. Different shades of light blipped on the doctor's face as they drove under streetlamps, past porch lights; the lights revolved over his face, fluttering like confetti, his nose was dark and then white, blinking almost like a clown's bulb.

"He probably would have died if you hadn't done that," Wendall said.

"Who—Chad? Died? Don't you believe it for a minute. Those kids are so tough you could hogtie 'em and throw 'em in a river, and they'd drift for days, snappin' up the trout when they got hungry, right up to the time the rope rotted apart and they could swim to shore. Disease goes through them kids like a clam through a gull. . . ."

"I still think he would have died," Wendall said.

Reaching over and putting his arm around the boy's shoulder, the doctor said, "Come here and snuggle up to your old granddad, Skunkhead. I haven't been very sociable lately, have I? Don't know what's got into me."

Wendall shifted over. The doctor returned both hands to the wheel as they entered the driveway. He drove into the barn, cut the motor, and turned off the lights. There were some crackling sounds as the motor cooled. Wendall nestled close against him, feeling his grandfather's warm body reaching out to enfold his own, the fat arthritic fingers over his shoulder, gently rubbing. After a while the doctor gave a snort and smiled a little. "The years go by so fast they make your ears whistle. . . ." His voice was dead tired. He clicked the key to one side so that the red light went on, then clicked it back and drew it out.

Without warning, Wendall's throat tightened. He wanted to speak, then arrested the urge, and, when almost immediately he wished he had said something, the time was already past when he could have. Feeling deprived and uncomfortable, he slid out from under his grandfather's arm.

They got out: Wendall helped slide the heavy barn door shut. They stood in the grass at the side of the driveway looking down over the garden toward the river. At the far end of the garden, Bernie Aja's victory pumpkin glimmered like a huge lead lump, a smoothly fallen meteor.

"That thing'll be so fat in a couple of days it will sink into the earth and disappear," said the doctor. He inspected the sky. "Looks like rain, tonight. Lots of rain."

They walked over to the back porch. At the door the doctor said, "Now you won't tell anything, will you?"

"About what?"

He tousled Wendall's hair and opened the door. "That's the spirit," he said.

THIRTY-ONE

On Halloween night, Tom and Wendall, accompanied by Sybil and the doctor, went trick-or-treating. They received favors of candy, fruit, popcorn, cookies, and even money from every house solicited except the Svenson habitat, where Dorothy opened the door, looked shocked, and exclaimed, "Oh, is it *that* night? Marie always kept track. . . ."

After the relatively peaceful Oler-Matthewson contingent had withdrawn from the Svenson house, other less peaceful groups descended on it. They first squished a bag of something that smelled suspiciously like the manure of a large domesticated animal through the mail slot in the front door, and followed up by wedging pins at various intervals into the doorbell. Dorothy came out each time, angrily removed the pin, and hurled a few choice invectives at the surrounding darkness. Finally, a nail was driven into the doorbell: Dorothy stationed herself on the porch and screamed bloody murder until she turned purple, then she called up the Olers and asked for someone to come over and undo the damage. A few minutes later Bernie Aja showed up with a hammer in one hand and a screwdriver in the other. He found Dorothy wrapped in a blanket, sitting on the front stoop, a carving fork held menacingly across her bosom.

"Evenin'," Bernie said.

"Evenin's rotten," Dorothy said.

"Well, hmm . . ." Bernie said. "Doorbell, is it?"

"You got eyes and ears, I hope." Dorothy swung her eyes around the front lawn, not for a minute going to be sucked into diverting her attention from whoever might be lurking in the shadows waiting to pounce on her house.

Bernie climbed the steps: with one jerk of his hammer he yanked out the nail and climbed back down the steps.

"Don't catch cold," he said. "It's a chilly night, y'know."

"The only thing I'll catch is some of those smart-alec hobgoblins," Dorothy said. "And when I do—" She made a jabbing motion with the carving fork.

"I wouldn't want to be one of them." Bernie said, backing away, bobbing his head. "Night, Miss Dorothy . . ."

"You're lucky you *aren't* one of them," Dorothy said. "Night, 'n' thanks."

She waited until midnight on the front stoop: when she got up she was so stiff she could hardly straighten her legs. Inside, she brewed a pot of tea, and was on her third cup when the doorbell rang again and continued to ring loudly without interruption. She went to the front and discovered another nail driven into the already badly mangled button. It being too late to call anyone for assistance, she dragged in a chair from the parlor, situated it to one side of the door, got a knife from the kitchen, and climbed onto the chair. She jammed the knife blade under the bell disk, and was just beginning to pry the metal cup out from the wall when the chair rocked over, pitching her downward. Her head struck forcefully against the hardwood floor, and the doorbell rang right through her instantaneous death and continued to ring for several hours.

Duffy Kahler waded across the river and crawled under the Olers' barn. He hadn't been there but a moment when a noise in the garden startled him, and down by the compost heap he saw several shadowy figures stooped over something.

A minute went by; the figures straightened. Duffy

counted four of them, slight of build, probably boys. Two walked close together, carrying something big between them; the others ran ahead and climbed up the lawn wall, slipping through the guard railing onto the sidewalk. On the other side of the street, its lights extinguished, an idling car was parked. The first two figures arrived at the wall and hoisted something huge and round up to the other boys who rocked it onto the sidewalk, then lugged it over to the car while their cohorts scaled the wall. Then the car drove slowly away; its lights did not flick on until after turning the corner onto Main Street.

The next morning, Bernie Aja's milk-fed Victory pumpkin was found on the steps of the post office–town hall. It had been hollowed out, and in its side, in place of a face, a swastika had been carved.

During a lunch hour recess, which was the same for both the elementary and high schools (they were located in the same building), Jimmy Wiggen searched out Wendall and said gloatingly, "Hey, I hear you people lost somethin' the other night."

Wendall gave Jimmy such a long and hard stare that it made the older boy uncomfortable. Then, speaking with icy calm, Wendall said, "Why don't you ram it up your rosy red rectum with a real red-hot railroad ramrod?"

Jimmy said, "Listen, ya little crud, don't ya swear at me if ya know what's good for ya. Ya watch out or ya'll get ya head broke, I don't take no crud, understand?"

Wendall repeated his ramrod epithet. Like steam, hate filled his head. His whole spinal column went numb; his muscles froze.

"Hey, Wendy. Hey, don't get mad, Wendy-girl," Jimmy teased. "Hey, Wendy—!"

Wendall drove his fist into Jimmy's crotch. Startled, the bigger boy staggered backwards a few steps. So mad he could hardly breathe, Wendall waded into him, spindly arms flailing like warped pinwheels. But as soon as Jimmy recovered himself, he pushed the boy aside, hit him in the face, bloodying his nose and lip, then knocked him down. Wendall landed on his back, scrambled to his feet, and Jimmy shoved him down again. Wendall got up and renewed his rush, Jimmy ducked aside and tripped him so he smashed down hard on his face in the dirt. Wendall arose, spitting and crying, and Jimmy hit him in the nose again. A crowd gathered, girls squealed and boys yelled "Fight! Fight!" His face gummy with tears, spittle, and blood, Wendall ran futilely at his enemy, who as before handled his charge with ease and sent him sprawling. This time the impetus of Wendall's fighting spirit exploded away into overwhelming fatigue and faintness; he had only just made it back to his feet when his knees buckled and he fell down for good. Kids giggled and walked away. "Ya crud," Jimmy Wiggen said. He kicked some dirt at the boy and scuffled scornfully off to join his friends. Wendall could not return to classes; he went straight home instead.

Even after he had cleaned up and calmed down, Wendall found himself bursting afresh into tears. Bitterly he recounted to Bernie Aja what had happened on the playground, claiming it proved beyond a doubt that Jimmy and his friends were responsible for destroying the pumpkin. But Bernie just shook his head and smiled forlornly and allowed it really didn't matter. "Maybe next year," he said sorrowfully. "You never can tell, y'know."

But during the days that followed, Wendall ached deeply for the honor of his family.

THIRTY-TWO

The first snow fell on election day, the eighth of November. The Oler family bundled up in the morning and trudged through a full-blown storm to the post office–town hall. While the grownups were inside voting, Tom and Wendall went to look at the ads for *Mr. Winkle Goes to War,* a film with Edward G. Robinson then playing at the Imperial. While appraising the photographs, they heard a voice behind them say, "Hello there, fellows. Are you gonna vote Republican or Democrat or what?"

The train man! Though taken by surprise, Wendall quickly composed himself and stared frostily away from him.

"Folks over voting?" Duffy asked.

Wendall said yes.

"Oh. You guys seen the picture?"

Wendall said no.

"Not worth it." Duffy shook his head. "I went last night thinking, Edward G. Robinson, this ought to be a top-notch picture, only it wasn't. It's a comedy, you know, it doesn't have anything to do with the war. Edward G. Robinson is a timid guy, if you can believe that. You familiar with his films? Well, a timid guy, no kidding. It's got nothing to do with the war."

They faced across the street to where people were hurrying in and out of the post office, heads bowed into the wind. The snow would not be a good one, it was too wet; already the street had turned to slush.

"I've been in the war," Duffy said, jabbing himself in the chest with his thumb. "And you can bet it wasn't a comedy." He chuckled. "Heck, you kids don't know anything about war, do you? Well, why should you? Do you know how far away the war is from us right now?" He withdrew his right hand and held it up. "This is us." He brought out the left hand and held it far from the other like a man telling a good fish story. "And this is the war." He wriggled the fingers on his hand and repeated, "The war. Do you know how many miles of ocean there are between this hand and this hand?"

"Which war do you mean?" said Wendall. "The European war, or the African war, or the Pacific war, or the Asian war?"

"Do I mean . . . Well, any war."

"I suppose between us and Europe there are roughly—"

"Three thousand miles!" Duffy blurted, lowering his hands. "Maybe even more." He swung his head to either side, then faced the boys directly and tried to smile disarmingly. "All the Nazis should be chopped into pieces with machetes," he said. Then: "Hey—what's the hurry? You don't like me? Hey, where are you going?"

Wendall pointed to the post office.

"Is his mother in there?" Duffy asked, nodding at Tom.

"Yes. We have to go."

"Wait a minute. How would you two soldiers like an ice cream cone—a sundae, anything you want—on me?"

"We have to go," Wendall repeated coldly, taking Tom's hand. Tom yanked his hand free. He said, "I don't wanna go, I wanna ice cream."

"If you don't come," said Wendall, "I'll kick you down the stairs when we get home."

"I'm not afraid of you. I wanna ice cream." Tom belched and sidled over to Duffy.

Wendall acquiesced reluctantly: "All right, but we have to hurry. . . ."

They took over a back booth in the Miss Stebbinsville, Tom on one side next to Duffy, Wendall alone on the other side, and they all ordered hot fudge sundaes. While Duffy wolfed down his ice cream, he talked about the war. He said that before the Americans destroyed the gas chambers they ought to do to the German people what the Germans had done to the Jews. If he were General Eisenhower, that was what he would do. Anybody caught speaking German would be executed. He wished he were back over there, he'd show those Krauts what was what. . . .

All the while Duffy talked, a funny foreboding sensation was growing in Wendall, and finally he saw very clearly that the man *was* crazy, and he said nervously, "Okay; Tom and I must leave now. We thank you for the ice cream, don't we, Tom?"

Tom said, "I don't wanna go. I wanna stay and hear some more stories about the war."

"Grandma said when it was five to ten we were to be on the steps of the post office to meet them."

"Yaah," spouted Tom, casting to Duffy for approval.

Wendall slipped out of the booth. "Okay for you, brother," he warned. "You're not going to be there, and I sure don't want to be on hand when you catch hell for not showing up," and he tramped out of the diner into a flurry of wet flakes.

He faked a saunter across the sidewalk, ears alerted for the creak of the door that would tell him Tom had relented, but by the time he lowered his booted foot into two inches of gray slush in the gutter, he had heard no sound, so he turned around, and, while continuing to back into the street, kept his eyes on the entrance to the Miss Stebbinsville.

Two things happened at once. The door to the diner sprang open and Duffy Kahler plunged outside. He hit the sidewalk running, his arms waving wildly, and disappeared around the edge of the building. At the same time Jim's station wagon came within an inch of flattening Wendall for good. Jim braked when he saw the boy walking backwards into the street, the car slid sideways, slewed out of control for a second, then the tires gripped, the car shuddered, straightened out, and swished so close by the boy that he felt a tick against his hand as a fraction of the taillight brushed it.

Jim was neither a fast nor an agile man, in particular when half scared to death. He opened the car door, lost his footing, and tumbled into the slushy street. It was to him, clods of wet snow dripping down his immense stomach, that Wendall breathlessly said, "Tom's in the diner with a lunatic!"

Jim grabbed the boy's hand and yanked him toward the Miss Stebbinsville. They stumbled into the white-suited soda jerk who was running full tilt at the door. The jerk pedaled backwards, shouting, "Stop that son of a bitch," recovered himself, and ran around Jim and Wendall out the door.

Deeper into the diner, the waitress who had served

the sundaes was leaning over the table at the booth in which they'd been sitting. They drew near; the girl looked around and stuttered, "He t-tried to k-kill the child!" The rag in her hand was red with blood.

Jim bent over and examined Tom, who, despite whatever had happened, still sat upright. Between Jim and the waitress, Wendall couldn't see a thing. Desperately, he dropped to his hands and knees and crawled through Jim's legs, under the table, and pulled himself up into the far seat beside Tom.

He blanched, immediately wishing he hadn't been so intrepid. A large white gash began just above the bridge of his cousin's nose and traveled zigzag like a streak of lightning into his hair.

"Somebody call a doctor?" Jim asked.

"Oh, dear, I don't know," the waitress said. "Oh, dear me . . ."

"Call one, fetch one," Jim ordered.

"He was crazy!" the girl said, letting out a hefty boohoo.

"Doctor!" Jim ordered.

"Oh, yes sir! I'm sorry, oh golly . . ." She fluttered toward the door, but was pushed back by the jerk, coming in with a rush, followed by the doctor, Cornelia, Sybil, John T., Bernie Aja, and a few other citizens.

"Well, Lord love a duck!" gruffed the doctor, instantly jovial, plunking his bag on the table. "Looks like we'll have to amputate his head."

Cornelia piped, "Oh!" and nearly fainted. When her knees went wobbly, Sybil took hold of her elbow and said, "Now, now, Mummy, it's only his head, and you know how hard and empty that is—"

"He's got a concussion," Cornelia moaned. "I just know it."

"By the time I get through with him, we'll have a zipper sewed on there so's he can take out the old rondo-sketiaptic dispeller any time he damned well pleases and clean out the detmoles," said the doctor. Jim withdrew from the scene, pushing past everybody to the rear: he waited unobtrusively by the end of the fountain to be called if needed. More people, murmuring and buzzing, crowded into the diner.

"Now, what happened?" the doctor asked. His blunt fingers deftly tore small strips of tape off a roll and he cut the strips into butterfly shapes.

The waitress said, "He tried to kill him!"

"He laid it to him with the ice cream dish," said the jerk.

"What's goin' on here? What happened?" Sheriff Flood elbowed through the crowd. "What'd he do? Who did it? Huh?"

"With the ice cream dish," the jerk repeated. He raised his arm, cupped his hand, and swung viciously down to simulate how the blow had been struck.

"Who, for Chrissakes?" John T. demanded.

"Nobody from around these parts," the jerk asserted. "Don't belong to this town."

"What'd he look like?" the sheriff asked.

"I think he had sort of red hair," said the jerk.

The waitress added, "His face was funny, messy . . . oh, golly . . ."

"Oky-doky," said the doctor to Tom, tilting the boy's head to admire his handicraft. "How's your gizzard?"

Weakly, Tom said, "Full of stones."

"That's what I like to hear. Now let's you and me shuck off all these ugly people and get ourselves sewed up." He lifted Tom out of the booth. "Reckon I'll have to use that special sewing machine for boneheads."

Sybil reached up and pinched Tom's nose as they went out. "It's about time someone bopped him, don't you think, Mummy?" she said cheerfully.

"Oh, Lord," said Cornelia. She sat down at the counter and placed her elbow into a half-filled cup of coffee. Some people drifted out of the diner, shaking their heads and muttering about a maniac, and someone guessed again it might be a Nazi escaped from the prison camp at Jactonberry.

John T. slid into the booth beside Wendall.

"Where were you?" he asked.

"I was going to get you people."

"What do you mean?"

"I told Tom he had better come away and he wouldn't, so I was going to the post office to fetch you."

"What the hell did you leave him for?"

Wendall turned his face away and began to fidget with the saltcellar.

"Got any idea who it might have been?" John T. insisted.

Wendall pouted. "Tom deserved it if he wouldn't come with me. I warned him a hundred times—"

The sheriff butted in. "Got any idea who it was? Ever seen him afore?"

"No," Wendall said firmly. These people angered him, and suddenly the man was no longer an enemy; suddenly he needed help, he needed protection. "No, I never saw him before," the boy reiterated.

"You sure?"

"Yessir. Positive."

John T. said, "Wendall, what's the matter with you?"

"Nothing is the matter with me. Can't you see?"

"You know something about that man—"

"I don't. I said I didn't. Of course nobody would believe me. I'm the little robber. I'm the ugly little brat responsible for whatever goes wrong."

"Aw, turn it off for Chrissakes," John T. said. "But so help me God—"

Their eyes caught and held, curious, alien, then swerved away from each other.

"All right," shouted Sheriff Flood. "Who else was witnesses?"

An hour later the Sheriff put in a statewide alert; then, with the aid of Mike Stenatto, he formed a small posse. Harry Garengelli supplied gas to whoever wanted it with or without coupons. Roadblocks were set up by the State Police on some major routes throughout the country, a vague description of the red-headed man was circulated, the prison camp at Jactonberry reported no one had recently escaped, and, finally, everything that could be done had been done.

The doctor sewed a "zipper" into Tom's head and brought him home; six big black stitches decorated the wound. Sheriff Flood came and talked with Tom, who responded with "I don't knows" and the sheriff didn't press him much because the boy was supposed to be in shock for a while yet. The fact is, Wendall had already cornered his cousin and said, "You have to promise me never to say anything about that man."

"Why?"

"Because we want him to be a secret between just you and me. We're the only people in the world who know about him, and we mustn't ever tell."

"Why'd he hit me?"

"He's sick. Listen, will you swear to God you won't ever tell about him, or say that I told you not to talk?"

"I don't know . . ."

Wendall wanted to say. "Then some night when you're asleep I'll get Grandpa's carving knife and cut out your gizzard and hang it on a nail in the attic until it's all shriveled up," but instead he purred, "Then I guess I won't ever be able to play with you again if you break faith like that. No more Uncle Wiggly either."

Now the reading of Uncle Wiggly stories was to Tom's spiritual survival what a series of well-executed belches was to his athletic ego: he squirmed but held out a little longer, sensing there was yet a fruit to be reaped in exchange for silence.

"If you do agree not to tell, however, I'll give you a dime every Saturday," Wendall said. Eyeing Tom sideways, he waited unhappily to see how Tom would take to the kicker.

"Oh . . . all right, I guess . . ." Tom said with smug reluctance.

"But if you ever tell, it'll be the worst thing in the world," Wendall said gravely. "Plus the fact that if you do blab, I'll castrate you, I really will."

"What's castrate?" Tom asked.

"Never mind what. You just believe it's awful, that's all."

Tom said, "I won't ever tell." And then: "It didn't hurt at all when he hit me," he said proudly. "It just got all bloody, didn't it?"

Wendall mumbled, "You don't have to brag about it, for God's sake," and went downstairs.

He came off the bottom step and turned right into the living room. Sybil was at the other end of the room before the piano. She riffled her fingers silently over the keys as if trying to play out in her mind a difficult piece before attempting it live. Then, with one finger, she played the first line of "Mary Had a Little Lamb." She mouthed the words as if to familiarize them to herself, played the line again, then, softly, she coordinated voice and piano.

When she was done, all the life flowed out of her face and her body, and her hands poised for a moment on the keys as if to play Beethoven; then all life left her fingers also, they were no longer poised to play but frozen in an eternal form never to make another sound. A breath of air would have shattered her. No longer brown but white was her hair—white as the snow swirling outside, splashing on the windows and on the shoulders of men all over the state looking for a maniac they could never find, men tramping into winter, frightened serious men with a purpose, searching for a phantom that, no matter how many ways they turned around and no matter how fast, they would never find. . . .

"Do you know who it is, Aunt Sybil?" Wendall asked fearfully.

"I don't want to talk about it just now."

Wendall put on his jacket, unsheathed the dueling cane, and skipped into the snowstorm, his heart singing with confused joy.

A customer told Irma Kahler about the incident in the Miss Stebbinsville, and she sensed right away that the criminal must have been her son. She went to the back storage room, brewed some coffee on a hot plate, and sat for a long while trying to decide what the right thing for her to now do would be.

Long ago she had ceased actively worrying about Duffy, for, thrilled to find herself in a position to aid him, she had contented herself with playing the silent yet helpful role she had adopted over the summer, unwilling to jeopardize that position by trying to wheedle her son home, or even speak to him, for that matter. There had been no doubt in her mind that he was sick, but she had not wanted to consider it a serious illness. And above all else she had not wanted to butt in because she felt herself awakening to a love that was requited simply by knowing Duffy was safe and fed reasonably well for the moment, and she had not allowed herself to look beyond that moment.

She closed her eyes, picturing his ghostly form flitting through the darkened store. She watched him from the stairs, she listened to the rustlings he made, the soft chink of tin cans against each other, the clean crinkle of a bread package, the rattle of coins he spilled from the open register into his pocket. . . .

For Christmas she was planning to buy him presents: new shoes, a coat, mittens, earmuffs, books—she was planning to wrap them—already she had bought the paper, ribbons—and she was going to leave them by the back door for him to take or reject as he wanted.

But that was all ruined now. Irma drank her coffee and felt old and weak and very small and very inadequate. In the evening, she said to her husband, "It was Duffy done it this morning to the Matthewson kid. I know."

She hadn't spoken of Duffy since their altercation many months ago. Hank Kahler looked at her surprised.

"We should forget," he said stiffly.

"I can't, I have to do something, I have to tell somebody because the boy is really in trouble."

"The boy is dead—"

She stretched her arm across the table and cuffed him. The blow was hard enough to knock him onto the floor. He scrambled up, rubbing his jaw, and said, "You are crazy."

"I'm trying to be a help. I'm trying to help a boy who needs it—our son, too."

"In a grave you need nothing."

Irma lowered her face onto her arms and gave way to despair.

Wrapped in an old overcoat, Duffy huddled at the head of the autoseat fighting the feeling that his body was about to swell to enormously puffed proportions and float him tumbling around the baggage room until he burst, spraying the walls and ceiling one final time with his thick blood and graying brain matter, destroying for once and for all the legend of his youth. He moaned, rocking woozily, his eyes closed, feet curled inward against each other. He had run back through the snowstorm instinctively, remembering nothing of his flight from the diner to the station. Now, the large snowflakes smashing against his window sounded like bullets hitting decayed flesh, his own flesh, and he wondered, terrified, where the hurt was, and when it would begin.

Later, when the wind changed, the sounds of the storm were transformed into footsteps: the queer stealthy footsteps of people hunting him. He stopped shivering and drowsed. There came to him an image of the townsfolk, all of them thin people with gray preoccupied faces and sad eyes, moving soundlessly through the trees, searching for him, each with a rifle slung over his shoulder. They passed and repassed the memorial, casting not a glance in its direction. Lying in the snow at the base of the memorial was his little son Tom whom he had struck dead, his blood, like an angry flower crown around his head, sprayed on the startling whiteness.

In his dream, Duffy crept from the baggage room and walked down the center of Main Street, and people turned their heads away from him, refusing to recognize him. The walk to the Green took him hours: his feet were frozen, his muscles refused to respond, and only with the greatest difficulty could he advance down the street. When finally he arrived at the Green, he knelt in the snow beside his son, and then the townspeople brought their eyes to bear on him. He was bewildered for a moment by their sorrowing gazes.

A rifle shot sounded and a bullet jarred into the back of his head, and he began to say the Lord's Prayer fast, unthinking, as he always had in church. Another shot sounded, then two more. He could feel lead hitting his back, he saw a shot that missed punch a hole in the snow before him. He struggled to rise, the air reverberated with gunshots. The impact of so many bullets tumbled him into the snow. He writhed and began to laugh. He laughed, and Sybil's laugh answered him. Snow melted; she came running down the park slope in the rain, whirlwind tails of leaves spinning away from her downward rush. He caught her hand and they danced around the edge of the pond. Their reflections, distorted and dancing, filled with water. Yellow boats, big maple and oak leaves, sailed on the rainpocked water. Sybil slipped and fell: Duffy did not let go of her hand as she slid wordlessly under the surface. He stooped until she was completely submerged, his own arms under almost to the shoulder. Then she turned into a flower, a bright flower of beautiful, brilliant crimson, pricked by the rain and garlanded by leaves, and when he pulled her out again it was the hand of Tom he held; it was the small body of his son he lay on the soft dying bank grass, and the ugly forehead wound was a pale purple color, drenched and bloodless. . . .

THIRTY-THREE

The sun melted off the snow, a week passed, and still no word of Duffy Kahler. Fear subsided, snow came again and buried beneath it the mechanics of the search; the public's curiosity dulled. The new snow soon melted away, leaving trees bare and stooped, and Thanksgiving arrived.

It was a beautiful blustery day: the family went to

church, then sat down to dinner, and with much gusto and wisecracking the doctor carved up the turkey. The men drank a lot of wine, and after dinner the doctor suggested they go for a drive. The suggestion was accepted and he toddled into the barn after the Studebaker. The rest of the family was gathered on the front porch when the car backed out of the barn. It seemed to all that the Studebaker was going a little too fast, and, sure enough, it whacked straight into one of the carriage port posts, cracking the post over to a mean angle. The doctor opened the door, laughing almost to the point of tears: John T. and Sybil were laughing with him. Cornelia's expression remained as joyless and wooden as a cigar store Indian, however.

"It isn't funny," she snapped. Her stone-face crumbled, it looked as if she might begin to bawl.

"It is so funny," said John T. "It's the first funny thing that's happened around here in a good long time."

"Oh, it's funny, all right," said Cornelia. "Now it'll have to be fixed—"

"Fixed? Fiddlesticks," said the doctor, patting the post affectionately. "We'll leave it this way, it's got personality. This carriage port always needed a little personality."

"And fixing will cost money—" went on Cornelia.

"Money!" interrupted John T. He smacked his palm against a porch column. "Money! Money! Money! That's all anybody in this stinking household thinks about is money. I'm sick of it, I'm fed up with money here, money there, money this, money that, can't we spend even one God damn minute without talking about, worrying about, money?"

He jerked open the screen door and slammed it as loud as he could behind him. He was so upset he tripped on the first stair and scrambled up on all fours, banging his palms down on each step. He shut the door to his room with such force that the entire house shuddered.

The little group on the porch looked at each other

in dismay, then disbanded, and the doctor drove the car back into the barn.

Later, Sybil sat for an hour on the edge of John T.'s bed softly rubbing his shoulders as sunset died within the room. John T. said he was ready to blow town, let his parents sink in their own mud, he'd had it. When he had calmed down, he told Sybil that if his life didn't change pretty soon he'd never be able to love anybody again: he could feel cold sheets of bitterness enameling his underskin, seeping through his emotions: "I want to go back to school, or get married, or die, Sibs," he said. "I'd do anything for a change, I really would. I just can't keep going no place much longer."

"The war is going to end soon and then everything will be different," Sybil said.

"No, I don't think it's ever going to end," John T. replied. "It fits this lousy world like a glove."

The following day, in the gorgeous sunswept afternoon, Sybil walked up to the park. She sat in the dry gloom of the pines and waited for Duffy Kahler. She thought the war had exchanged her son's real father for the man she married: and she considered it inevitable that she should eventually come to love him. She hoped that one day Duffy would make her pregnant, and that a new child, his very own and born of love this time, would heal some of his war hurt, and perhaps restore him to the platform from which, four years ago, he had been so ready to leap headlong into a life of joyful success.

But she waited alone throughout the afternoon; Duffy never came.

During that last week of November, Marty Haldenstein resigned from the library. He gave a short notice, and then walked quietly and unbitterly out of his office, never to return. Thereafter he stuck pretty much to his room, reading, working in his darkroom with old negatives, or just lying in bed, his chest swollen, his throat sore, every cough threatening to shake his feeble frame of its remaining life. He would not see a doctor—he gritted his teeth, determined to die with dignity and to die alone. Often he locked his door and went through all the preparations to suicide, but he could not pull the trigger of his pistol. He bore the pain that had been his lifelong companion, and sometimes, in a near swoon, he would feel himself nearly moved to tears, thinking of how the parasitic pain would one day kill him, and in doing so, kill itself. He was proud in his silent suffering, and this was the only pride life had allowed him. He took his meals in the Miss Stebbinsville, in particular enjoying his dinner, which was often served by Ercel Perry. The girl always had a kind smile for him, and he drew comfort from her eyes that he guessed could see beyond his superficial wounds. With Christmas coming, he would have liked to buy her a present, but could bring himself only to leave generous tips the times she served him. One night he lay in bed with the pistol on the coverlet over his chest, and he thought that great wings were wrapped around the house, he thought he could hear giant feathers scratching against his windows. Then Ercel Perry, docile and white skinned, appeared at his bedside, smiling her kind lonely smile. She was naked, her breasts were blue, her heavy flanks shone like marble, her lips were wet, her eyes dark shadows. They stared at each other a long time; then Marty handed her the gun. She held it in her hands, kissing it, and a second later aimed it at him and pulled the trigger. The pellet driving into his forehead made a snapping sound as it had in the bark of the apple tree. He lost sight of her, the feathers closed over him, dusting his skin which was suddenly cold and as wrinkleless as glass, and no blood issued from the hole in his white expansive skull. It disappointed him to be brought cruelly awake by wrenching coughs. He continued, uncomplainingly, to live.

November wound up. The doctor was his old animated self a few days before the Army–Navy football game, he talked of Blanchard and Davis, he speculated with Wendall that Army would lose by a touchdown even though they had a better team—he could feel it in his bones, he said. Wendall checked the game out with Jim who said no, Army was definitely superior, nothing Navy could do short of a miracle would beat them; he predicted a two-touchdown victory for the West Pointers, and that is the exact margin by which they won.

Thereafter, the doctor felt himself overcome by a wide-spread listlessness, his arms became leaden and heavy to lift, the agility of his arthritic fingers left him little by little, his bumpy red knees swelled and throbbed as if he had been kneeling for years on rough stones. Often he sat in hot baths Cornelia had drawn for him, smoking, the penguin balanced on the flat porcelain edge of the tub, and he soaped his wounds gently despairing and secretly remonstrating his creation, the detmoles for catching up with him and slowly hauling his rondo-sketiaptic dispeller down. The more Cornelia nagged him about economic problems, the more he ignored her beseechings, putting off, smoothing over, wiping out payments due with little jokes, embarrassed by himself, unhappy, weary, and unable to face up. He suggested once, and he was sincere, that they sell the house, cut down on everything, and Cornelia's eyes bristled fiercely, she said she would hear of no such thing, come hell or high water they were going to live as they were accustomed to living, and she continued to give a thousand suggestions, she beleaguered him with a thousand small alarms until he was blue in the face, and he allowed an insurance policy to lapse and didn't care, he came to the realization that his body really was full of giving up, it no longer mattered if he pulled his weight with the team, he was tired of toil, sickness, and pain, he'd had enough of crises, tension, and broken hearts—the burdens of others had filled him, numbed him to the core, and he couldn't cope any longer, he wanted a vacation, he longed to sleep. It seemed the goodness in him hadn't worked out; it seemed his lifetime of taking care had backfired. He felt terribly alone in the heart of his family; he said little, smiled wistfully, and carried on.

The house, as winter really took hold, became an icebox, for, in order to conserve fuel, the furnace was run but seldom. After the first weeks in December when snow had come to stay Bernie Aja helped Tom and Wendall shovel a large clear space on the front lawn and water it down for an ice skating rink. Just as there was a good ice surface, however, a thaw struck and ruined it. Then a foot of snow fell, mingling with the slush of the thaw, and the project was abandoned; the boys had to be content with trying to lift hockey pucks off a waxed board upstairs in the barn. Wendall learned all about hockey from Jim and transmitted his knowledge to Tom, and they pretended Tom's scar had been made by a fast-flying puck instead of an ice cream dish, and this pleased Tom no end.

In the war, the Allies, who had seemed to be mopping up the European enemy, suffered a reversal, and the Germans broke back into once-liberated Luxembourg. Wendall worried, clipped out the newspapers as always, and spent much time in front of mirrors flexing his soon to be massive muscles and daydreaming about the great athlete-soldier he would one day be, and in order to enhance his physical image he even took to going for long spells without wearing glasses, but finally had to give this up after misjudging a step and plummeting all the way downstairs from the second landing, spraining every muscle and ligament in his body, and badly bruising his ego to boot.

Then, as he hauled himself up joint by joint after this colorful spill, he realized that Christmas was almost upon them. . . .

Wendall had ten dollars and fifty cents in his jar beneath the barn. He took it out and counted and recounted, planning how he would use it for Christmas presents. On a piece of paper he wrote down the name of each person in the family, and beside it the sum he could spend on his or her present. At first he thought to divvy up the money equally: if Fred were included, that meant shelling out $1.50 apiece.

But after a moment's deep mulling he decided, somewhat arbitrarily, that Cornelia just plain wasn't worth more than a dollar, and he attached her fifty cents to the doctor's gift. Next, he reasoned that because Bernie Aja was the *handyman* and not really an *integral* part of the family, expenditure on him shouldn't run over a dollar either, and he switched that excess over to Fred's gift. The more he thought about his father's gift, however, the more it seemed silly even to attempt buying one. There was the problem of postage, of where to send the package; and in all likelihood Fred wouldn't receive the thing until March or April anyway, and he might not even be alive then.

That made two dollars just floating around free: Wendall counted it back into the jar.

Now he reviewed Tom's case, and the more he thought about his little cousin, the more he wondered what in the name of Sam Hill made Tom a candidate in any way for such an expansive donation. After all, for the past month, promptly on every Saturday, he'd been forced to pony up a dime to the little bastard just to assure his shut-upness. Already he'd given the boy at least half a dollar. . . .

Wendall counted fifty cents into the jar—and plinked off two additional dimes just for good measure.

At this point the doctor came into mind. Two dollars was a lot to spend on anyone, and besides, if he was going to give his grandfather cigarettes as planned, well, two packs more or less didn't make a whale of a lot of difference.

He counted Cornelia's fifty cents into the jar.

That left John T. and Sybil to reckon with. John T. had been sour grapes ever since the incident in the diner; in fact, he'd been downright hostile at times, always accusing Wendall—if not with his voice, at least with his eyes—of having withheld information from the sheriff. To be truthful, John T. had been just plain cold, and you could bet your bottom dollar he wasn't going to shell out for Wendall, probably wouldn't give him anything at all, so why heap money

—a lot or a little—on a gift for him? It was one thing if someone liked you; but if he hated you—

Wendal added seventy cents to the jar.

For a while, then, he turned Sybil over in his mind. He sensed that between them there was a bond: they both had keys to the secret of the train man—he knew his aunt had had contact with him in one way or another, though she'd never said anything, of course. And he could tell something was going to happen. If you'd put it to him he wouldn't for the life of him have been able to say what, but he had a feeling—

No matter how you looked at it then, he and Sybil were kindred spirits. Yet, having taken fifty cents off the doctor's sum, it would hardly be fair to leave hers intact. For being head of the family simply entitled his grandfather to the best, or something equal to the best, no way around it. So what could he do but lop fifty cents off the amount he planned to spend on Sybil? That was not only fair—it was right and moral.

How fascinating: already he'd saved over four dollars!

Highly pleased with himself, Wendall rehid the jar, stuffed the gift money in his pocket, and headed downtown.

Still and all, he thought, squeezing the money in his pocket: six dollars is a lot to throw away just like that. . . .

. . . and by the time he reached the Svenson house he knew everyone in the family hated him. Their respective eyes had followed him down the street, sending cartoon dots and knives into his back; their faces bobbed around him like fierce balloons, lips snarling; every look they'd cast at him during the past two months suddenly became loaded with hidden dastardly meaning. And as he went by the Svensons', their voices even came into play. Cornelia nagged; John T. spoke in curt surly sentences; the doctor was vague, never sincere, his jokes were in bad taste; Sybil was pious in order to make him feel guilty for not saying his prayers often enough; Bernie Aja's silence was sullen, unpleasant; and Tom's nasal twang thumped irritatingly against his eardrums, filling his head with cocky growls, belches, and idiotic floop sounds.

It wasn't hard, being thus beset upon by the chorus of their nasty voices, to come to the decision that they could all go soak their heads as far as he was concerned. Let them give each other gifts: he'd save his money for something worthwhile.

Guilt came and nudged him gently; he relented a little. It wouldn't be right to just pull the rug out like that. After all, he owed them at least a token. Even if they planned to give him nothing—

Christmas morning crystallized out of the blur behind his eyes. Wendall, his arms loaded with pretty packages, traipsed into the living room. The family, shocked, halted their unwrapping. In a silence fat with embarrassment, Wendall solemnly distributed his gifts. A watch and a sport coat for the doctor; a mink stole for Cornelia; canvases and paints galore for Sybil, an entire cowboy outfit for Tom; an electric sander for Bernie Aja; and out in the driveway, a motorcycle for John T. Then Wendall took a chair in the background where he sat stoically with folded arms, a martyr's smile carved on his lips, as they were forced to face the horrible fact that they'd gotten nothing for him. The scene was poignant enough to bring tears from even the most hardened of eyes. . . .

Floating past the sport and news shop, Wendall happened to glance in, and was brought out of his reverie by the sight of Jim, his head, like a stormy moon, absorbed and frowning over the paper world of sports.

Wendall felt a twinge—now there sat somebody desperately in need of a Christmas present. But who did he have to brighten the end of his year? A heart-wrenching tableau came to mind: Jim, wearing a Santa Claus costume, was stretched out on his bed, the mitt on his left hand, tossing a softball up and catching it. Over the radio came Christmas bells and choral voices singing "Hallelujah," and in between Hallelujahs, a jolly fat voice ho-ho-ho'd, and never in the history of the world was a man more forgotten, more forlorn, more alone, than Jim at this moment.

Then there came a noise, a gentle tap on the door. Jim sat up, frowning, turned down the radio and took off his baseball mitt, and lay the ball carefully in the center of his pillow. Slowly he stood up, the bed-springs squeaking in relief; he went to the door and opened it wide.

The angel Wendall—his aureole blazing, a white linen cloth wrapped around his athletic limbs—stood on the threshold, bearing a gift wrapped in powder-blue paper. He bowed low and handed the gift to Jim, who took it gingerly, bowing back. "Merry Christmas," said Wendall, smiling piously, and before Jim could reply he had turned and airily descended the stairs. . . .

Someone had nodded to him and said Hello. Turning around Wendall spied the hunched and hurrying figure of Marty Haldenstein already half a block away.

He took a step forward, wanting to run and catch up with the librarian and apologize for not having said Hello back. But he hesitated: what was the use? What did Marty care for his greetings? They were all washed up, there was nothing more between them.

Maybe if I gave *him* something for Christmas, the boy thought. Again the angel Wendall drifted onto the inner scene. Coated in dazzle, he knocked on Marty's door. There was no answer. He tried the doorknob and found it locked. Leaning over, he kissed the knob—and then it turned easily, allowing him access to the room. But Marty wasn't there. After searching everywhere he was drawn to the open window. Snow was falling; some had already blown in and accumulated on the window seat. He kneeled, peering down into the yard, and discovered Marty asleep in the hammock. No breeze molested the snowfall, the ground was white, and Marty himself wore a cloak of small dry flakes. Little clouds of vapor clung around his face. Wendall gave a loving flick of the package he held, and the gift twirled lazily down through the air, settling on Marty's stomach as gently as a butterfly. . . .

He came to his senses in Gruber's Five and Dime. Up one row, down another he went, handling things, resisting the temptation to slide them in his pockets, putting them back—

He drew up short. The store was pretty deserted; only a couple of salegirls opposed him. If he were fast, clever, and above all nonchalant, just think of all the money he could save. And it wasn't as if he were a tenderfoot. . . .

Eyes dimming with suave shiftiness, heart quickening a beat, Wendall "Pretty Boy" Oler pussyfooted down an aisle to the cosmetic counter and with a quick twitch of his agile wrist took care of both Cornelia's and Sybil's presents. The bottles of perfume snuggled deep in his ample pockets, his lips pursed and whistling a casual tune, he sidled two aisles leftward to the toy counter, and in no time a box of crayons, a mouse that squeaked, and a set of jacks joined the perfume.

Wendall hesitated; he looked this way and that way; he flexed his fingers and his innocent smile. The coast was clear. Deftly, his finger curled around the bowl of a pipe, and he tingled all over, thinking what pleasure Bernie Aja would derive out of that.

There remained but the doctor and John T. to go. A coiled tape measure fell pray to his wandering gaze: John T. was constantly involved in precise things, so why not?

That left only his grandfather. His eyes narrowed. The way to the door was clear. No blue uniforms in sight. His upper lip sneered slightly, baring a spot of bright fang; his fingers zipped confidently through the air and pounced on a pretty paperweight, swallowing it in an instant.

And his pockets were loaded; he had to walk carefully so as not to set things clinking.

On his way up front he passed the pet counter, and halted in front of some goldfish. He watched them swim around for a while, and was soon drawn to them: he wanted one for himself. He could keep it up in the attic, hidden away from everyone. It thrilled him to think of himself up there in that dim silence, lying on his stomach, watching his fish swim about, twitching its tail and grimacing its little mouth, way up there with only the dust and the moths for company.

But if the fish could give him such a thrill, think what they could do for Jim and Marty. He pondered this, became convinced, and soon he had to buy some for them. A fish could take the keen edge off loneliness, a fish could be a companion, something alive that both Jim and Marty might talk to on Christmas, a fish was something that depended on you, you could love it, and it would love you in return.

Five minutes later he walked out of the store carrying two small bowls containing one fish apiece, and they had cost him a total of one dollar and eighty cents.

On the way home, the thrill of his free catch and ultimate purchase suddenly wore off, and by the time he arrived at the Coolidge Street bridge his acquisitions and the manner of obtaining them had made him downright mournful. Setting the two fishbowls on the bridge railing, he gazed into the water and hated himself.

What had gotten into him? How could he have so misconstrued the spirit of giving? The shame, if he wrapped those things and actually doled them out as presents, would be almost unbearable.

That made him mad. In the old days he'd stolen with impunity: everything he'd ever given to Helen and Fred had been stolen. And it sure hadn't bothered him then. It had delighted him when they'd thanked him for the gifts. It had elated him to be such a con man. And they'd never even vaguely suspected him of stealing—or, suddenly, had they?

The river was only frozen over in still places near either bank. Lifting one of the bowls, Wendall upturned it. Like a gold coin, the fish sparkled for a moment in its bubbling sheet of water, then entered the dark river currents with scarcely a splash and disappeared. Wendall dropped the bowl in after it and gave the other fish its similar freedom. Angrily, he winged the remaining bowl off to the side so that it struck against a glazed rock in the frozen bank mud and shattered.

Then, cruelly and swiftly, he emptied his pockets, hurling each item with all his might at the water below. The perfume, crayons, jacks, and paperweight sank right away: the tape measure unraveled and was carried to shore; the mouse and the pipe stayed in midstream, gathered momentum, and were soon carried around the bend out of sight.

THIRTY-FOUR

On Christmas Eve, Cornelia served a light supper of tomato soup and sandwiches late, because the doctor had taken longer than expected to make some calls. Minus Bernie Aja who had eaten earlier and gone to a movie, the family sat down at the dining room table and attacked their soup.

"Well," said Cornelia over the din of masculine slurps, "Who's sick now?"

"Oh, lots of people," said the doctor. "Christmas fever, nothing serious. On the way back I stopped in at Oaklands'; three out of their five kids have German measels. I'd call that downright unpatriotic."

John T. said, "Biological warfare: I saw a U-boat in the river yesterday morning."

Cornelia said, "Who are the Oaklands?"

"Prescott family. Missus works in the factory, husband's in the service, New London, I think. Nice family of kids, every one of 'em. Sassy as frogs and peppy as the devil."

"They're poor, aren't they?" said Cornelia.

"Well, yes, I guess they are poor."

"Are you going to send them a bill?"

"Hey!" interrupted John T. "Christmas Eve, remember?"

"I only want to know, can they pay for your father's visit, that's all," Cornelia said, her voice rising.

"Well, my gosh, what's there to pay for?" said the doctor. "Just a quick stop on my way home, hardly five minutes, to check on some little sick feller."

"Are you going to send them a bill?" Cornelia insisted.

"Gosh, I don't see what for," said the doctor. "It's a pleasure to do something for folks in straits like—"

"Like who, like us?" Cornelia fixed her hands on the arms of the chair and leaned forward. "Who keeps our creditors from the door? Where's our Doctor Oler, our angel who pays all our bills, puts gas in our car, pays the food and electric bills . . . where's that angel, Frederick? We've got things of our own to pay, we've got a loan, insurance, a mortgage . . . how long are they going to wait—forever? We've got mouths, one, two, three, four, five, six mouths, our *own* mouths to feed. Frederick, we can't afford to be soft with the Oaklands, with that kind of people in this town, we've got . . . we've got troubles enough of our own. . . ."

She signaled the apologetic end of her short tirade with a flimsy shake of her hand.

At her first word, Wendall had poked his fingers in his ears and tried not to hear what she said, but he had heard, of course, and every word had jolted him like a punch. His head burst into flame as word after word battered home, his heart swelled and screamed for silence, and when he could bear it no longer, he shouted, "Stop it, dammit!" his words coming in unison with John T.'s anguished, "Christmas Eve, for Crissakes!"

"Well, well *sure* I'll send them a bill, of course I will, you don't need to worry about that," said the doctor. He winked nervously at Wendall. "Old granny's a goin' tonight, ain't she?" Cornelia got up, and when she came around to clear the doctor's empty bowl, he gave her an awkward pat on the fanny, saying, "Yessir, must be them detmoles . . ."

"Oh, yessir," she said wearily. "Those detmoles . . ."

"I—can't—stand—it," said John T., bringing his closed fists slowly onto the table.

Dinner over, there remained nothing more to do than decorate the tree, hang up the stockings, sing a few carols, and go to bed. The family filed into the living room and went to work. Silently they wound strings of popcorn and cranberries and cut-out stars around the tree. On the branches they balanced gingerbread men. Painted eggshells and pine cones took their places with the stars. An angel, of white cotton and limp cloth wings with the golden top of a tin can for a halo, adorned the tip of the tree.

Everyone drew in a breath and exclaimed how beautiful it was. Then, amid the usual ribbing concerning the coal lumps Santa Claus would put in them, the stockings were hung.

Carol singing came next. John T. took it upon himself to lead the group. They got no farther than the first verse of "Silent Night," however, because Sybil, who for some time had been staring fixedly at the Christmas tree, began to cry. Strange large tears welled unchecked from her eyes; the singing faltered and petered out.

"I was eleven when I made that angel," Sybil said.

"Lord love a duck," said the doctor uneasily. "Was it that long ago? Time goes so fast it makes your ears whistle."

Sybil looked straight at her father. "Freddy helped me to make it."

Standing, she smoothed the wrinkles out of her dress. As both the doctor and John T. arose, she said, "I don't know what's hit me. I feel like going upstairs and committing suicide. Why do I feel so God damn desolate?"

John T. touched her shoulder. "Take it easy, Sibs; take it easy, gal."

The doctor said, "No, honey . . ." He took her in his arms. She sobbed, and the doctor's nose expanded and grew very red as if it were about to explode. "Everything is going to be all right," he said, "so don't you worry about a thing."

"Let's everyone sing now," said Cornelia, her voice strident with woe. And she sang, "Silent night, holy night . . ."

Sybil pushed out of her father's arms and said, "I hate this Christmas, I can't help it, but I hate it."

" . . . all is calm, all is bright . . ."

John T. led his sister from the room, and the doctor followed close on their heels. Cornelia brought the first verse to a limping finish and had not the heart to go on. She stood up and all she could think to say was, "Well; well, well . . ." Her eyes flicked around, searching for something to latch onto. She eventually bustled from the room, leaving Tom and Wendall to finish celebrating Christmas Eve by themselves.

Some carolers arrived outside. The boys went onto the front porch to hear them. Out of the group of ten or so, Wendall recognized only Ercel Perry. While they were singing "Little Town of Bethlehem," Bernie Aja turned off Prescott and stopped on the sidewalk near the driveway, afraid to come on farther for fear of interrupting. Well muffled up in coat, hat and mittens, only a patch of his face shone out. Wendall remembered his story about night-flying the mail through the '27 flood, and how he'd almost been frozen to death. The boy could imagine Bernie's plane winging through the cold night in a mute and irrevocable silence, stars from the Bethlehem song going by the plane's wing tips, the stars gathering speed, the stars twirling by like diamond flakes as the snowy earth came closer and the lure of other places was being frozen out of Bernie Aja, his wings so iced and heavy and beautiful, dragging him forever downward with their weight. . . .

As the carolers were leaving, Ercel gave Wendall a small red-ribboned package to be put under the Christmas tree for John T.

"Something real original," she whispered in his ear;

"a tie clip. Tell him I'll stop by at eleven-thirty to meet him for the midnight service."

The group trudged on to another house, and, with Bernie Aja, Tom and Wendall went inside where Cornelia took them in tow and put them hastily to bed.

Once everyone had cleared out of the room, Sybil lay on her bed and grew calm. Outside the window she could see stars in the black sky shining cleanly like holes punched through a dark drawing paper. The room seemed stuffy, so she got up and opened the window: carolers' voices, lifted softly into the night, came through the aperture. She smiled, and the despair that a moment ago had caused her to upset the evening drained away. She breathed deeply, raised the window higher, and was swathed in cold air and fantastic starlight. Words—Milton's—came to mind, and she repeated them aloud:

"But peaceful was the night
Wherein the Prince of light
His reign of peace upon the earth began . . ."

Sybil knelt by her bed and prayed. She prayed for David and John T., for Duffy, for Fred and her child and parents. She prayed for Wendall; she said the Lord's Prayer. She prayed for ghosts, for soldiers, for starving people, for dying people, and for Bernie Aja. She rubbed her head on the quilt and moved her lips, saying as she had when but a little girl: "God bless Mummy and Daddy and Grandma and Grandpa and Freddy and Johnny and me, me, me . . ." She smiled and, hearing John T.'s squeaky little-boy's voice and Freddy's deeper voice canting with her, said reverently: "Now I lay me down to sleep, a bag of peanuts at my feet; if in the morn I should not wake, I'll go to heaven with a bellyache. . . ."

At the end of an hour she turned on a light and dressed for church. She dragged her gifts out of hiding, went downstairs, apologized for her outburst, kissed her mother and father and bit John T.'s ears, helped stuff full the stockings, and afterwards went to the midnight service with her parents, brother, and Ercel Perry.

When the service was over, and having told her parents she would walk home later, Sybil kneeled on her prayer stool listening to Marty Haldenstein's quiet organ music, her eyes fixed on the candle shadows that rippled over small stained-glass windows built high in the wall over the altar. She heard several people—the minister, an acolyte—stirring about the church, some lights went out, others were dimmed, and with a final sighing note, Marty brought his music to an end. Sybil watched him close up the organ for the night; there were clicks as he snapped off buttons and pushed in stops, a subdued bang when he lowered the wooden keyboard cover. In exiting down a side aisle, he caught sight of her.

She smiled: he nodded and motioned to her with his hand. Puzzled, she arose and walked up the main aisle, meeting him at the door.

"I don't know if it is propitious for me to tell you this," Marty began, speaking low and very rapidly, "but I feel I ought to. I saw you that day with Duffy Kahler. Oh, don't look alarmed, I have said nothing. I am much too restrained for that. But I followed him to where he lives: do you know where that is?"

"No, I honestly don't."

"Would you like me to take you there? It is not so very far from here. I have often wondered if I should have told you. But I was unable to act, I did not know . . ."

"Please take me there. I want to go right now."

They went by way of the narrow trail behind the Miss Stebbensville. The snowy path was uneven and lumpy, the footing difficult: once Marty lost his balance and, had it not been for Sybil's quick support, he might have fallen. He coughed a long time, each gasping breath he had to draw in after every convulsion setting off an even more painful one. They crossed Liberty Street and followed another footpath across the lot to where it ended at the wisps of brush marking the far boundary of the field. There they rested a minute; Sybil blew on her hands; the grain elevator cast a fiery cold shadow on them. Marty coughed and spit into a handkerchief, then led Sybil to the parking lot. They had to climb over a snowbank to get onto the plowed area.

"He's in there," said Marty.

The warped boards of the station were a scarred gravestone color. Sybil could not believe, if Duffy were inside, that he was anything but a corpse in this cold.

They traversed the lot: the inch or so of packed snow under their feet squeaked when they walked on it as if made of a pliable plastic material.

At the station Marty whispered, "Be careful, now. We'll go to the window."

He led her along the wall to the window nearest the tracks. With his mittened hand he rubbed a small clear spot in the gritty pane and looked inside. Sybil waited, fearing Duffy would not be there, fearing he might be dead. She faced across Main Street to the cold silver-studded window of the hardware store, then shifted her gaze to the thin lead wandering of the train tracks, following them into the dark hills, the frozen mountains beyond.

"He is there," said Marty. "He seems to be sleeping."

Cupping her face to cut out reflections, Sybil peered in through the spot Marty had rubbed clear. Thick dust on the other side of the pane considerably cut her view. Dimly she could make out shadows, and as her eyes grew accustomed to the darkness, these shapes took shape. She recognized cans and bottles, some magazines, a pair of boots, and the blocky shape of a trunk. Then her eye slanted to a near corner and encountered a shape that became a body. She raised her hands and pressed them against the cold glass.

"If I tapped and woke him and you were here he might be afraid," she said.

"I can leave if you would like."

"Is he frozen? Is he alive? It's been below zero

for weeks. Could he possibly have died? No one would ever know. How can I get in there?"

"I believe the door to the room is locked. But the walls, you may have noticed, do not rise all the way to the ceiling."

"Maybe I shouldn't disturb him at all. . . ."

"I saw him hit you, and I don't doubt it was he who struck your son. I would imagine he is sick, but I have not had the heart to reveal his whereabouts to the sheriff. Sometimes, though, I am inclined to believe that he could seriously hurt someone. The guilt would be a terrible thing to bear. But if I had turned him in it would have been an unpleasant thing to bear also. For months I have shared this burden at least with you that I know of."

Sybil leaned against the wall near the window and picked at a thread on the shoulder of the librarian's overcoat.

"Marty," she said gently, "has anything in your life ever turned out good?"

"Oh. Of course," he said, embarrassed. "I have nothing to complain about."

"Have you ever been loved?"

"Oh. Well. You know."

"I'm sorry. I'm sorry for all your suffering . . ."

"It doesn't matter."

She kissed him on the lips.

"Merry Christmas."

Wrenching away, Marty ran across the parking lot to Main Street. There he slowed and turned around, his face twisted with anguish; a second later his feet carried him out of sight.

Sybil leaned against the wall for a minute, weighing consequences, and decided she would have to see Duffy, she would have to touch him, make sure he was all right, let him know she—what? Loved him? Pitied him? Slowly, still mulling over the advisability of her plan, she went into the station. The enclosed area was colder than the outdoors: she pulled her collar up and fastened the top button.

She first tried the baggage room door and found it

locked. So she entered the men's room and climbed cautiously onto the sink, and pulled herself up, swinging a leg over the partition and attaining a precarious balance. She dared not suddenly drop in with him, because he might be startled, and, in his panic, attack her.

"Duffy," she said. "Duffy, wake up."

The first time she spoke the name, his eyes opened. Her face and hair swayed above him like an angel: he could not move; he had no idea who or what she was. He stared goggle-eyed; she was a vision, a dream.

"Duffy, may I come down? I want to, please."

He recognized her with that, jumped off the couch, and kicked over a can of coins, sending pieces of silver rolling across the floor. The noise, its sudden blast and ringing, cut Sybil loose: she rolled over and down, hung for one terrifying moment extended, her vulnerable back to him, then let herself drop to the floor. She spun around prepared to defend herself.

"I didn't come here to hurt you, Duffy. I don't even want to ask you questions. I just want to know if you're all right. That's all I care about. If you want I'll leave right away."

He crawled around the floor picking up his spilled money. Sybil sat on the foot of the autoseat.

"It's all right if I stay a little while, then?"

He came over to her feet to get the can and looked up at her, his face bleak as old snow.

"Why don't you say anything?" she asked.

He dropped a handful of coins into the can: "Did you come here because I hit the little boy?"

"No. I understand you didn't mean to. I don't care."

"Is he dead?"

"No. Of course not. You hardly scratched him. Didn't you know that?"

"I thought I killed him. I thought they would be looking for me more than ever. They're going to shoot me when they find me, aren't they?"

"No," she said, shaking her head and beginning to

cry. "No, no, no . . ." She shook her head, shut her eyes, and could not stop crying. Duffy knelt and unbuttoned her coat and felt her breasts, and began to cry himself. Nervously, ineptly, he forced her back onto his small couch and climbed onto her, pushing away the wings of her coat and sliding up her dress. He cried, and his wet face slipped over hers. Their lips touched and fell away. Sybil tried to help him, but he was uncoordinated, clothes kept getting in the way, he moaned softly and had a small orgasm, and with a feeble snarl hugged her to him, squeezing with all his might. She did not realize fully what had happened until she felt the wet material of his pants against her leg. For a minute she stared past his glittering cheek at her smooth thighs and small knees rising on either side of his hips, cradling him. Then, like a malevolent hand, the cold slid under her skirt and across her belly. She let her legs down, her teeth began to chatter.

"Let me up, Duffy."

He seemed not to hear.

"Let me up, please. I'm cold."

She was sorry for the way he must feel.

He made no move.

"I'm going to push you off, then."

She nudged her hands inward, twisted her wrists, and placed her palms flat against his chest. She pushed experimentally; he did not insist on holding her tightly to him. She shifted, sliding out from beneath him: he rolled over, off the couch, onto the floor. He crossed his arms, hugging himself, and, eyes open, lips set, faced the ceiling.

Sybil sat up, drawing the hem of her skirt down past her knees. She fitted her toes under his ribs and he remained still. Her blouse was open, he had clawed down her bra, one breast was exposed. She touched the nipple with her cold fingertips and was about to rearrange herself when his left hand, the broken one, rose; the fingers pushed her own hand aside. She allowed him to touch her, but would not look down. His breathing was still quick, hers had slowed. His touch failed to move her. It was feeble and inadequate, wanting, passive, helpless—a wounded gesture. And as she stared out the dusty window, she felt with deepest despair that the hand that touched her now was the hand of the world, and outside she saw the sky grow larger than a million lives, and it spread cold and dead, forlorn and star-bitten, it became too big for angels, it was empty, this sky, dark and all-crushing and Godless, silently freezing the earth with its bitter gleam. . . .

Gently she lifted his hand away and buttoned her blouse, her coat, and stood up. His eyes following her like blind wells, she walked around him, climbed onto the trunk, and, looking down from a great untouchable height, she felt her body flush once and for all in the zero air, then she pulled herself awkwardly over the partition.

Outside, she looked once more through the window, and, seeing Duffy stretched as before on the floor, tapped on the pane, whispering, "Get on the couch. Button up. You'll catch cold."

But he would not hear her: his face was blank with dreams.

THIRTY-FIVE

It was the end of a lovely afternoon: streetlamps had not yet gone on. It had only just stopped snowing, and a few large flakes, like lagging leaves, fell out of the sky where a certain forest blueness was focusing to let through the stars.

Wendall spied a figure gliding through the shadow at the corner of Main and Coolidge, and he knew the hour had come. Taking the dueling cane from the umbrella rack, he edged out the front door and walked down the slope of the lawn to a point equidistant with the porch and the river. Behind him the stalks of dead flowers in the garden formed an icicle fringe, and through this shone the candlelight glow of a few jack-o-lanterns.

The figure was John T. On the sidewalk even with Wendall he stopped, lifted his foot to the fence rail, and raised his hand in greeting, then grasped the railing with both hands, and his feet left the walk. He slowly ascended the air, his feet cleared the top of the railing, one of his hands let go as his body turned, and, back to Wendall, his other hand pushed off, but very slowly so that the boy could see his fingers begin to open and go straight and hesitate for a moment as if stuck to the metal before letting go. Falling, John T. revolved and landed lightly in the snow on his good leg, sending up opaque bubbles that rose and expanded and stayed a long time in the air.

The house door opened: other members of the family crossed the porch and headed serenely down the lawn to take up their places. Tom was in front, dressed in his pajamas; there was a serious look on his face and his red hair was not curly, but rather long, silken, and burnished-looking.

Behind him, dressed in a white nightgown, walked Sybil. She carried the goldfish bowl with the garnets in it. A light was shining through the bowl so that the color of the gems in a round spotlight skimmed over the snow ahead of her, to the right of Tom.

Cornelia followed her daughter. She was also dressed in her nightgown and had a silly turban thing wrapped around her head.

Next came the doctor. He wore a pointed gold cap on his head, and his nose was icy blue. A stethoscope hung around his neck, his arthritic hands were clasped over his stomach. All he had on was a pair of underpants and his dew-kicking slippers. Peering out from behind one of his hands was the purple centipedic head of a large appendix scar. Slung over one shoulder was a kind of crossbow contraption, and stashed in a quiver on his back were some asparagus forks.

Bernie Aja brought up the rear. His head, so bald

normally, was covered with curly white hair. Around his arms and legs he had tied evergreen boughs, so that he looked like the early men who tried to fly by tying feathers to their limbs before jumping off cliffs to their deaths.

They came down the lawn, marching sedately, their feet stirring up the snowy bubbles. The bubbles rose to about head height, expanded, and hung on the currentless air. Unlike soap bubbles, when they brushed against someone's head they did not break but merely floated off in another direction. The group made its way to where John T. was standing and formed a line like a choir, facing Wendall, John T. on one end, Bernie Aja on the other end.

They waited. In a few moments Jim climbed over the bank from the river and stood for a second in a cluster of frozen peony stalks. His mouth was clamped on a long cigar; he was dressed like the doctor, in only his shorts, and his huge stomach was also marked by a ragged appendix scar. On his left hand he wore a baseball mitt. Obviously embarrassed, he swung his pudgy arms forward and back a couple of times and took two awkward hops forward. A mass of bubbles flew up each time he landed, almost obscuring him. When they had cleared somewhat, he swung his arms forward and back again, and advanced another two hops. In this manner he proceeded to the group and assumed his place beside John T. Before the sweat bursting out of his facial pores could get much below his cheeks it froze, endowing his face with a white drippy beard like a candle.

There were yet a few people to come: one of them turned off Coolidge into the driveway, and off the driveway onto the lawn where his bicycle began to skid. The spokes glittered, seeming to twirl backwards, and when the bike fell, Jimmy Wiggen floated agilely off it, balancing Bernie Aja's Victory pumpkin on the back of one hand. He ran eagerly toward the assemblage and circled the group three times, but when no one paid the slightest attention to him, he slowed down, stopped, and dropped the pumpkin, disappearing for a minute in a colossal display of snow bubbles. Then he plunked himself down on the pumpkin and stuck out his tongue at Wendall. The tongue was instantly frozen, it turned purple, and Jimmy could no more withdraw it from the icy air than the man in the moon.

Mike Stenatto was suddenly standing behind Jimmy. Gently, he raised his hand and placed an ice cream dish upside down on the boy's head. As he did so, there was a movement at John T.'s feet, and Ercel Perry's head broke through the snow.

Now they were ready to begin.

Wendall withdrew the cane handle, displaying the sword. He held it in front of his nose, parallel to the ground. A feeling filled the air as if the world had drawn in a deep winter's breath and was holding it. The bubbles twirled lazily, weaving patterns on a plane inches above their heads. Wendall quivered the tip of the sword and the silence receded back beyond the limits of silence into zones of past history, into periods of magic lore, and an overpowering squeeze developed in the air, then all the mouths facing the boy opened and from every one there issued at first only a breathy sound, then the voices swelled and joined together in harmonious song . . . *Silent night, holy night* . . . and the people began to move, they began a slow-motion ramble over the snowy lawn, all eyes closed, all mouths open, and singing. Everyone moved except Ercel Perry, who was up to her neck in snow, and Jimmy Wiggen, who was stuck fast to the pumpkin . . . *All is calm, all is bright* . . . and Wendall no longer had to lead with his sword, so he walked among them, and they began to cry, and their faces took on beards of frozen tears in the shape of candle drippings. As Wendall drifted along he stabbed his sword into the bottom of a snow bubble, brought the bubble down, and slid it up the shaft almost to the handle; then he reached up and pricked another bubble and slid it up the shaft, and then another, so that by the time he sat down near Ercel Perry's head he had a whole shish kebab of bubbles . . . *Round yon Virgin, mother and child* . . . and he could feel his head getting heavy with the frozen tear beard, and more bubbles were rising everywhere as John T. and Cornelia and the doctor and Sybil and Tom and Jim and Mike Stenatto and Bernie Aja wandered around, crying and singing . . . *Holy infant, so tender and mild* . . . and pretty soon it was hard to see the people because of the bubbles, but they went on singing, and Wendall could hear Jim plunking his fist into the baseball glove every few seconds, and there was also the swishing of evergreen boughs tied to Bernie Aja's limbs, and before the bubbles closed over everything, Wendall had a last glimpse of Jimmy Wiggen, still seated on the pumpkin, his tongue frozen out, the ice cream dish upturned on his head . . . *Sleep in heavenly peace* . . . and then bubbles closed over him, everything became confused, and near Wendall, Ercel Perry stopped singing, and there was no more noise, no more bubbles, no more anything, just a forever and star-studded darkness, and Ercel opened her mouth, she nodded with her head, and Wendall followed her eyes to a figure perched on the far horizon and it was the train man, who was really Marty Haldenstein wearing a mask, and as this figure raised its hand in a funny futile gesture Wendall had seen somewhere before—a kind of unhappy, incomplete salute—the boy whispered, "Wait a minute; wait, I want to help you," and he reached out his arms to show he was sincere, to show he wanted to touch and hold and protect, and then he was alone and his grandparents and uncle and aunt and cousin and all the others were with the figure, all of their hands joined and walking in silhouette along the distant horizon as if along the blade of a dream, and he felt so hopelessly far away, he raised his sword and said, *"Alakadetmole; . . ."* but against whom? against what? they were so far away they were ant people, and then they walked right out of sight, and the void behind was stiff with a squeeze that threatened to crush in the boy until his heart slooped right out of his mouth, and although he wanted in the worst way to shout "I love you!" to the people who had just disappeared, the squeeze prevented him, it kept the words in his body where they seemed to grow and, like a fever, blister all his internal tissue, and he thought if he could not get the words out he would surely die, and he strained with all his might, but "I love you!" was trapped inside him, he could not push it out, he was suffocating, he could no longer move his arms, he no longer dared to open his mouth, he shut his eyes and felt they were forever closed. . . .

Wendall awoke—his eyes focused. Beside the bed stood Tom.

"Don't cry," he said, "You'll drown."

THIRTY-SIX

At five A.M. on New Year's morning, tired but no longer drunk after a night of partying, John T. and Sybil and Ercel Perry went skating on Bloody Pond.

They slipped, skidded, and tumbled around for half an hour, then sat on the edge of the pond gazing into the distance where soft splashes of silver gilded the crests of mountains rimming the valley. Above, stars glinted in a curious sharp way as the dark drifted westward and a cloth of worn gray emerged from the horizon and climbed to an apex above their heads, drawing out a green mist that lay like a false snow in the V's between mountains.

"1945," Sybil said moodily. "Everything's going to be all right."

"Yeah," said John T. "Everything's going to be fine."

Ercel said, "1945. Lord love a duck."

"That's right," said John T., smiling broadly. "Lord love a duck . . ."

"I wish Daddy and Mummy and Freddy were here," said Sybil. "If they could see how beautiful it is, they'd know things were going to be okay."

"Yeah . . ." John T. sleepily nuzzled his head against Ercel's neck.

Sybil got up and walked away from them. She wanted to descend and write the new year in the dust on Duffy's window; backwards it would have to be so he could read it from within. But not talk to him: could she ever again talk to him? touch him? was it possible to help him, ever? or help anybody, ever?

The green mist came down out of the mountains and was broken by a chill wind into many thin streams of haze that drifted into the white streets of Stebbinsville and soon lay about everywhere.

"Everything's going to be all right," Sybil said again, yet her voice was so thick with impending doom it gave her goose pimples.

A week later, John T. and the doctor had a fight.

When John T. sat down to supper, Cornelia immediately said, "If you had any more grease under those nails they'd be so heavy you wouldn't be able to lift your hands," and as usual John T. ignored her. But then the doctor said, "Better go clean up." He didn't look at his son, but kept his head bent as if ashamed. Surprised, John T. gave him a good long puzzled stare, then scraped back his chair, and said "Yes *sir,*" and went into the pantry to wash up. He came back and sullenly ate his dinner, and not much was said by anybody for the duration of the meal.

Afterwards the doctor went down cellar to where John T. was working on the jukebox and apologized.

"Things are a little tight," he said. "I just don't feel my old self."

"Things have always been a little tight," said John T. "Don't look at me."

"Oh, I don't blame you. You've pulled more than your share of weight with the team. I'm the first to realize that. I'm sorry I got grouchy up there. I don't want any detmoles to clog our rapport," he said trying to playfully squeeze his son's shoulder.

John T. backed away from his touch. "Our rapport," he said sarcastically. "That's a good one. If we ever had a rapport I'd like to eat my Goddam hat."

The doctor held up his hand feebly and shook his head.

"Oh, yeah," John T. charged bitterly. "Oh, we got a rapport that's polished as a Parisian whore, we really do, Pop. Why, we're so far away . . . why . . . we can't even *see* each other . . ."

The doctor's shoulders drooped first in shock, then further in defeat, and then he felt himself give way to stirrings of anger.

"Not even once have we ever talked together," John T. said. "It's all jokes and detmoles while I've been rotting away inside. Advice—Boy, I never got any from you. My good-natured Pop. Helps everybody. Save your life if you need it, but boy, you've never even tried with your own family, you never even came close to knowing me or Freddy or Sybil, you . . ."

The doctor drew himself up and his body became so cold that he could not imagine the sensation to be anything other than the final crippling manifestation of death, as fiercely he accused: "Well, John T., you sure don't know me either."

John T. lost control and began to cry. He blurted, "Oh, Jesus Christ!" and ran from the cellar.

As he awkwardly climbed the stairs to the pantry, the doctor recognized the truth in all John T. had said. His anguish declared: You have been a fool . . . but he already knew that; he'd known it for a hell of along time, really. He smiled, feeling lost and said aloud, "Judas-pries' . . . ." and then his head went empty, but his feet still carried him upward.

Of Sybil, John T. demanded: "How long does a kid have to humor his parents? Why don't we just walk the hell out of here?"

"What's a family for, then?" Sybil asked.

"It's for torment. It's for taking you and me and grinding us down little by little, year by year, until we're just shavings like in an oil pan. It's the big nag. Everybody has to love everybody. It doesn't make any difference if you like somebody or not, you've got family ties, you got to like them, it's a law."

"What will happen to Daddy?"

"He'll grow older; he'll die, for Chrissakes."

"Do you want to see him die?"

"I almost care . . ."

"I think I could take anything in the world except Daddy's death. If he dies before I do I think I'll kill myself."

"You're watching it," said John T. "It's been going on for a long time. And we've been going with him."

"I want him to be happy, Johnny. I want him to be old and happy; I want people to be kind to him as he has to them."

"Yeah, he's been great to us. God bless our happy home."

"Can't we do anything to help?"

"Sure. Hold each other's hand on the way to the graveyard." John T. said.

In a letter to Fred, Sybil wrote:

> . . . you are thousands of miles away from us, Freddy darling, and we love you but we don't think of you very often because we are so preoccupied with our own problems. Nobody knows really what is happening. Daddy's been his usual negligent self about collecting money and paying bills, but I shouldn't imagine we're any more in debt than we've been for the past twenty years. But the pinch is on, the emotional one, it's always been on, hasn't it? and I think Daddy's tired and burning out or something, and of course dear

Mummy doesn't know what's going on, she's trying to be so good and strong, we're all trying to be that way, but the more we try the more we miss each other, and I think we're all very decent people, but whatever is happening doesn't care that we're being good, it just lurks around without a name, and nobody understands it, nobody can even find it.

The war will be over soon, won't it? And will you come home to us? We need you here desperately, though I fear you would only be another person to love and be helplessly far away from. What's made us such individuals? What's kept us so far apart together for so many years? Mummy's always saying that in spite of the tension and everything we're a very "close-knit" family. Johnny says he wants to spit in her eye when he hears that. . . .

Don't get killed, Freddy darling. I pray for you continually, but I don't know if God hears me very well, as I imagine there must be a lot of people down on their knees with a lot of prayers for the ones they love right about now. Do you think there are interpreters up there, or does He understand all languages? Even Japanese? In any case, if you see a bullet coming, you better not trust in me, you better duck. . . .

One midnight the doctor got out of bed and dressed himself warmly. Cornelia awoke and asked him where he was going.

"Oh, just for a little drive," he said.

He backed out of the barn and turned around: Cornelia watched him from their unlighted window. He drove away.

Slowly, he cruised down deserted Main Street and waited a full five minutes at the stoplight, watching it switch from red to green to red again. He followed Main as far as the station, crossed the tracks, and made a U-turn, then entered the parking lot, inched softly around it, and drove back down Main, waiting another five minutes at the stoplight. It soothed him, the controlled changing of the lights; it dispersed some of the restlessness he felt.

He went left on Rutland, going by his office, pulled into the parking lot back of the Miss Stebbinsville, and went in for a cup of coffee. Years had passed since he'd been in a diner at that late hour. It was fun, everything smelled so good. Briskly he rubbed his hands and ordered a cup of coffee. The coffee tasted like the best that had ever been brewed, and the dim yellow atmosphere of the diner, its smells, its luxuriant sizzles, were something he had long ago forgotten. He drank up in loneliness, paid—tipping extravagantly—returned to the car, and drove home.

"Did you have a good time?" Cornelia asked.

"Yes, it's a nice night."

"Quiet."

"Yes, quiet."

His hands stiffened at his sides: he tried to wriggle them and couldn't. Four times he had to get up and go to the bathroom. At three o'clock he finally got to sleep.

THIRTY-SEVEN

Wendall decided he must do something for the family. The tail end of January filled him with the need to give. He wanted to make amends for his Christmas fiasco, and the itch to please his relatives began to torment him day and night.

Had he a million dollars he first would have bought a motorcycle for John T. In daydreams he often pictured himself steering the bike into the driveway, a big red ribbon tied to the handlebars. He rocked it back on its stand, then sauntered casually down to the cellar where John T. was hard at work on the jukebox.

Debonairly, he said, "Hello, Uncle John . . ."

"Can't you see I'm busy?"

"Oh, I just"—letting out a little air, not quite a sigh—"dropped in to let you know you might find something in the driveway if you looked."

"Yeah. A rock or something real exciting like that."

"Ah, well"—raising his eyebrows, letting out that faint sigh again—"you just might find something, that's all."

Condescendingly curious, John T. finally said, "Oh, I'll humor the kid just to get him off my back," and left the cellar. Wendall ran and hid in the cupola. From there he heard John T.'s delirious whoop; he watched his uncle run back into the cellar, then heard doors slamming all over the house as John T. yelled, "Where's Wendall? Oh, where oh where is that lovable kid?" and Wendall smiled loftily from his anonymous throne above the town—

What he struck upon at last was to give a picture to each member of the family. Not that he could draw or paint very well, but he could cut out images from magazines and paste them onto shirt cardboards in collage form, then put them in dime-store frames. This way the gifts, though amateurish, would at least be something that was of his own sweat and blood.

The doctor furnished him with plenty of shirt cardboards. Then he went through magazines and newspapers, ripping out pages that might be useful and storing the torn pages under his mattress. When he had enough pictures and had bought some glue and snitched a pair of Cornelia's scissors, he set to work making the collages.

He completed his grandfather's first: it was a hockey player shooting a flying pigeon at a big baseball mitt, superimposed on a black and white background made up of fans at college football games. Next, John T.'s had a fancy old touring car crashing head on into a motorcycle driven by a hippopotamus. Tom's was a big Santa Claus with a fishing rod in his hand and a butterfly at the end of the line coming out of a stream full of footballs, tomatoes and war bonds. Sybil's was a polar bear riding on a blimp over some white blossoming dogwood trees. Bernie Aja's was a mole with a flashlight tied to its back, the beam of which was aimed at a can of motor oil with a skunk on the label. And Cornelia's had four white doorjambs covered with fingerprints, and over them crawled a big brown centipede with a parachute opening out of its behind.

With crayons, Wendall colored in some of the blank areas, then snipped away at the cardboards until they fitted perfectly into the frames. He wrapped and marked the gifts, but then he was unaccountably ashamed of them, afraid they wouldn't be understood, and choosing to wait until the time was ripe, he hid them behind a trunk in an attic corner.

He worried himself sick, wanting to give away the collages. He dreamed a thousand times of each surprised and pleased face as hands all around the dinner table rumpled off the gray wrapping paper. He dreamed a thousand times that these simple gifts would save the family, boost it out of the doldrums and send it happily into spring—but the time for giving them never seemed to be ripe.

Wendall suffered, and every day he could see each and every one of the Oler household walking unsuspectingly farther away from his gifts. He writhed and sweated, but his hands were tied away from giving, and he wished someone would stumble across the packages quite by accident, but no one did.

So the days went by, and in the end, instead of doing something for the family, Wendall only contributed to its further discomfort by turning John T. against him at a moment when it seemed that for once they were all going to be loose and happy.

Church was just over. The doctor, Cornelia, and Bernie Aja went home in the Studebaker: the others —John T., Ercel Perry, Sybil, Wendall and Tom— returned by foot. That is, John T. and Ercel went by foot, hauling a toboggan on which the others were seated.

The streets were packed with several inches of good slick snow. Bending forward, the long towrope curled around their waists, John T. and Ercel broke into a run. They careened down Rutland Avenue, and, while trying to negotiate the turn onto Prescott, the toboggan slewed to the side, hit a lump, tipped up, and chucked its three passengers into a snowbank. They scrambled to their feet, but John T. and Ercel had already taken off hell bent for election, and they would have left their charges in the lurch had not Ercel slipped and fallen, taking John T. with her, so that by the time they could recover themselves, Tom, Sybil, and Wendall were smugly seated back on the waxed slats ordering their horses to get on the ball and pull again.

In the tenement area they entered shadow, then whizzed back into sunshine, and this time John T. and Ercel stepped deliberately aside. Holding the rope taut, they let the toboggan wing by. It spun out, the rear end crashed into a snowbank, sending Tom, Sybil, and Wendall skating another ten yards on their noses.

"Kill them!" bellowed Sybil. She jumped to her feet and rushed at John T. and Ercel, who, having unwound themselves, were making for the entrance to the Jubliee Café. When Sybil reached the Café, the enemy were already safely leaning against the other side of the glass door, their breath all but obscuring them in window frost. John T. rubbed a circle on the glass and squinched his lips, shooting buck teeth at his sister.

"All right for you—Get some snowballs—Wendall! Tomas!"

They scrambled to do her bidding, and in no time reported back, their arms loaded with projectiles.

"Okay. Let's all heave to."

The door, abandoned by the besieged, swung inward: off balance, the attackers stumbled forward.

Willie Bayle turned around with an empty French

fry basket in his hand. "Hey!" he cried. "Not in here!"

"Yeah," said John T., cringing beside Ercel in the one and only booth in the corner to the left of the door. "You heard what the man said, Sibs."

Both he and Ercel threw up their arms and ducked: the first snowball hit the window inches above John T.'s head, the second clipped the top of his head, the third splashed off Ercel's elbow, the fourth hit with a loud *clop* against the side of her head, and the fifth hit John T. dead in the chest as he heaved out of the booth and rushed at his sister. Tom, who still had one snowball his mother hadn't snatched from his arms, let fly in the direction of his onrushing uncle. The missile looped two feet over John T.'s head and descended on Willie Bayle's bald pate as he lifted up the wooden slab at the end of the counter on his way out to stop the nonsense.

John T. collided with Sybil and they fell squealing to the floor. "I'm gonna grind you into mincemeat!" John T. proclaimed, whereupon Tom, knowing a good rassle when he saw one, lowered his head, ran smack into his uncle's stomach, and almost succeeded in knocking him over backwards. Swept up by the hysteria of the moment, Wendall found the guts to leap into the pile-up. Even as he did so he felt Ercel's hand grab the hood of his parka, and, his glasses flying off, he hooked onto her arm, flexed his fabulous biceps of steel, and dragged her into the mess.

"I'll scalp you all! Out! Out, out!" shouted Willie Bayle. A fly swatter entered the fray. Wendall glimpsed daylight for a second and saw that the swatter handle disappeared into the owner's clenched fist. Then John T.'s boot scraped across the boy's face. His first reaction was to bite it, but when his teeth were nearly torn out by a buckle, he grabbed the boot and yanked. It came off quite easily, shoe and all. Then an altogether too golden opportunity to miss presented itself—his uncle's other boot.

"Hey," John T. said when he felt what Wendall had done. "Wait just a damn minute!"

Willie Bayle jerked Wendall out of the tangle. "You

come back here, you son of a gun!" called John T., rocking up. Wendall made for the door with both galoshes tucked under his arms. He pulled the door open, swivel-hipped nicely to avoid John T.'s desperate lunge, and pranced onto the sidewalk.

On his knees in the doorway, John T. threatened, "You come back here, boy!"

Wendall climbed over a snowbank, crossed the street, and thumbed his nose.

"I'll give you ten . . ." John T. stood up.

"Throw 'em in the river," crooned Sybil, cuffing her brother over the head with a mitten.

"Into the river with all of you," wailed Willie Bayle, giving Tom a light boot in the seat of his snowsuit. "Now clear out, the whole miserable lot, and close the damn door behind you!"

On ten, John T. hurled himself forward. Wendall had been anticipating as much. At his uncle's first move, he ran diagonally away from him toward the mouth of Chestnut Street. John T. scurried to cut him off, his face contorted in exaggerated pain at the clash of frozen snowstuff against his stocking feet.

Wendall made it by him and poured on the steam. Thirty yards down the street he angled off, dogged it over a snowbank onto the sidewalk, and stretched his arms, a boot in each hand, over the bridge railing. John T. halted: Ercel, Sybil, and Tom drew up behind him.

"One step closer and over they go," Wendall threatened. The river was frozen over except for one point some twenty yards downstream where rocks created a small open area.

"You wouldn't dare," said John T.

"I certainly would."

"You do and I'll throw you after them." The smile on John T.'s face grew tight. He hopped onto first one foot, then the other. "Okay," he said quietly. "Game's finished. Hand 'em over."

"No."

John T. took two steps forward. "Listen, don't be stupid—"

"You had better stop."

"Nope, not a chance."

"Okay for you, then—"

John T. was three yards away when Wendall heaved one boot with all his might. There was a hollow cracking noise as it struck and skidded over the snowy crust. It went straight into the open water and sank from sight.

The boy started to throw the other, then he couldn't. He dropped the boot on the sidewalk and retreated a few steps. John T. came forward and picked it up.

"Well it served you right," Wendall said. "I told you if you came a step nearer that's what I would do."

John T. slid his hand into the boot and yanked out the shoe. He put the shoe on the foot it fit, and the boot on the other foot. "Thanks one hell of a lot," he said.

"I don't care," Wendall said. "Your toes can freeze for all I care! And anyway, I warned you!"

But he did so horribly care, and without waiting for Sybil to give him his glasses, he ran away sobbing.

THIRTY-EIGHT

The first week in February a swindle occurred.

A man came to the house asking for Bernie Aja. A handsome blond fellow named Joe Morgan, he hailed from Buffalo, New York, but had only just been shipped back from Europe, and was on a two-week leave before heading for the West Coast and eventually an assignment in the Pacific. He said he had been in Jerry Aja's company, and he bore a letter from the boy to his father.

Bernie nervously opened the letter and began to read aloud. Jerry wrote that, being indisposed at the moment, he was dictating to a friend. But when Bernie came to the part where Jerry described his wounds, he fell silent; only his lips moved through to the completion of the letter. At the end he looked up and said, "He's in New York. He's goin' to lose a leg." Joe Morgan hung his head and swiped at the fringe of the rug with his foot.

"It's pretty bad, but he's takin' it like a real soldier, Mr. Aja," he said.

The letter requested two hundred fifty dollars that Jerry needed to pay off immediate hospital expenses. It also begged his father not to come down to the city; not until the operation had been successfully terminated, at least. It gave an address in the city, not a hospital, but the home of a friend where delivery would be quicker, then added that Joe Morgan could be trusted to carry the money back to New York if Bernie so desired.

Joe said he must leave for the city the following evening, and the doctor invited him to spend the night in the Coolidge Street house. Both Tom and Wendall cottoned to the soldier, for he had an infectious smile, a colorful way of talking once he warmed up, and the tales he told of the fighting he and Jerry had been through in Europe were authentic hair-raising sagas straight from the horse's mouth. Jerry, Joe said, was one of the best soldiers he had ever seen. He described in particular a patrol he had gone on with Jerry during a nighttime raid of a gasoline depot when the younger Aja had singlehandedly destroyed everything living and liquid that was Nazi in sight. From his wallet Joe then took out a snapshot of Jerry and his wife and gave it to Bernie, apologizing for not having remembered to give it to him right away. The handyman was at first stunned to learn his son had married, then overjoyed. Joe didn't know the wife's address, but he knew Jerry would get in touch with his father very shortly and bring him up to date.

Next morning, Bernie went to the bank and withdrew two hundred fifty dollars which he gave to Joe Morgan, and that evening the family put the soldier on the train, wished him all the luck in the world, and waved good-bye enthusiastically.

"That's what I call a pretty amusin' fellow," said the doctor.

"When is he gonna come back?" Tom asked eagerly.

Bernie Aja said nothing, but throughout the next few days he kept smiling at odd moments. He would be shoveling snow or mending something electrical, when of a sudden a good feeling would seize him and he would hum a forgotten air, light up a pipe, and puff it vigorously. At night he went to bed early as always, but he could never drop right into sleep as was his custom. Instead, he thought about Jerry, he reviewed the letter which he had read so many times he knew it by heart, he tried to imagine how Jerry's face would light up when Joe Morgan gave him the money. He couldn't wait for Jerry's next letter, and he hinted to the doctor and Cornelia that he might be asking for a week or so off soon so as to go to the city and see how his boy was recuperating. At noontimes he took to asking casually if there had been any mail other than catalogs for him that day. He carried the picture of Jerry and his wife around in his wallet, stopping often to have a look at it, and once he asked Wendall what he thought the girl's name might be. The boy suggested Elaine; Bernie said he guessed it was Ruth. "I might even be a granddaddy by now," he said. The thought tickled him pink and he felt fifty years younger.

At the end of a week's time Bernie received a letter, not from his son, but from the Federal Bureau of Invesitgation. It asked him if a soldier, masquerading under such and such an alias, had solicited a sum of money from him under false pretenses. The letter explained that this certain soldier, now on leave, had looted the tags and papers off the bodies of a dozen American comrades killed in action, and, on his return to the States, had looked up the families of these men, feeding each family a cock-and-bull story about money its son needed for fictional medical expenses. Minus their papers, the boys' deaths had never been reported by the War Department, of course. They were extremely sorry to break the news in this fashion. . . .

Surprisingly enough, after all was said and done, one hundred thirty dollars of Bernie Aja's money was returned.

Then there was an ice storm. It had rained, then temperatures dropped to below zero, driving became impossible, walking a chore, and many of the main power lines supplying town snapped. Rationing was lifted until the lines could be fixed: Kahler's and the other stores in town that dealt with perishable meats and dairy products had a heyday.

As did Tom and Wendall. School had been called off, and when the two boys weren't with the rest of the younger townfolk tackling Killer Hill with sleds and toboggans, they amused themselves gliding down the slope of the front lawn and seeing how near they could come to the river without actually falling in. As it turned out, had they been betting, Wendall would have lost. When he opened his eyes as much as he could, Tom was floating high above him framed in a hazy sun that rolled along the top of the embankment; six inches beneath him the river murmured; and fifteen yards away, overturned against the opposite embankment, lay his wrecked sled. He touched his nose, which was already incredibly puffed up, and let out a feeble whimper.

Thus, as school resumed after a two-day vacation, Wendall found himself confined to his bed, glowering at the world from beneath a warm blanket, his nose broken and his eyes as black as the Lone Ranger's mask.

Then, before breathing through his nasal passages had been comfortably reestablished, the boy came down with croup and was obliged to goop himself up with Vick's VapoRub, wrap a towel around his neck, and breathe in steam twenty-four hours a day.

Once the pain in his nose had gone away, however, he could not complain. His hours, though sweaty, were pleasant and ofttimes exciting. Despite having once declared that soap operas were "intellectual horse dung for ninnies," he suddenly found his ears trembling like poppies in the wind trying to pick up every melodramatic syllable of *Young Doctor Malone, Ma Perkins, Backstage Wife, Stella Dallas, Lorenzo Jones, Young Widder Brown, Terry and the Pirates, Dick Tracy, Just Plain Bill,* and *Front Page Farrell,* in that order.

And so he languished, pursuing and adding to his scrapbooks and drinking orange juice and Ovaltine while the radio babbled on. He was beginning to wonder how painful it would be to, say, chop off a pinkie so as to prolong his stay in the sack, when the formidable form of Cornelia presented itself in the doorway. "Up and off with you this morning, slugabed" is what she said, and back into the greasy grind of everyday living he trudged.

Sometimes during the long lunch hour recess, if the day were really cold or overcast, Wendall would go into the empty school auditorium with a book after his meal, and, taking a seat midway down the center aisle, he would read until the bell called him back to afternoon classes. One day he was thus entrenched and absorbed, when Jimmy Wiggen and a friend, Monroe Sickles, came down the aisle and stopped at his seat.

"Well, look who's here," Jimmy said.

Wendall closed his book and stared straight ahead at the stage.

"Don't talk much, does he?" observed Monroe.

Jimmy chucked Wendall under the chin: "He likes to fight, though, don't ya, Wendy-girl?"

Wendall pressed his lips firmly together, determined not to lose his temper or cry.

"Careful. Don't scare him too much," said Monroe. "Ya don't want him to crap in his pants."

"He's a girl," said Jimmy. "He's got a girl's name, and he talks high like a sissy."

"Aw, lookat him, he's gonna cry," said Monroe.

"You gonna cry?" Jimmy asked. "You gonna cry about the big fat punkin somebody busted all up?"

Wendall swallowed: his entire body was cradled in a hot blush.

"Talk or we'll kill ya," Jimmy said. He grabbed the boy's arm.

"Hey, I think he just farted," Monroe said. "I got nugies."

"Wait a minute. I'm the oldest, I got first nugies." Jimmie made a fist, one knuckle protruding, and jabbed Wendall's arm just below the shoulder ten times, then Monroe crowded eagerly in.

"Hey, how many ya give him?"

" 'Bout ten."

"I gotta double it then, cause I'm younger." Monroe slugged the boy twenty times in the same place. Tears came to Wendall's eyes, but he blinked them back and neither spoke nor made a move to defend himself.

"Let's take him backstage and murder him," Jimmy said, picking up Wendall's book. "Hey, lookat this. A smart book full of poems by Robert Frost. Ya like smart books, don't ya, Wendy-girl?" He ripped out several pages, crumpled them and bounced the wad off the boy's head. "C'mon, Monroe. Let's get him back there and murdered before he makes me sick."

Monroe prodded Wendall to his feet, and, twisting the boy's skinny arm behind his back, shoved him up the steps onto the stage. Off in a wing they pushed him into a bathroom and sat him down harshly on the toilet lid.

"I seen a light cord on the floor out there," Jimmy said. "Go get it."

Monroe came back swinging an electric extension cord. With a pocket knife, Jimmy cut the plastic plug off one end, then stripped the rubber insulation off a foot of the wire.

"We'll electrocute him to death, just like at Sing-Sing," Jimmy said. "Gimme ya hands, ya little crud."

Monroe jostled Wendall to his feet and jerked his hands behind his back. Jimmy wrapped the exposed end of the cord tightly around the boy's wrists.

"Okay. Fill up the sink."

His friend complied. Jimmy forced Wendall against

the bowl and dunked his hands in the water. Kneeling on the floor, Monroe held the plug near an outlet.

"Look," Jimmy said. "Look what he's doin'." Monroe advanced the plug near the socket, drew it back, then inched it teasingly forward again.

"Boy, is he ever gonna get fried," Jimmy said.

"I hate to be the one to do it." Monroe laughed.

"Nobody'll miss the little crud." Jimmy took some gum from his pocket and offered a stick to Wendall, waving it under the boy's nose. "Want some?" he asked. "Well, that's too bad, ya can't have any."

In the middle of their laughter over that, the first bell rang.

"Saved by the ding-dong," Jimmy said. "Why'n'tcha tie his legs, Monroe, then we'll blow. Leave him for the rats."

"Yeah." Monroe wrapped the cord around Wendall's ankles and tied a knot. Jimmy took off the boy's glasses, and, along with the book, threw them in the toilet. "Better pee a little to give it flavor," he said, and both he and Monroe relieved themselves.

Half an hour later a janitor discovered Wendall under the sink. After the man had untied him, the boy rolled up his sleeve and retrieved his glasses. Then he washed up and was sent to the principal, Dr. Cagnery, who quizzed him for fifteen minutes. Wendall explained that he and some friends had been playing and they had left him thinking he could get himself undone, that's all there was to it, When asked the names of his friends, Wendall said he didn't want to tell. The more Cagnery pumped him, the less the boy revealed.

For the next few days Cornelia hounded Wendall for information as to who had committed the heinous crime, but he would divulge nothing, and in due time the matter was forgotten. Then one day Jimmy Wiggen brushed up against Wendall on the playground and said, "Sorry we wrecked ya book," loping away before the boy could answer anything.

Wendall walked around the rest of that day emphatically elated.

* * *

At home, Wendall and Tom played war in Russia and the Alps, they had colossal battles with .75-millimeter snowballs, and each time Tom died and Wendall stood over him looking down at the brilliant scar on his forehead, he wished to hell it had been himself who had stayed behind in the Miss Stebbinsville that day instead of Tom.

The newspapers had long since stopped giving play to the red-haired attacker; he had been swallowed up by the winter, and folks conjectured he was most likely in another country by now. For a while, Wendall also forgot Duffy, but then, in the early weeks of February, he became quite conscious of the man again. For no particular reason he sensed that Duffy was back, or awakening preparatory to his return—

And then quite suddenly, Wendall met him again.

He went down cellar one afternoon to take a look at the jukebox. When he turned on the light at the foot of the stairs, he thought he heard something move. He could see there was no one in the main room, and he doubted very much that the jukebox had disturbed its metallic slumber, so he checked the coal and wood bins and found nothing, then surveyed the cubicle for the furnace and the room for storing natural vegetables, and lastly he opened the door to the perserve room.

There were four high rows of shelves in the room. At the end of one of these rows, in the low slanted light coming from the open door, Wendall spotted a pair of army boots, the edges wet, the blunt toes pointing straight at him. He couldn't see the rest of the man's body, but he could hear him breathing, waiting for him to make the first move.

"I found you," the boy said. "Where have you been?"

There was no response. Wendall wondered, did the man think that perhaps he was bluffing, that he really couldn't see him? Was his heart beating as fast as the hearts of the pigeons he and Tom used to carry downtown to the doctor? He almost wished for a stethoscope that he might walk across the room, stop on the edge of the shadow, and reach into the darkness and lay the end of the instrument on the man's chest. Was he wearing a shirt? Or was he bare-chested? And his skin —was it cold?

Wendall took half a step forward. Abruptly the atmosphere changed. The man's breathing quickened. His left boot moved nervously inward, the toe scraping over the floor with a faint sound, stopping when the boots were touching each other, pigeon-toed.

Then the horrible thought occurred to Wendall, what if there weren't any more of the man after the boots? What if above the line of light cast by the open door there was nothing, just the darkness, blankness, the wall?

He snapped out of it. One of the man's boots moved again. Wendall sensed he was going to act, and a chill ran down his spine. "I don't want to bother you," he said, backing up. "I want to be friends. I want to be helpful. Good-bye. . . ."

He tiptoed upstairs and waited a while, giving the man a chance to escape, then went down again, switched on the light in the preserve room, and found the only trace left was a damp spot on the floor at the end of the row.

That night Wendall had a nightmare about the boots at the edge of the darkness, everything black above them, and the possible real danger of Duffy woke him up and made his skin crawl. The man had gone away after hitting Tom, and now he was back as someone very different. . . .

The fact is—he wasn't there. Above those boots there was no man at all.

THIRTY-NINE

John T. drove the Studebaker into the park. Even with Bloody Pond, he swerved off the road, advancing about ten yards before the car bogged down in snow and stalled.

"Here we are," he said giddily, reaching under the seat for a flask of bourbon. He unscrewed the cap and took a bitter swig. Lights clashed across the windshield, his head swelled, but he licked his chops and said, "*Mmm*-boy! Is that ever good!"

Ercel shrunk against her door and stared moodily into the frostily lit town, the black hills beyond.

"Yessir," said John T., tugging off his boots and shoes and setting his feet on Ercel's lap. "Two months into another year, two months into another dollar. 1945. It's already been around too long. I want a new year, this one's worn out." He nodded emphatically. The windows frosted, enclosing them. What little warmth had been in the car seeped out.

"Like a touch?" John T. asked.

"No thank you."

"Tell me," he said. "What's a nice teetotaling wench like you doing with a bastard like me?"

She ignored him. Her breath came out measured; her pallid face clung darkly against the windowpane.

John T. lifted a foot and tried to sneak it under her arms. She pushed it down. He took another drink and didn't care about anything anymore.

"I got skates in back. I'm gonna finish this bottle and go skatin', that's what," he said.

"You go right ahead, I don't mind."

"You don't mind anything, do you? You can just wait and wait and wait and wait and wait, and wait some more. What talent. But what I'd like to know is: what are you waiting for?"

The metal of the car sucked up cold and aimed it from all sides at them: Ercel shivered. John T. missed his lips, spilling a little bourbon on the collar of his jacket.

"You shoud try some, it's good." He wiped his mouth, dizzily thinking the moment was really no good at all, it was lousy. But funny-lousy. Him sitting there with somebody he was supposed to love, his big feet in her lap, getting soused. Romantic as hell.

"Other people take off their clothes and lie together.

It keeps them warm," he said. "They make love, it keeps them warm, get it?"

Ercel laid her head against the window and stared through white frost and white snow at the empty center of the earth. She would wait until John T. had finished the bottle and gotten sick, then she would try to think of some way to get him home. Cold chiseled into a round spot on her forehead where it touched the window: she sat up straight and breathing deeply—her breath unfurled against the windshield, sweeping back over her like a wave of sea spray.

John T. tocked the bottom of the flask on the steering wheel. "Guess we're not goin' anywhere for a while. Might as well enjoy it."

He tried to wipe a hole in the windshield, but the newly formed ice wouldn't rub clear.

"Trapped," he giggled. "We've been digested by an iceberg."

That made him laugh. Ercel didn't react, so he ground his heel into her lap with a sharp movement. She knocked his foot onto the floor. He drank again. He hadn't believed it possible to go through a bottle as fast as he almost had. His buttocks molded themselves into the seat. He didn't want to move, ever. His guts were furry, his shoulders ached with a lovely pain, his face floated around the inside of the car like a beautiful white basketball in a tomb. Romeo and Juliet. Died in the snows of winter. Touched each other with hearts of glass. Hung in the air all naked like stars above the town while church bells tolled. Rolled over each other with skins of ice and made love in the air above the town. All below dreaming of sugarplums, stuffed full of resolutions; the dogs laid their wondrous big-eyed heads in the snow and were sore afraid of the two white bodies up there. And no ding-a-ling noise against the purple night, against the sky, against a pageantry of twinkling diamonds—they were the saddest little naked people in the whole fucking universe—

"I'm gonna go get Sibs," John T. said. "Sibs'll wanna drink with me, Sibs is okay. I love her, I really do.

You stay guard the chariot 'gainst the wolves. I'll bring you some skates, too. Freddy's old ones." He reached under the seat and brought up another flask which he tossed in her lap. "Keep that warm with your little handsy-wansies. Don't drink it all 'fore I get back. Ho ho."

He bumped the door open with his shoulder. "Start the car if you want, get a little warmth in now I'm gone if you want."

"Are you coming back?"

"John T. always returns to his little Island Of Security."

He capped his flask, shoved it into his coat pocket, and stamped away from the car. He chose to cross the pond, slipped and fell, got up, ran a few feet, and flung himself down, unheedful of how he landed. He skidded a few yards, uncontrolled, laughing. Getting up, he heard the car start and go into an idle. He couldn't see into the vehicle; exhaust rose behind it like a squirrel tail.

Gaining the road, he leaned forward and tried to leap down into the town. He floated for a tenth of a second, then struck his chin with great force against the ground. No more of that, he thought, slapping his jaw with his hand. But it had been so funny he had to laugh. Jump into town, indeed! How nuts could you get?

The Coolidge Street house was dark. He tiptoed onto the porch, inside, upstairs. The warmth of the house hurt him; he wanted to get Sybil quickly as possible and return to the outdoors. Breathing became difficult, his head wouldn't stay straight, his eyes refused to go where he aimed them, his stomach closed like a fist around a big apple of nausea. On top of that, his feet stung—he'd forgotten to put on his damn shoes!

Softly, he entered his sister's room, debated for a second on how best to wake her, then lost his balance and fell on her. She repressed a cry, recognizing his face the instant her eyes opened.

"Shh, Sibs. Getcha things on. Skating party. I'm all liquored up."

"Johnny . . ."

"Get dressed." He fumbled around, was aware of touching her breast, and mumbled "Scuse me." He fell, not as delicately as he might have wished, onto the floor. *"Shh-h-h . . ."* he said. "Bring your skates. Ercel's guarding the car in the park. Drove it off the road." He clamped a hand over his mouth to keep from haw-hawing over that one. When he thought he had himself in control, he said, "Got some detmoles in the—" and he was going to say "carburetor," but it was so funny he sprayed an unintelligible word out with an awkward muffled sound, and laughed internally so uproariously and so long his sides ached. Sybil dressed quickly, saying, "Hush, you'll wake up somebody," every few seconds, but by the time she knelt over him to say she was ready, he had got her laughing too, so that her cheeks were puffed from trying to contain herself. "H-h-how's your gizzard?" John T. managed to garble out, and Sybil just did say "Full of stones," when, sensing that they were both going to burst into hilarious screams, she pushed her lips against John T.'s to silence them both. All their laughter skimmed away in an instant, Sybil lifted her mouth back, aware that John T. had gotten an erection. She waited for just a second, feeling him grow against her, then he said, "Jesus, let's go," and they got up, both trembling.

"Jesus," said John T. again at the door: they tiptoed downstairs and started back.

"Maybe you want a drink?" John T. said, giving her the flask. She opened it, they halted while she drank. The liquor scorched her throat, bringing tears to her eyes. She wiped them and said, "Wow. Potent stuff."

They climbed higher, the blades to the white figure skates slung over Sybil's shoulder clinking from time to time. Twice more they drank before entering the park, so by the time the pond and the car came into view, Sybil was feeling somewhat mellow. At the edge of the pond they sat down to lace up, and John T. remembered he had forgotten to get Freddy's skates for Ercel. Tough luck on her: he went up to the car for his own skates and the other bottle of liquor. When he opened the door, the warmth made him feel sick again. Ercel, who had been lying curled on the seat, sat up.

"Gimme the other bottle," he said. "I forgot your skates. I'm sorry."

"Oh." She felt around on the seat and located the flask behind her.

"What's the matter, you didn't drink it all?"

"I suppose I should have."

John T. slammed the door and bolted down to the pond. Sybil stood up shakily. "Hit 'em!" John T. yelled, his fingers bending all over the place like flower stalks as he tried to pull tight his laces. Sybil glided onto the ice and skated slowly in a circle, her head streaking by gray clouds. Some lights in town went out; the few that remained were tiny and silver.

John T. cursed, fighting with his laces, and finally got them somewhat tightened. He stood up, stumbled; then his feet found wings. He gave a little hop and stroked strongly. Leaning forward, he was just executing a beautiful low-flying cut to the left when he collided with his sister and they both went down. Sybil sat a little ways from him, hands clasping her ankles, head tilted back, hair hanging down. John T. skidded the bottle over the ice to her. "I don't want any more," he said. "I've had it."

He got up and skated around the edge of the pond and his head cleared. Sybil skated behind him. She put her hands on his waist; he eased up—she pushed him. No lights, not even a streetlamp now shone below. A grave, John T. thought. Everything is a grave. "Oh hell and damnation," he said. "Fire and brimstone," he added.

First the blank black-eyed walls of tiny houses circled his head, then the car, a dark patch of pines, and the valley again, and the impenetrable hills bumping the distance.

And then, "Hey!" he shouted, breaking away from Sybil. He scrambled up the hill in his skates and opened the door on Ercel's side.

"Hey," he said. "Hey, hello!"

Ercel smiled at him.

"You got a blue nose," John T. said.

"Very blue," she answered.

"I love you," John T. said. "I love you!"

Ercel got out of the car and hugged him: they kissed and lost their heads in steamy breath and kissed again, and Ercel said, "This is what I wait for," and John T. felt like too big a baby to be crying, but he was, damn it all, and he couldn't stop.

FORTY

On Valentine's Day, Wendall received a card from Elaine Bergle. His heart tumbled so far the corns on his toes turned blood-red.

Elaine was nothing much to look at. She had freckles, a pug nose, dull eyes, a tight little mouth, a few spaces where teeth were missing, and a very weak chin. But her hair was something again: it was raven-black, alway glossy, and she wore pink and yellow ribbons in its like exotic butterflies.

Wendall fell with a tremendous thud heard only by himself, of course, and he became suitor extraordinary, one hundred percent dedicated to the panting pursuit of Miss Bergle.

He stole careful slanty-eyed, cross-eyed, and corner-eyed glances at her during classes, but not once did her small head turn toward his, not once did their eyes meet.

A recess came. Wendall followed Elaine down the hall, his features clothed with a nonchalance that could only be mistaken for terror. The girl stopped once at a drinking fountain and dabbled her lips in the weak jet. Wendall leaned against the wall ten yards away, planning how he would walk up behind her, just as if he were casually awaiting his turn at the fountain, and when she turned around he would smile, lower his eyelids a mite, and say, "How do you do, Elaine. I was so delighted to receive your card this morning. How thoughtful of you to think of me. You know, really, we must get together one of these afternoons for a drink at Hood's . . ."

Too late! Flouncing her ribbons, the object of his passion continued on down the hall, dragging him with her at the end of an invisible string. She descended the stairs and went out to the playground. It was a cold windy day; the sky was overcast; the air smelled of snow. Elaine walked over past the Junglegym and leaned with her back against the nearby fence, hands thrust deep into her overcoat pockets, her face darkened with a scowl. Wendall assumed a similarly inactive attitude near the drinking fountain on the other side of the playground, and waited to see what would happen.

Nothing happened. No one approached Elaine, no one yelled at her. Once a ball bounced near her and she started to lift a hand out of her pocket to retrieve it, then thought better and refrained. When the bell rang, she left her station and walked back inside, not even casting a furtive glance at Wendall as she went by him.

Love and pity swelled within the boy's breast. Oh, if only he could reach out and touch her, caress her, call her his little bunny rabbit, buy her things—

Buy her things!

"Courtin' a lassie, eh?" said the pimpled clerk in the RX store, handing over a huge box of Valentine chocolates which had been reduced to a dollar now that the big day was over.

"None of your business," Wendall snapped, fairly running from the store.

A moment later, even before he'd gotten as far as Perry Street, he recognized the plan to give her the chocolates for what it was: sheer, utter, and disastrously brash insanity.

Tom and Sybil were pleased yet puzzled about the chocolates: this did not deter them from downing the box in a gulp, however.

One day, two days went by: the farness of Elaine Bergle became increasingly wounding. Wendall thought if his love were not soon requited, he would perish in the abysmal flames of his own ferocious, almost mythical, ardor. In his dreams he took to riding the school bus with Elaine. Descending Killer Hill, the driver suddenly screamed, "My brakes! They're shot!" and, panic-stricken, he flung himself into the aisle, tears in his eyes—

At which point the angel Wendall reappears in our narrative. Swiftly he moved up the aisle, stern and calm. All around him kids—young ones, old ones, even high school ones are yelling and crying, as Death, in the lurid form of what will happen to this bus at the bottom of the hill, faces them squarely in their adolescent mugs. Unafraid, stepping scornfully over the prostrate form of the driver, Wendall slips easily behind the wheel. Trees, cars, and shocked pedestrians flash by outside. The smell of burning rubber fills the air. Using only one hand, Wendall takes control of the runaway bus. It bounces over the sidewalk, narrowly passes between two trees, and churns through somebody's flower garden. Then he guides it back on the road, shooting over the bridge, and slowing as it comes to the rise in Coolidge Street. Slowly our hero turns his head: directly our hero's steely blue eyes meet the eyes of our heroine, seated just across the aisle. The other kids are silent, desperately grateful, and, of course, absolutely awestricken at the iron nerves and winning way of this small boy, this Clark Kent of Stebbinsville. . . .

Actually, Elaine Bergle lived but a few blocks from the school, and she walked home at the end of every day. Wendall began to follow her, hoping, always hoping, for a freak meeting. Perhaps, when about halfway home, she would remember something she'd forgotten, turn around and, running back, bump full tilt into him. She'd raise her eyes, and, realizing who he was, give herself up fully to the Herculean support of his brawny arms. Then again—

But every day, regular as clockwork, Elaine made the short journey home without mishap. Day in, day out, it was the same. Wendall picked her up in the school yard and, following at a safe distance, trailed her home, and then stood for a minute or so on the sidewalk in front of her house, searching for her face in a window, but the face never showed, and, always a sadder but wiser man, he would reroute his dragging steps for home.

He remembered the story about Him and Clo Spinelli and he soon felt at one with Jim. When he entered the sport and news shop he regarded the fat man with a new compassion. Kindred spirits, they: and life, having spanked them with her fickle palm . . .

The time came (a week after all this had begun), when Wendall realized it was no use going on. His case was hopeless: his dreams were now filled with scenes that brought tears to his eyes. Here were Elaine and he, all dressed up in their finest, groomed and curried like two little fillies, sitting on the deserted steps of St. John's Church. Around them rice was scattered —there'd been a wedding. But now the street before them was deserted, everyone—everyone in town—was somewhere else, and evening, peaceful and rosy, was lowering out of the pastel sky, wetting the church grass with a yellow dew, and neither he nor Elaine spoke, they were both mute, withdrawn, thinking, thinking, but unable, in the end, in all the ends, to speak. . . .

And again, they were dressed in their same finest, this time in an autumn woods somewhere. They came to a long moss-covered log stretched across a small ravine. Wendall stepped onto it first, and, slowly, his arms outstretched for balance, began to cross. Elaine followed behind him. The forest was quiet; occasionally a leaf fell, taking its time, twirling and dying and leaving an autumn eddy in the air. Halfway across, Wendall looked up and discovered some people grouped in a semicircle around the far end of the log: Marty Haldenstein and Jim and B. J. Twine and the doctor and Irma Kahler and Sybil and the man on the train, and behind them were others, many others. They were waiting for him and Elaine to complete the crossing and set their feet in this new autumn land, where leaves fall languorously, always in a dream. . . .

And so in the end he gave up on Elaine. He actively ignored her for a while, and pretty soon he was no longer conscious of her, and shortly after that he forgot about her altogether.

Marty Haldenstein was in love with both Ercel Perry and Sybil Matthewson.

It was too stupid.

Ercel served him night after night, she was always kind to him, and he always caught a reflection in her eyes which seemed to spring from a source of sadness similiar to his own. And Sybil had kissed him on the lips—when, ever, had a girl kissed him on the lips?—and wished him a Merry Christmas.

That Merry Christmas echoed through his waking hours, through his dreams; it became his doomsday chant; choruses of black-robed Sybil Matthewsons and Ercel Perrys sang it to him, and he groveled before them, begging them to touch him, kiss him again . . . but they were stern and cold, now; their voices were like stone, their eyes backed him into chilly corners. And he coughed; he coughed long and painfully, trying for once and for all to upchuck his livingness, spit it out on the yellow comforter of his bed where he could watch that vile thing pulse once, pulse twice, and die.

There came a time, however, when he could wait no longer, and he determined to take care of things with his own hand. One evening he went to bed shortly after nine, but just a half hour later, unable to sleep and tormented by the pain racking his chest, he threw off the covers and drew on his clothes over his pajamas, and, cramming the CO2 pistol and the box of pellets into his coat pocket, he hurried outside.

The snow helped. It was coming down at a sharp slant, thick and protective, shifting with the wind, and it sucked the frantic last thoughts away from his brain, transposing his panic into a physical exterior turmoil and leaving his mind blank. Lowering his head against the storm, flakes stinging his cheeks and grabbing his hair, he started downhill, only to reverse himself after a brace of steps and head up to South Maple where he went right and ran for the park. The lit windows of houses, given a windy lace quality by the snow, fell behind him like soft flares as he plunged into the park.

He headed for the pines. There he would be able to die and lie undiscovered for days. He would be like a statue when at last they did find him, frozen and ethereal, unwarm to the core, bones brittle and brain shriveled to a dry pit, and his skin mercurially smooth.

But he collapsed before he got to the woods. He fought to his feet once, batting the snow away with his arms, yet it drove him back, it filled his mouth so he could hardly breathe, it rushed into his lungs—Marty fell, rose again, and, when next he fell, the snowflakes tumbled him around, and his hands clutched at solid ground to keep from rolling. . . .

He lay flat, gasping and blind. The storm beat at him; he crouched beneath it and worked the pistol out of his pocket. He took off his gloves; they were blown away. He fumbled with the gun, cursing and coughing; he spotted the overturned box of pellets right under his nose, but couldn't for a long time pick one up with his frozen fingers. At last he succeeded in pinching one and inserting it in the chamber, but it was backwards, so he banged the weapon upside down in his hand until the pellet fell out, and the next time he got it in right, closed the breech, and cocked the gun. He struggled to sit up, snow swept along the road spinning with great gyric wings around him and over him. Already he was numb, already he was in death's grasp being lifted—where? To what land? To what grave? His chest belched inside of him, the pain afraid and begging for another minute, one more fierce, all tormenting minute. His hair lifted off his head, sending silver fingers into the wind; his eyes were battered and blinking from the glare of a million minuscule flashbulbs; he felt the gun barrel stabbing in his cheek, and as he made to pull the trigger, a great pale moth swooped down out of the storm's turbulent nest, and he grabbed for its wings, and with a deep engulfing sob, he pulled tightly on the trigger. He heard a snap and felt a sting in his cheek, but it did not even tip him over. He waited for the burning bullet trail, like a comet, to go searing through his brain, drilling out his life, but no such thing happened. It stunned him beyond belief, five seconds after the fatal act, to realize that he had not killed himself.

He dropped the gun on the road. Jim's words, *sometimes they leak,* mocked him. How horrible! Way back in August had he not screwed the cap on tight when the CO2 cartridge went in? The gas had seeped out, there had been no force behind the pellet: it was impossible, preposterous. He stood up and swayed irresolutely.

It wasn't fair.

It was ghastly.

He moaned and ran back the way he had come.

He staggered into the boardinghouse, getting as far as the parlor, where he sank gratefully into an armchair. A fire was dying on the grate. He thought at first no one else was in the room—then he discovered B. J. Twine off to one side of the fireplace. The old man was asleep, cane grasped tightly in his mottled hands. His face, in this sleep, was like a late autumn apple fallen from the bough, half hidden in the grass, browning and withering as winter came on.

Marty thought: How long can the living go on living? He thought: I will go to him, I will kneel before him, I will ask him to give me his place—He touched his cheek; his fingers came away bloody. With a supreme effort he lunged out of the chair and raced upstairs to his room. Locking the door behind him, he went to the bathroom. His cheek, at the spot where the pellet had entered, was a little puffed and bleeding. He dropped his head in despair; something clinked into the washbowl and slid down the drain before his hand could catch it. Patting his cheek with his fingertips, he felt a hole, not even deep—hardly more than lacerated skin, in fact.

"Oh, no. Oh, no . . ." he whispered.

He washed, stuck on a Band-Aid, and exhausted, went to sleep.

FORTY-ONE

Wendall awoke knowing that Duffy Kahler was on the other side of the door. He slipped out of bed and stole softly to a corner across the room and crouched between Tom's bureau and the wall. The man opened the door and advanced over the threshold. A smell spread in the room—unwashed body, unwashed clothes.

He said, "Where are you? I don't want to hurt you."

He has a knife, Wendall thought.

"Where are you? I know this is your room. Where are you?"

Wendall whispered, "You go away."

"I can't see you . . ."

"I told you to go away."

"The door downstairs is locked," he said. "How come it's locked?"

He must be referring to Sybil's room: Wendall said nothing.

"It's locked," he repeated. "Did you lock it? Do you have the key? If you don't give me the key, I'll kill you."

"I said go away."

"You don't know what it's like. You've never seen it." He moved a little farther into the room. "You'll disintegrate, you'll fly apart, that's what. You don't want that, do you? Then give me the key to her room. I have to have it. Right now give me the key or I'll disintegrate you, I'm not kidding."

"Go away!"

"Oh, you don't like me, do you? Well, I don't care. If you give me the key, I'll leave the room, wouldn't you like that, for me to go away?" He was careful when he moved; he tested the floor ahead of him before taking a step. Did he think the boards were mined, did he think at the slightest pressure they would blow up?

"You go away, you bastard."

"I don't want to hurt you, believe me. I'd like to leave you, I really would. But first I have to have the key and if you don't give me the key—*where are you?"*

He inched forward and found Wendall's bed, and his hands patted up and down the quilt. He stopped and picked it up.

"Where are you?"

"What are you going to do?"

"Nothing." Silhouetted against the window, he held the pillow to his chest, rocking. "I don't want to do anything. I just want to see you. I'm cold. I'm so cold. Does the other little boy sleep with his mother downstairs? He's my little boy, did you know that? I didn't want to be his father—Do you think he's dead?"

Wendall said, "I have a sword and if you don't leave right now I'm going to kill you."

Duffy deserted the window's frame. The springs squeaked on Wendall's bed and released as he stumbled against it. Light momentarily sprang into the room, a strip of it fell over the bed, in it danced the giant distorted shadow of a man hugging a pillow to his chest, and as suddenly as it had come, the light shrank away from the bed and out the closing door. Duffy had gone, Wendall was alone.

He threw open the window. Rectangles of light from the second floor blazed out and fell onto the shiny old snow on the lawn. There were steps and muffled voices in other sections of the house. Directly below Wendall a window scraped up: the man emerged onto the roof of the front porch. Another rectangle of light, this time from Sybil's room, fell across the porch roof. The man blinked uncertainly in the brightness.

He still carried the pillow, which he raised to his face to ward off the light. Taking a step backwards, he lost his footing, one leg swung up, the other slid with the icy slope of the roof, a cry escaped his lips. For a split second his eyes sparkled; the back of his head slamming hard against the frozen coating on the roof sent a shower of icy sparks into the air as he disappeared from sight over the edge of the roof. Ice pebbles cascaded after him.

More light, this time from the first floor, spotted the driveway, extending onto the lawn. The front door banged open: footsteps clattered across the porch and down the carriage port steps. Wendall heard cursing—John T.'s. From directly beneath him came excited babbling—Cornelia was hard at it. The window to Sybil's room opened and his grandmother's head poked out.

"Have you got him, the monster?" she shrieked.

John T.'s voice came up angrily: "I got the bastard. He's half unconscious . . . bleeding . . . won't let go of the damn pillow . . . where the hell did he get that?"

"Frederick called the sheriff! I hope he's dead!" The window cracked shut, snapping icicles loose from the sill.

Then Wendall heard John T. say, *"Oh my God!"*

Neglecting to put on either slippers or a robe, he woke up Tom, and they barreled downstairs to the front porch.

Around the corner of Coolidge and Main raced Sheriff Flood's pickup truck, the lights swinging hectically from one side of the road to the other. He braked in front of the driveway and came around the back of the truck. Just as he placed a foot in the drive he halted, and his face went out of kilter. John T. was walking under the carriage port toward the sheriff. He had his arm around Duffy's shoulder, and Duffy made no resistance. He was bleeding from a cut on the temple and was still holding the pillow at his side. With a great pang of despair, Wendall sank back against the living room window. From the corner of his eye he saw Sybil leaning with her forehead against the half-open porch door: her eyes were closed, her lips moving, and as her stunned face blurred into miserable soft gray hues, Wendall realized she was crying.

Sheriff Flood gasped and said, "Duffy . . . Duffy Kahler?" and John T. nodded, and the sheriff stood there as if he'd been struck dumb on the spot while John T. and Duffy walked up to him.

"Duffy Kahler," he said again, shaking his head: he didn't understand. Then Duffy's legs went weak, and both John T. and the sheriff had to grab him. They strained to keep him up. His eyes were still open; his head lolled in the direction of the porch; he acted as if he were passed out. The sheriff and John T. walked him over to the truck and lifted him into the cab, and then because they couldn't push him any farther into it, they both went around to the other side and entered by the driver's door. In the confusion, the pillow had been shut in the door; half of it stuck out from the crack like a giant marshmallow.

Sheriff Flood shifted the truck into gear, backed up a little, and swung around in the street, heading up Coolidge. The truck crossed the bridge and turned right onto Main. Its taillights drifted out of sight.

The day after Duffy was apprehended, Hank Kahler did not go to work. He got up early for breakfast, then sat in the living room staring out a window at the bare crisp tree branches across the street. Irma spent some time in the morning with Duffy and the sheriff. She learned a little of her son's recent past—he gave out vague descriptions of wandering in Morocco after his plane was downed in flames, made short mention of Nazi bullets and a police bullet in his back, then told the frightening tale of his return to the United States and his commitment to a mental hospital from which he escaped, and finished with the sporadic details of his subsequent flight and fight for survival, after which he would say no more.

Irma came dejectedly home and fixed herself and her husband a light lunch. She didn't have the gumption to open the market, and so sat with Hank, staring bleakly out the window. They exchanged no words for the better part of an hour. Then Hank cleared his throat and said, "Well . . ." and Irma grunted in reply. Hank stood up, left the house, and went up to the Green. After looking at the memorial a few minutes, he turned heel and walked to the station. Already someone had thrown a rock through the baggage room window. He approached, looked inside at the mess for a few seconds, then crossed the railroad tracks heading east on 684. He hoofed it with a determined gait for about a mile, after which he began to hitchhike.

From a window Irma had watched him go to the Green. As soon as he walked out of her company she had known he wasn't coming back.

When the inquiries in Stebbinsville were over, Duffy was sent to the state hospital in Waterbury, and after a few weeks there he was transferred to a smaller institution downstate. Late in March he climbed over what hospital authorities called an "unscalable wall" and disappeared into the foothills. Again he was on the run. And heading slowly and unswervingly north.

FORTY-TWO

It was Palm Sunday and things were slow. His feet up on the desk in his office, Harry Garengelli was reading a comic book when he glanced up and saw Wendall standing in the open doorway. It looked as if he'd been stationed there quite some time.

"Evenin', Slugger," Harry said. "Didn't hear you."

Wendall swallowed, and nodded. "Evenin'," he said. Harry wondered if the boy were sick; he certainly had a pale tint to him.

"Come to take that motorcycle out for a spin?" he said, swinging his feet off the desk. He reached in his pocket, found a nickel and gave it to Wendall. "Here; fish yourself a Coke outta that machine."

Wendall stuck the coin in its slot, waited for the bottle to drop, then said, "As a matter of fact, it is about the motorcycle that I came to see you, Mr. Garengelli."

"Yessir, what about it'?'

"I want to buy it," Wendall said. He had to snap the head of the bottle four times under the opener before he got the cap off.

"Well, I'll be damned," Harry said softly. "You wanna buy it, huh? Well, I'll be really damned. . . ."

"All I have for a down payment is six dollars. It would take me a long time to pay, but in the end I would pay it all, I promise. And I thought that since you didn't use it at all, that you wouldn't mind the wait."

Harry frowned. "You can't ride that motorcycle. You're way too young for a license."

"Oh, it isn't for me," Wendall said hastily. "I don't care about driving it; I couldn't, of course."

Harry rubbed his chin. "John T. been pretty fidgety lately, that it?"

Wendall looked down and wiped the perspiration off his Coke.

"I see," Harry said. "So you aim to buy that blasted machine, huh? Well, I don't see why not. . . ."

Wendall raised his head quickly.

"I'm willing to pay whatever you paid for it, Mr. Garengelli. Later on this spring I plan to get jobs around town. Cutting lawns and that sort of thing, and helping Bernie Aja around our place, and I think that I'll be able to earn a good deal of money."

"I paid a hundred and a quarter for that hunk of tail pipe," Harry said.

"One hundred and twenty-five dollars?"

"The same."

"That's a lot all right." Wendall's skin went clammy and his stomach felt awful.

"I'm in no real hurry for money," Harry said.

"Could we work out some sort of deal?" Wendall hardly dared breathe.

"I don't see why not."

"You would trust me for the money?"

"You don't look like the sort of rascal welches on his debts," Harry said.

"How long would you give me to pay?"

Harry squinted and cast a long view out the dirty front window and across the street, giving himself the air of intense internal figuring. When he swung back to the boy he said, "I figure 1960's as good a year as any."

Wendall said, "I'll be twenty-seven."

"Will you now? I'll be damned."

"You'll be almost dead by then," Wendall said.

"Nobody will count me out before my time," Harry said.

"Don't you still think we should sign a paper—an agreement?"

"I'll take your word."

"What about payments? You know, monthly, weekly . . ."

"Let's say every Christmas you send old Harry eight bucks. Fair enough?"

"That's all?"

Harry scratched his ear thoughtfully. "One thing," he said. "When you gonna send somebody over for the bike?"

"Oh, don't worry about that: I'll take it with me."

"I see. Just, uh, ride it on down the block, that it?"

"I'll walk it. That's not hard."

"It ain't a mosquito you'll be walkin'."

"I think I can manage it all right. I've gained quite a lot of weight, you know."

"Suit yourself," Harry said. "Want me to back it out for you?"

"I *would* appreciate that—"

Harry clicked a nickel on the desk. "Help yourself it another pop while I'm about it. Won't take a minute."

Fresh drink in hand, Wendall walked outside and watched Harry back the Harley out past the grease pit. The boy's stomach dropped. The motorcycle looked like a locomotive. He sauntered over and patted the leather seat. "She looks okay," he said. "I guess I'll just take her from here."

"Sure I can't give you a hand?" Harry asked.

"No thanks. I'm all right."

"Okay. Glad to've been of service."

Wendall took hold of the handlebars and pressed his hip against the side of the Harley to keep it from flopping over.

"It don't tip 'til after the kickstand's up," Harry said. "Just give it a extra little shove forward and the stand'll flip up."

"Oh, sure. Well, I certainly do thank you, Mr. Garengelli . . ."

"Any time," Harry said, easing on back to his office.

Wendall pushed the Harley forward; the stand sprang up; the machine wobbled away, forcing him to tug ferociously toward himself to right it. Then, in somewhat tentative control, he inched out of the gas station and across the street.

In front of the Svenson place his luck ran out. One of the thick tires caught in a sidewalk cement heave and tipped the motorcycle over onto the boy. Unhurt, Wendall scrambled to his feet and tried to lift the bike, but he might just as well have tried lifting a mountain as that five hundred pounds of steel and chrome lying flat on its side before him like a lazy prize pig.

The boy sat down on the FOR SALE sign in the fringe of the lawn, and regarded the sparkling, but dead weight before him. He did not despair. Making the purchase had exhilarated him far too much for that. The whole thing was a fairy tale come true: John T. would have to worship him after this, no two ways about it.

So, in a mild state of ecstasy, Wendall waited for

someone to come by to help him right the motorcycle, and pretty soon that someone came by in the form of Joel Spender, and Joel was pretty drunk.

The garbageman assessed the situation even before Wendall asked his help and his heart leapt at the opportunity.

"Shoo, boy," he said. "I can uplift that thing with my little finger." He leaned over to grab the handlebars, lost his balance, went sprawling, and it was then Wendall began to have his doubts.

Joel hastily regathered his forces and brushed himself off. "Guess I can handle this bastard." He laughed, flexing his fingers a moment before pitching in again.

This time, grunting, cursing, and puffing, he coaxed the Harley right side up, but when Wendall moved to take over, Joel waved him back.

"Hold on a minute, boy," he said. "I got 'er up, I aim to get 'er started, too, if that's all right by you."

"I don't want it started," Wendall said.

"Well, she's gonna get started," Joel said, sitting astride the saddle. "Guess I know how to kick her up. Din't I ride one of these God damn things when I was a kid? I ain't no greenhorn, you mark me."

He pumped and kicked and pumped and kicked for five minutes, and just as Wendall thought with relief that he was going to give up, the engine turned over. Joel let out a whoop, twisted the gas on full, clicked " 'er" into gear, and popped the clutch.

The Harley bucked like a demon. Wendall flung himself onto the lawn as the big bike half turned, and, reared on the back tire, squealed up the Svensons' front walk. Joel kept the gas twisted on flat out, but he wasn't driving, he was clinging for dear life.

When the motorcycle's rear tire struck the bottom porch step, the front tire slammed down hard on the fourth step, and as the rear tire came up at the start of a first somersault, Joel left his precarious perch and sailed four feet out sideways, catching a porch post straight in his stomach so that his knees socked around one side of the pole, bammed into his mouth, and would have knocked out all his teeth had he owned any. The Harley landed backside down on the top step, then surged forward into another revolution and with a deafeningly dental crunch, imbedded itself in the front door.

The house quivered on impact: the front door trembled, and, after a few seconds—ripped entirely off its hinges—caved inward.

Joel stoppled off the porch and staggered zigazg across the lawn. He stalled momentarily in front of Wendall and slapped a dirty hand on the boy's shoulder.

"Haw, haw, haw," he roared. "Son of a bitch!"

Then he stopped laughing and peered at Wendall.

"Hey!" he said. "Hey, shoo, boy. What're you so mad about? That was *funny!*"

"What do you know about it?" Wendall said.

"Well, *hell!*" Joel spat, tossed his head, and, rubbing his jaw and guffawing sporadically, he wobbled chaotically away.

Wendall clenched his fists and walked dazedly back up Main Street to the gas station.

"I don't believe it," said John T., kicking the bent hulk of the motorcycle lying near the pumps at Garengelli's. "It absolutely defies the imagination, that's all."

"The kid wanted it for you," Harry said. "He was gonna pay me eight bucks for the next fifteen years. He was sincere about it."

John T. turned on him. "Sincere? You kidding me? He's the biggest little con man in the whole God damn world. *For me:* that has to be the biggest laugh of the season!"

"Well . . . okay." Harry wiped his nose and placed his foot on the crumpled tailpipe. "Let's lug this thing inside and shut up about it. . . ."

Early Easter morning, Chad and Tabby Spender showed up at the Coolidge Street house pulling a wagon. On the wagon sat a large crate, and in the crate were two white rabbits.

"We raise 'em out back," Chad said to Wendall and Tom. "We got lots so it don't hurt us none to give out these 'uns. Ma says it's a reterbution 'count of what Pa done and nothin' was never said of it. That female there's about to sling out a batch. Give a hand here, Tab."

Tabby helped him lift off the crate. They set it near the porch steps and quickly retreated from the scene.

Wendall looked at Tom. "I guess they're ours," he said. Kneeling, he stuck his finger in the cage and the bigger rabbit bit it. Wendall kicked the cage so hard it turned over, and the female rabbit let out a falsetto squeal that made both boys jump.

"I didn't know they made *noise!*" Tom exclaimed.

"I'm going to *torture* the bastards!" Wendall moaned, sucking on his bleeding finger.

"I won't have that animal in the house," Cornelia said.

"But it's about to *foal,*" Wendall said.

"I positively won't have it."

"It's raining out. The temperature couldn't be above thirty-five. In the barn the little rabbits will freeze to death."

"I told you I refuse to allow it."

"I suppose you just want to let them die?"

"They won't die. Animals are meant for the outdoors. That's where they belong."

"Then they'll all die," Wendall said. "And I hope you'll feel nice."

"I'll feel just fine," Cornelia said, "as long as they don't die in my house."

It didn't take "Sabertooth" (for so Tom christened her) very long to "sling out a batch." On Tuesday morning after Easter, Wendall went early to the barn and discovered six tiny pink bodies nestled up against her stomach. He sat down in amazement and stared at them. The proud papa, Joe DiMaggio (Wendall's brainstorm), lay languidly stretched out on some straw in a corner of the gun room, wiggling his nose.

Wendall ran to the house and informed the family of the newcomers. The doctor rubbed his hands and said he guessed by the end of the week there'd be another fifteen or twenty added to that batch; John T. said he guessed they wouldn't go hungry now with all the potential stew in the barn; and Sybil made a crack about the new rabbit-fur coat growing for her out there.

Indignantly, Wendall said, "You're all a bunch of cannibals!"

"If she'd had motorcycles instead of rabbits, maybe we wouldn't be so snooty," John T. said.

"If she'd had bombs, maybe I would have dumped them on your bed," Wendall replied. "Come on, Tom. Let's go out and look at them ourselves since nobody else is interested."

After much thought and discussion, Tom named his three rabbits Lilac, Funny Bunny, and Dragon; Wendall called his Dromedary, Rommel, and Abednego.

"We'll raise them and sell them as pets, crossbreed them and everything, and earn a lot of money," Wendall said, and Tom wasn't at all adverse to that.

All day in school Wendall thought about the rabbits. He wrote their names in the margins of his books and in his notebooks. He thought some day he would bring them to school to show the other children. He pictured himself behind Miss Flaxitte's desk, dressed in top hat and tails, drawing Lilac, Funny Bunny, and Dragon out of a hat, shaking Dromedary and Rommel forth from his sleeves, and popping Abednego out of a paper bag.

But most of the thrill of the rabbits was simply in owning a pet. In California they'd once owned a Siamese cat, but it hadn't been his, it had belonged to Helen. When it was a kitten he tried to play with it, but Helen always stopped him, claiming he played too rough and would develop mean habits in the animal. Whenever he chanced to be with the kitten and she caught him, she gave him a scolding, and she even took to locking the poor thing in her room so Wendall couldn't possibly get at it.

Consequently, Wendall determined to make things as miserable as possible for the beast. A water gun had been his principal instrument of torture. Every time he found himself alone with the kitten, he cornered it and systematically drenched it. He wanted to kill it, but was afraid to; yet he made plans—everything from mixing ant poison with its cat food, to simply beating it flat with a baseball bat or dropping Helen's iron on it.

Eventually the kitten became a cat, and one night it left the house and became lost. Helen went berserk. She blamed Wendall for letting it out and beat him with a belt in the kitchen, then she got so hysterical she threw a chair at him and even a small log from beside the fireplace. In the middle of this tantrum, Fred came home; he immediately sent Wendall up to the corner for a newspaper and some ice cream. When the boy returned, Helen was calm again because the cat hadn't been out after all, Fred had discovered it sound asleep behind the refrigerator.

That snapped the boy's patience. The next chance he got he grabbed the docile animal, dropped it in the washing machine, and turned the knob to ON. The beating he received the next day when Helen came upon the dead body was worth it. And there had never been another pet in that house.

Thinking about the killing now gave Wendall goose pimples. It had been a heinous thing to do, yet the boy who had done it existed no longer. And he would atone doubly for the past by bringing up his rabbits in the most pampered, luxurious manner possible.

Jubliantly, he hurried home from school . . . and came upon the six tiny offspring scattered over the gunroom floor, all dead. Huddled in a corner, Joe DiMaggio and Sabertooth looked cunningly at the boy through sleepy murderous eyes. Wendall was too shocked for a minute to realize what had happened. And when it hit him he went wild. He screamed insults at the cowering rabbits. Then he ran into the toolroom and gathered an armload of small flowerpots and came back and threw the pots at the homicidal pair. They scampered around, squealing when struck, but Wendall was too blind with tears to do much damage. It wasn't long before Bernie Aja heard the commotion; he came and halted the boy midway through the proceedings, and led him crying from the barn.

"An animal don't understand it's killin'," Bernie said. "So it ain't fair to punish him for it."

A fine rain was falling. And, though it was late at night, a distant hazy moon was visible, riding softly in the gray sky.

The front door to the Coolidge Street house opened, and Wendall, dressed only in a bathrobe and slippers, emerged. He headed for the plot beside the barn where the rabbits had been buried. He felt uneasy and on the verge of tears: he was fresh from a terrible nightmare. It had begun as something wild and slick, something to laugh about. He and Tom, dressed in very brassy army uniforms and with guns slung over their shoulders, were riding along a deserted road, up toward the Front where they could hear the mute rumblings of slaughter. It was a sunny day with a slight breeze blowing the tree leaves silver alongside the road. Wendall drove rapidly, feeling the bugs splat against his teeth and cheeks. They climbed over some mountains and descended a number of curvy scenic roads, and soon there began to appear signs of devastation beside the route. Tanks upturned and smoking; big guns lying askew; soldiers face down and rotting. Something familiar in the attitude of one of the bodies struck Wendall, so he stopped the motorcycle and went to inspect. When he turned the corpse over he found himself staring into Sybil's grinning face. And then, with the next body it had been the doctor's face, then John T.'s, then Jim's, and so on. Everyone he had known, including Fred and Helen and the man on the train, turned up dead and grinning on this battlefield. Frightened, Wendall returned to the motorcycle and doggedly continued on. The mountains receded behind them. There were no more sounds of battle ahead, only a thin screen of smoke. Through the smoke Wendall saw large white lumps moving slowly around. Then, quite suddenly, the smoke lifted and huge white rabbits wearing helmets were exposed, they dotted the plain, hopping one step, two steps, and stopping to twitch their noses and inspect Wendall and Tom with their pink laconic eyes. Wendall braked hard and the cycle shimmied all over the road. When it stopped, Bernie Aja rose out of a ditch, shouting and waving his arms. "They don't understand!" he yelled. "It ain't fair to punish 'em!"

And Wendall had awoken.

He stood in front of the six white crosses he and Tom had constructed and inscribed, and felt he couldn't bear the deaths of those little animals. He hated the parent rabbits inside the barn; the urge to stride in and kill them was almost overpowering. He knelt and said a prayer for Lilac, Funny Bunny, Dragon, Dromedary, Rommel, and Abednego. Then he lay prone, whispering to the little dead animals under the earth, "Yea, though I walk through the valley of the shadow of death, I will fear no evil. . . ." He waited, listening for a reply, then repeated, "Yea, though I walk through the valley of the shadow of death, I will fear no evil!" And he walked ahead of them through that valley, he was the protector again, the Wizard of Loneliness, the world's loneliness, and all manner of bird and beast and man trailed behind him . . . he was a pied piper, a savior, a soldier, a lover, an understander of all things living . . . and with his lips pressed into the fresh earth, his head pushing over one of the crosses, he said, "I'm sorry, I'm sorry," down into the dirt, down into the tiny dead rabbit ears. "I'm sorry, I'm sorry, I'm sorry . . ."

"Wendall!" Sybil shook his shoulder, tugging him up to his knees. "It can't be helped," she said hastily. "It's not the end of the world. These things can't be helped."

"It's not just them, it's everything," Wendall whimpered. “I don’t feel right. I feel awful. I don’t want to live anymore.”

“That’s not so. You’ll get over it, I promise you—”

“I can’t. I don’t want to. I don’t ever want to.”

“Stop crying,” she said. “Stop it this instant.”

“No. No-o-o, I won’t. I don’t have to.”

“Stop it!” She slapped him.

He sucked in a sharp breath and ended all moaning, all tears, all movement, all noise.

“You can’t let faith be shaken so easily, don’t you see?” She stopped, and this went through her head: A war makes you aware of the values you have and it makes you question them, much more so if you are removed from it, if you have the guilt of not being in it. The moral suffering doesn’t happen in the frontlines, it happens at the farthest point away from those lines. It happens right here, in one subtle way or another, it puts us all face to face with being a human being—And she said, “I have faith. You must have faith. You must never let it be shaken. Never let your faith be shaken. Don’t be afraid to believe in people. Please believe in people. Believe in me and Tomas, and Daddy; please believe in us all, please do, we love you, please don’t cry . . .” And Wendall buried his head against her breast, he didn’t think about a thing—

He shut his eyes and clung tight, getting wet, and he thought about nothing.

They clung together, hair sparkling; fragile beyond belief, they dared not move.

FORTY-THREE

John T. rubbed on Ercel: he wanted to be mean, to torture her with words, to poke her guts so full of holes she couldn’t stand up and be strong and silent and loving anymore. He wanted her to give him up, to crawl away from him in disgust and leave him alone to be consumed by the misery the stinking war and Duffy Kahler had drubbed him with, the stinking town had drubbed him with, and that his stinking family had drubbed him with—

"Maybe if you stuffed a brick in your virginity it would keep better," he spat at her one night.

Ercel was fifteen feet into the grain elevator clearing, facing him.

"You really want to have intercourse . . ." she said weakly.

"Hey. Whatever gave you that idea?"

He sat down, crossing his legs. It seemed to him the burnt timbers behind her that for so many years had held aloft were about to collapse on her head. He tore up a tuft of weed and weighed it in his hand.

"Well then; maybe we should," she said.

She stood very still, hands hanging by her sides, shoulders sagged, one knee bent a little. Confused, John T. said, "All of a sudden you decide it's a good idea, huh? Don't do me any favors."

"If I don't, you'll go crazy. You're already crazy. I think you're as unhappy as a boy can get, John T. I think if I don't let your ego take me, you might really steal whatever's left of that motorcycle out of Harry's garage one night and drive it into the Bixby quarry, into a tree . . . I don't know what frightful thing. I guess, finally, that intercourse is the best way to let you be a man. I don't want you to be a thing floating in the quarry with only a dead face for me to kiss."

John T. shook his head, warding off with his arms what she had said. His eyes climbed up the elevator. "Do you remember the day Duffy went up to the top of that thing?" he said. "Well, he might just as well have kept climbing right then and there into heaven for all the good his life ever did him."

"I wasn't there . . . I didn't know Duffy that well."

"Well, you should have known him. Everybody should have known him. I loved him. He was the only kid I ever knew I could talk to. I loved him, and anybody who says I didn't is a liar! *Duffy was my friend!"*

And with that he realized those words weren't true —Duffy had never been anything more than a comrade, a surface. John T. had never let anyone be more than a surface; he'd never forgotten himself long enough to do that.

Realizing this, his head went white with hate and he yelled: *"I want peace!"*

"I love you, John T."

"Stop beating me over the head with love! Stop standing there! Stop being so Goddam quiet!"

"Won't you ever stand up and stop feeling sorry for yourself?"

"Sure, why not?" He stood up. "Now what do I do? Do I come over and drop to my knees in front of you and kiss your twat and say thank you for saving my ego by giving me permission to fuck you?"

She turned around, went past the elevator up the embankment to the railroad tracks, and walked slowly toward the station, not once looking back. She walked dumbly and irrevocably away from him as if from a drowning, hunched and beaten and cavernously unhappy, her limbs loose and totally undefiant.

John T. fell over in the grass. "That did it," he moaned. "I killed it. I killed everything. . . ."

No matter where you went, death in one form or another was the answer.

Wendall stood in the cupola watching the rain. It filled the air with fine silver streaks, falling on the cupola roof without a sound. The shingles on the house began to glisten: blades of brown grass on the lawn seemed miraculously to assume a greenish tint; the dry stalks in the garden gave way to stirrings of leaf sprouts at their bases. It was a nondescript time of the year, neither winter's end, nor spring's beginning—the mid-April purgatory of New England weather. The sky for a few days would be neither this nor that—displaying a fraction of cloud here, a ray of sunshine there, but on the whole maintaining a bizarre grayness which looked still, yet was always changing; which promised sun, yet gave but these fine dragged-out precipitations that soothed the earth after its long affair with winter.

It was a nervous time, pinched between the seasons, threatening change at every puff of wind: and it mirrored the spirit of people on earth. Wendall tilted his glasses, squinted his eyes, and shifted his feet every few minutes, nervous and on tenterhooks, waiting for a change.

First and foremost in his mind was the war: he couldn't wait for it to end and for Fred to come home. He thought the first thing he would do would be to bring his father up to the cupola for a look at the place. And he would explain a few things to him.

"Down there, where you see the old pumpkin vines, that's Bernie Aja's compost heap," he said, pointing to where he meant. Besides him, Fred nodded and pursed his lips.

"Last year we grew a pumpkin there, milk fed it and all, and by the time October came around it was big enough to win the state fair," Wendall said. "It didn't though, because Jimmy Wiggen and some of his friends stole it and destroyed it. I tried to beat Jimmy up for that, and he laid it to me good. Bloodied up my nose something terrible. I hated him then, but I don't hate him anymore. We're not even enemies. It's really funny. . . ."

Wendall shook his head, smiling reflectively. "Over to the right, in the middle of the garden path, is where Marty Haldenstein had his blind when we took pictures of hummingbirds. A little later I'll show you pictures. I haven't seen Marty lately. He said he knew you, was in a photography club with you. . . ."

Fred said yes, he was, and his eyes showed he remembered Marty, they'd been together and talked together, though what had ever transpired no one could tell.

Wendall moved to the carriage port post. "That's where Grandpa backed up last Thanksgiving," he said. "You should have seen the way we all laughed.

All except Grandma, that is. She had a cat about it, she really did."

Fred rested his gaze on the damaged post until Wendall advanced his attention to the porch roof. "There are some loose shingles near the hall window where Duffy Kahler banged his head when he fell," the boy said. He talked about that night for a while, describing how the man had been in his room and later fallen, and how Sybil had been crying, and the pillow had been sticking out the closed pickup truck door when they drove away. And in a barely audible whisper, he told Fred something no one else knew. "Tom," he said, "is Duffy's son. Not even Tom knows that. I guess it's a secret you and I and Sybil will carry to our graves, don't you think?"

Sharing that knowledge made Fred uncomfortable, and he coughed nervously. Hurriedly, Wendall said, "When I came here, I wanted to run away. I hated everybody. And for the longest time just getting away was at the back of my mind. I stole a lot of money—did you know I stole money?—and I was going to use it to escape, yet I never did. And after a while I stopped wanting to run away. I can't remember when that was."

Embarrassed by these confidences, Fred turned away.

"Hey," Wendall said urgently. "I have so many things to show you. For instance, I can throw pretty well now. I'm even sort of adept. I can catch a baseball. I have a mitt. John T. says it was your mitt. Hey, Fred, look!" He unbuttoned his cuff, rolled up his shirt sleeve, and made a muscle. "Feel that."

Freds big hand came down and pinched the muscle.

"What do you think?" Wendall asked.

"You've changed," Fred said. "You've changed a lot."

"I'm better, aren't I? I've changed for the better, haven't I? You know, if Helen were alive right now, I wouldn't hate her anymore, I really wouldn't. I would try very hard to be nice to her. I would love her. I *do* love her. I love her very much. She was my *mother—*"

And then he knew that when Fred returned he was going to ask him a question, a very simple and meaningful question. He could even hear the tone of voice he would use, although he wasn't certain when and where he would ask it. Perhaps they would be on the porch, say near the end of a beautiful day. Or else they might be in the gloom of the barn, in the gun room right after Wendall had told Fred about the .410, and the story of the rabbits. Then again, they might be sitting on the front lawn, haloed in fireflies, while Wendall told about sledding over the bank and breaking his nose. In any case, the time and the setting were not important, and what had gone before or what would come after was not important. It was just that moment, and the tone of voice he would use, modulated and sincere in just the right and deepest way so that Fred would understand immediately what he was asking and what he himself must answer, and the question would be very simple, it would be this:

Fred, do you mind if I start calling you Dad?

Wendall was alone, the rain still falling. "Fred," he spoke to the misted air, "I hope you are safe. And if there are mosquitoes, I hope they aren't biting you. . . .

"Or if they are," he said, hardly daring to listen to his own words, hearing Sybil's voice pronouncing them, "don't, for the love of God, begin to scratch. . . ."

FORTY-FOUR

Spring was magnificent. Snows melted, ice broke up in the rivers, cold winds blew March into April. The air was cool, the sky a transparent green color; new grasses smelled of snow, in the woods and in roadside ditches layers of wet black autumn leaves steamed, and on the faces of rocks lording over country roads there still could be seen rose-colored falls of ice that would last well into June.

Every day that went by with Duffy still at large preyed on people's nerves. Folks locked up their houses at night against him. In Putney, Duffy walked down the main street in broad daylight, and before anyone could think to arrest him, he was gone. Three nights later a farmer turned his flashlight and a shotgun on a man in his chicken coop, and the man ran right through a wire fence, taking the fence and probably a lot of buckshot with him. He'll go off in the woods and die like a fox, some old hands said. The state and local police and some volunteers combed miles of woods, but they couldn't find a body. Then, four miles north of Proctorsville, a motorist slowed down for a hitchhiker, recognized the madman from newspaper photos, and sped up again, reporting to the police in the nearby town. And the search shifted, as did Duffy. He was next seen near Woodstock; so people in houses all around White River Junction began making sure their doors and windows were doubly latched at night. But nobody heard anything for a while, then a woman in Bethel opened her car door one afternoon and found Duffy asleep in the back seat. She closed the door and ran for the sheriff, and when he arrived the car was empty.

Duffy Kahler's whole body was strained to the outermost limits of endurance. Every blood cell, bone, and muscle fiber was charged to carry him up through the Vermont April to his hometown. In his mind a thousand times he burst across the railroad tracks, running and floating like a sprinter into the town, making for the memorial, *his memorial,* while lined all up and down the street the townsfolk shot at him with rifles and pistols, and with glee he knew they would not bring him down, not before he cast himself twitching at the base of that memorial, and after that he cared not a whit what happened.

Nobody was going to stop him. He was like a shadow in the woods, he was like a ghost, he was the invisible man nobody could catch. He moved night and day, he hardly slept, he ate anything—herbs, leaves, old snow; he drank from ice-cold creeks; he heard hounds baying, he fled from people running across pastures, he snuck through towns at night, he walked brazenly through them during the day, and he was lucky, nobody could catch him. When he made a wrong turning he knew it instinctively, he backtracked and followed the right road, the right stream, he walked through the right valley. He slipped on a rock and broke his hand again—he didn't care. Oh how he was going to cross those railroad tracks running like a deer while they shot him. Oh what gracious leaps into the air he would make, how lightly would land his feet upon the pavement. Oh what sleep awaited him upon the Green.

He licked his lips and peered between branches, he peered around the corner of a building. He spied his inessential figure gliding through plate-glass windows —Duffy going home. His body rose to the task and made him super supple; his life sense was immaculate, super strong in this ultimate heroic drive. He performed impossible feats of the senses and feats of the body, nothing let him down, he would get there; he would get there, all right; he would get to Stebbinsville.

No doubt about it.

April ended; May began.

* * *

Wendall sat in the attic thinking about Fred. He thought: I am important to Fred and he is important to me. We are father and son. Touching his penis, he thought of Fred's having a similar instrument; with it he had put some sperm into Helen, and Wendall had been born. It had been a very troublesome birth, through Caesarian, and after that any discussion of birth frightened Helen and disgusted her.

But it was because of them and between them that he had been born, and they had probably loved each other when he was conceived. And afterwards, although he had hated Helen, Fred had loved her, he had always known that.

Her death must have been a blow to Fred. It must have killed him inside in one way or another. He must have felt the way Wendall felt when the rabbits died.

It struck him funny to think of his father loving Helen. Fred never said anything: he just comforted her, and smiled at her when she wanted him to smile, and was morose when she didn't feel well and it would have been an insult to feel otherwise, and if she didn't want him to do something, he didn't do it, so of course he spoiled her, and she became a bitch, but he loved her, and she in her way must have loved him, and behind their door at night where Wendall had never been, all things must have been equal, and the days meant nothing.

Wendall stood up: moths winged off into the side shadows. He went to the window and poked dried and dangling wasps with his finger, and tears made depthless channels down his cheeks. Around him the clocks had no time on their faces because there is no time for love.

Now Duffy Kahler came to mind. He was coming back, Wendall knew that; everybody knew that. No one knew why. But then no one knew anything about Duffy: no one knew, for instance, that he had fathered the very child he had wanted to kill. But everyone knew he was dangerous. So the best thing that could happen to Duffy was that he be found, that he be captured, that he be shot, or put away.

Duffy was a kind of guilt running up through the state. He was a thing that all people had made and misused, sent off, and ignored, and come back again the way he wasn't supposed to do. He was coming home to a place that had no more home for him. He was a man with no more time going to a place that was lost. He was destructive and being destroyed, and for no reason except that he was a man without reason and without control, running to a place—just plain running to a place.

Running to it the same way B. J. Twine went toward it on the arm of his nurse; running to it the same way Wendall and John T. had gone toward it when they traveled on the motorcycle to the lost pond; running to it the same way Jim had repeatedly trudged toward it when he courted Clo Spinelli; running to it the same way Marty Haldenstein went toward it when he befriended Wendall, read him *Green Mansions,* held his hand—

And after you reached the place and the clocks were forever stopped behind you, there was still a little yellow grass where the blind had stood, or perhaps a scar such as the one Tom carried on his forehead.

Because nothing ever really stops. Because people can't not go on. No matter how much one man or a bullet or a white rabbit shakes their faith, they can't not go on. Because faith is blind, yet it is inherent—it just has to be learned.

Wendall walked through the attic and the boards creaked and the little moths flew out of his path, and the sun lowered and disappeared: darkness came. Out there, to the east or to the west, Duffy was running. Wendall could feel the man's blood in his own blood. He could feel the aimlessness, and the hope, the physical weakness and strength, the futility and the thirst, and the total befuddlement, and much much more.

He knelt.

He couldn't stop crying.

And he couldn't articulate his agony.

FORTY-FIVE

On May seventh the doctor left home early, but instead of walking to his office he took the Studebaker; his legs were tired, and he could hardly make fists of his hands around the steering wheel. Once at his office he saw a few patients, then abruptly closed up. His head felt funny; loose and awkward and unable to think; as if his mind were a puppet and all the strings had been cut, and his thoughts were all in a heap, unable to move. It was still early in the morning, a little after ten o'clock.

He walked around to Hood's, and the first thing Mike, who was busily swishing a broom around in the sawdust, said was, "Did they sign?"

"Did they sign what?"

"Did they sign *what?* Did they sign the surrender! Did the German guy sign the paper yet? Is it over? Because soon as it's over I got this Victory Sundae I'm gonna put out . . ." And he went on to describe the sundae, a concoction of three differet kinds of ice cream—vanilla, strawberry, and blueberry—topped with whipped cream, a few cherries, almond crunch, and a little paper American flag stuck into the summit. He had purchased over a hundred flags from Gruber's Five and Dime.

"I don't know," the doctor replied. "I don't know if they signed or not." He could hardly hear his own voice.

"Well, what can I do you for?" Mike asked, moving behind the counter.

"Mike, I came here to ask you a favor."

"Sure thing. What kind of favor?"

"I need some money. I'm in straits, Mike. Of course. it's nothing serious, and I'd be able to pay . . ."

That wasn't what he'd come in to do. That wasn't it at all.

"Sorry, I can't help you."

"But . . ."

"Listen, Fred. I don't loan money I ain't got. The bank's where you wanna go for a loan, not me."

The doctor couldn't stop himself. There was no control— He said, "Mike, do you remember what I did for you when your son died?"

Mike narrowed his eyes and put both palms flat on the counter: "Say that again?"

"I can't. You heard me."

Mike said, "Listen, I don't know what in hell you're drivin' at askin' me for dough, but I know one thing: you *gave* me that when the kid died. You remember? It wasn't no loan, nothin' like that. I come to pay the bill and you told me. 'Don't you worry about it, Mike. It's all took care of, and you don't got a thing to worry about.' I didn't figure it that way, but you just patted me on the shoulder, you told me you had enough so's it wouldn't hurt you to pay, and you give me this long sermon about how it did you more good'n it would ever do me, and I still insisted it be a loan, and you said, no, it was either a gift or nothing at all, so maybe I was a chump, but I thanked you for that, I thanked you for givin' my wife and me that gift with no strings attached. No strings attached, remember? It wasn't no loan, you *gave* me that dough. That means I got no obligations, Mike. No obligations at all. You can't tell me you didn't say that."

"No, I can't."

"Then what do you want, comin' in here like this, tryin' to put the squeeze on me?"

"Nothing . . . nothing, Mike. I think I could use a Coke." Out of his vest pocket he fished a nickel and clicked it onto the counter. Mike shoved it back at him.

"Keep your dough. This one's on the house. No strings attached."

The doctor drank the Coke, left Hood's, and returned to his office. He really was deaf, and he had trouble breathing. He mounted the steps to his office but did not go in. He stood in front of his door, and after five minutes or so he tore off the sign saying there were more old drunks in the world than old doctors, and ripped it up. Pieces of the sign fluttered over the pavement. Joel Spender was at that moment passing by and the paper fell at his feet. Looking up he said. "War's over, huh?" and the doctor neither affirmed nor denied this statement.

He tottered down the steps and went back to Main Street, this time to Jim's. Jim said, " 'Lo, Fred. What brings you by?"

The doctor leaned on the counter catching his breath for a second. He had no idea what had brought him by. He was running scared, he felt full of panic, he had no objective. His hands and knees throbbed; the bridge of his false teeth ached. He started to speak and couldn't think of anything to say. Yet he moved his lips and what came out was this: "Jim, everything that was fine in my life is what I *used* to do."

Jim said, "Why're you holdin' that glass?"

The doctor looked at his hands and discovered he still held the Coke glass from Hood's.

"Oh," he said stupidly.

"What's the matter?" Jim asked.

The doctor shook his head, said "Judas-pries'," and walked out.

From the sport and news shop it was just a short way across Perry Street to the bank. He entered the building, walked to the center of the floor, and stopped. The thought occurred to him that if he had brought along John T.'s shotgun he might have had a go at robbing the place. That cleared the air a little and made him smile. He said, "Oh, what the hell," and raised the hand that held the glass. In that glass was the weight of all the years, all the right things that had turned out wrong, all the dream things that had never materialized, all the bodies he had cared for and nurtured only to have them die in the end—all these things, all the futile efforts of a lifetime he lifted, and then, with a quick snap of his wrist, he speeded the glass down to the floor where it shattered, spraying fragments over his feet. Then he turned around and walked out into the sunshine. He stood in front of the bank trying to get his bearings straight.

"That was stupid," he said, "Lord love a duck."

He returned to the car and drove home.

Wendall had been allowed to play hooky from school so as to listen for surrender news. Sitting on the front steps with the kitchen radio on an extension in his lap, he saw the car come in. The doctor parked under the carriage port; Wendall descended to open the door for him. The doctor brushed by and went into the living room: Wendall followed. With a sigh the doctor sank into a leather chair beside the fireplace.

"Well, that's that," he said quietly. "It's all over, and I sure wish I'd done it different. Isn't that the damnedest, though, to wind up sayin' that? Seems like I spent my whole lifetime in a tizzy doin' everything under the sun so's I wouldn't wind up sayin' I wished I'd done it different. Hardly makes sense, does it, Skunkhead?"

He closed his eyes. "Well, I'm sorry. Yessir, I'm sorry I didn't do it right. It's funny how I thought so many folks loved me, and it wasn't right at all. Seems my bein' good just hurt everybody it shouldn't have all the time. Carted peace around to everyone but my own family. Or did I? Did I at all?"

Tubes of woe, in place of arteries and veins, were running through his body. Briefly, his three young children came to mind. Suppressing giggles, they walked into his downtown office with maple seeds stuck to their noses. "Lord love a duck," he had said then, and it had carried through the years. . . .

"I gave them childhood," he whispered weakly. "They loved me . . ."

The phone rang. Cornelia took it upstairs. A minute later she was in the room, or rather, in the doorway—she could bring herself to advance no farther.

"How did you think that would help us?" she asked dully.

"Cornelia, all my life I tried to be an honest, a moral man. I tried to be useful, I was liked. . . ."

"Did you really think it would help us? Is that what you thought? What kind of a fool idea was in your mind? We're ruined."

"Oh, it's not so bad," he murmured. But he knew that wasn't true. She was right. He could have dropped a bomb on the town, or strangled one of his patients in broad daylight, and it would have meant the same thing as throwing down that glass. Either way he was finished. That one stupid act was the period: he was retired. And he didn't understand how it had happened, it had just fallen this morning like a little acorn out of all his tiredness.

Unfamiliar anger came to the doctor; he tensed, wanting to flee, wanting to drive away, go up in the hills . . . *and he would, by God.* If it had to be alone, then it would be alone. He'd follow the old roads, turn a corner, spy Camel's Hump in the distance—and he would drive on farther . . . A vision flared up before him, the road leading him through the mountains toward the sun, and to his ears came the old college songs, the cheer of a football crowd, somewhere beyond the next summit college girls jostled through the streets of a city wearing yellow and white chrysanthemums on their bosoms, and after that, after the game, when the sidewalks were deserted and he was young again and leaves were new, snow would began to fall. . . .

Cornelia jerked hesitantly into the room. She drew behind the chair and laid her hand timidly on the doctor's shoulder. At her touch, he opened his eyes and smiled with benevolent sadness. For a moment they waited in this forlorn and familial pose, almost withdrawn into the one they had theoretically become long ago at the start of their lives together. It was as if they had slipped through every artifact of the life around them into a place all their own where each for a moment perfectly understood the heart and soul of the other, and in understanding this, had created that peace for which all men yearn, and Wendall was struck by the absolute beauty of their closeness, he wanted to get up and go to them, he felt the irresistible urge to climb onto the doctor's lap, to make himself a part of their moment, to wrap himself forever in his grandmother's graceful touch and his grandfather's vague gentleness . . . but even while he was moving to do so, the doctor stood up, lurched brusquely by Cornelia, and went out the door.

The Studebaker failed to start the first time, then the engine caught, and, too quickly, as if a young man were at the wheel, the car backed into the street. At that moment, the factory whistle began to blow, church bells started to ring. The doctor floored the gas pedal, the tires squealed as he went over the bridge rounding the corner onto Main.

Wendall and Cornelia waited on the porch, ears strained. Bernie Aja came out of the barn. When they heard the crash all three began to run.

At the gas station, John T. looked up from the pumps as the Studebaker went by. Puzzled, he followed it with his eyes down the street, and horrified, witnessed the accident.

Sybil also saw the accident. When the factory whistle began to blow, she ran out of the gift shop onto the sidewalk. She felt as if her legs had suddenly been filled with helium; she wanted to rise to the sky. She cried for joy, clasped her hands to her breast, and screamed "Hooray! Hooray! Hooray!" jumping in place like a schoolgirl, tears flooding her cheeks, tears coming so freely they literally spattered in the air.

And then she saw Duffy Kahler running down the middle of the street, and for just this moment there was no car on the street.

His eyes black, spittle flying off his beard, his mouth wide open sucking for air. Duffy ran by her. His pants were torn, his knees showed through, he wore no shoes. Sybil called his name and sprinted into the street after him.

Ercel Perry had just bought a white blouse in the Thrift Shop on Rutland Avenue. As she walked toward Main Street, the Volunteer fire chief's station wagon, Lou Feterson at the wheel, went by, a little fast, Ercel thought, but then Lou was announcing through a megaphone atop the wagon: "The war's over! It's all over!" As he went by, Ercel hurried her step, happiness welling within her. She had no idea where she should go, but headed for the Green.

When the factory whistle and church bells cut loose, Jim got off his stool, squeezed by the counter and stationed himself in the doorway to his shop. On his right several blocks down the street, he saw Sybil exit from the gift shop and begin to jump and shout for joy. He smiled. Then he caught sight of Duffy Kahler running in the street. He saw the traffic light go red on Main, green for Rutland, and as it did so, his head was brought around by the accelerating sound of the Studebaker.

Next door, Irma Kahler got to the entrance of the market two seconds before the crash took place.

The doctor did not see Duffy until he was ten yards in front of the car. Instinctively, he swerved right to avoid hitting him. All he saw as he collided with the rear door of the fire chief's station wagon was Duffy's mad face swinging away from his window and out of sight behind his shoulders.

The collision slammed the cars together side by side, catching Duffy between them, and all his bones broke at once; he had no time for a cry.

Sybil stood in the middle of the street, full in the sunlight, her hands raised to her mouth. Ercel Perry stood on the coner, a paper bag at her feet. Mike Stenatto and Jim and Irma Kahler were nailed open-mouthed to their stoops. John T. and Harry had run up the street and stopped twenty feet short of the accident. Behind them were Cornelia and Bernie Aja and Wendall. Lou Feterson sat in his car behind the steering wheel, and the doctor sat in his car behind the steering wheel, and neither man was too badly hurt, but between them Duffy Kahler was dead.

And then the church bells shut off, the factory whistle died—a resonance trembled in the air, the speaker atop the station wagon was still humming.

Seconds were glued to time, they couldn't tick off.

Nobody could move forward; nobody could move back.

Sybil spotted a white hand near the rear tire of the station wagon, and she remembered the night that hand had been the hand of the world touched to her breast as the sky outside the baggage room window expanded into a Godless bitter nightmare—and she thought: I couldn't respond to that hand, I couldn't do anything—why couldn't I do anything?—and the sun turned black.

Ercel Perry thought: This is a death and it isn't fair because the war is over. She saw past the accident to John T.'s stricken face and something funny about his face hit her, because he suddenly looked free.

Mike Stenatto thought: That son of a bitch. Then he raised his fist and shook it at the cars and screamed once, "You son of a bitch!" The thing is, he didn't know who he was screaming at.

Jim had to sit down. He didn't understand. He wanted to walk away and hide. But he was too weak to move.

Irma Kahler turned around and faced into her store where cans gleamed in the cool and shaded interior. If she had only told somone this would not have happened. Now she had nothing to live for.

John T.'s first impulse was to scream, fall down, grovel, tear his hair, and rent the air with woe, bellowing that of all the things that had happened to him, this had to cap everything off. And then his body twitched, and his agony was all over, like a balloon the old John T. popped and didn't exist anymore, and the new John T. felt himself flooded with a stern calmness, and he hesitated just another second or two to make sure the new thing had taken hold before going into action.

Cornelia thought it was her fault, all along she'd hoped things would get better, and they hadn't, and she'd made a fool out of herself, she hadn't shut up for one minute all these years, she'd just been the biggest most Godawful yackety-bub in the world, but she hadn't *done* anything, she'd never once done anything to make things better.

To Wendall, the strained composition of white grownup faces—each nailed to its neighbor by the brute force of shock—was terrifying. Suddenly stopped little acts of living glared out grotesquely—Ercel's package at her feet, Jim's unlit cigar, a rag in Mike Stenatto's hand—And the boy felt as if the air were filled with the strange squeeze of his dreams. Looking at these people, these adults, he recognized people so tender and emotionally helpless that a leaf could have crushed them, and the bright sunlight on their faces and in their eyes illuminated a feeling of crippledness so intense that the boy expected to see limbs turn to wax and be melted and deformed before his eyes in the final turbulent climax of their dismay.

And he recalled these people in his dreams. He could see them now, flashlights in their hands, tramping through the winter forest of pines to find himself and John T., and they were looking for someone, they followed him to the grave site. . . . Then he recalled them on the hilltop from which he smote the world's evils with his sword, and he remembered how afterwards a fairy grass grew over a plain of defeated bodies and they, the victors, the survivors, danced in ecstasy over that unreal ground, beneath an unreal moon. . . . And lastly he recalled his Christmas dream when he wandered among them singing "Silent Night" in the snow, and later they walked into obscurity beyond the horizon leaving him alone, and his despair on awakening from that dream had been no less than the despair he now felt—for his hands were tired, Duffy Kahler was dead, the act that had killed him was committed, the people involved in the act could not suddenly be withdrawn and made to smile . . . there was absolutely nothing to do, and nothing in the world could save these people from all the hurt this day would give; no one, at his mightiest, could hold up a sword and stem the chain of repercussions, there was absolutely no way to unblame the doctor from his deed, and the body crushed between those cars was forever dead, and what made it so unbearable was that in every face the boy saw reflected his own agony, in every still-clutched hand he saw his own hand—so much so that he felt if he cried every eye present would match him tear for tear, and if he raised his hand, every other hand would rise with it and move with it. . . .

Then, as the church bells began to ring again and the factory whistle sounded, John T. moved—he ran forward and opened the door to the Studebaker and pulled out his father; Ercel ran to assist him. Harry Garengelli ran to the station wagon and helped Lou Feterson out. Cornelia swayed and went to her husband. Sybil walked over to her father and kissed him. The sheriff appeared—he and John T. and Bernie Aja and Mike Stenatto bent over the rear end of the Studebaker and swung it out a little, opening a V between vehicles into which Wendall could see.

He could not bear the sight, and turned away. Down at the corner of Perry Street he saw Marty Haldenstein standing. They stared at each other, and Wendall felt they were all alone, forever alone, this little sick man and he.

Marty lifted a hand from his overcoat pocket. He raised it indecisively—perhaps he meant simply to wave, perhaps he meant to explain that he was afraid to approach any nearer to the accident. And with that motion, Wendall understood Marty; he understood the longing that had brought the librarian to him, and the need that had made him respond, and the fear that had terminated their friendship—and nothing in the boy's life could ever be the same after this day because these few startling seconds face to distant face with Marty comprised that moment when he finally understood that because of his heart, he was one of the most mortal and vulnerable beings in the universe.

FORTY-SIX

The manslaughter charge against the doctor was quickly dropped, but it didn't matter—he was through anyway. Sybil, Wendall, and Tom cleaned out his office; Wiggen, Cadwell, and Hempe expanded, taking over the rooms. The furniture was auctioned off, and the simpler tools of the doctor's trade went into the Coolidge Street attic.

The family moved through May and part of June in clouds of darkness. Cornelia was silent for once, Sybil was tender and afraid for what might happen to them, John T. was quiet and kind, puzzled by his new self and the sudden absence of rancor in his nature. The doctor felt old and ashamed; he read the newspapers, listened to the radio, and puttered in the garden, and after the car was fixed, Cornelia consented at last to some drives into the hills. The spring was soft and beautiful, but the far mountains, though green and fresh, were without the majestic magic that had so often captivated the doctor in bygone days.

Summer did not manifest itself with as much heat as the previous year: the level of the river stayed high, and there was rain often enough to keep tree leaves dark green. Wendall and Tom watched their old haunts and hideouts flower again; they sat in the protection of deep foliage and drew lazy pictures with twigs in the dirt. Wendall was not so interested in war games as he had been before; he had changed, he had mellowed. He read books aloud to Tom on the lawn, he explored with him, but his tone was subdued, and no longer did he derive satisfaction from ordering his younger cousin about.

Then a FOR SALE went up in the grass near the front walk, and Wendall wondered where they would all go once the house was sold. He dared not ask, but the answer was not long in coming. Cornelia and the doctor decided they were going to leave town and go down to Boston where relatives on her side of the family had offered them a town apartment. Sybil said she would go to Boston also, and John T. announced he was going to marry Ercel, remain in Stebbinsville for another year, working, then he might return to B. U. and finish his education.

Wendall waited, haplessly, to discover what was to be done with himself. The solution to that problem arrived one day in the form of a letter from Fred, who was getting discharged in November and planned to come east for his son, then head back to California. "He's still afraid of us," Sybil said. "He doesn't realize he no longer need be."

July and August were quiet, uneventful months. Jim came over often to see the doctor, they discussed the pennant races and attended D.C. baseball games, and everywhere they went, Wendall tagged along. The doctor paled, got thinner, and moved stiffly, but some of his old humor returned. At baseball games he never yelled very loud for fear of calling attention to himself, but he told Wendall everything that was going to happen before it did, and he got a kick out of being wrong most of the time. Wendall kept a scorecard so that after the game, in the evening on the front porch, he and his grandfather could re-create the afternoon's plays. The boy also threw a tennis ball against the barn doors for at least an hour a day, and he began to find his feet could move without tripping him, and his hands seemed also to have acquired a bit of dexterity so that the ball did not as often bounce the long journey down the driveway and into the street.

Early in September, Chad Spender pulled a red wagon piled high with books up the front walk to the porch steps. When Wendall answered the doorbell, Chad gave him an envelope. It contained a letter from Marty Haldenstein; the gist of it was that Marty planned to leave Stebbinsville shortly and go to Arizona, and he thought Wendall might appreciate the books. Wendall offered Chad a quarter even though the boy said Mr. Haldenstein had already given him a couple of bucks. They unloaded the books, and as soon as Chad had gone away with his wagon, Wendall searched nervously through the volumes for *Green Mansions,* but it wasn't there.

One night in late September, Irma Kahler awoke to a sound in her room. She thought it was a burglar, but: "It's only me," Hank Kahler said—"I come back." He sat at the foot of her bed and neither of them spoke for half an hour. When they were good and into the mutual silence that had existed between them for years, Hank nodded his head and said, "Okay," and went to his own room, and that was that.

On October twelfth, John T. and Ercel were married: Harry Garengelli was the best man. Wendall and Tom got a fit of giggles when they saw John T. mincing around in formal wear. The young marrieds took a week's honeymoon over to Lake Champlain. They made love for the first time in a dingy motel room near the shore of the lake. It was early evening, sunlight came through a window and feathered their young limbs with gold, and when John T. had his first climax in her, Ercel began to cry. She cried all through the evening with John T. quiet and proud, smoking beside her, and when they got up to go out for something to eat, Ercel took her husband's hand, letting him lead her the way she had always wanted him to. When they returned to Stebbinsville, they rented some rooms at Margaret Simpson's, and the Coolidge Street house seemed empty, the jukebox was forgotten.

In the last week of October, the doctor died in his sleep. Cornelia awoke in the morning feeling that the room was extra cold; she turned to her husband right away, and had no words for this moment. She stared at his face a while, then went and told Sybil.

When Wendall learned, he felt as if he himself were going to die. He lay on his bed, alternately sobbing and listening to the creepy stealthy movement of shocked people on the floors below. Ercel Perry came upstairs and sat on his bed for a short time, stroking his hair, but when she suggested he come downstairs he said no, and would not speak with her anymore.

After the body had been removed from the house, Wendall did several strange things. First, he went up to the attic and stamped on all his collages until the glass in each frame was busted into small pieces. Next, he went downstairs to his grandparents' bathroom and "stole" the penguin ashtray which he wrapped up in woolen socks and hid in a corner of his closet. Then he went outdoors and wandered aimlessly around the grounds, ending up in the playhouse. There he sat for quite some time as waves of ink-black desolation swept over him. Suddenly, overcome with hurt and anger, he leapt up, and, with the broomstick horse from the attic, began to bash out the windows. John T. barged in in the middle of the boy's rage and struggled to subdue him. Wendall bit and kicked his uncle; John T. had to sit on his chest until the boy finally cried himself out and apologized.

That afternoon Bernie Aja bought some glass from Bitte's Hardware and helped Wendall caulk in the new panes. They both cried as they worked: Bernie made no noise, but sometimes he would halt the repairs and, lifting his head, give a long low sigh and a pair of tears would leave his eyes.

At the funeral it snowed. The flakes fell softly in the graveyard, red and yellow leaves were still on all the trees. Wendall looked past the little group of mourners to where, along the curved crest of the hill, he saw the old man, B. J. Twine, supported by his nurse, struggling up to inspect his burying place. The snow caught in everybody's hair, it clung to black veils, and the ground, a gentle white, looked good to sleep under.

The house was finally sold, and some men came to get most of the furniture which would later be auctioned off. Bernie Aja moved into a room at the Pavilion Hotel, but he came over every day and took care of the grounds. Cornelia said she guessed when the new owners moved in they would keep him on to look after things, but Bernie said he reckoned he would retire and just puff his pipe and look at movies for a while, he was getting pretty old.

Fred came home in time for Thanksgiving, taller and stronger-looking than Wendall had remembered. His eyes were cold, his face sternly immobile and a little frightening. Things were awkward that first week. Fred said little even when spoken to. The empty house made him moody. He wouldn't go to the graveyard because he was not "ready yet." He walked around town and saw some people, and smoked and slept a lot, and puttered up in the attic or out in the barn, and not ten words passed between himself and his son.

On December first, Cornelia, Sybil and Tom boarded a train for Boston, and right after they had left, Fred went with Wendall over to the cemetery for his first look at the doctor's grave. It was covered with leaves, the trees around were bleak and bare. Fred kicked some of the leaves away and saw that the grass had all died. Wendall took his hand and they looked at the leaves and the streak in them where Fred had kicked, and they both wanted to cry, but neither did.

One more week they stayed in town, sleeping in blankets on the living room floor, eating their meals at the Jubilee Café or the Miss Stebbinsville. After his work at the gas station, John T. often came over, and he and Fred walked around and talked about all the things that had happened in the old house. While the house was still theirs they wanted to get everything straight in their minds so they would have it later on. They remembered much of the pain, and a lot of the good things also. They sat on the floors of empty rooms voices echoing even though they spoke quietly, and in that one week they became closer than they had been all their lives.

Then Fred bought a car, a Buick. He and Wendall and John T. and Ercel loaded it up with a lot of junk from the attic, and on a cold morning they were ready to leave. That morning Wendall ran downtown to the sporting goods store. It had just started to snow; a thin film of white covered the sidewalk. Jim was sitting behind the counter, cigar, glasses, frown, and *Sporting News* all in their accustomed places.

"I'm going away," Wendall said breathlessly. "I came to say good-bye."

Jim thought about that for a moment, then he said, "Where you goin'?"

"To California."

"California," Jim said, nodding approvingly. "You'll be next door to the Rose Bowl."

They shook hands quickly and Wendall went outside. He was about to break back for home, when he thought better of it. He went up the street to Hood's, ducked in for just a second, and said good-bye to Mike Stenatto. Blushing, he ran self-consciously back toward the sport and news shop, but stopped again, this time in front of Kahler's Market. Bounding inside, he hurried back to the cash register and mumbled, "I'm leaving now, Mrs. Kahler. I just wanted to say good-bye and good luck," and he patted the counter with his hand, but before she could reply he had run out.

He ran through the snow feeling funnier than he ever had in his life. Flakes sprinkled his hair, and his eyes were rimmed with tears. Something caught in his chest and he gritted his teeth and ran home as fast as he could.

A few minutes later he and Fred drove over to the garage to say good-bye to John T. and Harry, then went up Conroy Street to see Ercel a last time, then drove back down Rutland, turned right on Main, and passed the train station, bumped over the tracks, and went right again on 684. Snow swept across the windshield, the wipers squeaked as they worked, the heater whizzed, flooding the car with warmth.

Wendall moved over beside Fred and after a few miles he tightened his fists in his lap and said, "Fred, I've been thinking about something . . ."

His father nodded but did not take his eyes off the road.

"I was wondering," Wendall said nervously, "if you would mind me calling you Dad?"

Fred looked down, surprised, then he took one hand off the wheel and tousled Wendall's hair.

"I'd like that very much," he said. "I'd like that very much indeed."

They looked at each other and smiled and Wendall said, "Okay, Dad . . ."

And though it sounded foreign, awkward, and childish, Wendall didn't mind. He felt certain that with time he would get used to it, and he felt supremely confident for a moment, but not because he had suddenly become a man: it was rather as if, at long last, he had succeeded in opening wide the door to his waning childhood.